GATES OF HELL

BOOK THREE OF THE LAST MARINES

William S. Frisbee, Jr.

Theogony Books
Coinjock, NC

Copyright © 2022 by William S. Frisbee, Jr.

All rights reserved. No part of this publication may be reproduced, distributed or transmitted in any form or by any means, including photocopying, recording, or other electronic or mechanical methods, without the prior written permission of the publisher, except in the case of brief quotations embodied in critical reviews and certain other noncommercial uses permitted by copyright law. For permission requests, write to the publisher, addressed "Attention: Permissions Coordinator," at the address below.

Chris Kennedy/Theogony Books
1097 Waterlily Rd.
Coinjock, NC 27923
https://chriskennedypublishing.com/

Publisher's Note: This is a work of fiction. Names, characters, places, and incidents are a product of the author's imagination. Locales and public names are sometimes used for atmospheric purposes. Any resemblance to actual people, living or dead, or to businesses, companies, events, institutions, or locales is completely coincidental.

Cover Design by J Caleb Design.

Ordering Information:
Quantity sales. Special discounts are available on quantity purchases by corporations, associations, and others. For details, contact the "Special Sales Department" at the address above.

Gates of Hell/William S. Frisbee, Jr.-- 1st ed.
ISBN: 978-1648555473

Chapter One: Green Hope

Aesir Lojtnant Hermod – VRAEC (Vapaus Republic Aesir Erikoisjoukot Cadre)

Green Hope was a backwater, and Hermod didn't like it. He couldn't put his finger on why or when it had started bothering him, but something about his mission and this planet was getting under his skin. This was the worst kind of mission, the kind with little chance of clashing with the SOG military. Maybe that was the problem?

The colonists had been forgotten about by the Social Organizational Governance, and this planet was a place most people went to be forgotten or were discarded. It was unremarkable in countless ways, from the predictable weather patterns to the predictable terraforming algae that covered the planet in massive patches. From space, it was green. The shallow oceans now teemed with fish and in many places around the planet, native Terran plants and animals had taken root with minimum modification. Nothing set Green Hope apart from the other colonies the SOG had founded to spread humanity across the stars. The SOG spread colonies just for the sake of spreading them, like a dangerous plague, or the algae they used to terraform.

The ferns were huge, and to Hermod and his team, they could be trees because of the way they towered high into the sky, feeding on the algae below and the sun above. The algae consumed the hard rock and soil, turning it into soft, healthy mulch and good topsoil for plants and created oxygen. There was nothing sinister or trouble-some.

On Green Hope, humans only lived on a single continent. There were science stations on the other fourteen continents, but they usu-ally weren't manned. This continent, called Able by the locals who were issued their imagination by the government, was in the temper-ate, more hospitable part of the planet. There was no way he wanted to live here. They couldn't pay him enough.

But what would it be like to live here? Day after day, the same surroundings, the same house, the same plants, the same bed? To live and love, while letting other people carry the burden of war. He glanced toward Hanz ahead of him. The big German had once been a colonist, decades ago. Big, dumb, and peaceful. Did he miss it? Never wondering if he was going to be dead within the week? Not being hunted? There were colonies the SOG didn't think about. Col-onies where a person could return to their peaceful roots. Build a home, a family, a future.

Hermod couldn't imagine Hanz as a big dumb colonist. He and Ailne were two of the most lethal hand-to-hand fighters in the Eri-koisjoukot cadres, and Hanz might be a tactical genius. Hermod knew he would have to cut him loose eventually, so he let him have his own team. Ailne would probably go with him.

Hermod didn't want another executive officer. Maybe when Hanz left it would be time to retire. Ninety years in Aesir Special Operations and thirty in the Erikoisjoukot cadres was a very long time. Few people lasted half that long. Skadi had a team. Magni had decommissioned his team, but still served. Grimnir was still active. It had been a decade or two since any new Aesir Erikoisjoukot teams had entered service. How long would it be before there were no spec ops teams in service? Would the fleet disappear into deep space? There was talk about that now. Everyone was tiring of the war that had no end in sight.

Like ghosts, the eight Aesir commandos and sixteen robotic mules seemed to glide through the vegetation. Most of them had made this trip before. Their ship, *Valkyrie 19,* had seen no SOG ships in orbit, not even cargo haulers, which wasn't unusual for this system. Its distance from the Torag and Voshka fronts further isolated it, since there was no need for patrol cutters or anything larger than a shuttle. Through breaks in the vegetation, he could see the distant sky elevator, four cables stretching toward the sky. There didn't appear to be any activity on the lines, which, again, was not unusual with no ships in orbit.

Green Hope wasn't an awful place. The atmosphere was breathable for unmodified humans, and if the government could stop intervening, it would be a great place to live in twenty years. If there hadn't been a risk of SOG-tailored biological agents or that Hermod didn't want to reveal his team's presence through chemical traces, he would have inflicted the local smells and humidity on them. It wouldn't be the first time the SOG had seeded a colony with chemical sensors designed to identify and record foreigners.

Hermod paused and looked around. The Aesir and mules appeared on his heads-up display as icons showing the individual, distance, and direction of travel.

Right now, everything was normal. His Aesir were spread out, and the entire formation looked like a big arrow with Hanz and Ailne walking point, Rorik on the left flank for security, and Jord on the right. The other team members were walking among the mules, four-legged, all-terrain robots loaded with supplies. They looked more like a combat patrol than a trading mission, but it was always good to be cautious with the SOG, especially these days. Erikoisjoukot discipline would keep them alive more efficiently than anything else.

But the Governance had its own plans. Expectations and policies dictated by faceless, uncaring bureaucrats light years away, with politically motivated five-year plans that had little to do with planetary conditions or the needs of the colony. Although the temperature never fell below seventy or rose above a hundred, the official winter was approaching so the colony manufactories were tasked with creating cold weather gear, parkas, boots, long johns, electric blankets, space heaters, snow blowers, and cold weather hats.

Each item created had a cost associated with it and was tallied and transmitted to Earth, where the bureaucracy would tally the items created and deployed against the designs used. Administrators could then gauge how many millions, or billions, of winter coats were created for colonists to stay warm on those distant, hostile planets. Then those administrators could brag about how their product and their designs were widely spread and used. They could stand before committees and report how many colonists relied on them and their designs. The administrators would then extrapolate, based on population growth patterns, and decide that more coats would be needed or they could justify holding back resources from the people who needed them.

In the colony, automated factories just churned out what the schedules told them to, and the colonist had to make do. More often than not, they found other ways to make it work.

The black market was frequently the lifeline that the people needed, and sometimes the Republic was part of that lifeline, trading extra cold weather gear created on Green Hope to people on colder worlds in exchange for other things. Each colony needed something, and frequently the bureaucrats back on Earth just didn't care.

One crucial item many colonists needed, and no five-year plan could predict, were medicines. The SOG controlled medicines to avoid "abuse," but in reality, it just let government officials inflict artificial shortages. Shortages were used to cull undesirables and punish people who did not have a high enough social credit.

On most colonies, everything revolved around "social credit," from food entitlements to clothing to health care. Every purchase was monitored, prices were adjusted based on social credit and scarcity.

There was always a need, and people could always find something to trade on the black market, whether it was items they had to produce but didn't need because they fit some administrator's five-year plan, or information, sympathy, or support.

Green Hope was a small colony struggling to survive, burdened with things they didn't need and denied things they did. The planet was closer to its star and radiation passing through the clouds was higher. This caused more virus mutations so the people of Green Hope never had enough medication for cancer or fresh viral outbreaks.

"Hermod, this is *Valkyrie 19*," Eversti Halko said on the Aesir's channel.

Hermod paused and looked around again.

"Go, *Valkyrie 19*."

"Still have no activity from Village Epsilon," Halko said. "Or the main colony at the elevator. It's like they are gone. Evacuated maybe?"

Hermod scowled. They had to be there. The Eversti was just missing it. From orbit there had been no signs of battle, no gutted and smoking buildings. Maybe they were indoors for some religious reason or some stupid SOG propaganda dictate. They had displayed no religious affiliation the last time Hermod's team was here, but the SOG liked to experiment with social requirements.

"I'm also not picking up anything on any civilian bands," Halko said. "I really don't like this."

"I like it even less," Hermod said. "I'm the one down here."

"Do you think the SOG closed down the colony?" Halko asked.

Hermod couldn't imagine why they would. There were plenty of other colonies that should be shut down but weren't. Boring was not a reason to shut down Green Hope.

"You're still picking up power readings, right?" Hermod asked.

"Yes. There's automated comm traffic. The manufactories are still producing stuff, although I suspect a couple may have shut down for lack of materials or maintenance."

"Fine," Hermod said. Village Epsilon was only another two kilometers away.

"SOG trap?" Hanz asked. He was a good man. He had served with Hermod for almost fifty years. Originally, he had come from a colony on a planet, DeutschHeimat, which was now a SOG protectorate. The last time they had been there, almost twenty years ago, Hanz and Ailne hadn't recognized it. The SOG had imported immigrants and exported residents in order to make the planet more culturally diverse, robbing the local colonists of their culture and heritage "for the greater good."

"Probably," Hermod said. He had seen reports of other Aesir teams ambushed by SOG Peacekeepers. "Let's bunker down the mules and most of the team, then I'll take a few Aesir and we'll scout it out."

"Zen," Hanz said as Hermod sent the command to assemble in a patrol hide.

Like ghostly wraiths, the Aesir formed a circle around Hermod, using the mules like wagons, weapons facing out.

"Ailne, Rorik, and John, with me," Hermod said.

"Zen," the three Aesir said, and kneeled near Hermod.

Hermod nodded at Hanz and led the three Aesir toward Epsilon. They formed up in a diamond, with Hermod on point, weapons facing away from the center. John took up rear security, constantly turning to check behind them.

Hermod's bad feeling got worse the closer they got to Epsilon.

* * * * *

Chapter Two: Epsilon

Aesir Lojtnant Hermod – VRAEC

Epsilon Village was quiet. Not even a dog barked. The sun would set in about an hour.

The village itself was a cluster of drab, modular, one-story buildings.

"Ailne," Hermod said. "Send a drone around for a kurkistus."

"Zen," Ailne said. She already had a drone ready. The small robot slid noiselessly out of her palm and sped toward the village.

They lay so their feet were touching and everyone looked in a different direction, Hermod watched the village on the far side of the cultivated fields. Nothing seemed out of place. No broken windows, no bodies, and no evidence of weapons fire, but Hermod felt that death had recently been visited on this village. Goosebumps rippled down his arm. A biological attack?

There were a couple new buildings, maybe immigrants, maybe kids growing up, but everything looked just like it had years ago when Hermod last came this way. Plain and boring with the suppressed atmosphere of SOG colonies everywhere.

The colonists had requested some medicines and supplies, but nothing in their message had indicated they were in dire need.

Something was wrong.

The pit in Hermod's gut grew heavier as he watched through the drone as it looked in window after window. In one room, chairs were knocked over, but there was no blood splatter. He requested that the drone's limited AI look for any evidence of weapon fire, pock marks on buildings, spent shell casings, broken windows, blood stains, bullet holes.

Nothing.

Had everyone been rounded up at gunpoint? Watching the drone's cameras as Ailne piloted it around the buildings, Hermod felt they were being watched.

Epsilon wasn't a big village, maybe sixty or seventy families totaling a hundred and fifty to three hundred people, at most. Just a bunch of people slapped down in the middle of nowhere and told to multiply while the Governance took care of all their needs.

The drone approached the school. The first thing he noticed was that all the doors were closed and the shades pulled down on all the windows. Everywhere else it had been random, though, as he thought about it, most of the shades on the west side of buildings were down, which meant whatever had happened had probably occurred in the evening since the sun rose in the east.

All the vehicles were neatly parked, not that there were many, mostly automated farm tractors. Most of the bikes were near the houses, which again indicated evening, as people were settling down, going about their chores, children returned from school, or adults returning from work at the commissary or manufactories. Maybe whatever had happened occurred at sunset or shortly after?

"Nobody," Ailne said. "Nothing."

"Zen," Hermod said.

"That school, though," Ailne said. "It's the only building we haven't really gotten a good look inside."

Hermod checked his overhead view and plotted a course. The school wasn't quite in the center of the village, City Hall was, but there were several buildings surrounding it.

Both manufactories were quiet with full resource bins. It looked like they had run through the night and nobody had arrived to empty them, or the night shift had been otherwise occupied.

"No blood stains or sign of combat?" Hermod asked.

"I'm not seeing anything," Ailne said.

Hermod was sure the school was a trap. But what kind?

If satellite imagery from *Valkyrie 19* was any clue, all the villages and the main colony center were also empty of people.

"Are you picking up any networks or anything?" Hermod asked John, his network intrusion specialist.

"Low level maintenance networks only," John said. "No traffic that doesn't appear automated. I'm not picking up any other communication or data networks on any bands. Just the maintenance. It would take me a while to get in. They have the newer firmware, from the looks of it, much harder to crack. There's also some odd static, but that could be sunspot activity."

"How long to crack into the network?" Hermod asked.

"Probably five or six hours," John said. "But then we'll be able to see anything on the maintenance networks. Not sure what that will get us, though. They have upgraded since we were here last."

Hermod nodded. If there were easy answers, or the SOG really was that incompetent, this war would have been over decades ago.

"Ailne and I will take overwatch," Hermod said. "John, Rorik, I want you to see what is in that school building."

"Zen," his team echoed. Hanz's icon on the heads-up display blipped, indicating he was paying attention and acknowledging what Hermod was doing.

Cautiously, as if they were being watched, both John and Rorik slipped into the town, while their drone hovered overhead, watching. Seconds later, Ailne sent up another drone to do a wider sweep around the two Aesir.

If it not for their IFF beacons, Hermod would have lost track of them. They had their camouflage active so anybody looking with human eyes would only see two ghosts crawling or sprinting from hiding spot to hiding spot. In seconds, they were hidden by the buildings and Hermod had to follow their progress with the drone. Ailne was an expert and kept the drone moving around, watching for any movement, any observers, any other drones.

Both her drones were newer model Aesir stealth drones and should be undetectable to most SOG sensors. With a free market and an innovate or die incentive, the Vapaus Republic was steadily pulling ahead of the SOG in technology, despite the teeming hordes of scientists the SOG employed.

At any moment, Hermod expected SOG gunships to appear on the horizon with drop shuttles to pour hordes of brown-uniformed Guardsmen into the region. Drone fighters would be the first sign.

The two Aesir made it to the school without incident. They peered the windows.

"No lights," John said, and Hermod watched as they tested the door. "It is unlocked."

"Proceed with extreme caution," Hermod said as he watched John check the door for booby traps before inserting a wire-cam so he could look around without opening the door any further.

A minute later, John pulled open the door. With Rorik at his back the two disappeared into the building. Ailne's drone followed them while the second drone stayed outside and slid into the sky for a better view of the surrounding area.

The sun would soon set in the distance, which didn't worry Hermod in the slightest. Aesir gear had no problem with the dark. The only people inconvenienced by the dark would be people without night vision equipment. The dark would make him feel better, less exposed, less visible to any spy satellites in orbit.

At this time of year near Epsilon Village, the nights were almost as long as the days. Hermod had originally planned to set up a patrol hide near the town so John could crack their systems and make sure there were no surprises. If everything had been clear, the Aesir would have approached in the morning. But nothing about this mission was going according to plan or expectations.

Hermod switched to John's view inside the school. No signs of damage, no signs of struggle, no blood spray or drag marks.

Had the SOG rounded everyone up and sent them off to some ideological assessment or re-alignment camp? It wouldn't be the first time, but they usually didn't take every person on the planet. The current population of Green Hope was around thirty thousand, spread out in about twenty villages or towns. Nothing unusual for a SOG colony and difficult for sedition to take root on the scale required for a purge.

John peered into each room as they passed them. All the shades were down, keeping everything dark.

Large, reinforced double doors blocked the entrance to the gym. As John and Rorik approached, Hermod's heart began beating faster, but he couldn't put his finger on why. There was something behind those doors he didn't want to see, he just knew it. He was half tempted to tell the two Aesir to pull back, but they still needed to know what was going on.

The gym was a special affair in most towns and villages. They were usually sunk into the ground and designed to serve as emergency shelters. Hardened from radiation, storms, and most natural disasters, it was a safe space in each village. Frequently, the city hall also had emergency shelters, but the schools, tasked with educating, indoctrinating, and protecting the future generations of socialist slaves, maintained shelters for children.

The sun set, disappearing over the horizon as John began checking the gym door. It was silent except for the movement of his Aesir. John slipped the wire-cam under the door and it bumped into something soft, something that might have been cloth. Or a body.

With their weapons aimed at the door John turned the latch.

Both doors opened and several bodies fell at John's and Rorik's feet. They backed a couple steps; Hermod jumped even though he wasn't there. The two Aesir were disciplined enough to not shoot the bodies, but Hermod wasn't sure he could have held his fire. There were bodies everywhere, men, women, and children. It was likely everyone from the village was here.

"I nearly pissed myself," John said.

"What the hell happened?" Rorik asked looking around.

John knelt to look at the nearest body. It was a boy, maybe fourteen or fifteen, with bleached hair. His nearly closed eyes stared sightlessly at the ceiling.

"Rigor mortis hasn't completely set in," John said, lifting a hand. There was resistance and it fell slowly. "But I would say he's been dead for over six hours."

Hermod triggered John's biological warfare sensors. The Aesir battle dress was fully self-contained and should have reported any problems but it didn't actively scan for biowarfare contaminants.

"Thanks." John examined the boy. There was blood on his shirt and arm, like he'd been bitten near the neck and on the arm, puncture wounds rather than something trying to eat him.

"Injected poison?" Rorik asked. "That could affect rigor mortis, I suspect."

John nodded as he looked at the other bodies. It was impossible to step into the gym without walking on the corpses.

"See how he died?" John said. "He was leaning against the door. He couldn't have been stacked in there. He died there."

"So, is it still in there?" Hermod said, more of a statement than a question.

"I've got nothing on thermals," Rorik said, looking across the ceiling to see if anything was hanging there. "No movement at all."

"Hermod, this is *Valkyrie 19*," the Eversti said.

"Go," Hermod said.

"We might have a problem," Halko said. "I just detected a transition. It's reading as a medium ship, maybe a light cruiser. I'm going to pull *19* back to the rally point. Keep your head down."

Hermod cursed silently. "Zen."

If this was some SOG test of a biological agent, Hermod had confidence in Republic biowarfare protocols and defenses, but why would the SOG do such a thing? The people of Green Hope weren't seditious or in rebellion, they just needed medical supplies the bureaucracy was slow to give them.

But what was up with the puncture marks? Not much blood had been spilled from the puncture marks. A drone?

John turned on a light, and Hermod thought the bodies looked extremely pale. There was a speck of blood on the boy's lips. John reached down and pulled back a lip.

"Hermod?"

Hermod focused on what John was seeing. The boy's teeth were misshapen, almost sharp, the canines more elongated. "This kid is not normal. Is there some new dental fashion or something in the colonies I haven't heard about?"

"I haven't heard of anything."

John reached up and shined his light directly on the boy's face. He pulled back an eyelid and revealed a solid black eye. He released it and it slid closed. "Now that is creepy."

"You should check others," Rorik said. "The kid's a teenager; they do some really weird things these days. Heck, in my day they did weird things. Back in school on Gimli, cylinder Gama, there was a craze for a few years where it was all the rage to have purple skin and gold eyes."

"I remember that," Hermod said. "Damn. I didn't know you were that young. I visited Gimli and thought we were being invaded by aliens."

John lifted an eyelid of an older woman. It was also midnight black.

John leapt back. "Shit!"

"What?" Rorik brought his weapon to his shoulder.

"Man," John said, obviously trying to relax. "I thought I saw her eye move."

Hermod triggered thermals. Nothing. All the bodies were room temperature. They were dead.

The boy opened his eyes and looked directly at John.

John's and Rorik's suit sensors logged movement within the gym. Eyes opened and heads turned to look at the Aesir.

* * *

V*alkyrie 19* lost their link with the Aesir team in a wave of static.

* * * * *

Chapter Three: Homestar

Gunnery Sergeant Wolf Mathison, USMC

Wolf Mathison set his face to make it easier to hide his disappointment as the shuttle slid into the hangar. There were no windows and the video links for passengers was disabled for security reasons. Not even Skadi had access. If there was a better way to stroll into a trap, Mathison was hard pressed to think of one.

The Republic Executive Council had to recognize he and his Marines were a danger. When it was decided they were no longer worth the risk they would be killed instantly. Though Skadi and Sif were pretty calm about the Marines being allowed on a homestar and did their best to mask their confusion and uncertainty, nobody, including Mathison and his Marines, thought it was a good idea. While he couldn't find an exact reason not to trust the council, that little voice was warning him that right now, without a ship of their own, the Marines were at the mercy of their hosts. There was nobody they could appeal to for arbitration or rescue.

Curiosity drove Mathison forward. Skadi and the other Aesir had described the homestars as sprawling city-ships in space, hiding between the stars, mining the remnants of exploded stars, and hiding from the SOG battle fleets that hunted them. He imagined the people of the Vapaus Republic were starving refugees, crammed into ghetto-like starships, eking out a bleak living while their Aesir and Vanir raided and fought the SOG to bring back critical supplies. It sounded like a life of hardship, danger, and little reward. What did they eat? How bland was their diet? Would that be a life worth living? Could he and his Marines find happiness and a future as refugees aboard an ancient starship on the run from the most powerful regime in history?

Skadi had mentioned how obsessive the Vanir were about security and how seriously they took their mission. They could even overrule the Executive Council in certain circumstances, but this time the Executive Council had overridden the Vanir to bring the Marines to Asgard, capital homestar of the Vanir Republic.

Politics had never much interested Mathison except how it related to his Marine Corps and the wars he fought. Presidents came and went, some had stupid policies, some were smart, some betrayed the armed forces, other didn't. Regardless, American presidents were only there for four or eight years before government policy took a sharp turn in the other direction when the other party took power. Both parties did their best to reverse the gains and policies of the other, keeping the United States on a road to the future, if one imagined the driver was drunk and couldn't decide which shoulder of the road they wanted to crash on.

In the United States, there were good years and bad, depending on how the driver swerved, but in the Vapaus Republic? There was probably at least one secret police force. It made sense for a government to have multiple agencies that did similar jobs. Like the Army and Marines. Keeping them in competition kept each from becoming dominant and pushed them to be better.

Too many thoughts went through Mathison's mind as he waited for the hatch to open. Would there be secret police operatives ready to escort him and his Marines away, to dissect them and remove their SCBIs? Skadi had insisted that Mathison and his team wear sidearms, but they would be worthless against heavily armored opponents.

Skadi was like Mathison, or so it seemed, in that she spent little time involved in Republic politics. She was a warrior, and her enemy was the SOG. Any information that did not have bearing on her ability to wage war was secondary. She seemed as clueless as Mathison why the council wanted to see the Marines or why they would risk the Vanir's wrath by violating their precious security protocols.

The tattoo on Skadi's eye was back, advertising she was an Erikoisjoukot Special Operations Team Leader. The big hulking masses of Niels, Bern, and Vili were nearby. A giant warrior princess guarded by other giants. Mathison felt strange being near other men as large as he was. Next to them, Stathis seemed tiny in comparison, and Sif was almost unnoticeable. The Aesir were armored, their battle dress showing the parade colors of black and gold. Sergeant Levin had managed to color coordinate the Marines with dark blue and scarlet, to set them apart from the Aesir. They were as close to Marine dress blues as Levin and Stathis could manage. Wearing armor made Mathison feel a little better, but it would offer little protection against blazers without the trauma plates.

Mathison felt like a peacock on parade. Freya had interfaced with his suit and used the settings Levin had set up to add her own touches, such as rank, ribbons, and medals. Mathison thought it looked like a salad had exploded over his heart. To Mathison's surprise even Stathis had ribbons that went past a single row: National Defense, Combat Action, Papua New Guinea campaign, space service medal, sea service medal, space combat service award, a Navy unit commendation, North Africa Expedition medal, and a meritorious unit commendation. Far too many for a mere private, and almost as many as Chief Winters. Levin also had a small salad on his chest, but then Levin had been a Raider for years. Usually, that space on their armor was reserved for rank insignia and the eagle, globe, and anchor. It let people know their Marine rank, and there was little else they needed.

Had Stathis really been around that long? He had been in a line infantry battalion for several years before coming to the Raiders. Mathison knew he had been busted back to private once or twice, maybe three times, but Stathis was clearly better traveled than he acted.

The medals felt gaudy and pretentious to Mathison. It wasn't like anyone would recognize the awards, and it wasn't like they would be given any new ones, though the SCBIs had taken certain liberties with the space service and Papua New Guinea ribbons.

Skadi looked at him and nodded. She seemed satisfied. Mathison wanted to scowl. Gunnery sergeant was a staff NCO rank. Dealing with civilians shouldn't be in his job description; that's what officers were for or someone from public affairs.

Damn it.

Mathison glanced at Winters. She was an officer, and she was *supposed* to outrank him. Could he push her to the front and have her deal with this circus?

The hatch finally slid open, and a chilly breeze blew through the cabin. Skadi and the other Aesir shuffled to the door.

"Are we allowed to get drunk, Gunny?" Stathis asked.

"Is there a way I could keep you from getting drunk and stupid?" Mathison asked.

Stathis pursed his lips and thought.

"Sure, Gunny," Stathis said after a moment. "But I don't want you to be unhappy. I learned early that the only happy gunny is a frothing-at-the-mouth-screaming-his-head-off gunny. Since I'm your only private, I have a lot of work ahead of me. It's a big responsibility, and I take it very seriously."

Mathison took a deep breath and opened his mouth, but what could he say to that?

The nice, clean, brightly lit shuttle bay might have been the last thing Mathison expected. The bay itself was big enough for several large shuttles, but currently their shuttle was the only one in it. Large, double doors slid open, and Mathison saw a welcoming party start toward them. The welcoming party comprised of two Aesir wearing their battle dress without trauma plates, which Mathison understood was like wearing their day-to-day utility uniform.

So much for a drab, aged landing bay on a cannibalized hulk of a ship.

One of the two was a massively tall, handsome man with piercing blue eyes, short, braided hair, a short well-combed beard, a mustache, and a scowl. The other Aesir looked to be as barrel-chested as Niels, but he was short, almost Stathis's height. Both looked serious.

Mathison looked around. A couple techs in Vanir uniforms were supervising robots arriving to service the shuttle, but otherwise the bay was empty.

Skadi and the two Aesir stopped when they met each other. The new Aesirs' eyes flickered over Mathison and his Marines before locking on Skadi.

"Hei and Skal. Hermod's team has gone missing," the tall one said by way of a greeting.

"Hei and Skal. Missing?" Skadi asked. "What do you mean missing?"

The tall one's eyes flickered to Mathison.

"Gunnery Sergeant Mathison—" Skadi motioned at him and then the taller Aesir "—this is Krenraali Lief, the senior-most Aesir of the Vapaus Republic."

"Honored to meet you, sir," Mathison said, stepping forward. Leif held out his hand. He had a good, firm handshake. The most senior? Were there so few Aesir he had the time to meet them now?

"Krenraali is general," Freya said, Mathison's SCBI or Sentient Cybernetic Biological Interface. *"While I don't have any real data, I suspect he is the equivalent of the Commandant of the Marine Corps."*

"I'm surprised he isn't being followed by a platoon of staff officers," Mathison said.

"No surprise, if he's trying to be low key and keep secrets," Freya said.

"This is my immediate superior officer, Aesir Everstiluutnantii Baldr," Skadi said, motioning to the other Vanir. "These are Marines Chief Warrant Officer Winters, Sergeant Levin, and Private Stathis."

"Yes," Freya said, *"they are trying to keep a very low profile. Everstiluutnantii is the equivalent of lieutenant colonel."*

Everyone shook hands, and Lief finally looked at Skadi.

"I realize you just got back," Lief said, "but I don't think we can wait. You are the only Erikoisjoukot team we have available at the moment. There might also be, um, complications."

Skadi frowned. "Why not a standard rescue team? A Drekkar combat group with a Jaeger battalion?"

"Nothing about this is normal," Baldr said. "We've read your reports. I'm not sure I want to risk a Drekkar combat group or a battlestar task force. I'm also short of Jaegers and marauders."

"*Valkyrie 19* believes it might be some new SOG biological warfare experiment," Lief said, and Mathison's blood went cold.

"Based on your reports," Lief continued, "we are inclined to believe it is something else. *Valkyrie 15* is getting an emergency resupply. *Tyr* is also going to be briefed, but *15* can respond more quickly. *Tyr* will not be available to support you, though."

She raised an eyebrow and looked at Lief.

"What is *Tyr* doing?" she asked.

"Classified," Lief said. "It also has our other Erikoisjoukot teams involved."

Mathison would pay money to know what was going through Skadi's mind. The woman was damned good at hiding her thoughts behind a facade of ice.

"Zen," Skadi said.

"You have a couple hours aboard the Midgard," Lief said and glanced at Sif. "Magni is still collecting information and will send you a notification when the briefing is ready. He is consulting with the Nakija and trying to get information from them, otherwise we would have turned the shuttle around before it landed."

"Zen," Skadi said. "Is there enough time to show the Marines around?"

Mathison saw Lief stop a brief scowl before it spread to the rest of his face, then he nodded, his face now carefully blank.

"Thank you for coming down, Krenraali," Skadi said.

"I wanted to see what was tearing apart the Executive Council," Lief said with a small smile, looking at Mathison and the other Marines.

"That bad?" Skadi asked.

"Yes," Lief said, his eyes returning her. "I hope they are on their best behavior. The Nakija Johtaja called in a lot of favors and invoked some pretty obscure articles on behalf of these Marines. The president and other Johtaja are furious."

"Which makes me wonder if the Executive Council knows you are here," Freya said. *"That would explain the secrecy and the Krenraali's attempt to get you out of here sooner rather than later. According to what little information I have, the Johtaja are like senior executives; it translates from the Finnish language as 'Managers' or 'Directors.' In this context, I would say they rank right below the president, but I have no idea how their authority system works. Based on available data, this likely involves politicking on the Executive Council."*

"Thank you, Krenraali," Skadi said.

"I am detecting multiple networks," Freya said. *"I'm not connecting without an invitation, though. They're more numerous and open here, not nearly as secure as aboard* Tyr. *And unlike the SOG networks in so many ways."*

"Be on your best behavior," Mathison said.

"Of course," Freya said. *"Although we could get offended by the constant directed scans."*

Lief looked at Mathison. "I have no control or authority over you and your Marines, so I can't order you. And your legal status is somewhat peculiar for many reasons."

"Yes, sir," Mathison said. Obviously, the Vapaus Republic was still struggling with the SCBI problem.

"While we might accept you as immigrants," Lief said, looking skeptical, "that would move you and your Marines to our civilian jurisdiction. There is Vanir oversight, but there is nothing normal about this situation."

"We understand, sir." And he almost did. If artificial intelligence of Freya's level was illegal, then there would be legal ramifications, and that was before security considerations. He could easily see them saying they would not allow him and his Marines aboard unless they removed their SCBIs, which was unlikely to happen.

"So, I'm not sure how to handle your situation. We are working with different authorities to get you and your SCBIs some kind of solution, but if you have ever dealt with lawyers and politicians, you know it's not a quick or simple process, especially when there are security classifications and secrecy involved. Until then, we are doing our best to ignore some ramifications."

"Understood, sir." Mathison tried not to let his disappointment show. Refugees with lawyers?

"That said, would you be willing to work with Lojtnant Skadi?" Lief asked. "I would like you and your Marines to join her team for now. She would act as liaison while we figure out a status for you and your Marines. We can classify you as members of an allied military, contractors, or foreign advisers. The official term is Liitoutuneet."

Mathison glanced at Levin and Winters. He didn't see any disagreement; of course, he didn't look at Stathis.

"We would be honored," Mathison said. "We can follow her orders."

Lief shook his head. "It is a peculiar chain of command situation, though. I would really like you to be under Sif's command. She is Nakija and Aesir, although she is different from Skadi. Also, if you were under her command, you would not be under direct Aesir command due to legal quirks."

Mathison glanced at Sif. Taking orders from a preteen girl? He knew she was a lot older than he was, but looking at her, listening to her voice, that would be difficult. Was this a test?

"Freya?" Mathison asked.

"You've done harder things," Freya said.

"Can do, sir," Mathison said aloud. Logically, it made sense. Logically, there was no reason not to, except she looked like she was twelve.

Lief nodded. "For the moment, I would prefer your SCBIs not access our networks. Not even the immigrant network. I suspect they could download more information than we want to expose to the SOG in the event of your capture. We don't have access to your storage buffers, you understand?"

Mathison nodded.

"Do they want to neuter us while they are at it?"

"I think they're terrified," Freya said. *"They need us, but they're terrified. The Nakija is probably the only reason we aren't already dead."*

"The mysterious Nakija," Mathison said. *"Why doesn't that make me feel better?"*

"You and me both," Freya said.

"I'm sorry," Lief said. "This is the real reason I came down here. I wanted to look you in the eye and tell you personally, not hide behind others. I've read the reports. This would be easier if you were actual aliens, Torag, or Voshka. Instead, you have a highly illegal and feared technology, you come from a nation that no longer exists, and you don't even come from our time."

"Understood, sir," Mathison said.

Lief nodded. "I will leave you in Skadi's and Sif's capable hands. If you have any problems, questions, or concerns, you are authorized to contact me directly. Thank you."

"You're welcome, sir," Mathison said, wondering if that meant he and his Marines would spend the next hour or two waiting in the brig.

"Since we have time, I will take the Marines on a quick tour," Skadi said.

Tour?

Lief frowned. "I'm not sure that's advisable."

"Remember how you assigned a certain member to my team," Skadi said. "How I advised against it?"

The krenraali scowled at Skadi.

"Great!" she said. "Payback's a bitch. I'm going to take them on a quick tour of Midgard. They've been around *Tyr*, except critical areas. I think it's worth showing them what and who they are fighting with and for."

Lief opened his mouth, but Skadi kept going.

"Thanks!" she said before lowering her voice to a more serious tone. "Glad you agree, Krenraali. It *is* a good idea, isn't it?"

Lief looked at her, waiting for her to continue. When she didn't, he nodded and turned away.

Baldr smiled at Skadi behind Leif's back and said, "Magni will let you know when he is ready."

*****

Chapter Four:
Tour

Lojtnant Skadi – VRAEC

Skadi knew she would pay for treating the krenraali that way. It would be subtle, of course, but after nearly fifty years under him she knew how he worked and exactly how far she could push him. Before Krenraali Lief could come up with some new plan, Skadi took the Marines to the nearest tram. Her military credentials let her commandeer one for their use. Niels joined her while Bern and Vili went to handle their own errands.

"You plan on taking them down to Ice Picks?" Niels asked.

"Yes," Skadi said. Well, now she was. She had just wanted to get them away from the docking stations, away from the military, so they could see what civilian life was like aboard the homestars. Ice Picks was a club that catered to military personnel. Any civilians there would be pro-military. It would also be a good way to introduce the Marines to the other military branches and subbranches. There were usually a lot of friendly people and most Erikoisjoukot liked to go there to relax. There were even some fighting rings to work off some steam.

They loaded onto the tram but there weren't enough seats.

"You want to sit down, ma'am?" Stathis asked, standing and offering his seat to her. Mathison also stood.

"No, thank you, Stathis," Skadi said. *What weird custom was this?*

Stathis nodded.

"Well, ma'am, you can if you like. I would rather stand so I can see the sights."

Skadi looked at the walls outside the windows. Did he know the view wasn't real or did he know it would change?

In seconds the walls disappeared, removing a view of some mountains. Skadi thought she did a good job hiding her smile as the Marines' eyes widened, and they looked around.

The tram transitioned smoothly into the cylinder. This one was called Turku after one of the oldest cities in Finland as well as one of the first cylinders. It was eight kilometers in length and full of two-story buildings and shops, surrounded by parks and short trees. A pleasant place.

"Impressive," Mathison said. "This is a spaceship, right?"

"Yes," Niels said. "This is one of eight cylinders."

"How was it created?" Mathison asked.

"First, they burrowed a big tunnel in an asteroid, then they built a rotating cylinder inside the tunnel. You can't see the asteroid on the outside anymore. They started with a nickel asteroid, excellent base material. Most of it ended up on the outer shell as radiation shielding and armor. The cylinders were built next; the rotation provides gravity. They then built engines aft, control centers, hydroponics, and more."

"So, they just put engines on an asteroid?" Stathis asked.

"Zen," Niels said.

"Impressive," Mathison said. "How many people?"

"Millions," Niels said. "I don't know the exact numbers, but there are several other homestars with comparable populations. This is a big fleet."

"That is awesome," Stathis said. "So many people going from place to place. How fast do the ships go?"

"Usually they don't move," Niels said, glancing at Skadi. He was getting close to discussing classified information. "Mostly, the fleet stays in deep space. There is plenty of interstellar garbage floating between the stars that we can use. We have no need to travel much except to escape the SOG."

"Kinda like mobile homes in trailer parks? Sweet. Have they ever found the fleet?" Stathis asked.

"Once," Niels said. "Long ago. It wasn't a large attack fleet and it got ripped apart. Since then the fleet has moved a few times. To hear them tell it, they found the fleet and wiped us out. The SOG tells funny stories."

"What about the Kisky Syndrome thingy?" Stathis asked, staring around.

The trams were on elevated platforms, so it was easy to see the fantastically designed houses. Some looked like fortresses, others looked like they were made of living plants. They varied, with no two houses the same.

Niels shrugged and glanced at her. The fleet had not moved in almost a decade. Kiska Syndrome kept the fleet stationary these days. But most civilians were fine with that. The current government was under pressure to avoid relocating, and now it was just considered an emergency measure. Most people in the fleet were thoroughly convinced the Vanir could keep them hidden and safe indefinitely.

The tram stopped and slid to the ground so they could disembark.

"It is like a fairyland," Stathis said, looking at a house with a holographic display of a forest that was constantly growing and being absorbed by itself. One tree would grow in front of others before fading backward as another tree grew to conceal it. If you stood still it looked like you were moving away from a forest.

"This way," Skadi said, and everyone fell in behind her.

The Ice Pick looked like a palace made of ice and there were holograms on the ceilings and walls of Vikings sledding in longboats, waving and cheering silently as if the longboat was a rollercoaster.

Entering the building was soothing, like entering a nice, cool cave. The walls looked made of ice and dampers reduced the volume inside the club, and there were no loud sounds. Tables cluttered the room, and the bar stretched wall to wall. Different sections enticed customers with holotable games. Several doors led off the main room to other forms of entertainment.

"Wow," Stathis said looking around. "Gunny, check out the babes."

Skadi did her best not to frown. Calling them babes might get the little private beat up, restrained, and thrown in a trash can… if he was lucky.

She shook her head and placed an order for drinks. She ordered drinks for the Marines and led them to a table where they had a good view of the club.

One woman turned around to examine the newcomers. She had what looked like bat wings painted over her eyes.

"Are they team leaders too, ma'am?" Stathis asked.

"They are HKTs," Skadi said.

"Hunter Killer Teams?" Mathison asked.

"Finns founded the Vapaus Republic. The government was originally Finnish, and we take a lot of our names, customs, and words from Scandinavian cultures," Skadi said. "HKT means hyökkäys kaapata tiimi, which translates as 'attack capture team.' They are Vanir who specialize in commando operations, attacking and taking enemy ships and space-based installations. The black eyeshadow is one of their traditions; like bats, they hunt in the dark."

"So, like, if the Vanir are Navy, then the HKTs are like Navy SEALs?" Stathis asked.

"Close." Skadi looked at Stathis. *Navy? Like on the water?* She didn't want to go into details. And she had no idea how space-based commandos were anything like a military branch involved in water boats.

"They aren't humongous like you Aesir, ma'am," Stathis said.

"Speed is better in ship-to-ship operations," Skadi said, shrugging. "In space, without gravity, size and mass are not the advantages you might think they are, so they don't bulk up."

"So why are the Aesir so big, ma'am?"

"Because we fight on the ground and in space," Skadi said. "We are more versatile and flexible. All-terrain, space, air, land, sea."

Stathis nodded but seemed to be having trouble taking his eyes off the HKT commandos.

"Are all of them girls?" Stathis asked.

Niels spit out part of his drink and tried to hide his smile. His flippant comment caught Skadi by surprise as well, but she hid it better. Did the little private want to start a fight with the HKTs?

"If you call them girls," Skadi said, "you will probably find out how good they are at hand-to-hand combat. It won't be a pleasant experience for you. They have no problem taking on larger people."

"I could take 'em," Stathis said.

"There are combat rings," Skadi said. "You wear special suits to keep you from getting hurt too bad, like your powered armor, but backward. They don't boost your punch, but weaken it so it doesn't hurt too badly. It's a great way to let off steam."

"Really?" Stathis asked and Skadi noticed his eyes slip over to Niels.

Was he really thinking of challenging Niels?

"Shut up and drink, Private," Mathison said. "I'll let you take a crack at me later."

"I know how that will end up, Gunny," Stathis said. "Me beaten to a pulp and you feeling your age, then I'll have to listen to you complain about your knees and back for the next week."

Skadi and Niels laughed, and Mathison scowled. She caught Winters and Levin smiling, too.

"Have you ever heard me complain about my knees and back recently?" Mathison asked. His attention focused elsewhere, he was only half paying attention.

Another group of Aesir arrived and found a table in the gaming area. Other Aesir were cheering each other on.

"Well, Gunny—"

"Shut up, Stathis," Mathison said, cutting him off before he could get started.

"Aye, Gunny," Stathis said, more than happy to turn his attention elsewhere.

Stathis hadn't been discouraged though, and she saw his eyes turn toward the HKTs. More HKTs had joined them. There were a few men and the black paint around their eyes made them look odd. Of course, others probably thought the tattoo on her eye was equally strange.

She hadn't worked with HKTs much, maybe once or twice in the last several decades. As Vanir, they never went planet side and the only interaction they had with the SOG, or most of the ghost colonies, involved surgical strikes against space assets. They indoctrinated the Vanir to avoid contact with non-Republic entities while the Erikoisjoukot teams specialized in it.

"Are they Erikoisjoukot, too?" Stathis asked, pointing at some Jaegers who walked in looking like they owned the place.

"They are Jaegers," Skadi said.

"Like in Jägermeister?" Stathis asked with a smile.

Skadi shrugged, not knowing what he was talking about.

"They're veteran Aesir," Skadi said. "More highly trained and combat focused than regular Aesir. They frequently provide backup and muscle for Erikoisjoukot teams and they are used to spearhead other assaults. You can tell they are Jaegers by their patches. Aesir with Jaeger certification add a hammer to their axe and sword. Erikoisjoukot get a dagger."

Skadi pointed at the emblem on her own breast. It had the standard crossed axe and sword of the Aesir, along with a vertical dagger and a horizontal hammer.

"Like Army Rangers?" Stathis asked, looking at Mathison.

The gunnery sergeant just shrugged.

Something happened near the gaming tables. Half of the Aesir were cheering, the other half booing. It looked like they were playing

Battle Space Commander on one of the larger tables. It had millions of variations and was quite popular. It was also a great trainer for NCOs and officers.

"Good beer," Stathis said. "Not that watered down stuff we get in America."

"How do you know?" Mathison asked. "Are you old enough to drink?"

"I'm twenty-two, Gunny," Stathis said. "I've been drinking since I was like fifteen."

"This reminds me of German beer," Mathison said. "Yeah. American beer was watered down. Watch yourself, Stathis, I'll bet this packs a punch. You'll probably be shitfaced before you expect it."

"Aye, Gunny," Stathis said and took a big, loud sip. "It's time for me to build up my tolerance again. I bet I lost it sleeping for hundreds of years. Do you need a nap, Gunny? I hear old people like naps."

Was Stathis taunting his gunnery sergeant?

"Shut up, Stathis," Levin said as the gunnery sergeant ignored him.

* * * * *

Chapter Five: Ice Pick

Gunnery Sergeant Wolf Mathison, USMC

The homestar was impressive, and Mathison didn't want to show how impressed he was. If they could mine what they needed and didn't have to worry about water and air, living in space like this couldn't be bad. The few people he had seen on the streets had seemed normal enough. The extravagant houses and parks were impressive, although it could be this was an upper-class cylinder. He doubted Skadi would take them slumming in the less reputable cylinders.

There was one thing that bothered him. There was no actual sky. No clouds, no sun. It looked like the secret SOG base, just much brighter and bigger. There was a mist in the center of the cylinder that almost hid the lights and track running down the center.

It was disorienting to look around and follow a road as it went up, circled above you, and came down on the other side.

The closest thing to clouds was the spinning mist in the central core. The mist swirled slowly and Mathison wasn't sure if they were stationary while the cylinder rotated around them or if they were moving more slowly than the cylinder.

"Plenty of network links available," Freya reported. *"It will be interesting if we ever get permission to connect."*

"You see any problems here?" Mathison asked.

"Nothing glaring," Freya said. *"I have seen what appear to be some vagrants sleeping in the street. This is not the upper end from what I've seen so far. The far end of the cylinder appears to have much more elaborate houses, some three stories. Most houses have gardens on the roof. There is room for improvement, but overall, things look sustainable. Doesn't look overcrowded. I do not have full information, and this could be the middle of the night with everyone sleeping, but I suspect that is not the case."*

Mathison nodded as he watched the cheering Aesir. It seemed a lively event and made him think of football games in the barracks. There were plenty of monitors and other displays. It could have been a typical sports bar, though the soft music was not what he would have selected. Lots of twang, like country, but there was a piano and maybe bagpipes? That was going to take some getting used to. Mathison usually preferred his music loud.

Mathison tuned it out and looked at the other patrons. This place obviously catered to military personnel. There were pedestals scattered around the room that showed holographic images of warriors in uniform. Each showed for a minute with a name, rank, date of birth, and a date of death. He noticed that only "Vanir" and "Aesir" were indicated beyond that.

The waiter, or waitress, it was hard to tell with the short hair and slim figure, brought them another round.

"How are we paying?" Mathison asked.

"I've got it," Skadi said.

"Tervehdys!" one of the Aesir yelled. Everyone stood and yelled 'Tervehdys' and took a drink, even Skadi and Niels stood. Which meant Mathison and his Marines stood and drank.

"What was that?" Stathis asked.

"Tervehdys means salute," Skadi said pointing at one of the holographic displays. "It's done when someone recognizes one of the fallen."

Mathison looked at his drink thinking he should drink to Vance, Heller, Lampkin, Kamanski, Patterson, Stevenson and all the others. He read the platoon roster in his mind's eye as though he was staring at a screen. He might not drink to them here, but he would always remember them.

"I don't know if that's super cool or annoying," Stathis said, his eyes watching the ever-changing holographs.

"It is rare," Skadi said. "There are literally tens of thousands of fallen. Although one can put in requests and those one served with may appear more frequently."

"Doesn't it disrupt their game?" Stathis asked looking at the Aesir who were yelling and jeering at each other again.

"Nope," Niels said. "It gets paused for a minute when the sensors hear 'tervehdys.' Some things are more important than a game. If they are that serious, they go elsewhere."

"Sensors are always listening?" Stathis asked.

"Yes," Niels.

"Everywhere?" Stathis asked, looking around. "Is it ever abused?"

Niels shrugged. "Never been a problem for me. Anyone abusing it gets an invitation to the fight rings."

"Zen," Skadi said, agreeing with him.

Constant surveillance? Who monitored, reviewed, and abused the recordings?

A voice yelled out from the entrance, and Mathison saw Bern. Bern waved at them but headed for the other Aesir. He was obviously well known because some of the Aesir stood to give him a bear hug or shake his hand.

Mathison watched Bern start a lively discussion with the other Aesir.

"Are all cylinders like this one?" Mathison asked Skadi. He needed to get his mind off the fallen or he would drink himself into oblivion.

"Mostly," Skadi said. "Well, except in appearances. This was one of the first and doesn't change as much, it's also the smallest. Some cylinders are considered very stylish among different groups. Civilians in the Vapaus Republic are an eclectic lot, always following some fashion or trend."

"They lose grasp of reality sometimes," Niels said. "They think fashion is more important than the SOG. Most civilians have never set foot on a planet, and those who have, have not done so in almost a century. The lives of the protected are soft and easy without solid perspective."

"A century? Like a hundred years?" Stathis asked. "People live that long?"

"Yes," Niels said. "That is one thing the Vapaus Republic does, it takes care of the people, even the asukas."

"Asukas?" Stathis asked.

"Non-citizens," Niels said. "Immigrants who haven't earned their citizenship."

Bern joined them. "Hei and skal. Vili's not here? He owes me drinks for carrying his fat ass halfway across Lisbon. Figures he wouldn't make it."

"Hei and skal," Niels and Skadi said.

"You can ping him," Niels said. "He can open a tab for you."

"Where is the fun if he isn't here to see me drink his money?"

"How does one earn citizenship or asukas status?" Stathis asked Niels as Bern rejoined the other Aesir.

"Serve twenty years in the military or civil service for citizenship; prove you can serve something bigger than yourself and do so honorably. Asukas are everyone else. Only citizens can vote in most elections, but some are open to asukas," Niels said.

"Seems extreme," Stathis said.

Niels shrugged.

"It makes sure the asukas don't vote themselves a benefit increase and crash the system," Niels said. "Or vote to surrender to the SOG."

"They are okay with not having any power?" Stathis asked.

"If they want such power they have to earn it," Niels said. "If they earn their rights, they understand them and care about them."

"Civil service?" Stathis asked.

"Policing, building, repairing and designing Republic ships, or an array of other government jobs," Niels said. "They will find something for you to do if you don't have the guts to serve in the military. It won't be easy and there could still be danger involved, but the government will find something for you. As a Republic, they have to. No free rides. It is part of our Constitution."

"So, they're paying for their ride on this spaceship?" Stathis asked.

"Shut up, Stathis," Mathison said.

"Aye, Gunny," Stathis said, his eyes wandering back to the HKT women. "I think that tattoo on their face is sexy."

"You are a private," Mathison said. "Privates think anything with a pair of boobs is sexy."

Realizing who was present, Mathison glanced at Skadi and Winters. "No offense, ladies."

Skadi shrugged like she didn't care, and Winters nodded as she took a sip of her drink.

"It is still early on Midgard," Skadi said. "Not a lot of places are open. When they do we will go for a walk. Or if you want to look around on your own, we can meet back here later."

Mathison looked around. Nobody seemed interested in leaving.

"Don't look at me, people," Mathison said to the Marines. "I'm not your mommy."

Levin smiled. "I'm good, Gunny. They've got beer here."

"And babes," Stathis said, still looking at the HKTs. He pulled his chair close to Mathison.

"What would be a good pickup line for an HKT?" Stathis asked in a low voice.

"Do you think we're drinking buddies now, Private?" Mathison asked.

Stathis looked at the drink in his hand and the drink in Mathison's.

"Shut up, Stathis."

Stathis looked at Levin, who smiled and shook his head.

The private leaned back and looked dejected.

Good. Though it might be fun to send him over and watch him get his ass kicked.

Mathison quickly discarded the thought. He wouldn't send one of his Marines to get their ass kicked by a stranger. Hopefully, he could steer Stathis toward something a little less dangerous.

Privates had to be constantly supervised, especially the younger ones. They would try to stick their dick into anything wet or warm. Mathison tried not to scowl as he looked at his beer. How much trouble could Stathis get into here? What legal standing did he and his Marines have? Who would he appeal if he needed to get Stathis released from custody? It wasn't like the USMC had a status of forces agreement with the Vapaus Republic.

Bern gestured toward the Marines. Over the music, Mathison heard "US Marines."

Damn. What's Bern telling them? Mathison saw the HKTs look in their direction. Unlike the Aesir, their looks were a bit more hostile.

"I should mention," Skadi said, apparently noticing the looks from the HKT. "The Vanir are a bit xenophobic. They are very loyal to the Republic but have a problem trusting people who aren't from the Republic."

"Bern is apparently telling them that Skadi's team rescued us from the SOG who had found us in stasis. He is leaving out many operational details," Freya reported.

"Great," Mathison said.

"Good to know," Mathison said to Skadi.

An Aesir from Bern's group stood and came over.

"Hei and Skal. Welcome, friends," the big man said. "I am called Hans by my Jaeger brothers. My brother Bern tells me you are from the past. A fanciful tale I do not believe. America?"

Mathison stood and nodded, holding out his hand.

"I'm Gunnery Sergeant Mathison," Mathison said then introduced the others.

"Bern was telling me you can fight," Hans said. Mathison nodded, knowing what was coming. Hans was a big man and looked young.

"Did Sisko Skadi or Kaveri Niels mention there are combat pits and how they work?" Hans asked.

"They just arrived, Hans," Skadi said. "Just got off the ship. It would be polite to let them relax and learn a bit about Midgard and our people first."

"Can I, Gunny?" Stathis said. Hans looked at Stathis in surprise.

"Can you what?" Mathison growled.

"You know," Stathis said and glanced at Hans.

"Seriously?" Mathison asked.

Hans grinned widely, but then frowned. "You sure, young man? You might want to gain a little weight first."

"You calling me small?" Stathis said.

"No offense, young man," Hans said. "But you might want to watch a round or two while the larger men test their skills."

"You want to test me?" Mathison asked Hans.

The big man smiled.

"You can take him," Freya said but Mathison wasn't so confident.

Arrogant prick.

Mathison didn't want to fight him. Even if the suits prevented them from really hurting each other, it wouldn't be easy or tame. Mathison couldn't afford to lose.

"I'm just curious to see if your unarmed combat methods are as good as ours. It has been a few hundred years," Hans said.

"Fine," Mathison said. He was curious as well. "But Stathis here handles my light work. You want to take me on, you have to prove you're worth my time. If you can't beat Stathis, why should I waste my time?"

Hans frowned and looked at Stathis.

"Can Stathis take him?" Mathison asked Freya.

"Most likely," Freya said. *"He will be assisted and boosted by Shrek. His chances are excellent."*

Mathison looked at Stathis and thought the private's grin might split his face. He saw the HKTs were watching intently.

"What are the rules?" Mathison asked.

"Don't you think you should have asked before you accepted the challenge?" Skadi asked, obviously not happy, but her anger appeared to be focused on Hans.

"If Stathis loses I will use it as a teaching moment," Mathison said, shrugging. Then he gave in to the temptation to needle Hans. "I suspect that as people get more civilized they lose the ability to fight."

"Oh ho!" Hans said. "You are mad at your Marine, huh?"

Mathison smiled. Hans seemed like a big jovial buffoon, but that didn't fool him. He saw the rough knuckles and the way Hans carried himself, like a pit fighter. He knew he shouldn't antagonize Hans but backing down held no appeal for him.

Skadi shook her head.

Was he biting off more than he could chew? Had martial arts come that far? Hans might have decades of experience. Damn. He was throwing Stathis to the wolves. How could they not improve their skills?

"I'll go easy on you," Hans said to Stathis.

Stathis just smiled. "Thanks, Gunny! I owe you big for this one."

"Don't disappoint me," Mathison said.

"I won't, Gunny. I promise."

"Don't make promises you can't keep," Mathison said.

Stathis looked ready to bounce out of his seat and take Hans on right then and there.

"This should be a good test," Freya said.

Mathison nodded. Stathis better not embarrass him. On a positive note, it would keep Stathis close and focused. This way he was less likely to get into trouble or say something inappropriate to one of the ladies. Hopefully.

* * * * *

Chapter Six: Martial Arts

Lojtnant Skadi – VRAEC

Stathis seemed full of energy. Skadi almost felt sorry for him. Hans was a Jaeger champion. He had several decades of experience and Stathis was only twenty-two? Hans was also almost twice the little Marine's weight. It made little sense. This would be painful to watch. Stathis might get hurt, and his ego would be shattered. The fact that Mathison was letting the little private go against Hans must mean Mathison was mad at him, although he seemed more amused by it all. Skadi didn't even want to see Mathison go against Hans. That fight might last a little longer, but the gunnery sergeant still didn't have that kind of experience.

Stathis' exuberance didn't wane as Niels helped him into the suit. Because of his size, Stathis had to use a suit commonly worn by HKT women. It was clean and contracted so it was more form fitting, but Stathis didn't seem the least bit concerned he was wearing a woman's armor.

"Any pointers, Gunny?" Stathis asked.

"Don't let him hit you," Mathison said sizing up Hans who was already stretching in the small arena. Nearby, Skadi saw some of the HKTs were coming to watch.

Stathis laughed.

Skadi couldn't help herself. "Why are you doing this, Stathis?"

Stathis looked up at her, surprised. "Why not, ma'am? Do you get better by not accepting challenges? Or do you get better by training with lions?"

"Paska," Skadi said. "You don't train with real lions. You will get eaten! That is a lion in there."

Stathis laughed as he stepped in the ring. Skadi didn't want to watch. Stathis was annoying, but she kind of liked him, in a stupid little brother kind of way.

"Kick his ass, Stathis," Mathison said. He didn't sound nervous, and Skadi was pretty sure he was just good at hiding it.

"Aye, Gunny," Stathis said. "David and Goliath."

"Don't hurt him too bad," Levin said.

"Aye, Sergeant."

With both combatants in the arena, the floor counted down from five.

It reached zero and they just stood there.

Stathis walked casually toward Hans.

Hans chuckled, as if he couldn't believe what he was seeing.

"Game on." Hans jabbed a fist at Stathis' head. It was fast and could have ended the fight there if it had hit.

Stathis slipped to the side so Hans' fist passed centimeters from Stathis' head.

"You missed."

"Huh." Hans shifted his hands into a boxing stance. Stathis raised his hands, almost mimicking Hans.

Hans jabbed again and followed up with a hook. Stathis slipped the jab and then ducked under the hook.

"Little man can't dodge forever," Hans said.

"Don't call me little," Stathis said.

Hans jabbed again, but this time Stathis slipped outside Hans' fist. Stathis' fist slipped under Hans' arm and slammed into the larger man's chin with a *whack!*

A buzzer sounded as Hans stepped back, shaking his head.

Skadi checked the board and was shocked to see the punch rated a six. It could have knocked Hans out without the suit. Skadi had seen Hans fight before and knew his punches were usually rated at a seven. For a little guy, Stathis hit damn hard.

Hans grunted after glancing at the scoreboard. He stepped forward and kicked at Stathis.

Stathis barely managed to step out of the way and grab Hans' foot, lifting it higher until he lost his balance and fell backward. But Stathis didn't let go of the foot, instead he kept lifting so the Aesir almost landed on his head and neck.

Hans slammed loudly onto the floor. The armor kept him from suffering any real injury, but Skadi knew the breath had been knocked out of big Jaeger.

Stathis stepped back and let Hans get up. Neither checked the scoreboard. Now the Jaeger was wary. He hunched his shoulders and tilted his body to face Stathis.

Skadi knew Hans was no longer smiling and was finally taking Stathis seriously. Stathis was about to find out how tough Hans was.

Hans roared and charged Stathis, clearly intending to tackle him and take him down.

Skadi wasn't sure, but it almost looked like Stathis angled to the side and leapt into Hans. One of the private's hands cupped the back of Hans' head and pulled it toward the Aesir's feet while Stathis ducked under the Jaeger's arm.

There was too much forward momentum and Hans had to roll so he didn't land on his face. Instead, he landed on his back, but Stathis was still holding the Aesir's arm. Stathis threw a leg over the Aesir's face and sat, pulling the Aesir's massive arm back.

The buzzer sounded.

"Broken arm," the indicator said.

Stathis did something else. The buzzer went off again.

"Broken wrist."

Stathis brought his heel down on the Jaeger's face.

"Fractured Orbital."

Stathis pushed off Hans, rolled backward, and stood.

Hans lay still for a few seconds. He had probably had his breath knocked out of him again by the fall. Hans' score was zero.

"Don't stop now," Stathis said. "You might get lucky."

Hans sat and pulled off his helmet. His nose was bleeding. He wiped the blood off and looked at Stathis. He glanced at Mathison who was standing silently, staring at the Aesir, his hands behind his back like he was not surprised.

"No," Hans said, shaking his head and smearing blood across his face. "I think I was ill prepared."

Some of his Aesir friends jeered at him. He waved a hand to silence them.

Hans pointed a finger at Stathis. "I owe you a drink. Maybe more than one." He looked at Mathison with a smile. "My apologies, Gunnery Sergeant, maybe someday I will meet you in this chamber."

Mathison nodded.

"Good luck," Stathis said, glancing at Mathison. "He kicks my ass all the time."

Hans looked at him and raised an eyebrow.

"Neat trick," an HKT said, coming over. He was taller than Stathis, but much smaller than any of the Aesir. He moved like a panther and the jagged black wings over his eyes and beak of a nose indicated he was a team leader. His blond hair was barely long enough to braid and he was clean shaven. "Beating up Aesir knuckle draggers is one thing, taking on a real commando is something else."

"You want to try?" Stathis asked the Vanir.

The HKT commander snorted. "We have better things to do than brawl with primitives."

"Which means you know you'll lose," Stathis said.

The commander smiled a cold smile of superiority.

"We won't sink that low," the HKT commander said and turned away. The other HKTs followed him.

Skadi saw he was from the *Thor*, one of the battlestars that was usually assigned to protect the homestars. He probably didn't get out much.

"What a prick," Stathis said when the commander was gone.

"HKTs are like that," Skadi said. "He was nicer than most; he deigned to speak with you."

*****

Chapter Seven: Briefing

Gunnery Sergeant Wolf Mathison, USMC

It was hard to believe what these so-called refugees had accomplished. Taking asteroids and turning them into cities and then into spaceships? Skadi wouldn't tell him how many homestars there were in the fleet, but there had to be several. Mathison understood there were more homestars than battlestars, but Skadi wouldn't give him numbers on those either. Were there problems finding crews?

He followed Skadi into a briefing room. Vili and Bern were already there. He found a seat and sank into the chair. It wasn't one of those hard, military-issue chairs. He could sleep in one of these. If he hadn't seen the *Tikari,* he would have thought the Aesir were pampered. They seemed to spare no comfort for the people aboard the homestars and they definitely weren't refugees by any stretch of the imagination, just well-equipped nomads.

The door slid open and the man who entered looked like he had walked off a recruiting poster, clean shaven, brown hair, brown eyes, straight teeth, and one of those charming, lady-killer smiles. He also had a spec ops team leader tattoo on his right eye. Behind him was Baldr.

"Hi, Skadi," he said in a way that seemed too familiar.

"Magni," Skadi said nodding. There wasn't quite ice in her voice.

"Hello," he said, and Mathison took an instant dislike to the man as he walked toward Mathison.

"My name is Magni," the man said, reaching out to shake Mathison's hand. "I'm Skadi's intelligence and briefing officer these days."

Mathison shook the offered hand. An intelligence officer? Military intelligence? Mathison tried not to wince. Could he like the guy any less?

Magni sat. "So, I've been going over your information and comparing that with what Eversti Halko brought back from Green Hope. In all three situations, it looks like semi-related biological warfare agents. The Nakija assures me that is not the case. Green Hope is a different situation from 402 Base in a couple ways, mostly less apparent violence and the changes to the people are different."

"The changes are different?" Vili asked.

Magni shrugged.

"Aboard 402, Curitiba, and TCG, the victims were transformed into creatures, violent and non-human in appearance. On Green Hope they appear human, but they do not appear alive or noticeably transformed."

"Not alive?" Stathis asked. "Told you there were zombies."

"Shut up, Stathis," Levin said.

Magni continued. "They could be alive. We don't have sufficient data. They were not generating heat like living creatures. When they were first found, Hermod's team believed they were dead because they were room temperature on thermals. This could be some type of camouflage mechanism, but analysis of the video from Hermod's upload does not show them breathing."

"Wait," Skadi said, "we have that much video? Why don't we know what happened?"

Magni frowned. "That bothers us most, really. Shortly after encountering the creatures, the links to the Aesir comm nodes went out due to interference. Same with the link to *Stalkkeri*, Hermod's stealth ship. The only thing that makes sense is if *Stalkkeri* was attacked or the link was shut down by someone on *Stalkkeri*."

"Any SOG warships in system?" Skadi asked.

"One arrived while Hermod was investigating." Magni shook his head. "Hermod is straitlaced and fanatical about his approach and security. You know how Erikoisjoukot are. They secured *Stalkkeri* first. He even had a pair of Aesir watching it. It could have been nuked or hammered from orbit, but *19* saw no evidence of that. Just *poof* and comms were gone. Orbiting spy satellites also detected nothing. They saw what looked like a running gun fight as Hermod's team attempted to retreat to *Stalkkeri*, but not much. *Stalkkeri* never took off. There was a lot of interference, which has our techs confused."

"So, *Stalkkeri* could still be there?" Mathison asked. It would be the first place to start searching to determine what went wrong.

Magni nodded.

"Were the Aesir armored and all, sir?" Stathis asked.

Magni nodded again. "It's standard procedure with SOG biological warfare protocols. Hermod and his team would not expose themselves unless they were sure."

"Zombies can't bite through armor, can they?" Stathis asked. "Zombies are strong, but it's hard to eat brains encased in armor. Space zombies, though, sound wicked. And the creatures on that station got their claws in our armor."

"Stathis," Levin said in a warning tone.

"Support?" Skadi asked.

"You will have *15*," Magni said. "*19* is likely still on station and can provide some support."

"Nothing else?" Skadi asked.

Magni shook his head. "Everyone else is pre-occupied. Details are classified, but between you, me, and the wall, there's a big operation about to go down."

Skadi nodded, and Mathison wondered if she felt left out.

"Sounds like a paska-lounas," Vili said. Mathison wasn't sure if he was referring to their mission or the big operation.

"The krenraali is pissed because he wants to allocate more resources to find Hermod," Magni said. He looked at Mathison. "I think the main reason you are being sent after Hermod and his team is because of your Marines."

"He doesn't trust us?" Mathison asked.

Magni shrugged. "Maybe. But he can use that mistrust to keep your team away from the operation by sending them after Hermod. Besides, this mission seems to be more in your realm."

"Awesome," Stathis said. "Can we be called Team Monster Killers?"

"Shut up, Stathis," Levin said.

"Theoretically it is Team Sif," Magni said. "Although Skadi is technically in command."

"How does that work, sir?" Levin asked.

"On paper, Sif is in command," Magni said. "In reality, we have ordered Sif to defer to Skadi."

Skadi scowled.

"So, Sif gets the glory, and Skadi gets the responsibility?" Stathis asked, earning several glares.

"Stathis?" Levin said, looking at the ceiling.

"I know, Sergeant," Stathis said. "'Shut up, Stathis.'"

"Paska," Skadi said.

"You should leave now," Magni said. "*15* is done with its refit. Lief wants you gone."

"Sooner," Baldr said. "Paska is an understatement."

Mathison didn't miss the look that passed between Magni and Skadi. Something was wrong.

"What?" Mathison asked.

"We need to go now," Skadi said, leaping out of her chair and heading for the door.

"Data is being transmitted to *15*," Baldr said. "Lief has a plan for this. Just get them out of here."

"An executive order has been ordered for your detention," Skadi said to Mathison. "They don't want you to leave. A Vanir security team is on its way."

"Vanir?" Mathison asked. *Why not Aesir?*

"No time to discuss," Skadi said.

Everyone scrambled to keep up with her.

* * * * *

Chapter Eight: Packaging

Lojtnant Skadi – VRAEC

Stupid, incompetent, immoral politicians. It was a surprise the Vapaus Republic had managed to survive for so long.

She knew what do to. She glanced behind her and saw everyone was following her. They were in an Aesir security zone. The Vanir didn't have access to cameras or networks in this area. She knew they would send a request to Aesir network operations, though, and Skadi didn't know if the Aesir network operations team could delay them, or for how long. It was unusual for the Vanir to make this type of request. It would be interesting to see how the Vanir made that request, but what was more important was getting out of here. Would the Vanir use overrides?

They weren't far from the shuttle bay, but the Vanir were probably planning to intercept them there. They controlled shuttle departures and arrivals. She led everyone into the bowels of the Aesir section until she arrived at supply. An Aesir supply keresantti looked at her.

"Team Skadi isn't usually late."

Skadi shrugged. Keresantti Jarvi Aalto used to be special operations before he decided to transfer to a less stressful job that let him gain a little weight. He was a good man and usually gave her everything she asked for if he had it, unlike some supply keresantti's who were far too anal about things. They probably thought she would fly off to SOG space and sell everything they issued her.

"You were expecting us?" Skadi asked.

"No, not exactly. But the krenraali mentioned you might not want to leave by shuttle, and that you might have guests."

"Well," Skadi said glancing at Mathison, "most of us will, but four will not."

Aalto looked at the Marines and nodded.

"That explains the helmets," Aalto said pointing at a set of helmets waiting nearby. "This will make it easier. I have six shipments about to go out. Been sending regular shipments to *15* since the krenraali warned me. Now you have arrived."

That took some weight off Skadi's shoulders.

"I've got your coffins over here," Aalto said directing Mathison toward some open boxes. His eyes fell on Stathis. "Oh, you got a little one. Is he still in diapers?"

"Just my height," Stathis said. "In other areas, I'm—"

"Shut up, Stathis," Levin said.

"—overly endowed," Stathis said more quietly, picking up a helmet and putting it on. It matched with his armor and locked.

Aalto shrugged and gave a small smile.

"I've got six packages to be delivered," Aalto said and handed Mathison and his Marines some extra oxygen canisters. "If I miss you might need these."

"If you miss?" Mathison asked.

"I don't usually miss."

Aalto motioned Stathis into one of the boxes.

"What's going on?" Stathis asked. He sounded nervous.

"Standard resupply," Aalto said. "We usually put our cargo in these boxes and shoot them at the ship. Shuttles are just for people."

"Shoot them?" Stathis climbed into the crate Aalto had pointed him to.

"Sure. You don't have any heart or brain conditions that would prevent a high gravity acceleration, do you? It isn't designed for people. We think it will work, but if you move you could unbalance the shipment and change the trajectory, so it misses the retrieval net or splatters against the hull. There's not much padding, so the acceleration will be very uncomfortable. Your armor might help a little. Don't breathe hard, either, because that changes the balance."

"Wait, what?" Stathis asked as Aalto added some packages to the box with Stathis.

"Nothing to worry about," Aalto said. "I think."

Stathis looked toward the gunnery sergeant.

Aalto shrugged and continued, "Either way, don't jostle these packages too hard; they are plastic explosives. Totally inert and they shouldn't explode, unless you hit them hard. Just stay still and you'll be fine. If the package changes course the Vanir might shoot you. They don't like things they don't understand."

"Wait," Stathis said. "I don't think this is a good idea. Is it too late to find another plan?"

Aalto closed the lid on Stathis then turned and smiled at Mathison.

"Maintain comm silence," Mathison said on the team link before Stathis could protest further.

Aalto pointed at boxes for Winters, Levin, and Mathison.

"Are you sure about this?" Skadi asked as the Marines climbed in and Aalto packed more stuff in with them.

"Sure," Aalto said. "They will reach *15* before you do."

"How will Bluebeard handle this?" Skadi asked Sif.

Sif looked far too serious for a twelve-year-old. "He will follow my orders."

"He didn't before when he refused to return to fleet before TCG," Skadi said.

Sif shrugged "This time he will."

"You think?" Skadi asked, and Sif glared at Skadi.

"Yes," Sif said. "If you want certainties in life, you are in the wrong profession."

Skadi gave Sif a small smile. "I like certainties when I can get them."

"Eversti Oja takes orders from the Nakija council. He is not in the Vanir chain of command."

That surprised Skadi. "But he is Vanir."

Sif nodded as she got in a box. "But currently detached to Nakija MT."

"What are you doing?" Skadi asked.

"Technically, the Marines are under my command," Sif said. "I won't send them somewhere I wouldn't go."

Skadi was still having a hard time seeing the apparent twelve-year-old as an experienced combat commander, but she was also a covert operative.

Aalto closed the lid on Sif and motioned at some other available crates.

"Anyone else?" Aalto asked.

"No. Will they be okay?" Skadi asked Aalto when the last lid was closed and the conveyor took hold of them, pulling them into the launch mechanism.

"Yes," Aalto said chuckling. "This isn't the first time I've done this."

"But—" Skadi thought about what he had told Stathis.

"One joy I still have in my job is screwing with cocky young Aesir," Aalto said. "He will be fine. He is so tightly packed in there it will take a lot of effort to do anything. But you need to hurry and get to your shuttle. I think the krenraali has some replacements for those Marines."

"Replacements?" Skadi asked.

"Not my circus," Aalto said and shrugged.

"Better not be your monkeys," Vili said as the last of the crates holding the Marines and Sif slid into the launch mechanism.

"We prepared Eversti Oja to receive the shipment," Aalto said. "Shouldn't you be elsewhere?"

Skadi nodded and led the others to the shuttle bays.

*****

Chapter Nine: Shuttle

Lojtnant Skadi – VRAEC

She stormed onto the shuttle and four pairs of eyes looked up at Skadi. They were dressed in Aesir armor, but set to the Marine colors.

Skadi smiled as she saw them and realized what the krenraali had done. She remembered reading an e-mail telling her these four had gone into Aesir training. As newcomers to the Vapaus Republic, they were considered immigrants and asukas until they earned their citizenship. They held a unique place in the VR military traditions. They fell under Aesir command and control, and that control had never passed to the Vanir or the poliisi so they would not have many records or information about them.

Jason Palmer had changed a lot in the last few months. He was larger and there was a hardness in his eyes. He was also completely bald. Gone was the look of youth and innocence. With him were Claire Rowley, Mike Thompson, and Jennifer Abrego, also from Lisbon, and they looked like Jason, with shaved heads and hard eyes. They were now larger, bulkier, and more heavily muscled, which told Skadi they had undergone genetic manipulation and physical upgrades. They weren't as large as Bern, Vili, or Niels, but they were not the small Lisbonians they used to be; they were on par with the physical size of most SOG Guardsmen. Skadi was confident they could walk out of a one-on-one fight.

The former Lisbonian rebels looked at Skadi and she did a quick calculation: four months. Which meant they would have just barely completed Aesir boot camp. Now was when they would usually be assigned to a regular operational battalion for additional training and evaluation. Since they were the rawest recruits with just barely enough training to keep them from instantly being killed in their first firefight the krenraali was using them as a decoy and bait for the Vanir.

Her eyes fell on the SOG scientist Tristan sitting in the back, trying to look inconspicuous. He was dressed as a civilian in an unremarkable blue jumpsuit and wouldn't meet her eyes. His presence was disturbing because it meant this was about more than just the Marines.

"Aesir Korpraali Gunsen and Aesirs Zanella, Kittell, and Bazer reporting for duty. Hei and skal," Palmer said, standing and slamming his right hand to his heart. Korpraali? He had earned honors in Aesir basic training. A good sign. She looked at each of them, locking their names into memory. Name tags provided by her cybernetics appeared above their heads, visible only to her.

When Aesir arrived at basic training they replaced their real names with Scandinavian ones. It helped them put away their old lives and embrace the new one. In the event of a compromise, it helped hide their identity from the SOG. It was also a subtle form of brainwashing, an attempt to bind their new identity to a proud tradition they could embrace and help them shed their past. Far too many new Aesir had a lot of past they wanted to forget. Skadi had watched the Aesir and Vanir transform over the last century. A hundred years ago, she would not have imagined what it had become.

"Skal." Skadi returned the salute and slid into the nearest seat.

Niels, Bern, and Vili took their seats as the hatch slammed shut. The shuttle wasted no time and pivoted for launch. An alert appeared on her internal display, telling her to prepare for launch. She wasn't sure who the pilot was, but the krenraali had to trust him or her. But if the pilot didn't know these weren't the Marines, then it really didn't matter.

Skadi wished security protocols allowed her to see what was going on outside the shuttle. She smiled as she thought of how the Vanir were likely scrambling to intercept the shuttle. Their sensors would show what they would expect. Four Aesir and four strangers who did not appear in their databases.

"We are being intercepted," a voice said, opening a command link to her. The identifier showed it as the pilot, a Vanir named Lojtnant Kivi Toro. "It's a wing of manned fighters. There's no escaping this."

Manned? There were Vanir in the ships? That was rare, but not unheard of. Physically manned meant they were using cyberwarfare protocols. They didn't expect the Marines to come peacefully.

"*Valkyrie 27* is raising hell, though, demanding you be allowed to dock for departure on a high priority mission. *Valkyrie 15* is departing the fleet on a priority mission assignment."

Skadi nodded, understanding Krenraali Lief's plan. Once the Vanir realized they had been had, they would release her to rendezvous with *15*, which would have the Marines aboard. It would give her two *Valkyries*, three if *19* was still on station. That was a decent amount of firepower, though not enough to challenge the *Tupolev*.

Without warning, Skadi's network access dropped as they shut it off.

The door slid open, and the co-pilot came out. Her cybernetics buzzed as intense jamming blanketed the shuttle.

"They just janked our network," the co-pilot said, glancing at the new Aesir. "We are being redirected to the Battlestar *Thor*. We are also receiving a lot of jamming, but they have remote control of the system."

"Thank you," Skadi said.

Palmer and the others looked concerned but Vili just smiled.

"This should be fun," Vili said. "It's been a while since Vanir jackboots worked me over. Just a reminder to our young brothers and sisters, keep your hands off your weapons and do what you are told. No heroics or you will be killed. Being full of pride at a time like this will get you killed and accomplish nothing. I suspect they will have a Vanir Hyökkäys Kaapata Tiimi or two to greet us."

"Thank you," Skadi said. "Everyone, place your weapons in the back. When the HKTs arrive, keep your hands in the air and do not argue. Do exactly what you are told. They should realize they screwed up soon enough."

"One hopes," Vili muttered. "The Vanir are big on regulations and protocol, not thinking."

Skadi felt the shuttle slide into a bay and the transition of gravity control to another body, but she didn't see the offered network links. This would be the *Thor*. Not a ship she had spent much time on. The commander of the *Thor* battle force was a crusty old Vanir woman named Kontra-amiraali Riikka Kalm. She was an old battle-axe who had commanded the ship since the destruction of Asgard. She was a Vanir fanatic through and through. Skadi doubted she had a soul or a shred of kindness in her body. She had lost her children in battles over the years and was merciless with SOG prisoners.

The Vanir were not taking any chances.

"Why can't I connect to the network?" Gunsen asked. It took some effort for Skadi to associate his Aesir name with him and tried not to think of him as Jason Palmer, former 2nd lieutenant of the Lisbon Rebel forces.

"Don't worry about it," Vili said, sitting back down. "It's Vanir security protocol."

"Helmets on," Skadi said and everyone complied.

"I don't have a helmet," Tristan said.

"Close your eyes," Skadi said, knowing what was coming.

"But we can't even see Aesir networks," Gunsen said.

"Yes," Vili said. "Long story. Hopefully, you will not be tortured with the telling."

"Does it have something to do with our armor pattern?" Gunsen asked. "And our orders not to reveal our identity to anyone other than Team Skadi? Only to reveal our identity when she authorizes us."

"Aivan niin," Vili said.

"Sorry?" Gunsen said.

"It means 'exactly,'" Vili said. "It is Finnish."

"Zen," Gunsen said, and Vili nodded.

The hatch opened, and in a flash the HKT team poured in, weapons ready and pointed in everyone's faces.

It was hard for Skadi to contain her anger. They were on the same side, but the armored HKT Vanir were treating them like dangerous criminals.

"Hands up, hands up!" they yelled, deafening everyone, their voices boosted with speakers. Strobes on the Vanir's shoulders flashed, making it hard for people without helmets to think or aim. Skadi was glad her helmet filtered it out, but the constant flashes were extremely disorienting and unpleasant.

"Helmets off!" one of the Vanir yelled.

"Hands up or helmets off," Vili asked conversationally. "Make up your minds."

"Shut up!" shouted another Vanir, shoving the muzzle of his blazer into Vili's visor. More Vanir poured in, ganging up on the Aesir. A pair of Vanir grabbed Skadi and she felt her suit power go off, plunging her into darkness with her blast shield down over her eyes. Her arms were yanked behind her back and bound. Skadi went limp, not because it would cause problems for the Vanir in powered armor, but because resistance would cause them to be more brutal. She could barely hear the commands being screamed around her as the Vanir bundled up her Aesir and carried them off the shuttle. They were not brutal, but they certainly weren't gentle in their handling.

Once off the shuttle, they placed her face down on the deck, and Skadi felt a knee in her back. She knew there was at least one blazer aimed at her head. She didn't hear any blazer fire, so she was confident everyone was complying.

She listened but she would hear no conversation from the HKTs since they would communicate trooper to trooper via encrypted link.

After a few minutes, she was lifted and placed in what felt like a box. This would be a prison box. A small coffin-sized container designed to cut off all communication and senses. A countermeasure against cybernetics. Hopefully, nobody was claustrophobic.

Erikoisjoukot training involved a prisoner of war training cycle, but that had been many, many decades ago. She had scored highly in that training evolution, but Skadi was confident the Vanir had updated reports of her during that time. The new Aesir should be okay, but the question was always who would break first? Gunsen, Zanella, Kittell, Bazer? Her bet was on Bazer, who had only been a private on Lisbon and would be the least experienced. In reality, it could be any of them. Skadi had seen much over the years.

Trying to figure out who was likely to break down and do something stupid was just a tactic to keep from thinking about what would happen to her. Skadi recognized that and embraced it. She was confident her team would be rock solid under duress. They were all veterans, and she knew them in every way except intimately. And probably better than their intimate partners.

The most sobering thought was that the Vanir were her people, not the enemy. That, if nothing else, hurt the most. This wasn't training, this was war, and they now considered her an enemy. This was no way to treat fellow warriors, especially warriors with a long history of honorable service.

How far would they go? How far would Kontra-amiraali Kalm go? How far would the Executive Council allow her to go?

Her specialized Erikoisjoukot internal cybernetics were immune to the Vanir jamming, and she watched the time tick away. She knew she was being watched and closely monitored, especially if they followed POW protocols. She had helped write some of those protocols several decades ago.

Skadi took a nap, difficult to do with her arms pulled tight behind her back and lying face down in the dark. This was probably going to take a while. Bastards.

*****

Chapter Ten:

Valkyrie 15

Gunnery Sergeant Wolf Mathison, USMC

The lid came off the crate, and Mathison looked around. It was the cargo bay of *Valkyrie 15* and there was no mistaking the transition into wormhole space minutes earlier.

Sif and Krog were there. Sif had her helmet off but she wasn't smiling.

"We made it, ma'am?" Mathison asked, pushing away packages and sitting up. She was now his commanding officer, so to speak. He had to set the example.

"Yes," Sif said, but Mathison couldn't read her face.

"Is something wrong?" Mathison asked.

"I don't know," Sif said. Mathison saw Bluebeard opening another crate. Levin sat up as Mathison pulled himself out. Everyone was present except for Skadi's team.

"Is Skadi aboard?" Mathison asked. She struck him as the kind who would be here. Sif shook her head.

"There were—" Sif paused and looked up at Mathison "—complications."

"What kind of complications?" Mathison asked, glancing at Stathis' crate and doing a quick count. They were all here. Did one hold a dead Marine? *Please, not that.*

"Skadi has been delayed," Sif said.

"What do you mean, 'delayed,' ma'am?" Mathison asked.

Sif frowned. "Her shuttle was intercepted and sent to the Battlestar *Thor.*"

"They'll let her go when they realize they don't have us, right?" Mathison asked.

"Hopefully," Sif said.

"What do you mean 'hopefully?'" Mathison asked.

"We received an arrest warrant for her team and your Marines," Sif said.

"What about you?" Mathison asked.

"The Vanir do not have any jurisdiction over the Nakija," Sif said. "Their jurisdiction over Aesir is questionable."

Mathison glanced at Bluebeard.

"He is Vanir in name only," Sif said. "His loyalty is to the Republic first and then to me."

Mathison nodded, not liking any of this. The cracks in the foundation of the great Vapaus Republic were finally appearing. An arrest warrant for him and his Marines? He was pretty sure they had broken no laws. If the Republic wanted to arrest him that did not bode well.

"What does this mean?" Mathison asked.

"It means someone doesn't want you leaving home fleet," Sif said. "It means someone is playing political games."

"And that someone wants to cut us up and dissect the SCBIs?" Mathison asked.

Sif frowned. "I don't know. But you are now under my protection."

Under the protection of a girl who didn't look to be older than twelve did not fill Mathison with confidence.

"So now we are on the run from the SOG *and* the Vanir?" Mathison asked, glancing again at Bluebeard.

"Yes," Sif said. "I won't lie to you, this is a surprise to me. It's completely uncharacteristic and underhanded. Something is wrong and until I know what and why, you will remain free."

Which also did not fill Mathison with confidence.

Krog pulled the lid off another crate.

"Can I move now?" Stathis said.

"Yes," Mathison said.

"But what about the explosives?" Stathis said.

Mathison picked up a packet and read the label.

"Meal ready to eat, chili with beans," Mathison said, reading out loud. "I think you have to eat these before anything explodes."

"MREs?" Stathis said, looking at a package. "I thought they were explosives?"

Mathison looked at another package. "Beans and rice. I'm willing to bet this came from an American contractor way back in our time. Eat this and your butt will definitely explode."

"That Aalto guy was messing with me." Stathis scowled, and Mathison laughed.

"I'll send him a thank you," Mathison said.

"And Shrek didn't even warn me," Stathis said.

"Enough whining," Mathison said. He looked at Sif. "What is the plan now, ma'am?"

"Continue mission," Sif said. "Skadi will catch up if she can."

Mathison raised an eyebrow.

"You are under my command," Sif said. "The mission is to find out what happened to Team Hermod. That is what I plan on doing. Is this beyond a Marine's ability?"

"There is nothing in this whole wide galaxy that a Marine cannot do," Mathison said.

"Oorah," Levin said.

"Then we need to go over insertion," Sif said. "We have another ship besides the *Tikari*. It is smaller, and my assigned stealth ship."

"Why don't you have a larger team, ma'am?" Mathison asked.

"My missions rarely have a high survival rate," Sif said, and Mathison heard the pain in her voice. "I don't get assigned easy ones. It has been just me for decades. On a positive note, we have a regular Aesir combat team for support. Although they aren't Erikoisjoukot, they are good. They are from the homestar *Deutsch-star*, mostly German, like Hermod's team. Jaegers are veterans and more highly trained than regular Aesir units. They rarely work with liittoutuneet forces and are usually dedicated combat elements for special combat missions or to provide support to Erikoisjoukot."

"German?" Levin asked.

"Yes. Europeans that came to Asgard after the Finns. Good people, strong moral convictions and values. They have maintained a lot of their heritage and culture, enough to rate their own homestar and they have heavily influenced the Republic."

"You do not need to fear me or my crew," Bluebeard said. "As Lady Sif said, we are Vanir but we also serve a higher cause. We take our orders from the Executive Council or Nakija. The Musta Toiminnot answer to the Nakija and council. We are the shield bearers of our people and the assassins who defend them."

"Thank you," Mathison said. There were too many allegiances and loyalties; it reminded him of the Middle East, with the nations, tribes, factions, and cities all demanding loyalty from people. Was the Vapaus Republic that dysfunctional? A German homestar? Everything ruled by Finns? How divided were they?

"Your rooms remain where they were," Sif said. "The Jaegers are berthed in another area."

"So, before we even begin the mission, we have already lost most of our experienced veterans," Winters said. Sif nodded.

"Welcome to the Vapaus Republic," Sif said, sounding more like a hardened veteran than a twelve-year-old.

*****

Chapter Eleven: Arrested

Lojtnant Skadi – VRAEC

Her timer reported she had been in the box for four hours when they finally opened it and started peeling off her armor. She had almost reached the limit of her suit's life support. She couldn't feel her arms because they had gone numb hours ago.

They removed her helmet, and she faced a Vanir komentaja she didn't recognize.

"I am Komentaja Kotila," she said. Her blond hair was pulled back and braided tightly into several strands. Her blue eyes were ice, and her scowl did not give Skadi confidence.

"You are being charged with treason," Kotila said. "The penalty for treason is death."

"Then quit bragging about it and kill me."

"Charged, not convicted."

"Whatever," Skadi said, meeting Kotila's eyes.

Kotila sighed, and Skadi saw the komentaja was sitting while a pair of Vanir techs worked to remove her armor. Nearby, four fully armored Vanir stood ready, their weapons pointed at her. At least they respected her abilities enough not to take any chances.

"I am to be your counsel," Kotila said.

"Whatever. I plead guilty. Can we get to the execution part?"

"You don't want the specifics?"

"It will be a kangaroo court. I don't expect honor, integrity, fairness, due process, or legality to have any part in this."

"Why?"

"Because you are Vanir," Skadi said. "I am Aesir. A jury of my peers should try me." Skadi looked around at the Vanir. "You are Vanir. I always thought protocol was what Vanir specialized in."

Kotila scowled. "Under Article Sixty-Eight of the Vapaus Republic Security code, a Vanir council can try you."

"Is that your excuse? You're invoking Sixty-Eight? Top secret tribunals? I demand Aesir representation."

"Not possible."

"And that is why the Vanir have discarded their honor."

"You don't think this issue should be classified?" Kotila said.

"Aesir already know. It was the Aesir who informed the Vanir. You claim I have information my commanders do not?"

Kotila scowled at Skadi, and a chill went down her spine.

"Or are all the Aesir on trial here?" Skadi asked. Were the Vanir going to turn on the Aesir?

"There are circumstances in this case that the Vanir do not think the Aesir are concerned about."

"You're lying."

"I'm here to help you," Kotila said. "I might be the only Vanir officer who will try."

Skadi shook her head. "Secret tribunals are a tactic of the SOG. We become that which we fight and fear."

"We are doing this for the safety and security of the Vapaus Republic."

"For the greater good, as dictated by the Vanir overlords. Will you be replacing the civilian government next? Obviously, the Vanir know best."

"Where are the Marines?" Kotila asked.

"Probably next door."

"They are Aesir recruits. Don't insult our intelligence."

Freed from her suit, the Vanir left her standing there cold and naked. Skadi half smiled. The room was chilled to make her more uncomfortable. Being naked was a common technique. It was supposed to make her feel alone and vulnerable. It did, but Skadi wasn't about to give Kotila the satisfaction.

Feeling was returning to her arms, but they tied them again so Skadi tried to put them out of her thoughts, nothing to be done. What would Krenraali Lief do when he found out she was being held?

Did he even know? What were they going to do with the rest of her team?

"We have already executed the Aesir recruits who were with you," Kotila said. "Their treason and attempts to deceive us were obvious. Wearing the colors of a foreign power while under Aesir command is an open and shut case."

Skadi took a deep breath. Was she lying? Legally, that was shaky ground, but Skadi wasn't a lawyer. What if the Aesir were under orders to do so? If they had already been executed, this situation was far more serious. Were the Vanir about to start a civil war?

"You can save the rest of your team by cooperating," Kotila said.

Skadi laughed, but it felt hollow and forced.

"No. You aren't my legal counsel. You're my interrogator."

Kotila shrugged. "I'm your only hope of survival."

"As I said, quit bragging about it and just kill me."

Kotila shook her head sadly.

"I'm not sure you understand. We have the codes to disable your torture prevention protocols. We know everything there is to know about you." Kotila paused for a long moment. "Where are the Marines?"

Skadi laughed, but even she heard a small touch of hysteria there. Did the Vanir? Time was on her side, but it was going to hurt, and it was probably going to tear apart the Vapaus Republic if the Aesir found out about it. Was this why her father had wanted so badly for her to become Vanir? Because he knew the Vanir would eventually turn on the Aesir? How far did the rot go, and when had it started?

* * * * *

Chapter Twelve: Transit

Gunnery Sergeant Wolf Mathison, USMC

It was Mathison's first briefing with the ground combat teams. An hour ago, *Valkyrie 15* had left wormhole space, and Sif summoned everyone into a briefing room while *Valkyrie* maneuvered for the next transition.

Twelve Aesir were already present when Mathison arrived. Sif led Mathison and his Marines into the room.

Cold, appraising eyes followed the Marines as they took their seats. Mathison was the only one who was their size, and they made Stathis look like a dwarf. Sif was like a mouse among elephants as she stood at the head of the table. Standing while they sat, she could look most of them in the eye.

"Team Sloss," Sif said, looking at one of the Aesir, a big man with buzz-cut brown hair and a less elaborate tattoo than Skadi's. His eyes were hard, and Mathison would have been surprised if the man ever smiled.

All the Aesir were wearing their armor without the trauma plates. There were a couple women who were almost indistinguishable from the men except in the chest area and that they were maybe an inch or two shorter on average. Except for the lack of daggers on their emblems, they looked exactly like Skadi's Erikoisjoukot.

"Team Mathison," Sif said looking at Mathison. "You already know about Erikoisjoukot teams. Team Sloss is a Jaeger team. Aesir Jaegers are veterans focused on combat and rapid assaults. Team Sloss are huskarls, veteran warriors with proven skill."

Sloss nodded.

Sif turned to Sloss and his teammates.

"Team Mathison is a United States Marine Raider team," Sif said. "They are very similar to Jaegers in that they are elite assault troops. They are also huskarls of proven skills."

"United States?" Sloss asked, and Mathison wondered if they had been briefed on anything.

"The SOG found them in stasis," Sif said. "Unarmed and alone, they escaped from a high security prison. I would not underestimate them. The SOG did and has paid for it multiple times."

Sloss nodded.

"I would think this mission requires more stealth," Mathison said. "And more finesse if we are dealing with colonists."

Sif nodded. "We will work with what we have. I expect Skadi to join us once she resolves her delay."

"What is the mission?" Sloss asked.

"An Erikoisjoukot team has gone missing," Sif said.

"Captured?" Sloss asked.

Sif shook her head. "I wish it were that simple. Krenraali Lief has cleared your team, so I will brief you in more detail later. This will just be an initial briefing. We are en route to Green Hope, where we will try to find out what happened to Team Hermod and, if possible, rescue them. If not, avenge them."

"The entire team?" Sloss asked.

"Yes, and this is classified extreme secret. Your team is one of few that has that classification," Sif said. The lights dimmed as she brought up video. "We will formulate a plan. It is my intention to insert your teams onto Green Hope, investigate where his ship landed, and then work our way from there. We are not sure exactly what happened to them, and we are not sure if the SOG is involved."

"The SOG might not be involved?" Sloss asked glancing toward his team like he had misheard and expected them to correct him.

"Correct," Sif said. "The base the Marines escaped from was conducting experiments on a vanhat artifact. Something was released from that artifact, and it may have gone to Green Hope. I will start at the beginning and fill you in on the mission to Base 402."

*****

Chapter Thirteen: Interrogation

Lojtnant Skadi – VRAEC

"Where is your krenraali hiding the Marines?" Kotila asked.

"You should ask him. Open a link, and I will ask him for you. All I know is that they're somewhere outside the galactic core," Skadi said. She was tired. They had not yet disabled the torture protocols of her cybernetics. Had they been bluffing when they said they had the codes?

"Vili already told us. We know, we just need confirmation."

"Then ask Bern," Skadi said. "Or has he been executed as well?"

"I'm trying to help you. You have served the Vapaus Republic for a long time. Honorably. Your record is impeccable. Why do you insist on behaving in this treasonous manner?"

"Treason is a matter of perspective. I remember my oath. Do you?"

"No, you don't. You endangered the free people of the Republic by exposing them to ancient and extremely dangerous technology. How in your twisted world view can you justify that? You have spent too much time away from home fleet."

"Or my worldview is not so narrow that I can't see a bigger picture," Skadi said.

Kotila shook her head, and Skadi's stomach growled. She hadn't eaten since before they had captured her.

"We have spent over a hundred years fighting the SOG," Kotila said. "Surely even you can see we are not winning. The SOG response to Lisbon was overwhelming. This is not a fight the Republic can win."

"So, we flee?" Skadi asked.

"Hiding on ships in deep space is not the answer," Kotila said. "This must be obvious, even to one of the Aesir. We are humans. We should live on a planet, under the open sky."

Skadi frowned. She had spent as little time as she could at home fleet. Every day spent aboard Midgard or a battlestar was another day she was not undermining or otherwise fighting the SOG.

"Our people grow tired of the hiding, being hunted, staring at the insides of ships, the inability to expand. People want more space, more freedom. We are fish in a tin, crowded and afraid," Kotila said. "Don't you think a hundred years is long enough?"

"How far do you plan to flee? Do you think humanity will finally throw off the boot heel of SOG oppression?"

"The SOG is no longer our problem. We should be concerned with ourselves, not others."

"Moving home fleet long distances is not a simple problem," Skadi said. "Kiska Syndrome cannot be dismissed by pretty words and good feelings."

"We think we have a solution for that. The inkeri generator will allow us to make very long jumps so the SOG cannot follow us. We have the option to go very far away. Far enough that it will take the SOG thousands of years to find us."

"Then why do you want the Marines?" Skadi asked.

"You don't need to worry about that," Kotila said. "They are a different issue. You should worry about yourself and the charges of treason."

Skadi didn't have the strength to laugh. She just wanted to sleep. Did her father know she was aboard the *Thor*?

"Vili has confessed everything he knows," Kotila said. "His execution has been stayed. He will probably be exiled to a secret colony when the fleet leaves. That could happen for you, too. All you have to do is cooperate. Tell us what you know."

"I'm not sure what's worse," Skadi said. "You trying to talk me to death or the fact that you are betraying your brothers and sisters in arms."

"I could ask you the same question," Kotila said. "Why are you betraying your brothers and sisters in arms? Why did you recklessly endanger them by bringing those artificial intelligences back? Who knows what kind of damage they will do?"

"There is a bigger problem," Skadi said.

"Of course, some ancient threat is trying to wipe out humanity. It won't be our problem once we leave. Let it try to find us in another part of the galaxy."

"You are a fool."

"I am ready for lunch," Kotila said. "The cafeteria on the *Thor* is one of the best in the fleet, you know. So many choices. I especially like the lasagna."

Skadi's stomach reminded her how empty it was. She forced a smile and looked at Kotila. "Now you are just being mean. Go enjoy your lunch. You know where to find me."

"Shall I bring you something back?"

Skadi shook her head. Kotila was just pretending to be nice.

"Niels will be executed tomorrow." Skadi felt her heart grow heavy. "His legal counsel has determined he will not be helpful. I'm sorry. I thought you should know."

Skadi pursed her dry lips and closed her eyes. Was Kotila telling the truth?

"At any rate," Kotila said, now smiling, "I'm going to go get lunch. I'll talk to you later."

Kotila left Skadi alone in her cold cell, lying naked on the floor.

Her arms and legs were numb. It was too cold to sleep, and her urine had pooled underneath her. Death would be a release.

She laid her head down and listened to the steady thrum of the surrounding vessel. Could she trigger her suicide protocol? Had any of the others?

No. She was Erikoisjoukot. She would treat this just like a training episode. While she was alive and breathing, there was hope, and she wasn't ready to give up yet. The good guys did not always win, but she wasn't ready to quit.

The music began, nearly deafening her. She could feel it in her bones. Mixed with the music was the sound of a baby crying.

So, they were at this stage now? It would be impossible to sleep normally with that much noise, and the crying baby was just sandpaper on her nerves.

*****

Chapter Fourteen: Green Hope System

Gunnery Sergeant Wolf Mathison, USMC

Mathison received a message on his internal display requesting his presence on the bridge, which was good. He needed a break from the reading. Whoever had compiled the intelligence reports on the SOG had no personality and had worked to make the material as boring as possible. They must have gotten pointers from US intelligence manuals.

The Shorr space transition alert sounded and halfway to the bridge he felt the skin-crawling sensation that told him the ship was entering wormhole space again and ended seconds later as they slid out.

Arriving on the bridge, Mathison found Sif and Bluebeard already present.

Sif looked at him and nodded.

Sloss entered as Mathison went to stand over the holographic plot. Data was coming in and more was fast appearing in the display.

"Looks like we are about six days out moving under stealth," Bluebeard said. "We can be there in half a day if you aren't worried about being seen."

Mathison waited for Sif to say something, but she remained silent.

"It will be a day or two before we can link into the relay left by *19*," Bluebeard said. "We are detecting SOG military traffic, though. There appears to be a small task force entering the system from farther out. It will take some time to identify them. Looks like a battleship, two destroyers, and a transport."

"The *Tupolev*," Sif said.

"Maybe," Bluebeard said. "Fits the data we have so far. Can't say for sure. I haven't heard if Team Hermod has a SOG stalker like Skadi does."

"It means the insertion will be more interesting," Sif said.

"Aye. Though they don't have enough ships to implement a blockade. Not to say they haven't deployed an extensive satellite network, but they couldn't hope to intercept us. They will likely get to the planet around the same time we do. Probably before. It doesn't excessively worry me." Bluebeard glanced at Mathison, and he knew the words were for him.

"A planet is a very big place and the *Tupolev* could not hope to cover even a fraction. It will be easier to spot a gnat in Turku than to find an Aesir combat team."

"Not if they know where to look," Mathison said.

"Zen," Bluebeard replied. "Hermod is smart and won't be obvious. The *Tupolev* can only focus on a small area. We just need to avoid that area."

Mathison nodded, catching Bluebeard's point.

"They are not worried about stealth," Bluebeard said. "So, they can move faster. Perhaps they are the dogs trying to flush out the birds, but I doubt it. They are moving at maximum speed."

"Which won't leave us much time," Sif said.

"Is this a race?" Bluebeard asked.

"No. It is a rescue mission."

"If *19* does not know where Hermod's team is then it is unlikely the SOG does," Bluebeard replied.

"One hopes," Sif said.

* * * * *

Chapter Fifteen: Battle

Gunnery Sergeant Wolf Mathison, USMC

The hangar was empty without Skadi, Vili, Bern, or Niels and almost hostile with Sloss and his Jaegers. Stathis was taking a nap while Levin and Winters were busy on consoles. Mathison rubbed his eyes and looked away from his own console. The SOG bureaucracy had to be intentional in its confusing design. An organization that was supposed to help and take care of people, like the SOG claimed, should be comprehensible by people, but there were so many bureaucracies, departments, ministries, and agencies with so much overlap and duplication it was amazing they got anything done.

Sloss' team kept their distance from the Marines. They were absorbed with their tablets or muted conversations.

They were waiting until the last minute to board the claustrophobic stealth ship and head toward the planet. Everything was packed and ready. Now they just had to wait for word to climb aboard Sif's ship and be packed in like sardines. Mathison didn't like that the *Tupolev* had beaten them to the planet, but there was a lot about the mission he didn't like.

The intercom chimed.

"Something is going on near the capital," Bluebeard reported. "The *Tupolev* just hit the outskirts with a kinetic strike. More shuttles are launching. From the looks of it, there's a big battle. The *Tupolev* sent down a company of troops to the capital before dawn and then the fight started. Now they're sending reinforcements."

"Nothing on Republic channels?" Sif asked.

Mathison scowled. It was going to be hard to pull Hermod's team out if they were getting hit by that much firepower. One thing everyone was thinking but nobody wanted to mention was the possibility that the SOG had discovered a way to jam Republic communications.

"We just got *Valkyrie 19* on link," Bluebeard said. "We're getting a full download now, but they report they have heard nothing new from Hermod, and the fighting just started. *Tupolev* showed up a few hours ago and immediately sent down shuttles. Just Guard units, not the Peacekeepers or ODTs, which show they don't have a target for them."

"Who is fighting?" Sif asked.

If it wasn't Hermod, who else could it be?

"They don't know," Bluebeard said. "Looks like a rebellion. Cloud cover is a problem. It's the rainy season, and we don't have any feeds into the SOG network."

"Is Hermod there?" Sif asked.

"Eversti Halko doesn't think so," Bluebeard said. "He can't rule it out, but if he's there he isn't answering. Most of the relays are reporting online, though there is a lot of interference."

"Why doesn't he think so? Where else could Hermod be?" Sif asked.

"Halko says they would have called for help or let him know otherwise if they could," Bluebeard said.

"Unless comms are compromised," Mathison said.

"We have a protocol for that," Bluebeard said. "Aesir have regular radios and enough strength to punch out of the atmosphere. If they were engaged in battle, they would have nothing to lose by sharing that information with *19*. There are also emergency frequencies and code words."

Mathison nodded. It wasn't good news. The Aesir were paranoid bastards; they seemed to have a plan for everything. The Erikoisjoukot should be trained for things like this. It's what they did, and they weren't novices. If Hermod's team was in trouble, why didn't they call for help, or at least let the other Aesir know things were bad?

"Then our original mission continues," Sif said. "We will see if Hermod's ship is still there."

She had to be thinking the same thing. Hermod would let his *Valkyrie* know if they were still alive. Unless they had a dramatic equipment failure. Was that possible?

"Zen," Bluebeard said. "Halko doesn't have much. Everything has been quiet since his return. There is absolutely no activity. He reported that it's like the colony is dead. If there is movement or activity, it's at night and they don't use lights. Seems to be the rainy season on the continent called Able by the locals."

"What about the capital?" Mathison asked.

"There is a space elevator there, since it is on the equator," Bluebeard said. "But the *Tupolev* is not docking, and they've only sent down assault shuttles and gunships."

"What's wrong with the elevator?" Sif asked.

"Halko doesn't know," Bluebeard said. "He said it is not that big. A class one, mostly automated for light cargoes, weather satellites and such. Four strand, crew of maybe two? He saw a pair of shuttles dock with it, though, probably to secure it in any case."

"Could an EMP burst or something have knocked out his electronics?" Mathison asked.

Sloss looked at Mathison.

"Seriously?" Sloss asked. "How primitive do you think our gear is?"

"Or something like HERF," Mathison said, thinking about the static interference and energy drain aboard 402. "Some new weapon?"

"If the SOG has something like that, then we are about to take a big bite out of a paska-lounas," Sloss said.

"Yes," Bluebeard said. "Hermod would find a way. Regular radio, smoke signals, something. Hermod is locked on and knows what he's doing."

"What if he was going to the capital to get a radio and got trapped?" Mathison asked.

Sloss stared at Mathison and shook his head.

"I'm sure he would let us know," Sif said, but Mathison heard the doubt in her voice.

Mathison scowled. Hopefully, she knew what she was talking about. There were too many ways a team could be cut off, but she knew Erikoisjoukot and Aesir protocols. But the way the power had been drained on 402 would eliminate most methods of communication.

"Load up," Bluebeard said. "We are making some good progress. I hope to have you landed by noon."

"Zen."

Sif pointed at her ship, which looked almost exactly like Skadi's, except smaller. The Marines and Jaegers were about to get intimate, because the stealth ship was not designed for so many people. Skadi's ship would feel spacious after this.

*****

Chapter Sixteen: Rescue

Lojtnant Skadi – VRAEC

Sonic vibrations, bright lights, and cold prevented her from sleeping. According to her cybernetics, she had been awake for over eighty hours, and it was seriously affecting her ability to think and concentrate. Her nanites would keep her limbs from suffering too much damage, but she knew it might be hours before she could walk, if they ever let her. Stress and her physical condition made her lack of sleep worse.

The cell stank but she didn't care as she lay in a pool of her own waste. She had stopped caring about that many hours, maybe days, ago. It might be the sleep cycle now. She wasn't sure and her interrogator—her "legal counsel"—was probably asleep in a nice soft bed. All Skadi had was a featureless metal room with a drain in the middle

Death would be a release. Why couldn't they let her die?

Why didn't she initiate her suicide protocols?

Because that would be surrendering. She was Skadi, the Ice Princess. She might lose battles, but she would win the war, or they would kill her. She would not give them the pleasure of breaking her.

What had she told them so far? Had she told them anything? No. Yes? It was important to feed them information as slowly as possible. Everyone broke eventually. If she refused completely, they would kill her, like Niels. Maybe that was the way to go? No. They wouldn't make it easy for her. She was the team leader. She was supposed to have all the answers. Why hadn't they shown her Niels' death? That would have had more impact, wouldn't it? She was sure they recorded it.

Or had they? Maybe that had been a faked recording? Or was she imagining it? Paska, it was hard to think, hard to remember. They could fake a video. Why had they killed Jason and Claire? No. That wasn't right. It was Gunsen and Zanella. Their names should be honored and remembered. Would Krenraali Lief remember them? Would he remember her? He had to know the Vanir had captured her. Right? But the Vanir had control of sensors for security reasons, so maybe not.

The door opened. The guards were probably here to hose her down with cold water again. Her cybernetics and nanites would keep her from getting too sick, but there was a price involved, and there would come a point when the nanites wouldn't have enough resources to keep her healthy. Or had the Vanir technicians already zapped her, destroying most of the nanites? That wouldn't have triggered her suicide protocol. Right?

She heard the guards talking and felt the bands holding her arms behind her loosen and the bands holding her legs come off.

The guards cursed. She couldn't move her arms or legs.

One guard was kneeling next to her. "Lojtnant, we are going to get you out of here. We need you to work with us and not resist."

Skadi wanted to laugh. They were resorting to games now? Pretend a rescue to dash her hopes? The Vanir were fanatics about security. There was no way this could be real.

"Sure," Skadi said. Let them think she believed them. Whatever made them happy. It wasn't like she had the strength to resist.

They pulled her to her feet, and she saw they were armored HKT. She had expected regular Vanir security troops. It was easier to pretend they would betray their commanders and effect a rescue, but HKT?

Maybe her dad's troops? No. *Tyr* had already left the fleet on whatever mission they had planned. Right? Was that her memory or what she wished?

She would play their game. Why not? She couldn't resist. Breaking the body was easy. They wanted to break her mind. Did they really think she was that stupid? She probably knew more about HKT capabilities than most HKT teams. She had been around long enough and conducted several missions with the HKTs. They were underestimating her, and that felt good.

If they really wanted to mess with her, though, they might put her aboard a skeid and take her through a couple of wormhole transitions. That would also put her outside the reach of the Aesir, or the Executive Council, as if they could be bothered with a couple Erikoisjoukot. Why would they care? Was an Aesir accused of treason worth tearing the Vapaus Republic apart over?

Was this how they planned to get her aboard the skeid? By pretending to rescue her?

"She's messed up," said one trooper .

"Nussia," came the angry reply.

The troopers gently picked her up and lay her on a stretcher.

"We have about a minute before the scan," said the first voice.

"Then let's get out of here," said the second voice, a deep man's voice.

"I'm going to sedate you," said the first voice. "We aren't sure of your condition and it's easier to transport an inert body than a resisting one. I'm sorry."

Skadi didn't recognize the voice, so there was no reason to trust him. Her world went dark.

*****

Chapter Seventeen: Infiltration

Gunnery Sergeant Wolf Mathison, USMC

This could be Earth, Mathison thought as he moved through the woods. The trees, ferns, and vines looked normal enough. Behind him, Stathis and two Aesir followed him like a shadow. The Jaeger team of four was trying to contact Hermod's ship. Mathison and his team were a tactical reserve while Sif and several other Aesir remained aboard her stealth ship *Tera* as a strategic reserve. Winters and Levin remained with Sif, which made Mathison feel better since they could act as a Marine reserve, or if things went badly, they would be more likely to survive.

It hadn't stopped raining since they landed, a light drizzle that allowed the plants and algae to thrive. The sun was up, but it was nothing more than a bright spot behind the thin gray clouds. It was dreary, but Mathison couldn't complain. Gravity felt a little odd; it was slightly less than on Earth but not significantly. It was just enough that it didn't feel right, but that was minor and easily ignored.

The two Aesir, Andre and Stahle, appeared to be good men. They followed Mathison like ghosts, and while they weren't Marines or Raiders, the warriors had enough in common that there wasn't much confusion. Mathison was sure that once the shooting started, the differences in tactics and techniques would become more obvious.

"Aarne," Sloss said on the mission link. "We are approaching the ship's location."

"Copy, Aarne," Sif said. "Bertta hold position."

"Bertta, zen," Mathison said holding up his hand. Sloss' first team was Aarne, while Mathison got Bertta, or Alpha and Bravo, as he thought of it. Sif's call sign was Aiti, which meant mother, but wasn't Bertta a girl's name? Saying "zen" instead of "aye" was odd, but when in Rome...

The four warriors settled down. Mathison nodded as he watched the two Jaegers pick a direction and start watching it. The mule, a funny four-legged, spiderlike bot carrying missiles and mortars, hunkered down behind Mathison. Mathison watched the front, Stathis the right, the Jaegers watched rear and left. Their current position gave them good concealment among the ferns and trees.

The light rain continued to fall around them. In the distance, he heard trickling water. Sif had set the biological protocols to dangerous, so Mathison couldn't smell the wet forest around him, but he could imagine it. On his display he saw Sloss and his team as markers two kilometers away. The resolution was fine enough he could see them spread out.

"Ship is gone," Sloss reported. "No sign of *Stalkkeri*. No wreckage, no sign of battle. It's just gone, but it was here."

"Zen," Sif said. "Pull back, and we'll move closer to the fighting around the capital and see what that's about."

"Aarne, zen," Sloss said.

"Bertta, zen," Mathison said, following Sloss' lead.

* * * * *

Chapter Eighteen: Battle

Gunnery Sergeant Wolf Mathison, USMC

He could have been one hill over from their previous position for all the difference it made in vegetation and weather. The sun was setting, and while Mathison considered that an advantage, a feeling of unease was developing as they approached the capital. Mathison didn't really know or care what locals called it. They had named it in the briefing, but everyone called it "the capital."

"I'm able to pick up SOG traffic," Freya said. *"Standard squad and platoon links. They're still faint, but we can crack them."*

"And?" Mathison asked.

"Sounds like they're fighting genetically modified rebels. They seem confused. They are calling the colonists mutants and it seems like the colonists are not leaving their houses."

"Mutants? What are they fighting with?"

"Unknown. The SOG troops are under orders to not enter the buildings. Apparently, when they do, they take very heavy casualties."

"So, what are they doing?"

"They're trying to secure the colony computer systems," Freya said. *"I suspect they want those systems because of recordings so they can get an idea of what's going on."*

"What's the problem, then? Don't they have enough troops? Can't they access the systems remotely?"

"Apparently not. The power is out, and the systems are in a bunker under the capitol building. They are also getting a lot of communications interference, like jamming. They have to either power them up so they can remotely access them, or they have to go in and physically capture the data."

"Do we have visual on the mutants?" Mathison asked.

"Negative. Just communication intercepts. Leadership elements have a more heavily encrypted link back to the shuttles, which are further encrypted and talk with the Tupolev.*"*

"It's getting dark, Gunny," Stathis said.

"So?" Mathison said.

"Isn't that when the zombies woke up and attacked Team Hermod?" Stathis asked.

"I think they're already awake," Mathison said. "The Soggies aren't fighting sleepers."

"Aye, Gunny," Stathis said. "Just pointing it out. *Valkyrie* didn't lose contact with Hermod's boys until nightfall."

"What are you getting at, Stathis?" Mathison said.

"The Soggies are fighting colonists who aren't leaving the buildings," Stathis said. "What if they aren't leaving because the sun is up?"

"So, you think the shit is about to hit the fan?" Mathison asked. The private was right, though. Coincidence?

"I'm a private," Stathis said. "You told me it is not my job to think, Gunny."

Mathison thought about it. Habit would be to tell Stathis to shut up.

"Don't be a dumbass," Mathison said. "I asked you a question."

"Well, Gunny," Stathis said, "I used to play a lot of video games before joining the Marines and any time I was restricted to quarters."

"Get to the point," Mathison said. He remembered implementing some of those restrictions.

"One thing all the video games like to do, especially the VR sets, is turn off the lights to scare people," Stathis said.

"Didn't I say something about a point?" Mathison said.

"Yes, Gunny," Stathis said. "Just saying, people are hardwired to be afraid of the dark. They say it's hardwired into humans."

"Typical psychology. Loss of primary source of information causes uncertainty and fear. We are not nocturnal; we are a diurnal species. Besides, these days we have all sorts of gear that lets us see and fight in the dark."

"I know, Gunny," Stathis said. "But why?"

"Stathis, you dumb shit," Mathison said. "This isn't the time for lessons."

"What if long ago we became diurnal because of *what was in the dark*, Gunny?" Stathis said.

"You lost me, Private."

"I've been thinking…"

"Mistake number one," Mathison muttered.

"That Nasaraf demon dude, wannabe, what if he is an actual demon? Demons don't like sunlight. What if deep down we knew this and still do?"

"You think the mutants aren't coming out because of the sunlight?"

"Yes, Gunny. Maybe the radiation of a primary star or something is painful for them. Which would be why demons and monsters like the dark and being underground."

"Scientifically it isn't impossible," Freya said. *"Although I will say it's likely implausible. The flaw in his theory is the creatures on TCG were out in the sunlight. Video links would help us a great deal to determine what's going on. There appears to be a more powerful radio not far from here. It might be a grounded shuttle."*

"I guess we will find out," Mathison said and opened a link to Sif.

"Aiti," Mathison said. "This is Berrta. We are going to divert toward what might be a grounded SOG shuttle acting as a relay. The intent is to break into the more secure SOG traffic."

"Zen," Sif said. "Let us know if we can help, Berrta."

"Aye, Aiti," Mathison said, not realizing until after he had said aye instead of zen. It was hard to break decades of Marine tradition and training.

Slipping through the woods like ghosts, Mathison led the way toward the radio source as the sun set. He expected to come under fire from the SOG troops at any moment. He reached the edge of the forest and looked out on a ruined field. He saw that there were no troops present, though there were two possibly abandoned shuttles sitting quietly in the field. Nearby, the smoking remains of a small house revealed the violence that had occurred much earlier.

One shuttle ramp was open and the turret was motionless, but Mathison was confident that it was still observing the surroundings.

Without warning, the turrets spun toward the house and began stitching the area with small-caliber blazer rounds. Something exploded, but Mathison didn't see what it was. Again, the turret fired but then fell silent. Something must have crossed the threshold without warning.

"We need to get closer," Freya said.

"And get shot?" Mathison asked.

"I can jam the turret sensors and keep it from shooting us. The Aesir suit has some interesting capabilities. Not sure if I can mask all four of us from both shuttles."

"Andre and Stahle," Mathison said on the Berrta team link. "Stay here. Stathis and I are going to get closer to see if we can crack into their network."

"Zen," they said, then took cover to provide overwatch. The mule moved forward and lined up a missile on the shuttle.

Mathison was about to step into the open when two figures exited the nearest shuttle. They had weapons up and began approaching whatever the turret had fired on. Neither was wearing trauma plates, so Mathison figured they were either the pilots or crew chiefs for the shuttle. At least they were smart enough not to get between the turret and its target.

Mathison took a deep breath and stepped into the open. His Aesir armor made him practically invisible, but that wouldn't work against an auto turret that didn't like him. Fortunately, the turret didn't move as Mathison and Stathis approached the open hatch. The Marines moved faster than the two crewmen and kept the targeted shuttle between them and the other shuttle, using the first one as a shield.

The two crewmen had their backs to the Marines and had almost reached the turret's target when the Marines got to the shuttle. While Stathis kept his weapon trained on the two crewmen, Mathison kept his weapon aimed at the shuttle.

"Accessing now," Freya said.

Mathison peered into the shuttle. It could have been any one of thousands of troop transports, with uncomfortable seats against the walls forcing loaded troops to stare at each other while their knees touched. There were a few small windows and Mathison could see into the cockpit at the other end. The door was open, and it didn't look like there was anyone there.

Mathison felt a little better now that they were close enough that the turret on top couldn't reach them. Stepping aboard the shuttle gave him even better cover and Stathis stayed close, boarding the shuttle while watching Mathison's back.

The turret began firing again, and he heard screams.

He peered out the nearest window in time to see a shadow flicker toward the two pilots. The turret tried to fire, but the shadow used the pilots as a shield and slammed into the first pilot before he could attack the shadow. Something was sprayed in the air as the surviving pilot screamed and tried to back up. A humanoid figure detached itself from the first pilot and leapt at the second. The turret caught the creature in mid-leap, saving the second pilot, but Mathison saw more shadows move.

"Something is interfering with the electronics," Freya reported. *"A recall is being ordered. All shuttles are being ordered to return to the* Tiananmen *and* Tupolev.*"*

"What was that?" Stathis asked, his SAW not leaving the ramp area.

The ramp closed and Mathison rushed up to look in the cockpit. It was empty.

"An emergency override," Freya reported. *"I can't block it."*

"What is going on?" Stathis asked, but then fell silent. Hopefully, his SCBI was telling him.

The engines powered up, and the shuttle slid into the sky.

"Good idea, Gunny," Stathis said. "Those things are nasty. But what about the two Aesir?"

"I'm not controlling the shuttle," Mathison said.

"Andre, Stahl," Mathison said on the team link. "Get back to Aiiti. The shuttle is on autopilot. If we can get control, we will meet you somewhere else."

"Zen," Andre and Stahl echoed. "Leaving us with these creatures, eh?"

"Not intentionally," Mathison said.

"We can handle them," Stahl said. "You be safe."

"Don't underestimate them," Mathison said. "Team Hermod might have."

"Zen," Stahl said.

"Zen," Mathison said as he watched the ground drop away. Stahl was supposed to be a senior Aesir. He seemed competent enough, but Mathison still felt he was being separated from his troops.

"Good news, bad news. With darkness, the creatures left the buildings and began to hunt the SOG troops," Freya reported. *"So far, the SOG has sustained over ninety percent casualties."*

"Is that the good news or bad news?" Mathison asked.

"The bad news is that I cannot get control of the shuttle," Freya said. *"It is running a hard coded program and following a beacon. We are on our way to the* Tiananmen*."*

"Can't we blow something?" Mathison said. *"Take manual control?"*

"They built it into the system," Freya said. *"An anti-mutiny protocol. I'm trying, but they may have over engineered this feature. Breaking it means we crash and die."*

"I don't think I brought enough ammo," Stathis said. "Could we go back and get some more? How many jackbooted thugs are on the *Tiananmen*? This might be an excellent training opportunity for the chief."

"Shut up, Stathis," Mathison said, feeling helpless.

"Bertta?" Sif said. "What is going on?"

Mathison explained, and Sif fell silent.

"You are likely to lose communication any minute," Sif said. "I'm transmitting some frequencies that I will monitor."

"Any suggestions?" Mathison asked.

"Don't get captured," Sif said. "But if you do, I will do everything in my power to rescue or kill you."

"Reassuring," Mathison said as the team link showed a lost signal.

"Kill us?" Stathis asked on a private link. "How is that reassuring?"

"Ask me that again on day four of the SOG marathon torture session," Mathison said.

"Gunny?" Stathis said. "If it is okay with you, I would rather die than get captured again."

"Permission granted," Mathison said.

"The override is coming from the Tupolev,*"* Freya reported. *"Apparently, not even the* Tiananmen *is trusted with those codes. But we are being sent to the* Tiananmen.*"*

"Do you think they're worried about hitchhikers?" Stathis asked.

"No," Freya reported. *"They saw the pilots get killed through video. I have masked our presence, and adjusted the weight of the shuttle to show it's empty. The pilots on the other shuttle did not see us. They have targeted some shuttles with kinetic strikes. The* Tupolev *is not taking any chances with the infection leaving the planet."*

"Never mind, Gunny," Stathis said. His SCBI must have informed him as well. "So, are we going to come off the shuttle shooting?"

"If we have to," Mathison said sitting in the pilot's seat. Stathis sat in the co-pilot's seat and started reaching for controls.

"Don't touch anything."

"I won't, Gunny. Shrek is just pointing out different controls. Heck, I might be able to fly this thing with Shrek's help."

Mathison stared at Stathis.

"Please don't try."

"Aye, Gunny. Or are we supposed to be saying zen?"

"Marine to Marine you say aye."

"Aye, Gunny." Stathis sounded relieved.

"Can you help me fly this?" Mathison asked Freya.

"Very likely. Do you want me to identify the different controls?"

"No," Mathison said. *"Not now."*

"I estimated our flight time at three hours. We are basically following the other shuttle."

The shuttle had a closed cockpit, but there were viewscreens along the sides that showed the planet falling away below them.

"I'm linking into the shuttle controls," Freya said. *"View only."*

The viewscreens lit up with information. A series of orange rings in front of the shuttle showed the flight path and Mathison saw other icons appear. Four were instantly obvious, but not yet visible. One ship was labeled SBS 7004, others were DDA 4749, DDA 4753, and TTR 2349.

"What are those?" Mathison asked.

"SBS is Specialized Battleship and the number is the hull number. The DDAs are Dedicated Destroyer—Assault, and TTR is Troop Transport—Regiment. The SBS is the Tupolev *and the TTR is the* Tiananmen,*"* Freya reported.

"And we are going right into the lion's den."

"We are going to the Tiananmen. *Not quite as bad."*

Just a regiment. That's all. Just a few thousand heavily armed jackbooted thugs, thought Mathison.

From above, the planet of Green Hope was beautiful and there was no evidence of the battle that had occurred below. Mathison wondered if Stahl and Andre had made it back. What would the creatures have done when the shuttles left?

"We're screwed, aren't we, Gunny?"

"No," Mathison lied. "We are heavily armed, armored, and we have the element of surprise. They've never screwed with Marine Raiders before."

"But that is a regimental troop ship."

"That's just suffered a ninety percent loss of their ground forces," Mathison said, not believing his own words. "They have to be reeling from the shock and dazed at so many lost."

"They still have two battalions and an ODT battalion aboard the Tiananmen,*"* Freya reported. *"On a side note, if we were to deviate course now, we are within range of the* Tupolev *and I doubt they would hesitate to fire upon us."*

"Shut up, killjoy," Mathison told Freya.

"So how do we get back to the Aesir?" Stathis asked.

"I'm working on it," Mathison said.

"You have a plan?" Stathis asked.

"If it was quiet enough for me to think I might come up with one."

"Sorry, Gunny," Stathis said and sat back. "I guess we have a few hours, so I'm going to get some sleep."

Mathison opened his mouth to tell Stathis to shut up or go do something, but there really wasn't anything for him to do. Getting some sleep now wasn't a bad thing. At least he couldn't get into trouble.

Maybe.

The distance to the *Tiananmen* closed. What kind of protocol did they have for dealing with unoccupied shuttles? Would they have a combat team waiting to clear it? Decontamination procedures? There were too many unknowns, but Mathison knew he would not be captured. Not again, not by the SOG. Death was preferable, and if he was going to die, he was going to hurt the bastards bad.

*****

Chapter Nineteen: Snekke

Lojtnant Skadi – VRAEC

The first thing she noticed when she woke up was that her body did not hurt, then she noticed the bed was soft. She was in an officer's cabin aboard a ship. Her cybernetics showed the option to link with the VRS *Ovela Kostaja*, which was a snekke class ship, or by SOG classifications, a heavy cruiser. Skadi had never been aboard and knew little about it. She wasn't even sure which fleet it belonged to, offensive or defensive.

Was this an elaborate ruse? She denied the link for now. Once she came online, whoever was in command would know.

A uniform had been laid out nearby and she had been cleaned up, but she still felt crusty and dirty. The quarters had a shower, and Skadi wondered if she would get to use it or if they would rush in at the last minute to dash her hopes.

Half an hour later, she was pulling on the uniform when the door chimed. A display above the door said "Kari Ramo" with no rank or other designation.

Now presentable, she told it to open.

A short, serious looking man stepped in. He looked like so many SOG citizens. He was unarmed and unarmored, but Skadi wasn't fool enough to think he wasn't dangerous. There was an aura about him, and Skadi wondered if he was one of the MT, or Musta Toiminnot, Black Operations, frequently called disciples of Loki by the Aesir. It was possible he was more machine than human, with subdermal armor and weapons.

He smiled when he saw her, but it was reserved.

"Hello, Skadi," he said. "My name is Kari Ramo and I'm one of the Nakija."

Skadi nodded. Were the Nakija in league with Kontra-amiraali Kalm and whoever else was in that camp? Was Kari here to read her mind or conduct some secret Nakija interrogation technique?

Skadi remained silent and tried to think of nothing other than what was going on. Would that make it harder or easier for him to read her mind? Could Nakija read minds?

"How are you feeling?" Kari asked.

"Better," Skadi said.

"Good," Kari said. "If it is any consolation, we also rescued Niels, Bern, Vili, Gunsen, Zanella, Kittell, Bazer, and Tristan."

"I was told all but Vili and Bern had been executed," Skadi said.

Kari scowled. "No. Come with me. Niels is still unconscious, but the rest are awake and moving around."

Was this for real? Diagnostics reported she wasn't in some VR simulation, but they might have her codes. There were no indications, though.

She followed Kari and found herself in a room with a similar configuration as the *Valkyries*. The Aesir rooms opened onto a central room full of chairs and tables, food dispensers, and monitors.

Vili looked up and smiled. He still had bags under his eyes and looked tired, but he was alive. Bern was beside him and smiled, too. The younger Aesir stood up in deference.

"Sit," Skadi said to Gunsen and the others but she couldn't keep from smiling when she saw them.

Both Vili and Bern hugged her.

"They told me they had executed you," Vili said. "I thought we were all dead meat."

"Same here," Bern said.

"Those kusipääs are going to pay," Vili said. "How low have the Vanir sunk?"

"Many know nothing more than war," Kari said. "The youth long for peace, for blue skies overhead, for the dream of a home world. The Vanir, like the Aesir, see the power of the SOG and the young do not think we can win against them. Even the older citizens of the Republic long for peace. It is something we have seen growing in Republic society, but we have been blind to the rot. The Nakija have a code."

"That is more than rot," Vili said. "That is treason, to torture and threaten honorable Aesir."

"It is a delicate situation," Kari said. "It is not simple or clear cut. Just because people may be sympathetic to the departure faction does not mean they will support a civil war."

"A civil war?" Skadi asked.

Kari scowled. "Maybe. The Nakija are trying to prevent it. We cannot use force; we can only sway hearts and minds, but even in that we have limits. That might be the only thing the Nakija agrees on. We will take action, but violence begets violence, and once the shooting starts it won't stop."

"Where does that leave us?" Skadi asked.

"There's a lot going on," Kari said. "Even the SOG is teetering on the brink of a civil war."

Skadi raised an eyebrow.

"The Erik teams are not told everything," Kari said. "The Governance Central Committee is having problems maintaining control. Sector fleets are becoming more powerful and independent. War Command, those fighting the Torag and the Voshka, is also growing stronger. Because of distances and communication lag, the Central Committee cannot exercise as much control. They cannot monitor their commanders and fleets as tightly as they must. That is the prime reason SOG Home Fleet is so powerful; the Central Committee can exert more control over it. They desperately need faster than light communications to maintain control over their growing empire."

"So, the SOG is teetering?" Skadi asked.

"Not obviously," Kari said. "They appear united and strong, but we are watching sector commanders amassing power and control on a scale of which the Central Committee is unaware. We've intercepted reports; one sector has developed a covert combat robotics program."

"Why tell us that now?" Skadi asked.

Kari sighed. "Because that may be irrelevant if we do not eliminate this new threat."

"Nasaraf and the others?" Skadi asked.

"Correct."

"Why don't we leave then?" Skadi asked.

"This threat has ties to wormhole space we don't understand," Kari said. "There is nowhere we can run from it. You saw how they are linked to wormholes and wormhole space. Until we understand why we don't dare move the fleet."

"What about the inkeri generators?" Skadi asked.

"We are not sure exactly why that helps or what it does in wormhole space. It does let us make longer jumps with no one suffering Kiska Syndrome, but that doesn't mean they can't follow us. We just don't know. And there are factors I can't share with you yet."

"That still doesn't answer the kirottu question!" Skadi says. "What do we do now? Hide until this civil war sorts itself out?"

"The Vapaus Republic needs you more than ever," Kari said. "External threats, internal threats, and I'm sure there are threats we don't know about. The Executive Council needs you out in the field, needs you to find out more about the Nasaraf threat."

"What about the Marines?" Skadi asked.

"For now, they are safely out of reach of the flight faction," Kari said. "We think. They are with Sif and they have left for Green Hope to find out what they can about Hermod. Sif also has an experienced team of Jaegers with her."

"You sound like you have a different mission for us," Skadi said.

"The Nakija do not," Kari said. "Krenraali Lief does."

"He knows?" Skadi asked.

"Yes, he knows. He wants you working on the Nasaraf problem, as well, but it isn't that simple. The Vanir are being torn apart. Our society is being torn apart, and the SOG is preparing to implode. If the SOG implodes on its own, it will be bloodier if we do not interfere."

Skadi nodded.

"The Vapaus Republic, in conjunction with the Golden Horde, will launch an assault on the sector capital of Zhukov and the SOG Thirty-Second Space Defense Fleet."

"You have got to be kidding," Skadi said.

"I am not," Kari said. "We have need of the Erikoisjoukot and, incidentally, that will get you away from the Vanir. The Musta Toiminnot can be trusted where the Vanir cannot."

"So, what do you want us to do?"

*****

Chapter Twenty: *Tiananmen*

Gunnery Sergeant Wolf Mathison, USMC

"*Atmosphere is being purged remotely,*" Freya reported.

Mathison checked his heads-up display. Out of four suits, two reported as fully pressurized and intact, the other two were unavailable. Stathis was still sprawled out on the co-pilot's seat and his vitals reported he was asleep. Their suits had forty-eight hours of air and power at current consumption levels, so Mathison wasn't worried about that, yet. Everything else was a major problem.

Mathison still didn't have a plan. Stealing another shuttle wasn't an option, not with return-to-base protocols Freya couldn't override, and that was assuming the shuttle wasn't blasted to pieces by the *Tupolev's* or the *Tiananmen's* close defense weapons.

Hitchhiking a ride back down to the planet was also probably not a good idea. A shuttle full of troops would probably notice strangers in their midst.

Taking a high-ranking officer or three hostage was also unlikely to work. Skadi had mentioned the SOG knew better than to negotiate with hostage takers. They would blow up the shuttle instead.

Freya couldn't even rig the shuttle's power plant to overload and detonate to prevent their capture.

Mathison watched the *Tiananmen* grow larger. It was a massive ship, nearly three kilometers long and was not designed to enter a planet's atmosphere. Even getting too close to some planets could cause structural damage. It wasn't as sturdy as a battlestar and it looked slow, ponderous, and fragile. A regimental transport was what Freya had called it, and it carried a reinforced regiment of over five thousand troops, support craft, and support personnel. Sif and the SOG called it a regiment, but Mathison classified it more as a brigade. Semantics. It was still a lot of troops. The crew numbered a few hundred. They had suffered heavy casualties, but there were still thousands of Guardsmen who had not been deployed, and that was just combat troops, not support. That was still far too many for only two Marines to fight.

The second shuttle adjusted course and headed toward a shuttle bay of the *Tiananmen*. The Marines' shuttle decelerated, flipped, and slid into an external rack. The process made Mathison nauseous. Because the shuttle was reporting that there were no humans on board, the system didn't worry about being gentle as it maneuvered the shuttle around and slapped it into the docking clamps. The shuttle came to rest after a few seconds. His stomach threatened rebellion and he almost started dry heaving.

Stathis woke up as the shuttle went through its final maneuvers and the clamps grabbed it. Had he really slept through the shuttle being whipped around? His armor would have stiffened to protect him, but still.

"Are they just going to keep us out here?" Stathis asked, shaking his head.

"Why not?" Mathison said. "There's no crew or anything to offload."

"Don't they have gunnies who make them clean everything up, Gunny?" Stathis asked.

Mathison shrugged.

"What is the plan, Gunny?" Stathis asked when Mathison didn't say anything.

"Don't get captured, don't get killed," Mathison said. "Simple enough that even a private can understand it."

"Are you sure you're my gunny?" Stathis asked.

"Shut up, Stathis."

"Aye, Gunny."

"I'm close enough to work on the Tiananmen*'s networks,"* Freya reported. *"It doesn't have the heaviest encryption or security, but it might take a little time."*

"We have about forty-six hours, then the air runs out, and we die. Take your time." Then Mathison told Stathis, "You have watch. Wake me up if anything changes."

"I thought you were working on a plan?"

"I've got one."

Stathis stared at Mathison, and the gunnery sergeant wished he could see the private's face.

"Is it need to know or something, Gunny?"

"Nope. I already I told you: don't get captured, don't get killed. Every minute we avoid that is a victory. So far, so good. Victory is ours."

* * * * *

Chapter Twenty-One: *Valkyrie 15*

Chief Warrant Officer Diamond Winters, USMC

Winters looked at Levin, who looked back at her. Without the gunnery sergeant, or even Stathis, Winters felt more alone.

They were in the briefing room of *Valkyrie 15,* and the Jaegers were filtering in. The sergeant looked at her like she was in charge of the Marines, and she didn't like that feeling.

"It's just us until the Gunny gets back, Chief," Sergeant Levin said.

She didn't know what to say, so she lied. "He'll be okay. Gunny is a tough bastard. He got us off that SOG research station."

"Aye. He has his work cut out for him, though, escaping from thousands of SOG Guards and getting past a battleship."

Sloss joined them at the table.

"Paska-lounas," Sloss said. "Why did your gunnery sergeant board the shuttle like that?"

"Better signal," Levin said. "Why didn't you warn us that could happen?"

"Didn't know," Sloss said, shrugging. "Never been dumb enough to board a SOG shuttle. They do stuff like that to prevent mutiny and to capture mutineers. I've worked with Sif before. She will try to get them back."

"You've worked with Sif?" Winters asked, hoping to find out more about the girl-woman who was leading them.

Sloss nodded thoughtfully. "Can't tell you details but we are her axe when she needs violence."

Sif walked in, sat down, and looked around the table.

"*Valkyrie 27* has arrived. They are requesting a linkup to transfer personnel."

"Skadi's back?" Levin asked.

"They didn't say," Sif said. "I assumed so, but now that you mention it there was no greeting or news from Skadi."

Warning bells went off in Winters' head.

"Are they that trusting?" Blitzen asked. *"The Vanir are fanatical about security, but that sounds complacent."*

"Is that normal?" Winter asked.

"No," Sif said, her eyes piercing Winters'. "It isn't. Nor was Eversti Nyland in command."

"Why?" asked Winters.

Sif pursed her lips. "Are Marines usually this paranoid? *27* knew the links and codes. What could be wrong? They are Vanir. They are the shields."

Winters shook her head.

Sif looked around. Sloss did not seem concerned, but Winters could tell the lack of information bothered Sif now.

"You shouldn't worry," Sif said. "I will ask when they get closer. They are still a few days away from our linkup location. It is common for *Valkyries* to rotate captains as well."

"What are we going to do about the gunny?" Winters asked.

Sif suddenly looked more disturbed.

"We have to wait," Sif said. "We cannot stand against a SOG *Drekkar*-class, especially not a newer one. Not with only three *Valkyries*, and make no mistake, the *Tupolev* will protect the *Tiananmen.* The two *Busse*-class vessels are also a problem. We lack the drone strike force and raw power needed to overwhelm the defenses of anything other than the *Tiananmen.* And we have no way to communicate to coordinate a rescue."

"Maybe you should just let the Republic handle it," Sloss said to Winters. "We understand the technology and protocols."

Winters scowled at the big man. "I didn't ask your opinion. He is my gunnery sergeant, my brother. What would you do if it was one of your Aesir?"

Sloss shrugged. "My Jaegers wouldn't be dumb enough to board the shuttle to begin with."

"Because you can't crack into their networks and systems," Winters said. "When all you have is a hammer, every problem looks like a nail, doesn't it?"

Sloss leaned forward and scowled at her.

"What do you know?" he asked. "Most of your knowledge is over three hundred years out of date."

"I learn," Winters said. "I adapt. Why can't you?"

"Enough," Sif said before Winters could say something she was sure she would regret. Sloss shrugged and dismissed her, which only made Winters angrier. Sloss was acting like a big, braindead lout.

"I'm not an Erikoisjoukot," Sloss said to Sif. "I shouldn't have to deal with muukalainen."

"Muukalainen means stranger or alien," Blitzen told Winters before she could ask. *"If I had to guess, based on his body language, he has a problem*

working with women. Alpha male ego. Maybe if he saw you fight... He also looks down on Sergeant Levin, if that's any consolation. He probably has problems with Sif, too."

Sif stood and approached Sloss, her anger clear.

"You are dismissed, Over-Sergeant Sloss," Sif said. "You and your party are not needed at this time, especially if you can't work with allies. I will call you when I need a hammer."

Sloss stood, towering over Sif, but she didn't back down.

"Zen, Kapten." Sloss left and his team silently filed out behind him.

Sif looked at Winters and Levin. Much of the fire seemed to leave her.

"I'm sorry," Sif said.

Winters nodded, mollified and surprised that Sif would take the Marine's side.

"Right now, all we can do is watch," Sif said. "Watch and wait. Maybe Skadi will have some ideas."

"She has more experience with the SOG?" Winters asked.

Sif shook her head sadly. "Not really, but she is more familiar with the use of selective violence. I'm familiar with SOG protocols and procedures, but less so on the combat side. In the last couple decades, I've worked more on the infiltration and subversion side of things, with more focus on the intelligence agencies and bureaus. Infiltration and subversion are not quick. We need something quick."

"If Skadi is on the ship," Winters said.

"Why do you think she isn't?" Sif asked.

"Because they intercepted her shuttle before it could dock with us, right? Sorry, you might trust the Vanir, but I do not."

"Who else would it be?" Sif asked. "Even if she is not aboard, they will be allies."

"Why did they try to stop us from leaving Midgard?" Winters asked. "Something is going on, and I don't understand it. Why should the Vanir give up once we left the fleet?"

Sif pursed her lips.

"I agree," Levin said. "You might trust the Vanir and Aesir, but from where I'm standing, the fact the Aesir had to sneak us out tells me things aren't copacetic between the two groups, which smells of political games." Levin nodded at Winters. "I think we've both seen enough American politics to understand how quickly the winds can shift. The fact your general will risk our lives to get us off Midgard tells me we should be very cautious."

Sif nodded.

"Do you trust Eversti Oja?" Winters asked.

Her narrowed eyes told Winters that was not a smart line of questioning.

"Yes," Sif said.

"He is Vanir though," Winters said.

"In name only," Sif said. "He is loyal to the Nakija."

"Yet you couldn't override him," Winters said, and Sif laughed.

"The Nakija and Vanir are loyal to the people of the Republic," Sif said. "He is loyal to them before me. I am a representative of the Nakija, but he is required to think for himself."

"I hope you're right," Winters said, convinced now more than ever that Skadi was not on *Valkyrie 27*. Why couldn't Sif see that? What could she and Levin do?

*****

Chapter Twenty-Two: Astral Messenger

Kapten Sif – VRAEC, Nakija Musta Toiminnot

Kat sat in the middle of her quarters and stared at the wall, set to display a sunset. It was a pleasure to shed her persona as Aesir commander and be who she was. No pressure, no need to appear strong, dominant, and always in control.

27 had replied that Skadi was not available to talk, and they wouldn't say why. They told Kat they would have her call when she was available. When pressed, they said she was running simulations, and she was not to be disturbed. Her senses told her to trust Winters and the Marines' intuition, which bothered her. Now Kat was getting a bad feeling about *27,* which was just a day away.

There was nothing new from the *Tupolev* battle group. She wished her disciplines were different, but they were the hand she had been dealt. Her plan probably wouldn't work, but she had to try. Really, she needed Skadi. There was no doubt in anyone's mind she was the premier special operations officer, and if anyone could come up with a plan to rescue the Marines, it would be her.

Eversti Hiltel, commander of *27*, was a certified Valkyrie Eversti. Sif had heard of him but never worked with him. The records aboard

15 said he was currently a liaison officer aboard the Battlestar *Thor*. He had a long, honorable service record. When asked, Hiltel had said that Eversti Nyland was undergoing additional training, along with most of his crew. It wasn't unheard of, crews rotated so they could get some rest and relaxation, undergo additional training, acquire new certifications, and otherwise get a break. Transporting a combat team, or running simple errands, was a typical mission for crews in transition.

Aboard *15*, the Marines and the Jaegers were sleeping. The ship was quiet. Only the Vanir on watch were awake.

Sif closed her eyes and concentrating on her breathing, focusing on putting her body to sleep while she kept her mind awake. Around her, she felt energy and warmth.

Breathe in, breathe out.

She tried to slow her breathing, increased the time to inhale then exhale. With each exhale she relaxed different parts of her body, starting with her toes and working her way up to her scalp, released tension, and when she breathed in, she imagined inhaling a relaxing light. There were no monsters waiting nearby. She had done this before and now, maybe, she could again. There weren't any other options.

Minutes later, she felt her body vibrate and euphoria flowed through her. She felt her different bodies, her physical and astral self. The harmony of the ship's song grew louder as the vibrations increased. She was at peace, safe.

For a moment, memories of the creature aboard the station haunted her thoughts, but she pushed them away before they could take root and pull her into a nightmare. That creature was not here.

She was not alone. She trusted others would come if she needed help. The knight would be close if she needed him.

She listened to her heartbeat slow and opened her astral eyes. Kari was sitting in front of her. He wore a gentle smile and a warm green aura. He was like a big brother to her, even though he was younger and her junior.

"A civil war is coming to the Vapaus Republic," Kari said to her, mind to mind, but without words. His thoughts were pure and could not hold deception or misunderstanding. "The Vanir are being torn apart, like our people. Some wish to stay and fight, others wish to flee into the depths of space, far from the SOG."

"The Aesir?" Kat asked.

"Few Aesir are divided. They are the blade that wish to fight. The Nakija have spent so much time looking out and away from the people that we have not seen this. We did not see the trees because of the forest. Our laws have protected our people, but the laws have concealed and protected the rot, as well. We were not watching for this and now it may be too late."

Kat understood.

"We are sending Skadi to Zhukov," Kari said. "There will be a major fleet action there."

"Why?" Her mind spun. That meant Skadi was not aboard *27*. Hiltel was lying.

"The Vanir who wish to stay and fight must prove themselves," Kari said. "They seek to hasten the collapse of the SOG."

"We have lost two Marines," Kat said. "They may have been captured and are with the *Tupolev* battle group."

"I will inform the council when I get the chance," Kari said. "I am not with the fleet."

A chill passed through Kat and she saw it pass through Kari. Fear in the astral realms was a powerful, destructive force and Kat recognized it.

"Something is wrong," Kari said.

The vibrant colors around them lost their shine and Kat felt her vibrations increase.

The ship disappeared, leaving the two astral travelers in a gray fog.

"Are you doing this?" Kari asked. Kat felt his fear and alarm. She did not answer, he knew it the instant he asked. Their minds were linked.

There was another presence. It wasn't unfamiliar, and she felt what could only be described as evil emanating from it. There was a mental sickness, a vile hatred and insanity lurking just beneath the surface of this entity. Something wanted to hurt her. It was like the creature aboard the secret SOG base but different, more powerful, more hateful.

"I sense you," a voice said inside her mind. Kat felt sick as terror welled up in her. Again, she was frozen, unable to return to her body.

"We must flee!" Kat told Kari but she saw he was also frozen with fear, but then she saw it wasn't his fear holding him in place, it was dread-filled curiosity.

She realized her own curiosity was holding her there as well.

Something moved past her in the mist, another presence, this one familiar and comforting. A shining beacon of silver and comfort.

"Your curiosity imprisons you," Kat whispered mind to mind to Kari.

"One of the tribes," the evil voice whispered. "Once again, we do battle."

A voice laughed at the evil, and Kari disappeared. Kat knew he had fled back to his body.

"Semper Fi, motherfucker," the voice said as Kat fled back to her own body. "Yeah, though I walk through the valley of death, I will fear no evil, for I am the baddest son of a bitch in the valley."

It was the knight from before, coming to do battle.

"Leave them alone," the knight said.

"You cannot defeat me," the demon said, and a shudder passed through Kat as she heard the truth there.

"Your time will come," the knight replied, moving forward, ready for battle. "Right now, I'm just going to piss in your matzo and shit on your challah."

Kat opened her eyes and stared at the sun setting on the wall before her. Her body felt warm and comfortable, but a chill passed through her. Fear still clawed at her heart as a high priority alert came in from Bluebeard.

Kat took a deep breath, wishing there was somebody to hold her. Her hands were shaking and she wanted to be in someone else's presence. Alone in her room, she felt like she was in danger, like the creature could appear at any moment from some dark corner. There was no knight here.

She ordered the lights to max as she looked around, half expecting the demon to be lurking there, looking back at her, preparing to attack.

The alarm buzzed again, demanding her attention.

She took another deep breath. Kat tried to cloak herself in the persona of an Aesir commander. "Answer."

"Sif," Bluebeard said on audio only. "The *Tupolev* task force just slipped into wormhole space. We have detected another ship on the periphery. It looks like the *Pankhurst* and it's coming closer to the system, trying to be stealthy."

Was this coincidence? Where had the *Tupolev* gone with the Marines?

There wasn't anything she could do for them. They were on their own. She did not want to wait to see what the *Pankhurst* would do.

"Acknowledged," Sif said. "Plot a course for the Zhukov system."

"After we link up with *27*?" Bluebeard asked.

Kat didn't want to link up with *27*. Skadi wasn't with them. Why were they lying?

If the Vanir and Aesir were tearing the Republic apart, who could she trust?

What had the demon meant by "one of the tribes?"

What was matzo and challah?

*****

Chapter Twenty-Three: Zhukov

Gunnery Sergeant Wolf Mathison, USMC

It was as though the SOG had forgotten about the supposedly empty shuttle latched to the outside of the *Tiananmen*. Mathison was okay with that, but oxygen was likely to become a problem before food and water. While Freya and Shrek worked on the *Tiananmen* network, Mathison pretended to sleep while Stathis practiced various reload drills and martial arts moves in the reduced gravity. Mathison kept waiting for Stathis to accidentally hit a button or fire off a round, thereby informing the *Tiananmen* that someone was present, but Stathis managed to avoid any of that. That fear kept him from sleep, but telling Stathis to stop just meant the private would find something else to do.

And it was good to see Stathis practicing. Unarmed combat in zero gravity was nothing like unarmed combat in gravity. Throwing a simple punch when you weren't braced was stupid. A punch was more likely to push you around than hurt an opponent. Two opposing points of contact against a single surface are required to deliver a good punch. If you can establish those two points of contact with your opponent, you can do some serious damage, if your contacts were solid. Usually, you just pushed them away. Jujitsu was ideal for zero gravity combat because it frequently required close contact with an opponent and had many moves that used the opponent's mass and limbs against them. Breaking an arm or neck was more practical than trying to punch someone in the face. Even stabbing could be problematic for the attacker because you had to stab with enough force to pierce armor and the lack of gravity or mass to push the attack home made that impossible. Jujitsu, combined with knife fighting, was lethal in zero gravity.

It was difficult practicing Jujitsu in space without an opponent.

Mathison watched Stathis, who was practicing hand slips, slipping a hand under an imaginary arm while anchored to the floor. It looked like a Wing Chun style with the moving, flowing hands, but Mathison remembered the last time the Raider platoon had undergone space combat certification, he had spent a lot of time doing that. Constant repetition built muscle memory. It was boring and sometimes mind numbing.

After more time than Mathison would have spent doing it, Stathis changed to strikes; hook the opponent with one arm and a leg, then deliver a blow from the body, usually an upper cut. Stathis did it slowly since he only had a single leg anchored to the floor, but he kept doing it over and over. His form wasn't bad, and he had enough control he didn't lose contact with the floor.

Mathison was about to correct Stathis' upper cut, his fist wasn't rotating properly to get enough torque, when Freya got his attention.

"I have access," Freya reported. *"Security isn't what it could be. Right now there's a lot of confusion and morale is low. They have taken heavy casualties. Second Battalion is undeployable. There are four infantry battalions, one armored battalion, and a support battalion of artillery and gunships. One battalion is an Orbital Drop Trooper battalion, considered elite, although not Peacekeeper caliber. They were about to be deployed when night fell, and the creatures slaughtered the second battalion. There's a lot of reorganization going on. The battalion commander, along with all the officers of the battalion, are facing charges: dereliction of duty and incompetence."*

"Was there any incompetence?" Mathison asked.

"Not from what I can tell," Freya said. *"That's really the least of my concerns, but I suspect it's standard procedure."*

That didn't surprise Mathison, but he really wanted to know if they would find someone to blame anyway, what they had learned, and if they were going to try again.

"Any way to get a message to Sif?" Mathison asked.

"They will notice any unusual transmissions. They really seem obsessed with mutinies and treason. Zero tolerance for unauthorized transmissions or receiving unauthorized transmissions."

"So that is a no."

"This is bad," Freya said moments later.

"They're mobilizing the troops to capture us kind of bad, or they have captured Hermod kind of bad?"

"Worse. They are preparing to transit. All troops are being sent to quarters. Apparently, they lock everyone up in their sleeping capsules for wormhole transitions."

"Where are we going?"

"I'm trying to find out," Freya said. *"I don't have access to the astrogation and bridge networks yet, but from what I've been able to glean from other communications, the* Tupolev *battle group is supposed to rendezvous with a larger fleet. They say it is for a training evolution, but I'm picking up traffic that they're to prepare for ship-to-ship combat. They are not preparing training missiles and ammunition."*

"Sounds like they are being sneaky. An ambush?"

"That sounds about right."

"Fleet action?" Mathison asked. The last thing he wanted was to be attached to the outside of a fat, slow troop transport like the *Tiananmen* while people were shooting at it, especially if it was the Republic doing the shooting. Friendly fire really wasn't as friendly as people liked to think. *"Against who?"*

"Unknown. I have a destination: Zhukov. They are going to stop, restock, and then they're to link up with a battleship squadron on the outskirts of Zhukov for a simulated raid on a Torag system. We are nowhere near the Torag front."

"So, somebody is going to get ambushed in Zhukov. Who?"

"Unknown. Who has the firepower to tangle with the SOG?" Freya asked, and Mathison winced. *"Actually, it could be the Republic or a group called the Golden Horde, or maybe they have discovered a pirate base and are going to raid it."*

"Or they know where home fleet is."

"That is a definite possibility."

"How can we warn them?"

"We can commit suicide," Freya said.

"I'm looking for another option," Mathison said. *"Preferably an option that doesn't involve us dying for people who wanted to arrest us."*

*****

Chapter Twenty-Four: Wormhole

Gunnery Sergeant Wolf Mathison, USMC

Freya couldn't tell Mathison if they would have problems transitioning in the shuttle. It was not a topic that had come up, and Mathison could imagine too many ways it could be fatal. Radiation was the biggest one. The shuttles had some radiation shielding but not nearly as much as the ship's hull. Was there some kind of protective field that only extended to the edge of the hull? Would the Kiska Syndrome be magnified? Was he about to go psychotic on Stathis, or vice versa? Apparently, nobody was stupid enough to be in a shuttle on the hull of a ship during transition.

There were too many questions, and it was too late to get inside the ship. Being in the shuttle should be better than being stuck directly to the outer hull when the ship slid into wormhole space.

Maybe.

"Are we going to be okay?" Stathis asked.

Mathison looked at Stathis. He didn't like to lie. "I don't know. It could get bad if this Kiska Syndrome crap is as bad as they claim. We could be in for a bumpy ride. This is a SOG ship, and they lock up their people for transition."

Freya began a countdown, and Mathison held his breath.

A shiver ran through his body, and he felt dread when she reached zero.

They were in wormhole space.

"Still alive," Mathison said, looking at Stathis.

"Doesn't radiation kill you slowly?" Stathis said. "How will you know your hair is falling out if you don't have any?"

"How will you know with your helmet on?" Mathison said, checking his suit's radiation counter. Nothing out of the ordinary. Vital signs showed normal as well.

"So, my hair could be falling out and I could be dying slowly without knowing it?" Stathis asked. "I don't feel well. I'm dying."

"Shut up, Stathis. The suits have a radiation indicator. Pull up your display and vital signs if you're worried."

"Oh," Stathis said, and fell silent.

"I'm detecting odd brainwave activity," Freya said seconds after Mathison figured they would survive. *"I'm releasing chemicals and programming nanites to restore and reverse the change. Shrek is doing the same."*

"Our brains are melting," Stathis said.

"Shut up Stathis," Mathison said.

"What do you mean?" Mathison asked Freya.

"Your neural pathways are altering slightly. Shrek and I do not understand it, but we are trying to limit these changes. We don't think they are beneficial," Freya said. *"On a positive note, our processing capabilities are improved greatly and this is allowing for faster analysis and counteraction."*

"Great," Mathison said. He didn't feel different, but would he?

"I don't want to change, Gunny," Stathis said.

"Well, you can't get any dumber."

"But I like being me, Gunny."

"Relax, Stathis. Trust your SCBI."

"But what if I become evil or something?"

"Then I'll shoot you,"

"What if *you* turn evil?"

"Then I'll shoot you twice. Besides, who says I'm not already evil?"

Stathis went quiet. Mathison looked at the private and waited for him to go for his weapon. Having seen Stathis in action, Mathison didn't know if he would be fast enough. Maybe he should try an easier approach.

"How long will this last?" Stathis asked.

"Five more minutes," Freya reported.

"Five minutes," Mathison said. "You aren't going to change much in five minutes."

"How do you know, Gunny?"

"Your SCBI will. Relax, Private Stathis. This is as bad as it gets."

Something flickered at the corner of Mathison's vision. He looked over but saw nothing had changed. Again, there was a movement at the edge of his vision.

"Freya, am I seeing things?"

"Not with your eyes. I can see what you see, however, your brain is responding as if it's seeing something, and I don't understand that. Maybe it's a residue of these changes?"

"So there really isn't anything there?"

"I see nothing," Freya reported. *"I do have recording ability. I triggered it with your first sighting. The replay shows nothing."*

"So, I'm bonkers?" Mathison said.

"We aren't alone in here," Stathis said.

"Yes, we are," Mathison said. "It's the weird brain activity making you think you're seeing things."

Stathis nodded and remained silent.

"I'm pretty sure I saw an ugly face," Stathis said. "Sharp teeth and squinty bug eyes."

"Shrek saw nothing," Freya reported.

"It's the wormhole space," Mathison said, hoping it was true. "You are imagining things."

"Aye, Gunny."

Looking around, Mathison saw an indistinct ghost walk through the shuttle behind them and across the troop compartment. It was definitely a biped and walking, but other details were blurry.

"Did you see that?" Mathison asked Freya.

"No," Freya said. *"Your brain patterns are currently stable except certain centers which are acting like they see something. What did you see?"*

"Did you see that?" Stathis asked. "That was a freaking ghost! It walked across the back." Stathis pointed to where Mathison had seen the phantom.

So much for imagining things. Mathison watched for monster faces.

"The fact that both of you saw something is outside of our understanding at the moment," Freya said.

"Only a few more minutes," Mathison said with a cold sinking feeling. If Freya or Shrek didn't see the ghost because their physical eyes did not see it, what did that mean?

"Gunny?" Stathis said. "I'm getting kinda creeped out."

Mathison saw Stathis' hand fall to his sidearm.

"Stand down, Stathis." Mathison putting an edge in his voice and Stathis took his hand off his pistol.

"How can we fight something like that?" Stathis asked.

"Harsh language," Mathison said. "Keep your hands off your weapons. I don't want you shooting holes in the shuttle."

"Aye, Gunny." Stathis sounded calmer, now. Score another one for NCO command presence.

Time passed, but neither Marine saw anything else. Finally, Mathison felt a warm sensation flow through his body as the *Tiananmen* entered normal space.

"We need to get out of this shuttle, Gunny," Stathis said.

Mathison couldn't argue. He did not want to be in the shuttle going through wormhole space again. It couldn't be any worse in a prison cell, could it? What would happen if they had been in wormhole space for longer?

"Can you get us into the Tiananmen*?"* Mathison asked Freya.

"I should be able to. There's a storage room near a shuttle bay you could use. I will change permissions so nobody else can access the space. That should keep visitors out. Unfortunately, senior officers will be able to override it. But it's a big ship, so you might be able stow away successfully if we maintain control of the network."

"How senior?"

"Just ship's officers; commander and up."

Which might work, unless it was a broom closet.

"Good," Mathison said. *"Better than here. With my luck, they'll decide to jettison the shuttle in deep space because it's useless weight. How do we get there?"*

"That will be tricky. If you ditch your trauma plates you will look more like SOG crew in space dress, but the SOG crew members do not walk around armed."

"So, we put our extra gear into a bag or something. Then we walk to the storeroom and lock ourselves in until an opportunity presents itself."

"Yes, but I'll also have to mask your presence, erasing it as we go. You can't fart aboard the Tiananmen *without it being recorded and analyzed for treason."*

"Any luck on finding out more from the bridge?"

"Yes and no," Freya said. *"The bridge and astrogation are on separate isolated subnets. I have no access to them."*

"And?" Mathison prompted.

"And they monitor even the officers for compliance," Freya said. *"I have observed a very interesting conversation between commissars. It appears the travel pods the troops sleep in are also incineration pods. They incinerated three troopers. Apparently they went crazy, a very severe case of Kiska Syndrome."*

"Great."

"It makes me think things might not be much better aboard the ship," Freya said.

"That's nice," Mathison said. *"Can we work on getting to that storeroom?"*

* * * * *

Chapter Twenty-Five: Storeroom

Gunnery Sergeant Wolf Mathison, USMC

The room was bigger than he had expected. There were several aisles, created using metal panels. There were crates stacked atop each other and magnetically attached to the walls. Boxes were coded, but they made little sense to Mathison until Freya accessed the inventory and displayed a pop-up in his vision showing the contents. There was everything here except weapons, explosives, and ammunition.

"You are the first line of defense against the total collapse of civilization and human decency," the intercom said.

Mathison wished he could mute it. It was getting old. The damned voice had not shut up since they had managed to get aboard the *Tiananmen*.

"You are the firstborn. You are the guardians of society, the heroes of the future. Without the order and standards implemented by the Central Committee, humanity would devolve into individuality and violence. The Social Organizational Governance depends on you. You are the sharpened sword, the well-aimed gun, the steel gauntlet of the righteous. You are the champions of social organization and civilization. You unite humanity and will bring about a socialist utopia."

"Can we shut that off?" Mathison asked Freya.

"Not easily. I'm filtering out the subliminal messaging, though. It is part of the mutiny defense mechanism. There are microphones throughout the ship that monitors sound levels. In places where there are not enough cameras, they use it like a radar system to map out people's location and actions. They use the wireless networks similarly."

"Seriously? Is that possible?"

"Yes. I am working to silence it in this room, but that could initiate a maintenance ticket and a crewman visiting with a replacement part. They are extremely paranoid aboard this ship and masking our presence is difficult. They behave like mutinies happen on a weekly basis or something. Not that I blame them, actually."

"Gunny?" Stathis asked. "Do you think they would notice if I shoot the speakers?"

"Probably," Mathison said. "But I'm wondering if that's a bad thing, unless they also pipe it into the prison cells and morgue."

Stathis stared at where the droning voice was coming from.

"You hold the line against lawlessness and social upheaval. You protect the weak, the young, the innocent. You defend our freedoms and our virtue," the voice went on. "It is your mission in life to fight treason, social injustice, and disloyalty to the Central Committee, the guardians of humanity. Violence brings peace. Mercy provokes betrayal. Compassion breeds selfishness."

Mathison walked around, checking what was in stock, when the voice changed and became louder.

“All personnel,” the voice said. “Jump stations. Report to jump stations immediately. Jump duration will be ten minutes. Anyone found outside their pod will be shot.”

“Can my jump station be out the airlock, Gunny?” Stathis said. “I really don’t want to go through that again.”

“Maybe it will be different inside the hull,” Mathison said.

The regular propaganda voice droned on.

“An open mind is weakness. You have been specially selected to serve in your current role. Your physical and mental capabilities have been carefully evaluated, and we have assigned you to the place that you can make the biggest contribution to the common good. You are exceptional and the free and happy people of the Governance appreciates your contribution. Sometimes your job may seem difficult, but your officers will not let your good work go unnoticed.”

Mathison rolled his eyes.

The icy chill of transition into the wormhole flowed through Mathison. He willed it to differ from the shuttle.

It wasn’t.

* * * * *

Chapter Twenty-Six: Inspection

Gunnery Sergeant Wolf Mathison, USMC

Neither of the Marines could move inside the cramped confines of the locker. Stathis was almost sitting on Mathison's head, and Mathison was sitting on their weapons and trauma plates while the three crew inventoried the storage room. Freya could only block the inventory for so long because the officers seemed to work overtime to keep the crew and troops busy. Mathison knew it was because it took their mind off the casualties and kept them out of trouble.

Over the last week, Mathison and Stathis had spent most of their time tapped into the video feeds watching the people of the *Tiananmen* go about their daily chores. There were few robots in use, which did not seem efficient, and most crew were nothing more than meat puppets for their headsets, which told them where to go and what to do. The headsets linked into the main *Tiananmen* network and databases so any crewman could fix or replace most pieces of equipment by following the instructions displayed on their retina by their headset.

Combat troops were kept busy with constant drills and exercise. It was depressing to watch the way the troops were treated, like every day was boot camp. The Guards had no free time, no time to unwind, and Mathison couldn't understand how they suffered through it. Many were like automatons. The crew and the troops were kept separated, which made sense since most of the crew were women and most of the Guards were men. It was easy enough to identify a person's branch with just a casual look due to the steroids fed to the troops. The crew were small like Stathis, and the Guards were usually big like Mathison.

Freya, or Shrek, had adjusted the shipboard inventory to compensate for the rations and other supplies Mathison and Stathis were using. They were both armored, minus their trauma plates, just in case. The nearby bathroom allowed them to avoid overloading their suit systems, but Freya was making Mathison paranoid that some SOG technician would notice the increase in facility use and begin investigating.

"Are those women, Gunny?" Stathis asked as he watched the video feed of the storage room and the crew going cabinet to cabinet.

Mathison looked at the three crew members. The baggy, shapeless, dark blue jumpsuits made them appear sexless and plain. The Governance did their best to hide the gender of their troops, which probably made it easier to think of them all as not being different or individually unique, like ants.

"Yes," Mathison said. "Watch their center of gravity. It's higher."

"Oh," Stathis said. "Those SOG rations give me gas."

Stathis shifted his hips again.

"Quit squirming," Mathison said. Whenever Stathis moved his hips, he pushed Mathison's head against the side of the locker.

"Gunny," Stathis sang. "I just killed a man. Put my butt against his head, cut a fart and now he's dead."

"Shut up, Stathis," Mathison said, thankful he was wearing his helmet and breathing recycled air.

"But those SOG rations give me gas," Stathis said. Mathison couldn't shake his head and there was something disturbing about Stathis farting next to his head. "It's uncomfortable."

"Wait until I put my boot up your ass," Mathison said. Stathis stopped squirming so much.

"Gunny," Stathis sang. "My tour had just begun—"

"I swear to god, I'm going to throat punch you, Stathis."

"Maybe if things don't work out with the Republic we can join the SOG ODTs."

"Seriously?" Stathis had seemed to enjoy watching the ODT battalion aboard the *Tiananmen* train.

"They seem pretty hard core, Gunny. Not Marine standards, mind you, but they are the best we've seen. They also get real powered armor and blazers, unlike the Guard. I'll bet with our SCBIs we could make ourselves officers."

"You want to be an officer, Stathis?"

"It would be an easy life. Just make sure we have the best NCOs. I think our SCBIs could arrange that. NCOs do all the work."

Mathison opened his mouth then shut it. Arguing with a private was a good way to get dragged into the gutter of stupidity and beat to death with inexperience.

"That's right, Private," Mathison said with the patience of a parent.

Some battles could not be won. And some battles were not worth fighting.

*****

Chapter Twenty-Seven: Colonel Feng

Gunnery Sergeant Wolf Mathison, USMC

Mathison did not want Stathis to go alone, but there were no other options. He expected alarms any second as he watched the private make his way through the corridors. The young Marine looked and acted just like one of the regular spacers, with his shaved head, baggy, dark blue jumpsuit that didn't fit, and the slouch. It tore at Mathison. He wanted to yell at the young man for slouching like a slob, but he was doing a great job emulating the SOG spaceberts.

While there were the occasional large spacers, there were very few small Guardsmen. He watched through the *Tiananmen's* cameras being displayed on his retina by Freya, geared up and ready to rush to Stathis' rescue. He didn't like sending a young, inexperienced private into harm's way. Not like this. But Freya assured him it wouldn't be a problem. Mathison knew anything that could go wrong would. And while it was difficult to tell him from one of the spacers, this was Stathis, and perhaps the only skill Mathison knew the young man was truly good at was fighting.

Stathis had spent hours watching the crew as they moved around the ship, and Shrek had downloaded some manuals for the two Marines to go over, but this was an acting job and that worried Mathison. How could a private be a competent actor?

One of them had to get more food, though, since the stock in the storage room was minimal. One would think they would spread emergency rations throughout the ship in large quantities, but the SOG, in its infinite wisdom, had decided to not put many in the storage room and the Marines had already gone through the small stash. Since Stathis was less obvious, both SCBIs agreed he had the best chance to move around the ship without being noticed. Mathison was just too big and memorable.

Mathison felt a little better as he watched the private walk down the corridor. The private acted like a natural spacer, and he was nearly to the supply commissary where the SCBIs had arranged for an order to be ready for him. It was just a small box, nothing big or noticeable. They were emergency rations, and the official story was that he was replacing some in a storeroom that had expired. On a large ship like this, Mathison hoped nobody would recognize a new face.

Stathis turned a corner and almost bumped into a SOG officer dressed from head to toe in gray so dark it was almost black. Stathis leapt out of the way and froze like the other spacers usually did.

Mathison had seen this officer several times. He saw the hammer and sword symbol on his uniform, the emblem of the ODT. Commissar lightning bolts and a colonel's eagle adorned his collar and shoulder tabs. Mathison's mouth went dry. The SCBIs had not seen him because that corridor had some broken sensor links.

"Stop," the colonel said.

Mathison brought up a dossier on the ship's net. Colonel Shing Feng, commissar colonel, ODT qualified and most of his record was classified at a level not even Freya could dig up. *Crap.*

"Yes, Friend Colonel," Stathis said, coming to a pretty good equivalent of SOG attention, hands at his sides, chin up as if exposing the throat, shoulders pushed way back.

"You don't look familiar, friend spacer," Colonel Feng said, like a predator who had spied prey.

"I'm sorry, Friend Colonel," Stathis said. "I seek to serve without recognition."

The colonel scowled at Stathis.

Mathison checked his rifle. Yes, he had a round chambered. The colonel had a sidearm, like all officers. Stathis had nothing except his bare hands. Mathison doubted he could get to Stathis in time. The young private was a level up and about five hundred meters to the rear of the ship. Stathis was good at unarmed combat, though. If he could take on an Aesir, he should be able to stomp some stuck-up, prissy commissar, but then the gig would be up and the SOG would hunt for them.

"What division are you?" the colonel asked.

"Blue division," Stathis said. "Under Lieutenant Bukolov, Friend Colonel."

"Are you one of the spacers we picked up at Tau Ceti?" the colonel asked.

"No, Friend Colonel," Stathis said and Mathison's blood went cold. Why the hell hadn't the private said yes? That was an easy out.

The colonel nodded, as if satisfied.

What?

"We didn't pick up anyone in Tau Ceti, did we?" the colonel asked. "What is your name?"

"I don't know about Tau Ceti, Friend Colonel," Stathis said. "This spacer's name is Zale Bobylev."

"Why don't you know if we picked up anyone in Tau Ceti?" the colonel asked.

Stathis shrugged, and Mathison wanted to strangle the private. *You don't shrug at commissars!*

"I don't have a lot of friends, Friend Colonel," Stathis said.

"Are you anti-social?" Feng asked, sounding more curious than angry.

"No, Friend Colonel," Stathis said quickly. "I mean, I don't have a lot of friends I talk to a lot."

"He's accessing the Tiananmen *data net,"* Freya told Mathison. *"I'm feeding him some bogus information."*

"Hm," the colonel said, looking at Stathis but reviewing the data Freya was feeding him.

"Fine, Spacer Bobylev," Feng said. "Go about your business."

"Thank you, Friend Colonel," Stathis said, popping out an open-hand salute, showing Feng the palm of his hand before sprinting down the hallway away from him.

Mathison let out the breath he'd been holding.

The commissar watched Stathis go, his face expressionless. There was something about the colonel that made Mathison nervous.

Stathis hadn't done half bad; that was a surprise.

The private made it to the commissary, picked up the package, and made it back to the storeroom without having to talk to anyone else.

"That colonel is a crafty bastard," Freya reported as Mathison opened one of the rations Stathis had brought back. *"He's actually going through Blue Division's watch roster looking for Bobylev."*

"And?" Mathison thought.

"Shrek and I have made sure he found what he was looking for. But he is a dangerous person. Even with such a large crew he can identify a spacer on sight alone."

"Maybe we can arrange for him to have an accident?"

"Maybe you *can. I can't do that."*

"Right," Mathison said. "Well, you get me a button, and I will make it happen."

"That might be an option," Freya said. *"I will review my protocols and conscience."*

"Good," Mathison said. He wished Stathis had been able to get something other than emergency rations. Was it the fate of humanity to always make emergency rations taste like rotting garbage?

Colonel Commissar Feng might have to be dealt with, especially if he started poking around more. Mathison scanned the logs Freya had dug up on him. He seemed to spend a lot of time talking with someone on the *Tupolev* and spent a lot of time with the ODTs. As a colonel it looked like everyone, including the captain, deferred to him, but Mathison wasn't sure if that was because he was a commissar or because of his connections to the person on the *Tupolev*.

* * * * *

Chapter Twenty-Eight: Zhukov

Gunnery Sergeant Wolf Mathison, USMC

Tiananmen docked at Kovpak Station. It was easier for Mathison and Stathis to transfer to the station than it had been to board the *Tiananmen.*

Freya and Shrek were able to quickly compromise Kovpak's sensors and find a weak spot where they could get across with their armor and gear. The crew and troops aboard the ship could not depart, but the officers could. There were numerous non-military ships docked and transferring cargo or passengers at the massive station; it was a perfect opportunity to get off the *Tiananmen*, with all the different people and cargo being shifted around.

The station was attached to three planetary tethers. Large cargo containers, some holding passengers, traveled the lines to and from the planet below. Freya and Shrek thought it would be their best opportunity to get away from the SOG military, which could discover them at any moment.

When the *Tiananmen* airlock to space slid open, Mathison got his first actual glimpse of Kovpak drifting above Zhukov. The vertigo was almost enough to send him scrambling back into the airlock.

It was hard to trust Freya as he walked across the hull of the *Tiananmen,* using the shuttles as concealment. One miscalculation on her part and the magnets in his boots wouldn't catch and he would drift into space where sensors would detect him and automated weapons would slice him to ribbons. Mathison kept his eyes on the hull and concentrated on putting one foot in front of the other as he followed Freya's instructions. He had the easy job. Freya and Shrek were currently linked to the *Tiananmen* and Kovpak, pointing cameras away from them, silencing alarms, and doing their best to mask the two Marines' progress as they made their way to a gantry that was plugged into the ship providing waste removal and power.

Looking down at the beautiful green and blue sphere "below" them was too distracting. He saw at least three closed defense turrets, any of which could suddenly spring to life and start shooting at him. With his weapons and trauma plates inside the bags they were carrying, Mathison felt defenseless and vulnerable.

It took thirty very long minutes to make their way to the nearest maintenance airlock and get inside Kovpak.

Mathison's skin crawled as he stepped into a public area and saw other people in real life for the first time in what felt like forever. Nobody glanced at them as they made their way toward the space elevator. Getting off Kovpak was a priority for Mathison. Even though it wasn't all military, there was a substantial military presence. All it would take was one alarm to mobilize forces against the Marines. Just one alert technician to notice a discrepancy in data. Mathison wanted to disappear among the civilian population on the planet below. Once there, Freya could generate an identity for the Marines, and they could pretend a life while Freya found a way to contact the Vapaus Republic. Mathison was half tempted to get a ride on one of the civilian ships to a smaller colony but there was no way to know if it was a dead end or if there would be Republic agents there.

Mathison's brown suit looked more like a Guard's while Stathis was wearing the dark blue colors of Star Force. Nobody dared look at them twice.

Even here, voices droned on telling people they were the best, wonderful, and valued by the Governance. It looked like people didn't even notice the voices.

"Capitalism is the ideology of pure evil and extreme selfishness. Only the government can ensure equity and justice."

Mathison and Stathis moved through the crowds, keeping their eyes down like everyone else. Useless cloth masks covered everyone's faces and bland, gray clothes masked their individuality. Many people had a single patch on each arm, but Mathison didn't know what any of the patches signified.

"We live in an age of peace and plenty," the voice droned, "but we are constantly under threat by those who want to oppress others with their individuality and differences. We must unite to fight those who seek to destroy our social unity. The revolution continues, comrades and friends. Stay strong. The Central Committee is on your side, fighting for the future of our children."

Freya and Shrek slid through the systems like digital ghosts, pointing cameras and microphones elsewhere. This part of the station was civilian and lacked the hardness of the military side.

"This is almost easy," Freya reported. *"The systems are old, and I see plenty of evidence that there are others who circumvent the system. Almost like it was designed so they can manipulate it."*

"By AI?" Mathison asked.

"No, probably SOG internal security or other officials, but the back doors seem to be in use by others. Smugglers and human traffickers if I had to guess. I already have a route to your private room aboard the elevator going down. Once we are planetside I'm sure we'll have other options."

"Any sign of the Republic?"

"I'm not sure. Though there are plenty of back doors, there seems to be a directive from SOG internal security to patch the firmware on many systems, which might close most back doors. That's going on as we speak, but the updates are nothing for us to worry about, though it erases previous activity."

"Will the updates be a problem later?"

"No," Freya said, *"from what I've seen, there are always new back doors. Though it may be easy to monitor who's using these back doors, there are still many flaws in the code, like a government committee programmed it. Very inefficient."*

"Life is beautiful. Let us cleanse it of all evil, oppression, and violence for future generations. Let our beloved children enjoy it to the fullest. We should not take advantage of our fellows, for their weakness is your opportunity to help them. Throw off your chains. It is your duty to enlighten and elevate our comrades, to help them prosper. For those who do not embrace the socialist unity, your days are numbered, and we will hunt you down. There will be no mercy for those who oppose social equity and our benevolent government. The government trains specialists to study and understand what is best for everyone. The Social Organizational Governance ensures that only the best, most qualified scientists are trained and employed. No other government in the history of humanity has done this."

"Is there any way to turn off that inane speaker?" Mathison asked.

Freya ignored his question. *"I've disabled the sub-harmonics. They make the lies more believable, and few people even know they are there. Be thankful for that."*

Poor bastards.

*****

Chapter Twenty-Nine: HKT

Kapten Sif – VRAEC, Nakija Musta Toiminnot

The *Pankhurst* was still lurking at the edge of the system as *Valkyrie 27* maneuvered to dock with *Valkyrie 15*.

Kat wanted to cancel the rendezvous, which was scheduled to occur within a few hours at current speeds. The sense of foreboding had followed her like an evil shadow since she had spoken to Kari. She was afraid to try astral projection again. Nasaraf had found her, but how could she be sure the knight would be there a third time? If he had survived.

Kat draped her Aesir commander persona about her as the door slid open. What had Nasaraf meant about tribes?

Winters and Levin entered the conference room as Sif sat there staring at the blank display. Both Marines were armored and carrying sidearms. That had encouraged the Jaeger team to reciprocate. She felt like a war was about to break out between the Aesir and the Marines at any moment and everyone had heavier weapons ready and available within their rooms.

Her biggest problem now was whether she could trust Sloss. She had worked with him off and on for over a decade. He was an excellent fighter but tended to be very focused. He did not handle subtlety or subterfuge. He was a high caliber weapon with only a single purpose. Direct combat. Give him a target and let him destroy it. She had expected nothing else from him or his team. His loyalty to the Republic was unquestioned.

This was different though.

Bluebeard entered after the Marines. His beard glittered under the bright lights. Sif wasn't sure if there was a Vanir regulation that covered glitter in a beard. Wouldn't it get caught up in air filtration systems or something? Bluebeard loved his children, though, and a promise was a promise.

Sif nodded at the big man.

"We have a problem," Sif said, not sure how she could explain everything to them.

Bluebeard raised an eyebrow as the Marines sat emotionlessly.

Bluebeard glanced at the Marines. "Either the Marines have a problem with the Vanir or there is a problem with the Jaegers."

"No," Sif said. She had known Bluebeard for many decades and never had reason to question his loyalty. She should not have to question it now, but she had to know where his loyalty lay. How would he define his loyalty?

"I think there is an HKT unit aboard *27*, and when they dock, they will storm this ship," Sif said. She felt the Marines' shock despite their emotionless faces, and she saw the shock on Bluebeard's face.

"That makes no sense," Bluebeard said. "Vanir do not make war on Vanir or Aesir. You must be mistaken."

"I wish I were," Sif said.

Bluebeard glanced at the Marines and noticed their lack of reaction.

"This concerns me," Bluebeard said, leaning back.

"Me as well, old friend."

"Please explain this to me."

"When we left home fleet there was an attempt to arrest the Marines."

"Which is why they were brought aboard in secret," Bluebeard said scowling. "But to dispatch an HKT team? They still allowed us to leave. Why would they resort to force instead of ordering us to return?"

"Because the Vanir are not in agreement. The council may not be in agreement."

"This sounds like a civil war. Vanir do not fight Vanir."

"They do now," Sif said softly.

"How did this happen?"

"With the development of the inkeri generator, we now have the option to take home fleet far away," Sif said. She had spent a lot of time thinking about this, and it was the only thing that made sense. "Some people want to leave; some want to stay and fight. The SOG show of force in the Lisbon system cast doubt on our ability to win."

"Aye, but can this not be discussed and voted upon?"

"I don't know. I don't think either faction would abide."

"How do you know this?"

"Nakija secrets," Sif said wincing.

Bluebeard nodded. "Why are not the Aesir here? Sloss?"

"I do not know where he and his squad stand," Sif said.

"You are wise." Bluebeard looked at the Marines and his eyes dropped to their holstered sidearms.

"We have mere hours, and I am out of ideas. You are master of this vessel, and I thought you should know."

"My crew trust me," Bluebeard said. "But if the Jaegers are not trustworthy, we will have lost. We are all brothers and sisters. We should not be fighting. How sure are you?"

"I have not yet spoken to Skadi. They keep making excuses, saying she is unavailable."

"Yes, I found that odd, too, but they are Vanir. We are the shields of our people. Why would they lie? I have thought little of it."

"And now?" Sif asked.

"The lie seems obvious in retrospect. They rely on my trust so they may betray it. They don't trust me to take action. Which means they oppose the Nakija and the council. They are breaking their oath."

Bluebeard's words relieved Sif.

"However," Bluebeard said, "we cannot shed our honor and abandon them. They are Vanir and have yet to behave dishonorably."

"What does that mean?" Sif asked.

"We must make rendezvous."

"And risk an HKT assault?"

"Yes. If nothing else, I must know how deep this rot goes."

"And if I am right?" Sif asked.

"You said yourself, not even the Nakija are all knowing, and they can make mistakes."

"Can we weather an HKT assault?"

Bluebeard pursed his lips. "The HKT specialize in taking out enemy ships. They have a distinct advantage in that they know a lot about us."

"What do we tell Sloss?" Winter asked.

Sif winced. He was the big unknown. Whichever way he went, his Aesir would follow him. They were all veterans, but they were fanatically loyal to Sloss.

"We should explain it to him and ask him," Bluebeard said. "It is the honorable thing to do."

"And if he decides we are wrong?" Sif asked. "Or he refuses to believe the reality of the situation?"

"Then we should be ready to take him and his team down," Bluebeard said.

Sif shook her head. Another no-win situation, but unlike others, this involved brothers and sisters.

"What if we jump for Zhukov?" Sif asked.

"Again, Sloss would want to know why. Will you then start lying to him?"

Sif scowled. Once the lies began they did not end. She had been in covert operations long enough to know that. Lies and deceit were for the enemy. If they became a tool for friends and allies then the lies became a way of life, and Sif did not want to go down that path, because it destroys people, heart, body, and soul.

"Tell him it is need to know?" Sif asked.

Bluebeard shook his head. "Sorry, lady. If that is what you order, then I will comply. But if Vanir are turning on Vanir and Aesir, he should know."

"We can't take the chance," Sif said. "I will ask Sloss to join us. While I trust him, I cannot take the chance he will disagree."

Sif was glad both Marines were armed.

*****

Chapter Thirty: Sloss

Sergeant Tal Levin, USMC

Sloss entered the room and paused when he saw everyone sitting there. Levin saw a look flash across his face.

"He is concerned," Lilith told Levin. *"And on his guard."*

Sif stood. The large Aesir made her seem small and fragile. Levin wondered how she could look so cool and calculated as she looked up at the big Jaeger commander. It looked like he could break her in half with one hand.

"You requested my presence, Sif?" Sloss said.

"I need you to assemble your Jaegers in the recreation room. I have a couple of announcements."

Levin stared at Sif. He could tell she had changed her mind about something but wasn't sure what. A quick glance at Chief Winters showed she hadn't caught it.

Damn. What would the Gunny do?

"May I ask what this is about?" Sloss asked.

"I will brief your team," Sif said. "But what I need right now is your loyalty."

Sloss glanced at Winters and Levin before locking eyes on Sif.

"Zen. We are Aesir," Sloss said, quoting part of the Aesir code. "Bound together through blood and tears. We are the blade of our people."

Sloss left to collect his team.

Sif turned to Winters. "Chief, you and Sergeant Levin are the most combat capable soldiers aboard. My intent is to place them in protective custody. I don't know if I can trust them, and I do not wish to endanger their lives for a cause they might not believe in."

Levin wanted to scowl when she called them soldiers, but he kept his face neutral.

"Understood, Sif," Winters said. "However, can we hold off the HKT without them?"

"If they try to storm our ship," Sif said. "We just need to escape. I do not want a pitched battle."

"And you think the Jaegers will ever trust you again?" Winters asked.

Sif looked sad as she broke eye contact with Winters. When she looked back there was ice there.

"This is best for them," Sif said. "I can't ask them to fight our battles. I won't pit Aesir against Vanir out of personal fear."

"If there is an HKT force on *27* don't you think the Vanir have already made that decision for you?" Winters asked.

"I've made my decision," Sif said. "Will you help me carry it out?"

Winters looked at Levin.

What would the Gunny do? Why was Winters looking at him?

Levin didn't know what to say, or whether to shrug or nod. This wasn't a good fight. This was dark and twisted with conflicting loyalties and no definition of good and evil, no obvious battle lines. Where was right and wrong?

Winters took a deep breath and looked back at Sif.

"We're with you," Winters said. "You're the one who kept Skadi's team from engaging us. I think I owe you that loyalty. You have done right by us. We will try to do right by you."

Sif's shoulders relaxed slightly.

"I don't want casualties," Sif said. "But we need to disarm and contain them. With Bluebeard's help, I think we can do this. They are my brothers and sisters. Do you understand?"

"Semper Fi," Winters said, and Levin nodded. Winters had the right idea. Loyalty would be returned. "It means Always Faithful."

Sif smiled, relieved. "I remember."

"Well," Winters said, and Levin heard an edge, "you called us soldiers, so I figured you probably forgot."

An amused smile came to Sif's lips. "My apologies, Marines. Here is my plan."

*****

Chapter Thirty-One: Defense

Chief Warrant Officer Diamond Winters, USMC

Valkyrie 27 was on its final approach. Winters gripped her blazer carbine. It could punch through walls, if she was required to use it, but then she would probably end up dead because that meant they had made it past Levin.

Sergeant Levin had come up with most of the plan, and Sif had approved it. Winters was out of her league planning such a defense, and she wasn't afraid to admit it. Levin gave her plenty of chances to override him, but she hadn't. They weren't facing off against the SOG's thugs. These were professional killers. The Navy SEALs of the Vapaus Republic. This was what they lived for, their bread and butter, the thing they excelled at. All she had was an apparent twelve-year-old-girl, a badass Marine sergeant, and a bunch of spacers who probably didn't handle weapons more than once a year. Nobody had any faith in *Valkyrie's* automatic boarding defenses against the HKTs. They would know exactly where the drop turrets were and could probably program mini missiles to take them out before they came anywhere near them.

Levin was positioned at the airlock with Sif. He had rigged the airlock to blow to stall any assault. With him were a couple armed and armored Vanir crew. Bluebeard's crew were loyal, and all Vanir were trained in repelling boarders. Levin didn't have a lot of confidence in them, and Winters had picked up on that. There were boarding robots and internal defenses, but Levin had insisted the HKTs probably wouldn't be slowed by such things. The HKT supposedly specialized in boarding and capturing ships.

She had briefly worked with SEALs during some fighting in the Philippines after becoming a special operations pilot. Her impression of the SEALs was that they were good, but their egos were more dangerous. They didn't wear their seat belts during the insertions and they were a secretive, elitist bunch. They had threatened her crew chief at gunpoint when he told them to put on their seat belts and that experience had forever made her dislike the arrogant bastards. The SEALs got results by frequently taking what she considered insane risks. Having worked in special operations, she knew how frequently the propaganda was more intense than reality, but propaganda always had a basis *in* reality.

Her SCBI, Blitzen, and Levin's SCBI were integrated with *Valkyrie 15's* sensors and internal monitoring systems to give both Marines a full view of what was going on. It was Winter's mission to keep the bridge secure and act as a tactical reserve. She had thought Levin was trying to keep her out of the fight, but he had explained that he didn't trust the Vanir crew and if the shit hit the fan, he wanted a Marine to come save him. The fear in her gut and doing as ordered warred with the idea of making Levin put her somewhere more dangerous. The fact he was an experienced infantry sergeant won out, or so she told herself.

It also bothered her that Sif, that small fragile slip of a girl, was stationed at the airlock. That would be the most dangerous location, but logic dictated that as mission commander she would be there to meet Skadi and her team.

Winters listened to Bluebeard talk with *27;* everything seemed routine. Blitzen couldn't detect any stress in the pilot's voice, but why was everyone insisting on an airlock match instead of using the sleds?

Maybe Sif was overreacting?

To her, the only thing unusual about this was that everyone was fully armed and armored and the pissed off Jaegers were locked in their quarters without weapons. Sif had not even told them why, which Winters didn't agree with, but Sif was the one in command. It was a side of the Aesir Winters had never imagined. One could easily mistake Sif for some awkward pre-pubescent girl—a bean pole about to turn into a woman. The cold, calculating eyes ruined that impression; she had a heart and soul of steel.

"We have a match," Bluebeard's officer, a man named Krog, said. "Cycling now."

Winters watched the viewscreen, and the hatch began to open.

The power went out. The emergency lights did not come and a sudden migraine made her bend over in pain, an EMP pulse.

Bluebeard started cursing, and Winters got the impression he was confused. She brought up a link with Levin. A display showed Sergeant Levin leaning back, and Winters got a view of what should be behind the sergeant. A high-pitched whine was coming from the airlock.

"What's going on?" Winters asked.

"Armored robots," Levin said. "Damned assholes. Heavily armored freaking robots. Can't even spit into the corridor without getting shot."

"You okay?" Winters asked.

"Minor wound," Levin said. "Nothing major. Lilith has nothing on them. Robots are armored. Not sure how they are being controlled."

"Can you stop them?" Winters asked.

"Do I have a choice?" Levin asked. "Get the power on or we won't be able to escape. How did they kill it?"

She didn't know, and from the sounds of it neither did Bluebeard.

"Unknown." Winters looked around her. The night vision in her helmet let her see in the dark, and aside from Bluebeard's crew standing around staring at their consoles and talking to each other, there wasn't much to see.

"We need to get the power back on or this is going to be a fight we can't win," Levin said.

Winters felt an explosion.

"Booyah," Levin said. Winters checked her view and saw that Levin was now shooting around the corner at something. Two wrecked robots lay shattered at Levin's feet.

Winters went to the bridge's door and pushed the button to open it. Nothing.

"They're controlling the bots via wire, in case they make it past us," Levin said. "SCBIs got nothing on them."

"Threats detected beyond the door," Blitzen said, and Winter's blood froze.

"They're here?" Winters asked.

The door to the bridge shattered. Winters was thrown against a console then bounced onto her face. Her suit protected her from the explosion, but she was seeing stars. Figures poured through the door. Boots landed on her back, and she felt something metallic against her head as weapons fire erupted. Through the rear view of her helmet, she saw three dark figures clustered around her, their hands or feet holding her down, their weapons locked on her.

Elsewhere on the bridge, she heard a scream cut short. The attackers were absolutely silent.

"They are on the bridge," Winters said to Levin. "They have me prisoner."

"I would not recommend resisting," Blitzen said.

"How many?" Levin asked.

Winters couldn't see all of them and she was careful not to move. She glanced to one side and saw Bluebeard's sightless eyes staring at her through a shattered helmet. She shuddered. What would they tell his children?

"At least eight," Winters said as two HKTs pulled her arms behind her. Another did something to her suit and the power went off.

"Shit," Winters said.

"I can still communicate with Lilith and Levin," Blitzen said.

"Tell them the power to my suit was cut, and I'm now blind and mute," Winters told Blitzen. *"It's all on Levin."*

Winters was pissed. How the hell had they gotten in and past Levin so quick?

"They are professionals," Blitzen said.

"I'm supposed to be a professional," Winters said. *"And so is Levin!"*

Minutes later, Levin came online. "Son of a bitch. They came in behind us. Shit, they're good. Hopefully we'll get adjoining cells."

"Sif said the HKTs know what they're doing," Blitzen said.

"But this is damned embarrassing," Winters said.

"Hopefully it won't be fatal as well," Blitzen said. *"The Vapaus Republic seems to be more decent than the SOG, at least."*

Two HKT troopers effortlessly lifted her and placed her in a bag. After zipping that up, they picked her up and put her on a cart as if she was a psychotic patient.

She couldn't get Bluebeard's eyes out of her head.

They had killed their own. What would they do to her and Blitzen?

"They have cut me off," Blitzen said. *"The bag is made of a material that blocks all communication."*

Winters felt alone again.

Their allies had turned on them.

Who was going to rescue the gunny?

* * * * *

Chapter Thirty-Two: Prisoner

Kapten Sif – VRAEC, Nakija Musta Toiminnot

She felt their hatred and animosity as they put her on a cart like a slab of meat. She had felt the deaths of nearby people, but she didn't know who they were or how they had died, and now she felt fear. It was suffocating and draining, pushing in on her. The fear threatened to overwhelm her, made it hard to think and listen.

The power was off in her suit so she couldn't see or hear.

The HKTs had to know who she was. She had shot one of them in the gut, but they had taken the casualty rather than kill her. She had fired on a brother, or sister, and she felt sick. It was an effort not to vomit in her helmet. Without power, she would probably suffocate and die in her own puke, a bad way to go. She had seen it happen in the past.

Moments later, they pulled off her helmet and put a bag over her head so she couldn't see. At least now she was less likely to drown in her own vomit. She still couldn't see through the pitch dark cloth. The air was stale, and she smelled blood. Had they killed Levin? There had been two crewmen with her and the sergeant; were they okay? So many emotions pushed down on her, and she couldn't separate them. A single shot, an execution. Sif went cold. Who had the HKT executed?

The only sounds were the HKTs moving around. She knew they were talking, but their helmets prevented her from hearing them. The bag they had put over her head had definitely been used before. She smelled stale vomit. They might have rinsed it off but not cleaned it thoroughly, a touch of cruelty she had not expected of them, because it would trigger her own nausea. Seconds later, they strapped her to a cart, tying her down so she was immobilized. It was hard to focus, hard to use her abilities. She had to regain her calm.

"Levin?" Sif asked.

Muffled sounds, and one of the HKTs lifted the hood enough to tape up her mouth.

Bastards.

"Be silent, bitch traitor," a digitized voice told her.

With her mouth taped there wasn't much she could say or do. She still couldn't focus.

The cart started rolling. It almost felt like a mobile bunk bed, and she sensed she was on the bottom; someone else was above her.

She closed her eyes and tried to keep the tears from flowing.

She took a deep breath through her nose and let it out to calm her mind and body. She tried not to think of the fact she had shot a Vanir or that people had died. They had executed people, murdered them in cold blood.

The cart moved for several minutes, probably transferring her to *Valkyrie 27*. She felt the razor-sharp, focused minds of the HKT around her, but there was nothing she could grasp.

What were they going to do to her? Would the Nakija council send a rescue team?

Finally, they stopped. She was pulled off the cart and placed in a chair, once again strapped down like she had the strength to break free.

They removed the hood and violently ripped the tape off her mouth. Sif winced.

"Why would you betray your oath?" the digitized voice asked.

They weren't going to let her stew then. They were starting the interrogation while the fear and adrenaline were still coursing through her system.

Sif looked around. All she saw was darkness and a dazzling light shining on her face.

What they didn't know was that she could sense the surrounding people. There were four of them, three men and a woman, and there was hatred in their hearts. How could they be Vanir?

"I have not fired upon and killed my brothers and sisters," Sif said. "I have not murdered them in cold blood. I have defended myself."

"Liar. You are an oath breaker," the voice said. "The lowest of the low. A traitor who endangered those she was sworn to protect. How do you plead?"

"Does it matter?" Sif asked.

"When you stand before the tribunal and your crimes are judged, you will need to enter a plea," the voice said.

"I do not recognize the authority or legitimacy of any tribunal that does not include an Aesir general or one of the Nakija," Sif said. "If they are not present, you have overstepped your bounds."

"You do not understand the gravity of your situation," the voice said. "We know you are a Nakija black ops agent, one of the secretive Musta Toiminnot. One would think your loyalty would be without question. You need to tell us more about the Musta Toiminnot and Nakija. We have plenty of time."

What did they know about the Nakija? Obviously not as much as they thought, and they clearly knew less about her and her abilities.

Sif calmed her breathing and focused, cast out her senses. When they had attacked *Valkyrie 15* they had forfeited their rights as Vapaus Republic citizens. The code of the Nakija no longer protected them. How much did they know? Not enough if darkness was their only defense.

"Who is the head traitor?" Sif asked as she regained her bearings and restored her inner calm. She could listen now, listen with more than her ears. The darkness and bright light made it easier to concentrate and use her other senses and abilities.

"You don't get to ask the questions here," the voice said.

"Amiral Valma Kyllonen," came the unspoken thought from one man. His mind was unprotected, open, vulnerable. He was not the one in charge, but he was an officer.

"What will you do with the Jaegers?" Sif asked.

"They will probably execute the ones who survived; we can't trust them," the unspoken thought came back, and she sensed regret. Another chink in the armor she could exploit. He would be her prey.

The ones who survived? They killed prisoners? They must have killed the Vanir. Why?

"You should worry about yourself, not the Jaegers," her interrogator said.

"Why are you doing this?" Sif asked. Now she felt her interrogator's emotions. The bastard was smug. A chink in his armor; she sent a tendril into his mind. People who angered easily were easily manipulated and controlled through their hate.

"We are doing it for the people of the Republic," her interrogator said. "So we do not have to live in fear, dreading the appearance of a SOG fleet."

"Who are you?" Sif asked.

"Kommendör Jani Salonen," he answered without his knowledge. Her prey, the weaker one, answered as Taavi Kallio. The third man was Kal Kopri, and the woman was Katrina Jarvinen, all Vanir. All officers and full of hate. They were traitors. They had violated their oath. There would be no mercy. They had unleashed her and put themselves outside the protection of her oath.

"If you do not cooperate, I may be your executioner," Jani said, and she felt that he looked forward to it.

"What do you want from me?" Sif asked to keep them talking. She didn't care much about the answers or the questions as she slid into Taavi's mind. He was a junior officer, a lojtnant. She wedged her way in.

"We want to know about the Marines, the Nakija, the Musta Toiminnot," Jani said. "Everything you know about them. We have time, but the sooner you tell us, the sooner you can be comfortable."

"We found them on a secret SOG space station," Sif said. Surely, they had that information. How long could she tell them what they already knew? Time was her ally, not theirs.

"They are good people," Sif said.

She felt Jani's anger and Taavi's sadness. More weaknesses in their armor that she forced open. She didn't widen Jani's since that could lead to violence, but Taavi, yes, she could manipulate Taavi. Jani's turn would come soon enough. This was now a game. But how to move the pieces for victory?

"I don't want opinions," Jani said, and she felt he wanted to strike her. How would the others react to a grown man striking a child? "I want facts. Tell me what I do not know, and you will live."

Jani was lying.

That was a problem. Vanir should have honor. The rot in the Vanir ranks was deeper and more dangerous than she had estimated. Now was the time to root it out. These petturi were about to learn. They were enemies of the people and anyone who killed people of the Republic would suffer. That was her mission in life. That was *her* code of honor. Her soul demanded it.

"You look like a little girl," Jani said, perhaps realizing what he was looking at and how it would appear to the others when he resorted to physical violence. "You don't fool me. You aren't an innocent child."

She nudged Jani. He was feeding his own emotions, but he could go further.

"You are a slut," Jani said, saying more than he should have as she pushed him. "The SOG has many pedophiles, but we won't fall for your behavior, for your lies, for your seductions, for your pretense of innocence. When we are done with you. I will take great pleasure in killing you slowly. You have betrayed the Republic; you have betrayed our people. Your whoring, lying days are over."

Next, she nudged Taavi. He was becoming more horrified at the hatred and brutality Jani was displaying. Even Kal and Katrina were becoming sick as they listened to Jani. Sif gave each a mental nudge, stroking their emotions as she stroked Jani's. The wedge between them was growing. It was easier to build on emotions than change or redirect them.

She closed her eyes, concentrated more. Jani didn't need her to feed his hatred and anger. He was on his path and didn't want to change. He ranted, working himself into a killing frenzy.

Taavi put a hand on Jani's arm to calm him and Jani snarled at him before turning back to Sif.

Taavi was becoming more concerned and doubt was forming there. Sif nudged that doubt, expanded it, fed it, helped it grow.

"Kommendör?" Kal said.

"Silence!" Jani hissed. "Don't you see what she is? How evil she is? The insidious, putrid vileness she represents? She is Nakija, a keeper of secrets, a purveyor of hatred and deception using petty parlor tricks and sleight of hand to exploit our people. They're worse than the Governance!"

Sif sensed Kal's horror. A small nudge increased that emotion.

Katrina backed up, a scream in her throat. This was not what she had signed up for.

Now Katrina and Kal looked at Sif and saw a small girl tied to a chair about to be murdered or tortured. At some level, they were decent people. Sif knew that and used it. Even the most vile humans frequently had a shred of decency.

"You have already sentenced me to death, then," Sif said. It wasn't a question, it was a bombshell.

Jani screamed at her, giving his hatred voice. Kal, Katrina, and Taavi reeled back in shock and surprise.

Sif was waiting for it. She nudged them all, pushed hard with her mind.

Jani drew his sidearm, aiming it at her, but Sif reached into his mind and froze him before he could pull the trigger. In that second, she pushed Taavi. The horrified lojtnant drew his sidearm before his crazed commander could shoot the helpless girl. Taavi hesitated, but Sif was ready, and Taavi fired against his will. The pistol blew a hole through Jani's head and sprayed the wall with gore. Taavi thought he did it and Sif allowed that emotion, fed it.

Katrina screamed. Sif pushed and Katrina fainted.

Kal drew his own weapon but didn't know who to shoot. Fear and guilt flashed through his mind. Sif caught it, used it, and wrapped it around his thoughts. He had failed Jani, had failed the cause. Sif pushed, magnifying the failure and fear. He had failed. His career was over. What would the amiral do? How would she handle his failure? He couldn't salvage this.

Sif pushed harder as he pointed his weapon at Taavi.

Kal couldn't kill a fellow Vanir. It wasn't in his nature. He was a good man trying to do his best for the people he was sworn to protect. He had failed. Jani had been about to murder this child in cold blood. This isn't what he had signed up for. He had been so wrong!

Sif pushed harder, straining.

Kal put the barrel against his head and pulled the trigger.

Numbly, Taavi looked at Kal's body and his brain matter coating the ceiling. He looked at Jani, then Katrina.

His eyes finally fell on Sif. His mind broke. She owned him.

The interrogation room was soundproof.

"Is anyone watching?" Sif asked.

"No," Taavi said. "The kommendör did not want witnesses."

"Release me," Sif said.

Taavi moved to release her as Sif planted more guilt and loathing in him. She pushed his broken mind, shattering it further, grinding it under her iron will. Her disgust at herself and her actions almost made her stop. This man had once been a trusted Vanir brother.

"What happened to the Jaegers?" Sif asked as Taavi released the straps.

"They are in prison cell Bertta," Taavi said. "They resisted when we told them they were to be moved to another prison cell. Two were killed."

Once Sif was free he handed her his sidearm.

She closed her eyes and used her powers to feel around her for others.

She was in the interrogation room aboard *Valkyrie 27*. She sensed unease from the bridge area. Anger, disgust, and fear emanated from the prison cells. Elation came from the Aesir quarters, which was probably where the HKTs were.

"What did you do to *Valkyrie 15*?" Sif asked.

"We used micro missiles," Taavi said. "Main, secondary, and tertiary power feeds were destroyed. It is a Vanir secret that this can be done. *15* will be destroyed later."

"The Marines?" Sif asked.

"In solitary confinement," Taavi said. "They are in a special cell, a Faraday cage. They should be completely isolated and unable to access *27's* systems. We have special bags with life support to transport them in. They are to be left there until rendezvous."

"How many HKTs are aboard this ship?" Sif asked.

"Three strike teams," Taavi answered. "The amiral didn't want to chance the Marines escaping or surviving."

"Who, where, and when is the rendezvous?" Sif asked.

"In five hours we will meet with the *Snekke* VR *Kotka*," Taavi said. "I don't know the commander."

There wasn't much time.

"Eversti Hiltel is attempting to contact the kommendör," Taavi said. "He says it is urgent."

"He will have to wait," Sif said, checking the ammunition in the pistol. It held fifteen rounds, now fourteen. She took the weapons from the others.

Sif paused and looked at Katrina, lying there on the floor defenseless. Katrina was a Vanir officer and would have killed Sif. She fingered Taavi's sidearm and considered how easy it would be to punish the Vanir for her betrayal. So easy.

Instead, Sif pushed her mind harder. An unconscious mind was frequently harder to manipulate, but she could increase the duration of her unconsciousness. She would deal with the traitor later, hopefully with a real tribunal. She would not be judge, jury, and executioner if she could help it. The Nakija were not oath breakers.

She used her mind to listen around her. The unease on the bridge was growing. Did they know about her escape?

She had to get the Marines out. There was no way she could take the ship alone.

* * * * *

Chapter Thirty-Three: Escape

Sergeant Tal Levin, USMC

The HKT were damned dangerous, and he had underestimated them. They had captured him and Lilith alive despite his best efforts, and that failure hurt him to his core. How could he have fallen for their ploy? How had they boarded the damned ship so fast? It had been a classic assault, though. Trap the defenders into thinking traditionally and in two dimensions, then mix it up and go three dimensional. Levin wanted to bang his head against the wall. If he had been the attacker, that is exactly what he would have done.

Despite being the most experienced combat veteran, he had screwed up. The gunnery sergeant and Stathis were gone. Now he and Chief Winters were prisoners, and who knew what these Vanir wanted or would do to them. His two-dimensional thinking had gotten them captured. So much for being a badass Marine Raider squad leader. He couldn't even fight his way out of whatever plastic bag they had put him in. The fact he hadn't suffocated yet was no consolation. Maybe he should just give up his eagle, globe, and anchor and go be another typical civilian screw up.

He replayed the last moments of the attack and his mistakes became more obvious. He should have had the two crewmen watching behind them. He should have had a backup set of claymores, placed more motion sensors around the ship. Relying on the bridge's ability to monitor the corridors had been a bad idea. Bluebeard had assured him that even with the main power out, secondary and tertiary power would allow him to monitor most of the ship.

Levin recognized his mistakes, now. He had surrendered the initiative to the HKT. He had let them dictate the battle and rules of engagement. They had thought three dimensionally against his two-dimensional planning. They had launched a multi-prong attack while he had only expected a single vector. They had let him think he was going to stop them at a bottleneck when they had no such limitations. A classic case of myopia. Levin had seen what he wanted to see. The HKT bastards had let him screw up and exploited his arrogance.

Why hadn't they just killed him?

He felt the straps holding him to the table loosen. Was it interrogation time? That was quick. Whatever they had done, Lilith couldn't talk with Blitzen, or anything else. It was just the two of them, and Levin wondered how they planned to interrogate him. How much did they really know about Lilith? Clearly enough to isolate him.

If they knew about Lilith, did that mean they could prevent her from blocking pain from torture like when the SOG had tried to torture him?

Whatever happened, Levin knew he would never trust someone who wasn't a Marine ever again. The Vapaus Republic had betrayed him and killed their own.

Power returned to his suit.

"We need to move fast," Sif said. She was the last person he had expected to see. How had she gotten out of her restraints? Did they not fit her small childlike body?

Behind her, a Vanir officer was standing with his back to them, staring at a wall.

"Where's the chief?" Levin asked, looking around. He was on the lower bunk in what was obviously a prison cell.

"In a bag on the bunk above you," Sif said. "I need your help to get her out, and then I need you and your SCBIs to help me take over this ship."

"The HKTs?" Levin asked.

"Unaware we've escaped," Sif said.

"Him?" Levin nodded toward the man while Sif undid the restraints on his arms.

"A contact. He's helping us."

How did she establish so many helpful contacts?

Sif pushed a pistol into his hands, and Levin checked to see a single round had been fired. He also noticed that Sif's contact was unarmed with an empty holster. That made little sense.

"Why doesn't he have a weapon?" Levin asked.

Sif narrowed her eyes and shook her head. He was just staring at the wall, not the door, the wall. What was wrong with him?

"The room is shielded and soundproofed," Lilith said. *"We need to get out of here. How nice do we play with the Vanir network security?"*

"Screw them," Levin told Lilith as he got Winters out of her bag. *"I want you to take ownership of the entire freaking vessel, and space those HKT bastards if you can. We aren't playing nice with the Republic anymore. They've abandoned the gunny and are treating us like some prize."*

"What about Sif?" Lilith asked.

"Temporary ally," Levin said. *"I don't trust any of these bastards anymore."*

"Aye," Lilith said. *"I now have a link with Blitzen. We are online."*

"Tell her we aren't playing," Levin said to Lilith. *"We are going to take this vessel and own it. I'm tired of being at the mercy of these Republic pricks."*

"She agrees," Lilith reported seconds later.

"Good," Levin said as Sif pushed a pistol into Winter's hand.

"Do you have a plan?" Levin asked.

"You two are the only ones I trust," Sif said in a low voice. Levin didn't miss the fact she did not include the Vanir officer. "We need to take the ship, fast and hard. You do anything and everything you have to. I would prefer not to inflict pain or suffering on the Jaegers, but they are the least of my concerns. They may be the only innocent people in this, but I don't know."

Levin nodded when Winters looked at him.

Why? He had screwed up the defense of *Valkyrie 15*.

"Raiders are good at attacking," Winters said. "I'm in the mood to kick some teeth in."

Levin nodded. Yes, Marines were much better at attacking than defending. *Maybe that had been his problem?*

"Let's see if we can subvert some systems," Levin said.

That was it. Raiders weren't defenders, neither were the HKTs, who probably thought they were safe now. They had won the first fight. They would be patting each other on the back, debriefing and feeling good about themselves, suffering the post-combat adrenaline withdrawal symptoms. It was the best time for them to attack.

"First problem…" Sif said. Levin looked at her and raised an eyebrow. "There are two HKT guards outside. They need to be put down, with prejudice."

"How did you get in past them?" Winters asked.

"I'll explain later," Sif said, but Levin heard "never." "Can you link with my cybernetics?"

"Basic link only," Levin said, frowning. Aesir cybernetics were secure in many ways. Basic data exchange was available, but the SCBIs were pretty sure they couldn't do anything the owner didn't allow.

"I'm giving you the cipher and code for the *27* systems," Sif said.

"What level?" Winters asked.

"Eversti level," Sif said, her voice low.

"How did you get that?" Winters asked, and Sif smiled.

"I'll explain later," Sif said. "You should be able to use them to gain control. When the outer door opens, your SCBIs should be able to link with *Valkyrie's* network. I'm hoping they can silence the alarms, disable sound sensors, and lock the hatches. You'll need to move fast. Sound sensors will hear any gunshots and alert the CIC. Alerting the CIC will cause them to react. I'm sure the HKTs have a squad ready."

"Is there anyone you don't want us to kill?" Levin asked.

"Me," Sif said. "Maybe the Jaegers, unless they get in our way."

Levin glanced at the Vanir officer. Sif noticed but remained silent. Her eyes were steel.

Before Sif could stop him, Levin stepped past her and wrapped his arm around the Vanir officer's head. With a step and a flex of his arm he broke the officer's neck before the Vanir could do anything. The officer collapsed in a heap, gurgling as he died.

Sif remained silent. She looked at the body then at Levin.

"The HKTs outside the hatch will move faster," Sif said.

Levin blinked in surprise. She was unfazed and unconcerned by her contact's death. Winters stared at Levin.

"Why did you?" Winters asked motioning at the body. She was also watching Sif to see her reaction.

"He was a traitor," Levin said, still staring at Sif. "If he wasn't betraying them, he was betraying us by not warning us."

If Levin was being honest with himself, he wasn't sure why he had done it other than to prove a point to Sif. He wanted her to understand that her life might be in danger; that he was done playing games. Levin wanted as few people around him as possible. Winters was a Marine. He trusted her. Sif? She was still an unknown, and right now he only needed an excuse to kill her.

"Ready?" Levin asked Lilith.

"I have the codes from Sif," Lilith said. *"They seem valid. Based on everything I know about the Aesir, she should not have these codes. Her cybernetics also seem different from Skadi's."*

At the door, Sif held up her hand. "Move fast, don't stop, don't hesitate. I tell you this because I'm pretty sure they have orders to kill you if they cannot contain you."

Levin nodded.

"They deserve no mercy," Sif continued. "They are oath breakers."

"Like him?" Levin asked pointing at the body in the room behind them.

Sif nodded and looked at Winters.

Levin wasn't sure if Winters had the killer trait. She was a Marine, but she was a pilot not a Raider. Killing someone face to face was very different from firing rockets or vehicle-mounted weapons.

"No mercy," Winters said. There was enough edge in her voice to satisfy Levin.

"What's the layout?" Levin asked, and Sif told him. "Here is the plan," Levin said.

*****

Chapter Thirty-Four: Counterstrike

Chief Warrant Officer Diamond Winters, USMC

The door slid open, but both Marines waited while Sif walked out.

"Silenced," Blitzen said, referring to the sound sensors that would report small-arms fire and set off every alarm on the ship.

Levin moved first and Winters responded without thinking, just like in training. Her pistol was already up and aimed, just far enough from her eye so the slide wouldn't blind her. She aimed her body, which aimed the pistol at the HKT guard at the other end of the hall, closer to them than Levin's target. The trooper was wearing his helmet, but the visor was up. Blitzen helped guide her aim, but only Winters could pull the trigger.

The HKTs head slammed backward as the round pierced his helmet, killing him before he could bring up his carbine. She hadn't even heard her shot. The indicator on her weapon showed there was one less round in the magazine.

She glanced at Sif and saw her looking around. Her weapon wasn't up. A quick glance behind her showed Levin's target was down as well.

She advanced on the HKT trooper to take his carbine. She tried not to think of the person she had just killed.

"It's ID locked," Blitzen reported. *"But it has been entered into the ship's inventory. Transmitting unlock code so you can use it."*

"Sweet," Winters said as she picked it up and looked it over. Safety, magazine release, and a selector switch. A button on the side extended a wicked silver bayonet.

Sif stripped the magazines from the body and put them in the bag she had taken from the cell.

"Lilith and I are locking down the ship and locking out the crew," Blitzen reported. *"Sif's access codes are high level. We do not have access to the captain's private systems or astrogation."*

"Why would she have such codes?" Winters asked.

"Lilith and I suspect she is not typical Aesir or Erikoisjoukot," Blitzen said. *"Too many things don't add up. She may be the equivalent of CIA paramilitary or CIA Operative."*

"Like a spy?" Winters asked, glancing at the girl. The girl who looked to be about eleven years old but was a lot older.

"Exactly," Blitzen said. *"She was not a regular part of Skadi's team and knew of the operative aboard the secret SOG station. Her childlike appearance is deceptive and might get her into, or out of, a lot of different situations. She is Nakija, and we aren't sure exactly what that means. In the Finnish language, the word means seer, visionary, or prophet."*

"Or psychic?" Winters asked. The gunny had said that. The implications hadn't sunk in until now. What was Sif capable of? Perhaps there was truth that she has some abilities.

"Psychic abilities have been hinted at, though not confirmed. I thought it might have been propaganda, but now that cannot be ruled out," Blitzen said as Winters hurried to catch up with Levin, who was preparing to go

through the next hatch. *"We are adjusting the oxygen mixture in the HKT quarters, bridge, and crew quarters. There is a locker ahead with firefighting gear. I suggest you acquire a breathing mask."*

Winters did as Blitzen instructed.

"Crew are being summoned and locked in their quarters," Blitzen reported.

"We need to capture the CIC," Levin said. "That's the only place to access the astrogation systems. Shit." He turned to face Sif. "We need to move a lot faster. The *Pankhurst* just engaged the *Kotka*."

Sif paled and her eyes widened.

"We cannot let the *Pankhurst* capture us," Sif said. For the first time since Winters had met her, Sif looked and acted scared. Her eyes darted toward the shadows.

"It is only three against what? Fifty? Sixty?" Levin said.

"Do we need the Jaegers?" Sif asked.

"Three against seventy?" Levin asked, checking his weapon. "We're pretty much screwed. But let's see how far we can go. How did the HKTs kill the power?"

"Missiles," Sif said. "*Valkyrie 15* is dead. They have placed a nuke aboard to make sure it's destroyed. We have to get out of this system. We have to escape the *Pankhurst*."

"Working on it," Levin said. "Calm down."

"If we can secure the bridge we can make a jump," Blitzen said. *"Random if need be. Something is really bothering Sif."*

"We take the bridge, or CIC," Levin said aloud for Sif's benefit. "Then we can force a jump, escape the *Pankhurst*. That will put us somewhere we can take more time to secure the ship. Is there anything you're not telling me?"

"Lots, but nothing that will make sense now," Sif said. "We have to get far away from the *Pankhurst.* Please."

Winters stared at Levin. He seemed too damned calm, confident. What the hell did he know that she didn't?

She could almost feel Sif's fear, and it was infectious.

Levin nodded. "Then follow me. Chief, I want you to watch our rear. We're going to move hard and fast. Lilith is showing me a route around the HKTs. Nobody knows they're locked in yet, but they will figure it out fast. Sif? You're behind me; backup shooter. Watch the flanks and front. Be ready with extra magazines."

"Sergeant Levin is asking that you watch Sif," Blitzen said. *"Lilith says he doesn't trust her."*

"Can do, Sergeant," Winters said. "I've got your back." Then to Blitzen, *"Tell him okay."*

"Stay close," Levin said as the door slid open, and he started moving. Winters watched Levin. From the waist up he was motionless, the captured carbine set against his shoulder and covering every angle. He seemed to glide down the hallway. Behind him, Sif followed, her pistol held ready.

"One of the HKTs just tried to leave their area and found the door locked," Blitzen said as she brought up a gray wireframe view of the ship and highlighted the recommended route in green. Within the wireframe she saw ghostly figures clustering around the door.

"I'm tapped into the ship monitoring system," Blitzen said. *"As senior Marine you may order me to open an airlock, the corridor, and then the door to the HKT ready room. You must push a button to initiate the kill. This will kill them even if it doesn't suck them into space. They are unlikely to survive either outcome. It does not look like they are wearing their armor."*

The door behind Winters slid shut and she heard it lock.

"You are ordered to do so," Winters said.

"Press the imaginary button in front of you," Blitzen said.

Winters pushed a spot on the wall like it was a button.

"In progress," Blitzen said.

Levin looked at Winters in surprise. Lilith must have told him what she had done.

Winters pointed herself forward so they couldn't see her face.

"Move it, Sergeant," Winters said, feeling sick. She had killed them like Levin had killed Sif's contact, without mercy. She was glad she couldn't see her victims. Would Levin see his? "We're running out of time."

"Aye, Chief." Levin spun, moving faster than before.

They passed through another hatch, and Winters heard it lock behind her.

Levin started up the ramp.

The CIC was the next level up.

*****

Chapter Thirty-Five: CIC

Sergeant Tal Levin, USMC

The hatch to the CIC slid open, and three Vanir looked up in surprise.

"Hands up!" Levin yelled, entering and moving to the right. He gave the corners a quick glance.

Levin shot the first Vanir between the eyes as he reached for his sidearm. Superheated flesh exploded. The second Vanir reached for his weapon out of reflex so Sif shot him. She came in behind Levin and went to the left. Out of the corner of his eye, he saw Chief Winters enter and close the CIC door behind her.

The last Vanir officer raised his hands higher but didn't look as scared as Levin wanted him to be.

"What do you think you can accomplish?" the Vanir asked.

Lilith displayed "Lieutenant Yrjo Pulli" above his head on his internal display.

"Shut up, Pulli," Levin said. He made sure nobody was hiding behind any of the consoles.

"This really is a bad time," Pulli said. "Unless you want to get captured by the SOG."

"That isn't the SOG," Sif said glancing at the magnified view of the *Pankhurst*. "That is a creature from your worst nightmare."

Pulli scowled, and Levin came to stand beside him. The silver blade slid out of the carbine with a *snick*, causing Pulli to flinch. Not as fearless as he was pretending.

"Step away from the console," Levin said.

"Depressurizing corridor to the CIC," Lilith reported. *"It will trap us in, but it will certainly delay any HKT response. There aren't many left alive. Most of the other areas, including the brig, are depressurized. The Jaegers are trapped but safe."*

"Copy that," Levin said to Lilith. He still couldn't believe the chief had given that order. Depressurization was a bad way to go. They wouldn't be explosively sucked out the airlock like in the movies. With decompression the air pressure dropped as the air flowed out following the path of least resistance. Most of the HKTs wouldn't survive unless they got oxygen.

Sif examined the displays.

"The *Pankhurst* just took out the *Kotka*," Sif said. "It's coming for us."

Pulli looked at the plot in surprise. "That isn't possible. The *Kotka* is one of our newest ships. It should easily be a match for a mere battle cruiser." He glanced at the display and went for his weapon. Levin shot him in the head and burnt flesh spattered across the consoles.

Chief Winters stepped up to the console.

"The chief and Blitzen will get us a fresh course and put us through a wormhole," Lilith told Levin. *"We need you to verify the operation of other ship systems. There are still some HKT active."*

A console lit up in Levin's vision, and he moved over.

"Pankhurst *is about to enter extreme range,"* Lilith reported.

"Missile launch!" Sif said, staring at the plot. "The *Pankhurst* has launched missiles. We really need to get out of here!"

"Chill," Winters said, sounding far too calm for Levin. If Sif was freaking out, there was something seriously wrong.

Lilith told him what buttons to push and which displays to look at. Levin had no clue about most of it, but Lilith did, and that was what mattered.

"Some bridge systems are hardwired only," Lilith explained. *"For security. There are wireless backups, but there have to be catastrophic failures and override codes entered."*

Levin glanced at the bodies. The nearest one was tagged "Eversti Ulto." So, he had shot the captain, or Sif had, Levin didn't remember which. Both officers were bearded and tall and now dead. Would that cause a problem?

"We don't have any coordinates for the fleet," Lilith reported. *"The Eversti had the code for that. It's just a bunch of encrypted numbers, maybe several passwords. But we can jump into a SOG system. Or as the chief said, deep space."*

Something started buzzing, stopped, buzzed again. Levin looked around. An alarm?

"Automated point defenses are firing," Lilith reported. *"Trying to lay down a wall of pellets to intercept the missiles, but the missiles can maneuver. It's a numbers game."*

"Stand by for transition," Winters said, grabbing hold of the panel.

The transition into and almost instantly out of wormhole space was rough.

The plot of near space reset and showed nothing. They were in the middle of nowhere.

"Where are we?" Levin asked.

"Hell if I know," Winters said.

"Lost in space!" Levin said with a smile.

"Shut up, Stathis," Winters said, and both Marines laughed.

"We need to secure the rest of the ship," Sif said, not understanding the humor.

It quickly sobered the Marines.

"Now the real killing begins," Levin said. He felt tired already.

"There are two HKTs in the bathroom," Lilith reported. *"They locked the door so I couldn't open it to vacuum, and they are disabling cameras. There are also six crew in the crew quarters who have done the same."*

"What about the ones in the ready room?" Levin asked.

"They all appear to be dead," Lilith reported. *"Currently, I estimate fourteen hostiles aboard, not counting the eight Jaegers. The Jaegers are still in their cells and remain unharmed."*

"Assign threat levels," Levin said. *"Ones with weapons or rapid access to weapons are high on the list, but anyone who can disable the vessel are top."*

Levin looked at the wireframe of the ship presented through his implants. The survivors were flagged, and Levin looked around, as though he could see through walls.

Corridors without air were highlighted in red and Levin began planning out how he would kill the survivors. It would be easiest to shoot a couple holes in a door or bulkhead and let the room they were in depressurize. A bad way to go, but Levin wasn't feeling very sympathetic at the moment. They had murdered the Vanir aboard the *15*.

"You have things under control here, Chief?" Levin asked, remembering the last time he had left her in a CIC.

"I think I do, Sergeant."

"Permission to go hunting, Chief?"

"Yes. But you do not have permission to get killed or seriously injured."

"Aye, Chief." Levin looked around and changed magazines. He would need something better to carry spare magazines in. The dead Vanir officers had cargo pockets on their jumpsuits. Would one fit him?

* * * * *

Chapter Thirty-Six: Zhukov

Lojtnant Skadi – VRAEC

Not all Erikoisjoukot missions involved heavy weapons and armor. Sometimes they involved acting as a security element for Musta Toiminnot operatives. It was one of Skadi's least favorite types of missions but with the hell that was about to be unleashed in the Zhukov system, there were not nearly enough Erikoisjoukot troops available. The MT operatives needed muscle, and they used as many of the flexible Erikoisjoukot trigger pullers they could find. Skadi wanted to punch Zari in the face for this. Glorified security guards was all they were. True, they were out of Vanir hands, but they also weren't investigating the Nasaraf problem, and who knew what Sif and the Marines were dealing with on Green Hope. Damned MT spooks.

Although her team had cover identities, it was mind numbing to sit around waiting on a razor's edge for SOG INSEC to swoop in and start shooting everyone. The concealable MT weapons were quite capable, but they weren't nearly as comforting as having her own blazer rifle and pistol. With MT, everything was discreet. Stealth and secrecy were more important than lethality.

Not that she had done many operations with MT. For most Erikoisjoukot, they were mostly rumor and myth. She rarely saw an entire MT team for security reasons. On one operation a few decades ago, she had been next door to another Erikoisjoukot team and not known it. That mission had not been a shining success, but everyone survived, and they had extracted the operatives. It wasn't until later that she learned about the other team and other operatives. MT was like that, which made sense. If INSEC came down and captured anyone, nobody would have any reliable information for them. Skadi was pretty sure they had given them false information, just in case. Lies within lies.

It was unpleasant, and MT spooks were some of the worst.

"The Disciples of Loki need security at the Haskell Bar and Grill," Niels told her. He was currently watching the operations channel on his cybernetics while Skadi watched people walking past outside the hotel.

"It's about a block away," Niels continued. "Tonight. Control Otto wants two Aesir there. No specifics. No contact. Operative will wear a Kino Football patch on the left arm, Daughters of Social Freedom patch on the right."

Skadi shook her head. With everyone wearing the same loose, gray clothes, patches were a way to express themselves, so people liked to change them regularly. It was the only individuality they were allowed on this Governance hell hole. The people of Zhukov had a little more freedom than most because they got to wear about nine different shades of gray. Almost festive. Which it might be, if gray was all you saw.

"They want us to wear patches twenty-two and seventy-six," Niels said. "And twelve with sixty. Also need a kit load out; one purse."

Bern looked in their bag and winced.

"Bastards," Bern said, pulling the patches out.

One was a rainbow triangle, and the other was a Trog Football patch.

"Obviously yours," Bern said handing Skadi the patches.

"Great. I get to pretend to be a lesbian for the night."

"Well, better than whoever gets these," said Bern. One patch said "Boy Love" and the other was "Funkers Fooseball."

"Since curfew will be in effect, you will be there all night," Niels said. "Not sure what kind of place this is. Mission brief also says to use the makeup kit to make yourself as pale as possible. Looks like the albino look is in. Red eyes, too."

Holding up the whip and chain patch and the patch of a little boy with a ball made Skadi wince. Sick bastards. Sometimes she wondered if the dregs living on core SOG worlds still understood human decency. On the flip side, it would keep people from looking too closely at them. SOG civilians were so damned paranoid about offending each other.

"Probably black market, if I had to guess," Skadi said. "If they were worried about SOG interference, we would be more heavily armed and prepped."

"Looks like the psycho struck again," Vili said, watching the news.

"Anything like TCG?" Skadi asked.

"Dunno," Vili said. "They aren't into reporting so much as fear mongering, and MT isn't sharing information. No mass murders in subways or anything. Lots of disappearances, though. More like a rampaging animal or something and people getting scared and leaving."

"A rampaging animal?" Skadi asked. "Here on Zhukov?"

Vili shrugged.

"There's way too much hardware in orbit for a repeat of TCG," Bern said. "That wasn't a sector HQ. Coming in here were what? Four dreadnoughts and about twenty battleships?"

"Somebody might have an inflated belief in our technological superiority," Vili said. "Not as much as what was over Lisbon, but damn, I hope someone knows what they are doing."

"Yeah," Vili said. "But my point is that whatever force Nasaraf had on TCG wasn't one or two. He had to insert his troops somehow, planet side and on the station, and I'm not talking about the drop pods."

"No idea how it inserted them," Bern said. "It was hard enough for us to get in undetected, and we had codes."

"No alerts about off-planet travelers having to report in," Vili said.

"What was that about?" Bern asked. "You think they discovered Nasaraf slipping in agents?"

Vili shrugged again.

The team thought about what the SOG news had reported. It was nearly impossible sometimes to separate the lies and propaganda from the truth.

They had accused the Vapaus Republic of releasing a virulent plague upon Tau Ceti Gold, a plague that transformed people into bloodthirsty killers, and it had many people scared, which might explain why there were so many patrol corvettes trying to shield the planet.

The SOG had reported that the only option they had had was to sterilize the planet. It was difficult for Skadi to imagine that place, with all the people, now a glowing radioactive wasteland.

Not even MT knew the truth about what had happened to TCG after Skadi and her team had left, or if they knew, they weren't sharing that information.

Skadi wished she had one of the Marines with her. Their SCBIs could have probably cracked into the SOG systems and gotten the information they needed. Maybe.

"A Marine would be nice right about now," Vili said. "I wouldn't mind a little roll in the sheets with that cute girl Winters."

"I don't think you're her type," Bern said.

"How would you know?" Vili asked.

Bern shrugged. "A hunch. She seemed more interested in Skadi than a knuckle dragger like you."

"I'm a fine specimen of manhood," Vili said.

"Is that what you tell the goats?" Bern asked.

"Goat!" Vili said.

"Was it a magical moment?" Bern asked.

"No," Vili said. "I told you I was drunk."

"Sure," Bern said.

"If you don't mind?" Skadi said and Vili and Bern fell silent.

"Baaaa," Bern said softly, mimicking a goat.

Vili gave Bern the finger.

Niels made kissing sounds.

"Lock it down," Skadi said, glaring at them.

"Find out more about these murders," Skadi said to Vili. "You know how the SOG likes to lie. Read between the lines and get me a report."

"Zen," Vili said.

"Baaaa," said Bern.

"Bern, you're coming with me," Skadi said and threw him the patches.

Bern rolled his eyes and put the patches on while Skadi began secreting various weapons about her body, a couple of wire pistols, her mini-blazer, two knives, a folding knife, and a string of mini grenades.

"Got anything you want me to put in this stupid purse?" Skadi asked.

"That purse is for me," Bern said with a sigh. Skadi checked the mission upload. Yes, Bern got the purse.

"These people are so damned confused," Vili said. "No wonder they trust the SOG. The boot heel is the only stable thing in their life. You should also put on gray lipstick, Bern. Gray. It certainly is your color."

* * * * *

Chapter Thirty-Seven: Propaganda

Gunnery Sergeant Wolf Mathison, USMC

Something was about to start bleeding, either the walls or Mathison's eyes. If he heard "for the greater good" one more time, he was going to start shooting at the damned video, which covered a wall in every room and could not be turned off. The apartment itself was drab and soul draining; the only color came from the video screen. Trying to cover it with a blanket made it get louder. Not only did the videos bombard citizens with propaganda, but they also allowed the monitoring of citizens. So, turning it off wasn't an option because they monitored it from other rooms and apartments. The sound waves and electromagnetic emissions were monitored and recorded from different sensors, which let investigators piece together activity from the recordings. The SCBIs could change the sensors in real time, but that took a lot of processing resources. Changing the final recordings was easier.

Which meant that Mathison could not shoot the video or turn it off without having the entire Zhukov City Police Department come down on them.

Currently, it was asking people who were unsatisfied with the government handling of some fishing incident to complain at a certain address.

Mathison saw Stathis typing away at a keyboard and referencing the screen.

"What the hell are you doing?" Mathison asked.

"Leaving a review and sharing my comments, Gunny. Those fishermen should be allowed to give away any of the fish they catch on their own time. It sucks that the mayor wants to send them to an ideological re-assessment camp for three years because of it."

"Are you fucking crazy?"

"Well, half the time the complaint links don't work, but this one does. I'm pretty sure they're going to track my response and get pissed."

"This does not strike you as a very bad, very stupid idea?"

Stathis looked up at Mathison. "No, Gunny."

"What the hell are you saying?" Was Stathis really that freaking dumb? Shit. Mathison looked around. They were ready to go at a moment's notice, but, damn, he didn't want to be forced to leave so soon.

"I'm saying the mayor has his head up his ass and should actually hold real elections, and that he might get a better response if people could report anonymously. I also asked what was wrong with the fisherman doing what he wants with the damned fish if he caught it on his own time," Stathis explained.

Mathison stared at Stathis. "You know they're probably going to dispatch a SWAT team because of those posts, right?"

"I hope so, Gunny. I'm getting bored, and this bullshit is getting on my nerves. Hopefully, they'll show the SWAT teams on the news."

"When did you start?"

"This morning, Gunny,"

"You didn't think to mention this to me?" Mathison asked, looking out the window, expecting to see gunships and a SWAT team stacking against the building. "You want to shoot it out with a SWAT team?"

"Oh," Stathis said, as if he just realized what Mathison was talking about. "Sure, I wouldn't mind a good firefight, but Shrek is redirecting the source to some SOG flunkies in the department of human resources, so they're the ones getting personal visits from the police. Shrek said we're good. There's no way they can track it back to us. I'm bored, Gunny, not stupid."

Mathison told himself that shooting Stathis would likely set off all sorts of alarms. He really wanted to shoot Stathis and tried not to scream.

"You didn't think to check with me?"

"I figured you were busy planning and doing gunny things. I knew you would want to stick it to the SOG, mess with them. You want me to stop? I was going to redirect to some flunkies in the governor's office next."

Stathis was probably destroying lives. Some poor bastard in the monolithic bureaucracy was suddenly getting the fright of their lives.

"Why human resources?" Mathison asked.

"Just out of high school, before I joined, I had a job doing tech support for a company. They were such a bunch of touchy-feely bastards. I figure here in the Governance they're the ones you have to bribe if you want a good job."

Mathison thought about it. "Carry on. Don't get us caught, or I will shoot you myself. If you find out who authorizes housing fashion, target that bastard next."

"Aye, Gunny."

Maybe it wasn't such a bad idea, keeping the police running around targeting government flunkies for subversion or dissent. They would eventually figure out the flunkies were harmless, but it would take time and resources.

Of course, then they would start looking for the source, but the SCBIs could handle that. He hoped.

Boredom was a terrible thing.

*****

Chapter Thirty-Eight: Zhukov City

Gunnery Sergeant Wolf Mathison, USMC

It was a chilly day. Mathison pulled the threadbare jacket more tightly around him. Like everything else the Governance issued, it was inadequate and didn't fit right. The streets were deserted, which could be due to the weather, the danger, or the curfew. Mathison didn't care. He wasn't being bombarded by propaganda in a bleak, soulless apartment. The cold helped clear his mind. His body wasn't old anymore, but his future looked bleak.

The Governance was a monolithic and oppressive organization that crushed dreams and lives. The evidence was all around him. Everywhere he looked, the blank eyes of people who had nothing to strive for stared back at him, sometimes masked by fear or depravity. Everywhere he looked, people struggled for an identity and the SOG crushed it to make them identical and interchangeable, like ants.

Coming to Zhukov City had been a bad idea. He hadn't seen a Guardsman in days, but then this wasn't living. Unlike TCG, Zhukov City wasn't as run down and in poor repair, but everything was still the same drab, joy-draining gray. Watching the local propaganda shows made Mathison sick. The sports channel couldn't even get it right because they fell over themselves trying to show how all the teams were equal. The local authorities of Zhukov's cities were on an equality spiel and there was no way the games he had watched were not fixed. Ten overweight men should still have enough mass to plow through ten overweight women. Mathison had never seen athletes run that slow and the men outweighed the women by at least fifty pounds. It was a poor joke watching them run around the field, pretending to knock each other over.

The planetary government called itself the People's Democratic Governance, but it spent too much time talking about how great things were on Earth and how they wanted things to be great here. While traveling Zhukov City, Mathison watched the news in different areas. Despite all the talk of equality, the news agencies, even in the same city, had very different messages for the local neighborhoods, which seemed to be organized based on skin color or sexual orientation, and in some places by favorite football teams.

Unable to turn off the apartment video, Mathison had decided a walk would be preferable to the announcer droning on and on about how people should pull together and support the glorious Guard and Space Force as they hunted down the vile pirates of the Vapaus Republic before they struck again. They showed far too many videos of TCG and Mathison was pretty sure most were computer generated. There had been no creatures composed of screaming human faces, and he had seen no videos of the actual creatures, just horrifying insectlike creatures, misshapen mutants or spiked manlike monstrosities.

There were also numerous reports about some place called Lisbon, where a recent rebellion had been crushed. The talking heads ranted and raved about the depravity, cannibalism, and fascism of the Vapaus-backed Lisbonian rebels, how they had used innocent children as human shields and how they had used nukes against brave SOG Guardsmen trying to save the children. They even accused the Republic of trying to help the Lisbonians so they could use the children for food. All that was on the videos was hatred, propaganda, and division.

The "entertainment" wasn't much better. It was all designed to drag people down and make them afraid.

Stathis was still in the apartment, sleeping. When he put in his earplugs, he was out like a light. A sleeping private meant he was less likely to get into trouble, so Mathison wasn't going to interfere with that.

The real problem was that Mathison had too much energy and could only sleep so much. He wanted to exercise, but there were no running tracks or gyms outside of military facilities. Streets in the neighborhood where they were hiding out were clean, and the minimal graffiti made it a better neighborhood, which was a point in the SOG's favor. Most of the cameras and sensors worked, but Freya assured him he was one person among millions. She had created a mask for him to help him avoid the authorities' attention, and though Mathison didn't like to trust it, staying in that drab apartment one more minute would crush his soul.

Sunlight was fading and would be completely gone in minutes. He was wearing his blazer pistol in a jury-rigged shoulder holster, and it was cold against his skin. He was finally getting used to walking around in civilian clothes and not having to fear every time he saw a police patrol.

Freya and Shrek were sorting through the SOG networks looking for any trace of the Vapaus Republic or their agents, but Mathison was beginning to think the Republic wasn't active in Zhukov City, or if they were, they were well hidden. Mathison didn't know where to go next. The SCBIs had fabricated a complete identity for him and Stathis, but they couldn't give them a purpose. Stathis was starting to talk about getting a job just to have something to do. That surprised Mathison. He figured the private would be ecstatic being able to lie around all day watching videos. Sometimes Stathis made no sense.

A horn sounded indicating the curfew was in effect.

Thinking about going back to the apartment bothered Mathison. The Marine barracks he had lived in most of his life had displayed more personality and flair. He slowed and decided he didn't want to go back just yet; he didn't want to sit or sleep in that prison. If Stathis needed him, the private would contact him. He was slightly out of range of their regular communicators, but Freya and Shrek could tap into the SOG civilian network to send each other messages.

The more he saw of this planet, the more he hated it. He despised the soul-crushing attempts to make everyone the same. The government's goal was to make people interchangeable and equally worthless. What bothered him most was that the people expected the government to take care of them and make everything better. It was nothing but false promises. By controlling the media and education, they controlled the people like sheep. There were no alternative viewpoints, no arguments, no questioning the "benevolent" government, no real accountability.

Darkness slowly crept over the city, and the grayness deepened. If he didn't bother with cybernetics, he could pretend there were more colors in the surrounding city. Weak lamps came on, providing the minimum lighting an unmodified human would need to see.

"Police patrol," Freya warned him. Yellow icons appeared in his internal heads-up display, showing police officers as they walked their rounds. There were eight of them, an unusually high number.

Mathison was in a park, and he crouched behind some bushes until they passed. The officers in this area didn't have night vision gear on their helmets, just large flashlights they occasionally turned on. Cheap bastards, or their local politicians, were.

"Halt!" one officer yelled, and Mathison's heart froze. Had they seen him?

"Not you," Freya said. *"They just spotted some poor bastard coming out of a nearby apartment."*

Mathison leaned over and looked around the shrub to watch.

The officers intercepted the two strangers, the one in charge had his helmet off. Hard eyes and short brown hair made one stranger look like a combat veteran. He wasn't a little man, but he looked older, maybe a retired Guardsman?

Zooming in his vision, one stranger looked familiar.

"That is Aesir Hermod," Freya said. She sounded as confused as Mathison.

"What is he doing here?" Mathison asked. "You should create a mask for him in the network."

Mathison zoomed in and looked at Hermod and the other Aesir more closely. Freya tagged him as Aesir Hanz Abelt. Had Sif and the others finally found Team Hermod and brought them here?

The large Aesir commander still had his team commander tattoo visible, which was a bad idea. Skadi had concealed hers on TCG, but Hermod was wearing it proudly, and he didn't seem the least bit concerned he had been stopped.

"I'm Sergeant Lescheva. What are you doing out here?" the senior officer asked, approaching Hermod. The Aesir was almost a head taller than the police officer, and Mathison watched the other officers surround Hermod and Hanz to keep them from running. Hermod did not seem the least bit concerned. Mathison saw him smile. Aesir were a confident bunch.

"His face is paler than his pictures," Freya noted. *"His eyes also seem to have a reddish tint. Seems to be the fashion of late."*

"Hunting," Hermod said, allowing the police officers to surround him.

"Probably doesn't get a lot of sun on his ship or hiding," Mathison said. "I'm pretty sure I'm as pale as Snow White myself. Always wearing armor and such. Not the biggest surprise."

"Hunting what?" the officer asked. His tone was threatening, but Hermod was merely amused.

"Remember TCG?" Freya said. *"Everyone spent time working on a tan to erase their pasty complexion. I'm getting some static. Might be Aesir jamming."*

"Prey," Hermod said.

"*Maybe he didn't have time?*" Mathison said. "*If they're looking for us, they might not have had a lot of prep time. I've seen paste-white people with red contacts around Zhukov. The commander's tattoo is odd though.*"

Mathison's internal display flickered as Freya quickly cycled through his optical sensors.

"Who are you?" the policeman asked.

"Your systems aren't telling you?" Hermod asked.

"He doesn't have much of a thermal signature," Freya said.

"Some kind of masking?" Mathison asked as a chill ran down his spine, and he got a sinking sensation in his gut.

"Temporary outage, dumbass," the policeman said. "You'd better fix your attitude, or you're going to have a couple of accidents on the way to your cell."

"Maybe," Freya said. *"But that could make him more obvious to some sensors. This isn't normal."*

"Really?" Hermod asked, amused.

"He asked you a question, putz," another policeman said and put his hands on Hermod's shoulder.

"Interesting," Freya said. *"The local network is down; lots of interference. It seems to center around Hermod, but now that I'm looking, there are several places throughout the city where it is happening. Quite a few actually. It's obviously Aesir technology. I'm surprised Skadi didn't mention or use it."*

"Maybe she did."

"No. I'm pretty sure I would have noticed or remembered. This is wrong, like what happened on Curitiba."

"Hermod doesn't look like one of the monsters," Mathison said. There was no evidence of change, except maybe the pale skin and red-rimmed eyes.

In the blink of an eye, Hermod grabbed the policeman's hand and pulled the officer forward. Mathison couldn't see what happened because Hermod turned away, but a spray of blood and a scream surprised Mathison.

Hanz moved in a blur of motion as he grabbed the officer nearest to him, pulling him into a hug.

Everything happened so fast. Mathison watched the two Aesir break the necks or backs of the police officers or bite their throats by pulling back their helmets to expose their necks.

Mathison sat back behind the bush and froze.

What the hell had he just seen? Had the Aesir actually gone for the patroller's throats and bitten them?

"I'm not comfortable with you contacting Hermod," Freya said. *"Something is very wrong."*

"No shit," Mathison said as he backed up, keeping a large tree between him and what had happened. He drew his blazer pistol but didn't take his eyes off the tree except to glance around.

When he looked back, he saw Hanz rounding the tree.

"I thought I heard someone," Hanz said. Blood covered his smiling face.

"I'm Gunnery Sergeant Mathison," he said. He wanted to point his weapon at the man, but if he was an ally, that wouldn't be polite. "You are Hanz Abelt?"

Hanz's smile grew as he came toward him.

"You are from the Republic, yes?" Hanz said.

"He doesn't know who you are," Freya said. *"If he's here to rescue you, he should know."*

"What are you doing here?" Mathison said.

"I have notified Stathis," Freya said. *"He should be armoring up now."*

"Hunting recruits," Hanz said, continuing to walk toward Mathison. Hermod was nowhere in sight.

"For who?" Mathison asked, walking backward. "Why don't you stop right there."

"Prey," Hanz said. He didn't stop. "You are Republic? Dakaral will be pleased."

Hanz stepped into a pool of light, and Mathison saw there was a reddish film or something on Hanz's eyes. Another chill went down Mathison's spine. Hanz was also pale. The pictures Mathison had seen of Hanz showed a large man with a tan. This Hanz was big, but the reddish eyes and paper-white skin was not Hanz.

Mathison raised his blazer and fired.

Hanz had started to move but Mathison's shot hit him in the arm. There was a flash and the superheated plasma round exploded. Hanz screamed and reeled away, his arm a smoking ruin.

Hanz turned and sprinted at Mathison, his face a mask of rage and hatred, his teeth bared. Mathison adjusted his aim and fired two rounds into Hanz's chest. At the same time, he noticed the Aesir's bloodstained teeth were pointed and razor sharp.

The first round hit, and Aesir Hanz's chest exploded. The second round completed the damage. The Aesir commando stopped and dropped to his knees. Mathison could have put his head through either hole. Steam rose from the wounds and Mathison saw the light fade from Hanz's eyes as he fell facedown.

Mathison turned and started running. Hermod was out there somewhere, and Mathison wanted to put as much distance as he could between him and whatever Hanz had been.

"The blazer rounds caused significantly more damage than usual," Freya said. *"Almost explosive."*

"Joy," Mathison said, trying to look everywhere at once as he sprinted out of the park and down a street. Hanz had moved fast, Hermod could probably move just as fast. *"How about we get out of here before we do an after-action report?"*

"Keep moving. I've almost pinpointed the disturbance that may be Hermod. Turn left at the next corner."

"How can you be sure it is Hermod?"

"I can't, but the data supports my theory. Turn left again ahead, into the doorway."

Mathison did as he was told, just in time to see a police car go flying past.

"When you took Hanz's arm off, I notified the police," Freya said. *"All hands alert. Let's see if they can track Hermod down. He is no longer human."*

Mathison took a deep breath as he looked around. He was only two blocks from the park.

"Stathis is still at the apartment," Freya said. *"He's awaiting orders."*

"What did I just see?" Mathison asked.

"Good question," Freya said. *"I don't have enough data."*

"Guess," Mathison said.

"The Pankhurst *made it to Green Hope, then Nasaraf began infiltrating and controlling the local population. Hermod arrived and was captured, or turned, along with his team. I suspect Nasaraf is refining his technique."*

"They were talking. They killed those cops with their bare hands and freaking teeth. Hermod wasn't even trying to hide his commander tattoo."

"Conflicting and insufficient data," Freya said.

"They were wearing gray, trying to blend in, at least a little."

"I think we can now identify the cause of the murders and disappearances. It appears the Pankhurst *has operatives here, and they are changing tactics."*

"This is very bad," Mathison said. *"I think we need to get off the planet."*

"I agree. We will need to do some prep work, though, physical IDs and such. We might have to contact the local black market and purchase what we need."

"With what?"

"Something… Let me see what we can find out."

"If Hermod attacked the police on the street, I'm pretty confident he isn't as worried about being discovered as he used to be."

"Which means he might have enough troops."

"To do what? What did they try to accomplish on TCG?"

"Insufficient data," Freya said.

Mathison wondered if there would be enough time to get off the planet. With the force in orbit, *Tikari* wouldn't be coming to extract them. Skadi and her team might still be on Green Hope looking for Hermod, if they arrived in time. *Valkyrie 15* was supposed to wait for them, and Mathison was pretty sure that Skadi and Sif didn't know where the *Tiananmen* had taken them.

"If you can get into the police systems, can you put out an alert for Hermod and his team? That might delay the takeover."

"Or accelerate the timetable," Freya said. *"I already put out an alert. I think I've found a place with black market contacts."*

"Have Stathis meet me there."

"You don't want to plan this out a little more?"

"I don't want to end up as chow for Hermod and his monsters," Mathison said. *"But we also can't let the contamination leave the planet."*

*****

Chapter Thirty-Nine: Grill

Lojtnant Skadi – VRAEC

The meet location was an all-night recreation center where people could arrive and stay all night. It was a curfew sanctuary that stayed open all night. Most people arrived as the sun set and left when it rose. Skadi was confident there would be every form of depravity there.

Brightly lit and welcoming, the main lobby was not a disappointment. She had to surrender some of her scrip before the bouncer, a retired Guardsman, let her enter. At least they had some standards, and it was a busy place. There were far too many young people here desperately trying to prove they were having fun, taking selfies and congregating in groups. They struck Skadi as sad and desperate to convince others they were happy. Everyone was making some effort to appear paste white, and more than a few were wearing red contacts. It was bizarre, but the SOG citizens seemed to take extreme pleasure in finding ways around the standard rules of appearance and conduct. Fashions changed weekly. Paste-white skin and red eyes was just the latest craze.

Bern had arrived before Skadi and found a chair in the main room where he pretended to read a tablet. They briefly made eye contact before Skadi found a place on the opposite side of the room. She sat and scowled at people, her eyes lingering longer than usual on the girls running around and giggling in their groups. Someone watching her might assume she was checking out the other women, but Skadi was more amused at what the other women were wearing. Apparently, some places allowed something more than drab gray clothes and it looked like people had thrown themselves on a rainbow explosion. Nothing matched and there was far too much color. Ah, youth. The older patrons, about a third of the people present, tended to wear gray.

The loud music made anything over five feet away indistinguishable noise. Skadi didn't know what was playing, but the poor bastard singing was having a bad day because a Golden Horde raider had landed on his dog or something. It was all noise and distraction.

"Can you hear me?" Niels said. He and Vili were at the safe house. The MT had equipped the Aesir with subdermal communicators that let her team communicate using Republic tech, while hopefully staying undetectable. Skadi didn't like them though since she didn't have a list of the relays and there was no way to change the link.

"Zen," Skadi subvocalized. People would have to watch her closely to see her throat moving.

"Zen," Bern said. "It's going to be a long night."

"One hopes it'll be a boring one," Niels said. "We have a few drones up around the Haskel Bar and Grill. So far, all is quiet. Do you have eyes on our protectee?"

"Yes," Skadi said.

Their protectee appeared to be a young man. He blended in well with the current crowd, unlike her and Bern. There were a few hulking brutes in the club, but not many. Skadi was willing to bet they were protectors for the local black market. She and Bern had likely already been identified. Skadi got the impression most people here were regulars. She hoped the MT knew what they were doing. The MT handlers probably wanted Bern and Skadi there as obvious muscle, a statement to the people running the black market that they had guards as well. It kept everyone honest.

Outside, the sun was setting. Skadi tried to relax. Sunrise was in nine hours, fourteen minutes, and thirty-three seconds. It was going to be a very long nine hours, fourteen minutes, and thirty-two seconds unless something bad happened.

Skadi hoped Niels was right and it was long and boring. So far, people were avoiding her and Bern. That couldn't last, though.

"The night begins," Niels said. "Curfew horn sounded. Looks like you are in for the duration."

"Oh, the excitement," Bern said.

"I'll bet you wish you had a goat about now," Vili said.

"Secure extra chatter," Skadi said.

"Zen," Vili said. He sounded smug. He had gotten the last word with Bern.

The link fell silent as everyone spent their time watching everyone else. Time dragged on.

Almost an hour later, Vili came online.

"Paska, paska, paska," Vili said. "Oh, paska-lounas for everyone. Paska just hit the fan."

"What?" Skadi said, adrenaline hitting her system.

"An alert just went out for Hermod and his team over the SOG police net," Vili said.

"What?" Skadi asked. Had she heard right? Hermod?

"They have his picture," Vili said. "It's being sent to all police officers. There's a kill command associated as well. They list him as extremely dangerous. No capture, kill only, treat as biologically contaminated. His entire team is here."

"Affirmative," Niels said. "Control Otto just informed us as well. They're scrambling to get more information. They said they know nothing about Hermod being on planet and are checking up the chain to see if he needs assist."

"Well," Skadi said. "I guess that's why they went missing on Green Hope. I didn't expect MT to be involved, though."

"Why are they wanted?" Skadi asked.

"Biological contamination," Vili said. "Doesn't say they are Republic, but it says they captured a ship and arrived here from Nugget in the Tau Ceti System. Says they're contaminated and must be eliminated at all costs. Other possibly contaminated individuals may appear with paste-white skin and reddish eyes."

"Hermod was nowhere near TCG," Skadi said, trying to make sense of it. The SOG liked to spin propaganda, but they were usually halfway decent at mixing the truth with the lies. Hermod had gone missing when the *Pankhurst* was in Tau Ceti or shortly thereafter. Right? Paste-white skin and red eyes? Wasn't that the latest fashion? That description now applied to a large number of the younger population now. If Hermod really had been infected, he wouldn't look like Hermod, or even human. Something else was going on.

"Well," Vili said. "He's wearing his commander tat in the pic; it's definitely Hermod. That's the name the SOG is using, too."

"That makes no sense," Skadi said as a nearby video screen changed channel to an alert message. Now she saw Hermod's face along with the other members of his team.

"Odd," Vili said.

"The entire situation is odd," Niels said.

"No, it's odd that Hanz isn't listed."

"What does that mean?" Bern asked.

"Let me call the SOG and ask," Vili said. "Maybe he's already in custody, or they don't know. It's an interesting omission."

Skadi saw their protectee turn and look at her. Obviously, he had just received the news. He looked at the video screen. People were being asked to report any sightings of Hermod. The screen cycled through his team. Vili was right. Hanz wasn't listed.

There had never been an Erikoisjoukot team outed on public SOG television before. Though they weren't calling them Aesir, Skadi was pretty sure once the military saw the alert they would recognize that commander's tattoo for what it was.

Skadi scanned the surrounding people and made doubly sure none were from Hermod's team. They would have to be found and evacuated sooner rather than later. Once the military figured out Hermod was Aesir, they might cordon off the city and start a door-to-door search. They would probably go crazy using DNA sniffers and analysis. Anyone not a Zhukov native would get extra scrutiny, and Skadi was pretty sure her team would not pass.

The main door opened, catching Skadi's attention since it was after curfew. Who was brave enough to risk arrest?

Skadi's eyes fell on Mathison and Stathis handing over some scrip to the bouncer at the door. They were wearing gray SOG civilian clothes, and it took a second for her memory to make the match as she stared at Mathison in surprise.

The two Marines entered and started looking around.

Skadi stood to get a better look, and her movement drew Mathison's attention.

The look of fear and anger on his face was unmistakable as he backed up and reached into his jacket. Stathis saw her as well and reached inside his jacket.

"Gun!" someone screamed as the two Marines drew their weapons. Skadi barely ducked in time as a blazer round flashed over her head. She felt the heat from its passing. When she looked up, both Marines had retreated out the door and people were screaming and running away. Everyone was panicking. He had come very close to killing her. It was only her speed and training that had kept her alive.

"Was that Mathison?" Bern asked.

"And Stathis," Skadi said. she wanted to punch Mathison in the face. Why would Mathison shoot at her and run? What had she done to him? Why was Hermod being hunted?

"I have them on drone," Niels said. "They're running north."

"Follow them," Skadi said. Her priority was the MT agent, but she wanted to chase them down. Had he really tried to kill her? "Don't lose them."

"Did he just shoot at you?" Vili asked.

"You need to get out of there, now," Niels said. "Badges are probably already on their way, and they're probably going to search everyone and scrutinize everything."

"I've got the protectee," Bern said, and Skadi saw he was standing at the man's side, his hand inside his jacket. Skadi pointed at another door and Bern steered their protectee toward it. Skadi moved to join them. Other people were struggling to escape. Obviously, nobody wanted to be here when badges showed up.

What the hell was Mathison thinking? Why did he shoot at her? Not just shoot at her, he had tried to kill her. The kirottu gunnery sergeant was hullu.

“Well,” Niels said. “The gunnery sergeant just shot our drone out of the sky.”

“Paska-lounas for everyone,” Vili said. “This is not getting any better. Is it too late to retire?”

*****

Chapter Forty: Retreat

Gunnery Sergeant Wolf Mathison, USMC

Mathison kept checking behind him as they ran down the street.

"Drone," Freya reported and highlighted the stealthy device.

Stathis turned and shot it with a single round before Mathison could.

"Nice shot, Stathis," Mathison said and pointed down another street before whoever had put the drone up could get another to their location.

"I liked Skadi," Stathis said. "I'm glad you missed her, but not. Is she one of them now?"

Mathison was also glad he had missed her, but at the same time pissed. If she had turned she needed to die, but he didn't want to be the one to do it. Why Skadi, damn it?

"She's as good as dead anyway. Can you think of any other reason she would be here, paste white with red eyes?" Mathison said.

"She didn't have her tattoo."

"But she was pretty pale."

"She wasn't killing people."

"Wanna go back and ask why? Hermod didn't start out killing the cops."

"How many Aesir has Nasaraf turned?" Stathis asked.

"Let me give her a call. You still want me to ask her if she wants to go out on a date with you?"

"I like my throat unripped out, Gunny."

"Turn here."

For several more minutes the two Marines ran through the streets, weapons in hand while Freya and Shrek masked their presence from the SOG street cameras and kept them from running into any police patrols.

Twenty minutes later, they were back in their apartment, pulling on their armor.

"We are so screwed," Stathis said. "So damned screwed."

"We aren't dead," Mathison said. "Just stay behind me. I'll get us out of here, somehow. If you have any ideas, don't hesitate."

"You're asking me for ideas?" Stathis asked, suddenly sounding panicked.

Mathison chuckled, which seemed to calm Stathis a little.

"Gunny, that isn't funny. When you ask me for ideas, I know we are screwed. Please don't mess with me like that."

"Well," Mathison said. "I have good news."

Stathis looked at Mathison hopefully.

"As the senior-most Marine on planet, it is my honor and privilege to promote you to private first class," Mathison said. "Congratulations Private First Class Zale Stathis."

Stathis stared at Mathison. "What does this mean, Gunny?"

"It means you get a pay raise."

"What?" His confusion was clear. "More pay?"

"Yes," Mathison said, patting the now-PFC on the shoulder.

"How much am I getting paid, Gunny?"

"Let me see." Mathison looking up like he was doing math. "Nothing plus nothing, minus a percent for taxes, plus nothing for combat pay, minus social security tax, carry the nothing. Let's see… it almost doubles your pay to nothing."

"Gunny…?" Stathis said, shaking his head, not sure what he could say, or get away with saying.

"Shut up, PFC Stathis," Mathison said, all business. "Get your gear ready. We might have to get out of this city sooner rather than later."

"Aye, Gunny. I guess we know why we can't find any evidence of the Republic. Nasaraf has turned them. Is it too late to find some quiet secret colony and retire on my new PFC pay?"

"You are an optimist, Stathis."

"Why are you sure she was turned?" Freya asked.

"How do you explain her being here instead of Green Hope?" Mathison asked. *"The red eyes? Pale skin?"*

"She could have come here first. Also she could have come here immediately after learning they had brought you here. White skin and red eyes is the latest fashion, though only a week or two old."

"Fashion is stupid. How did that become fashionable? Skadi doesn't strike me as fashion minded, and Hanz was not being fashionable. That shit was real."

"Unless Hermod and his team helped inspire this latest craze," Freya said. *"Or people have seen footage from Nugget. Though the creatures of Nugget were not paste white."*

"And how did she learn we were here? What are the chances that she arrived at Green Hope, found out we were here, and then abandoned the search for Her-

mod to come here? I don't recall any pale-skinned people on Nugget. Just fat slugs and monsters."

"Maybe she learned Hermod had come here? You did not hit her, by the way."

"I tried," Mathison said, but he wasn't entirely sure that was true. *"Where's the rest of her team?"*

"Reviewing footage, it appears Bern was there, as well. However, regular SOG cameras and monitors are offline or not installed in that area. Apparently, the black market pays the right people for privacy. I tapped into the local footage."

"But nobody else?"

"No, not on anything I could access. That area is a black hole as far as SOG surveillance goes. There wasn't any odd interference I could detect."

"Maybe the interference only occurs when they get ready to start killing."

"The rest of Hermod's team was absent. So, if that's a regular meeting place for the black market why was she there instead of out hunting for me or Hermod?"

"Looking for leads?"

"What are the chances we'd end up in the same place? Really? Hanz was certainly no longer human, and if Skadi is here, she had to come with Hermod. There are no other explanations. What are the chances that both teams would show up here with white skin, red eyes, and unaware of each other?"

"Extremely remote," Freya said.

"Exactly, two hundred and twelve occupied planets and she ends up here, in this city? She is not here for us, and I don't think there's any way we can contact her. She looked surprised to see us."

"Sif gave you those radio frequencies."

"Then let's try them," Mathison said. *"Sif should be listening."*

"I can do that, but we need to get a radio that's powerful enough."

"You can't transmit on those frequencies?"

"I have many capabilities," Freya said. *"Transmitting natively and with sufficient power on that frequency is not one of them."*

"So we need to hijack a radio."

"If only it were that easy. The SOG will hear it, as well, and while we can encrypt it, there is no guarantee the SOG will not be able to decrypt it. The SOG doesn't like unauthorized radio transmissions. Records show they make them nuke-happy."

"So, we can send a message and a meeting place, but there's a good chance the SOG will beat the Republic there."

"Exactly. This is a heavily populated system, a sector capital, so I'm pretty sure the authorities will be more alert to odd, random, encrypted transmissions."

"That would put all Republic operations in jeopardy too, wouldn't it? If they are here because of Hermod, we'll be pissing in their cheerios and endangering their operations."

"Which we probably did by releasing Hermod's information to the authorities," Freya said.

"And with me shooting at Skadi. That will make us enemy number one for the Republic. If Blitzen or Lilith were in the networks, would you have encountered them?"

"Probably. Especially if they were working with Skadi."

"So obviously Levin and the chief aren't here."

"That is a certainty. Unless they are in space and not part of the on-planet mission."

"Unlikely. And if they were okay, then Skadi wouldn't hesitate to use them," Mathison said.

"Yes."

"So has the Republic turned on us completely? Sneaking us off Midgard obviously caused a problem, and I don't like the implications."

"Maybe Stathis' idea of finding a secret colony and retiring has merit?"

"No, not without Levin and Winters. No Marine left behind and screw the SOG. The bastards nuked the USA and my beloved Marine Corps. Payback is a vengeful bitch with herpes. If Skadi's here and isn't looking for us then something really screwy is going on."

"So, are we going to piss in the SOG's cheerios? What do you propose we do next?"

"Drink lots of water. Dehydrated people don't piss much."

"You have a plan?" Freya said. *"I thought you were the idiot, so I'm pretty sure I won't like it."*

"Yes. With the Republic compromised and untrustworthy, it's time to drink the Kool-Aid. Fortes fortuna juvat."

"Fortune favors the bold. I really hope you don't mean what I think you mean."

"Stathis, how would you like to join the SOG Space Fleet? Maybe it's time to promote you again. I'm thinking you'd make a good ensign."

"Isn't that like a second lieutenant?"

"Close."

"Gunny, I'm a private first class. I'm not dumb enough to be a second lieutenant."

"You'll do fine."

"Ow, that hurts, Gunny."

"I've been nurse maid to privates and second lieutenants for a good part of my life," Mathison said. "Sometimes there's not a lot of difference."

*****

Chapter Forty-One: Escape

Lojtnant Skadi – VRAEC

The trip back to the apartment had involved dodging badges but now they were safely off the street.

"Who the hell was that?" the protectee asked as Vili peered out the window. His MT issued carbine was now assembled and ready. Skadi was pulling on her battle dress. It didn't have nearly as much protection or advantages as her regular Aesir armor, but at a quick glance it wouldn't be noticeable.

"A US Marine," Skadi said, still trying to make sense of what had happened.

"What?" he asked.

Niels explained while Skadi finished putting on her suit.

"Why did he shoot at you?" the protectee asked.

"I have no idea," Skadi said. "Maybe he's met the Vanir recently."

"What is that supposed to mean?" the protectee asked.

"What is your name?" Skadi asked.

"Call me Vince," the man said.

"Well, Vince, if your handlers haven't told you what is going on, then I'm not going to."

Vince glared at her.

"We have our orders," Niels said. "We're to make our way to the spaceport at sunrise. They'll have extraction available."

Skadi looked at Vince.

"Did you accomplish your mission?" Skadi asked.

"No," Vince said. "It was going well until your friend showed up and started shooting. It's your fault my mission went to hell. Now we'll probably have the entire planet hunting us."

"Won't sunrise be too late?" Bern asked. "I don't think that will work well for us if the SOG wants to cordon off the city and go door to door."

"Control Otto says they have a plan," Niels said.

"I don't have a good feeling about this," Vili said.

"I agree," Bern said.

"They have canceled the alert," Vili reported, sounding confused. He was listening to several SOG police bands.

"Canceled?" Skadi asked.

"They are saying 'test complete,'" Vili said.

"MT has that much pull?" Skadi asked, looking at Vince.

Vince also looked surprised, but just shrugged.

"Is evac still a go?" Skadi asked Niels.

A few seconds later, Niels replied, "Affirmative. Control Otto says they don't know why the alert was canceled."

Skadi didn't like it. MT sounded incompetent and uncoordinated. Too compartmentalized with the different groups not telling each other what they were up to. How did they function?

"What about our mission?" Skadi asked, wondering if the Marines SCBIs were involved.

Vince winced. "Not going to happen now. Any hint of Republic involvement in the system would compromise it."

"What was it?" Skadi asked.

"I can't tell you," Vince said.

Skadi scowled then shrugged. She couldn't make him tell her, but she was willing to bet it had to do with the upcoming Vanir attack. How many lives would the failed mission cost the Republic?

"Can we get it back on track?" Skadi asked. Vince frowned and shook his head. Mission failure bothered her.

"You don't understand how much of a disaster that was," Vince said, but Skadi had conducted enough covert operations to know exactly how it could be a major disaster. Of course, everyone seemed to think their mission was most important.

"Any word on the Marines from Control Otto?" Skadi asked.

"Nothing," Niels said. "If I had to guess, they were as surprised as we were. Right now, Control Otto wants us to hold position until they have an exfiltration route ready."

"Shouldn't they have had that ready before the mission?" Skadi asked.

Niels shrugged. "One would think."

"That's a lot of hardware driving by," Vili said from the window. "Looks like they put a call in to the local military base."

"Discharging blazers in a public area can do that," Niels said. "Local badges have probably never even seen a blazer fired. Why couldn't those damned Marines have used something a little more subtle?"

"I was reading about them," Vili said. "One nickname for them is Jarheads and something about eating crayons. They aren't known for their intelligence."

"They seemed pretty damned smart to me," Skadi said.

"Maybe they were just referring to regular grunts," Vili said. "I don't know. People call Aesir stupid, too. They don't have a clue what we do or how difficult things are."

"They're smart enough to stay off the grid," Bern said.

"Could they be the ones who canceled the alert on Hermod?" Niels asked.

"Maybe," Skadi said. "Which might mean they're working with Hermod. They must have found him on Green Hope and come here."

"But what?" Niels asked. "And why shoot at you?"

"Not enough information," Skadi said.

Where was Sif?

* * * * *

Chapter Forty-Two: Corvette

Gunnery Sergeant Wolf Mathison, USMC

It felt strange to be wearing a SOG fleet officer's uniform as he strode across the tarmac toward the SOG corvette. The ship had no name, just a number, 77842. Fleet command had grounded the ship while the crew underwent loyalty evaluation for some infraction or other. Freya was working to ensure the corvette was prepared and ready for when the eight-man crew was available again, which wasn't to be for another month. The actual captain had reported his crew and was currently vacationing somewhere on a coast. Freya had blocked several recalls to the captain so they had time. The XO of the ship was scheduled to be replaced, but that was another order Freya had rerouted to the wrong department where it would subsequently be ignored.

Until then, per SOG standard operating procedures, the corvette would remain grounded but ready. While parked in its bay, there were several umbilicals that provided power, water, sewage, and hardwired network access to the SOG military networks.

There were several other corvettes in the area, each with a pair of guards at the main entrance.

Stathis walked behind him and to the left. Behind Stathis was a small, wheeled robot carrying all their gear, their weapons, and their armor. It wasn't a big robot, just what most officers would use to transport their personal effects.

As he approached, the two guards snapped to attention and saluted Mathison.

"Good evening, Captain," the first guard said. Mathison nodded like he had seen twenty other captains do as they approached their ship. He passed them, walked up to the hatch, and put his palm against the reader. If Freya had messed something up, the two guards would be alerted and all hell would break loose. Stathis had slowed down a little so he would be next to the guards if the hatch didn't open.

A light flashed green, and the hatch slid open. Mathison was careful not to let his relief show as he stepped aboard. Stathis and the robot followed him.

The main hatch opened into a small airlock. The inner airlock door was already open.

When the outer hatch slid shut, Mathison looked back.

"Ship is secure," Freya reported. *"We are the only ones here. I'm erasing our presence from the guard's log."*

"That was easy," Stathis said. "Like taking candy from a baby."

"No," Freya said. *"It wasn't."*

'Shut up, Stathis," Mathison said. "We still have work to do."

"Aye, Gunny."

The corvette was a small ship, barely larger than Skadi's *Tikari*, and it was going to be their home for a while.

Mathison made his way to the bridge and looked around. There were five stations on the bridge, or CIC, which made it crowded: captain, XO, navigation, weapons, and sensors.

He sat in the captain's chair and examined the controls as Freya brought up a holographic overlay.

"First, we need to take full ownership of the ship," Freya said.

"What are we going to name her?" Stathis asked.

"Name? Her?" Mathison asked, now distracted.

"Our ship?" Stathis said.

"*Patriot*," Mathison said. It was the first thing that came to mind, and he was afraid of anything that Stathis might pick.

"That is awesome," Stathis said. "Better than what I was going to suggest."

Mathison grunted acknowledgment as he logged into the system as directed by Freya.

"You aren't going to ask me what I was going to suggest, Gunny?"

"Nope."

"I was going to recommend Wolf," Stathis said. "Your first name. That's a cool name. The USS *Wolf*."

Mathison grunted. Yes, it was cool.

"You need to get to work," Mathison said. "We need to connect wireless to the hard link so our SCBIs can access the hard link networks."

"Aye, Gunny. Or should I call you 'captain' now? I kinda like the ring of Lieutenant Stathis."

"Don't call me 'captain.' Unless you're calling me a bastard."

Stathis took a breath and Mathison turned and looked at him.

"Aye, Gunny," Stathis said after a brief pause.

"The sooner we get access to the SOG hard link networks, the sooner we can get off this rock. I really don't want to be here when Hermod comes out of hiding. And the SOG is building up their fleet here for something. I'd like to miss that as well."

"Damn straight, Gunny. This many SOG ships give me the creeps."

"Several orbital ships are sending down Guard units," Freya reported. *"Hard burn. They're coming down in drop pods and assault shuttles."*

"It's begun. Are they coming here?"

"I don't have full access yet, but right now it looks like they're landing on the outskirts of the city. They are likely to establish a cordon, surround the city, and move in. I estimate it will take them about three weeks to search the entire city. They'll likely consider military facilities secure."

"So, as long as we don't leave our new ship we should be okay?" Mathison asked.

"Correct. We should have enough time. Correction. I'm picking up several heavy landers being directed to this base from one of the orbital troop transports."

"Will they go ship to ship?"

"I don't know. I will begin monitoring communications. You and Stathis need to work faster to get us direct access to the hard link network. I've also started monitoring radio communications in case Sif tries to send us anything, but the sooner we get access to the network the better."

"No kidding," Mathison said.

* * * * *

Chapter Forty-Three: Closing Net

Lojtnant Skadi – VRAEC

It was a long day watching military transports drive by on the road outside their hideout and nerve-wracking to think the SOG could surround the apartment complex to prepare for a sweep at any moment. Control Otto had told them to stay in position and Skadi liked to think they had more information on the situation, but this wouldn't be the first time Republic operators had their wires crossed with other teams'.

The coffee they had in their apartment didn't meet minimum military standards, and Skadi was starting to wonder if it had any caffeine in it.

A link opened from Control Otto to Skadi on the Aesir link.

"Erik-twenty-seven," the controller said. "This is Control Otto. I need to ask some questions."

"Go," Skadi said. She sat and got comfortable. Nearby, Niels looked at her and rolled his eyes.

"We have the recordings," Otto said. "It definitely looks like the Marines named Mathison and Stathis."

Skadi nodded though Otto couldn't see her. Sometimes people liked to state the obvious to set a line of inquiry. Intelligence types were like that. State the obvious and work from there.

"Any reason you can think of that they would shoot at you?" Otto asked.

"They learned how the Vanir betrayed them?" Skadi said.

"How would they learn that?" Otto asked.

"Maybe you should ask them," Skadi said. Did they think she was psychic? Didn't they have Nakija they could question?

"Where would they go to ground?" Otto asked.

"They have internal SCBIs that can hack the SOG networks like you wouldn't believe," Skadi said. "They can probably go to ground wherever they want. If I had to guess, they would avoid the SOG military facilities because they've run into issues with them before. On Koros Nine they tripped a fly paper trap, and on TCG they showed extreme caution with the local MilNets."

"So, they could be hiding anywhere in the city?" Otto asked.

"That would be my guess," Skadi said. "As far from the military as they could get. They were wearing civilian clothes when they shot at me."

"How did they get here? Weren't they supposed to be on Green Hope?"

"So was Hermod," Skadi said. "What's the status with that alert? Did the MT cancel that?"

"Not to my knowledge," Otto said. "That cancelation came from INSEC."

Skadi paused. It came from internal SOG security? They certainly had the authority, but why would they? A chill ran down her spine. Was INSEC aware?

"Is the attack still on?" Skadi asked. If INSEC knew about the impending attack, they might have a trap ready and they wouldn't want anything to tip it off.

"I can't discuss that," Otto said, but he sounded unhappy. Was it too late to cancel the attack? She couldn't think of a single good reason INSEC would cancel the alert unless they knew and wanted the Republic to attack.

"Do we really need to evacuate?" Skadi asked.

"We are detecting evidence of assault drops being prepared," Otto said. "The SOG might decide to drop a couple Guard divisions around Zhukov City."

Skadi did not like that. She hadn't had access to the *Tikari* since the MT had smuggled her in on merchant transport.

"Shouldn't you be getting us out of here?" Skadi asked.

"We are having problems," Otto said, and Skadi froze. This was not the time to "have problems."

"What problems?" Skadi asked.

"This information is confidential," Otto said, "however, the cat might already be out of the bag. Over the decades, we've been putting back doors into various SOG systems. Planting certain vulnerabilities in the firmware for some devices, creating hidden accounts in others."

"And?" Skadi said.

"We've discovered some of these back doors have been compromised," Otto said. "In one case, the firmware was completely updated, and now we're locked out. We suspect INSEC is on to us, so we're activating some deep cover operatives."

"This is not filling me with confidence," Skadi said. "Could Hermod be involved?"

"Possible, but I don't think so. The compromise appears to be Vanir, not specifically MT or Aesir related."

"Do you think it could be the traitors?" Niels asked Skadi on a private link. Skadi frowned. Could the Vanir have sunk low enough to betray their brothers and sisters? Or would the Vanir even bother to show up?

"When did you notice this?" Skadi asked.

"Weeks ago," Otto said. "We were reviewing everything and discovered it."

"Which might eliminate the Marines," Skadi said.

"But not Hermod," Niels replied. "Unless he's with the rebel Vanir."

"Why would Hermod be involved?" Otto asked.

"Why are Hermod and his team here?" Niels said. "Well, except Hanz. The alert did not include Hanz."

"We noticed that, and we are investigating," Otto said.

"None of this really means squat if INSEC captures us," Skadi said. "I really hope you're working on a plan to get us the hell out of here."

"We are," Otto said. "But now you know the problem."

"Paska," Skadi said.

"No *Tikari,* no *Valkyrie,*" Niels said on a private team link. "And now we find out they've compromised our handlers? Can it get any worse?"

"You forgot Nasaraf," Vili said. "I'm sure he's got something to share. One hopes the *Ovela Kostaja* is safe."

"Anything else?" Skadi asked her team.

"Well," Vili said. "I see dismounted Guardsmen outside. That can't be good."

* * * * *

Chapter Forty-Four: Valkyrie Command

Chief Warrant Officer Diamond Winters, USMC

The *Valkyrie 27* wasn't too difficult to understand, though Blitzen did most of the understanding and Winters just pushed the occasional button. Most functions aboard the *27* were automated, and Winters suspected the reason for six crew was more a precaution than a requirement. It should be possible for two people to run the vessel. The big question was, what next? Could she and Levin rescue the gunnery sergeant and Stathis?

Once the *27* was secure and under her control, and nothing major was going on, Winters turned her attention to Sif, who was sitting in her chair patiently watching Winters.

"The HKT killed two of the Jaegers," Levin said when he came in. "They're pissed and Sloss wants blood. We need to find a place to drop them off. I doubt they can escape their cells or take over the ship, but I would rather not tempt them."

Winters turned to Sif.

"Any recommendations on where we can put you and your Jaegers?" Winters asked.

"I would rather continue with you," Sif said.

"No offense," Winters said, "but I don't know if we can trust you either."

Sif nodded as if expecting it.

"Are you going to give me a reason to trust you?" Winters asked when Sif remained silent.

"If I have not earned your trust by freeing you, I don't know how I can," Sif said. "You are in command."

Winters leaned back as Levin sat. He looked exhausted. Winters glanced at him.

"Bots are fixing the damage, ma'am," Levin said, looking around the bridge. "If I can make a suggestion?"

Winters nodded.

"We need sleep," Levin said. "We appear to be safe for the moment, in deep space where nobody can find us. The ship appears secure, and while I don't know about you, it's getting hard for me to stay awake. I could take some stims, but in my experience that doesn't always help. Do you want me to stand watch while you get some sleep?"

Winters looked between Levin and Sif, uncertain. Was there a reason he wanted her to rest? Was he planning something? Blitzen would know, right? She had contact with his SCBI.

"You go ahead and rest, Sergeant," Winters said. "I didn't spend the last hour fighting through the ship. You've earned it."

"Thank you, ma'am," Levin said. "I'll be in one of the crew cabins. Wake me when you need to, even if it's just twenty minutes."

"Thank you, Sergeant," Winters said. He seemed sincere, but she knew he'd need more than twenty minutes.

Winters turned her attention back to Sif. She still had too many questions. She decided to start digging.

"How did you escape?"

"My abilities let me influence the mind of my interrogators," Sif said. "I had them turn on each other and pushed them to their logical conclusion. Then I used the last Vanir's guilt and weakness to control him so I could rescue you."

"And the HKTs in the hallway?"

"They expected the Vanir officer. I masked their awareness of me. They saw me but they didn't recognize me or associate anything unusual with my presence. Like the color of the walls. You notice but you don't notice. I can't use that to hide others, though; it takes too much. It isn't as easy as I make it sound."

"Are you influencing me?"

"No. I would have to influence you *and* your SCBI."

"You can do that?" Winters asked, slightly alarmed.

"I haven't tried."

"Why not?"

"Do you know the difference between a republic and a democracy?" Sif asked.

"Yes. But you tell me."

Sif nodded. "A democracy is mob rule, a republic is a nation of laws. In a democracy, the majority can bend laws to exploit a minority. In a republic, everyone should have equal protection."

"Your point?"

"The Vapaus Republic is not a democracy. We have laws. We Nakija also have laws and rules that we abide by. One of those laws involves using our abilities against citizens and allies. We do not change the laws for our convenience. I don't get to vote on that."

"Weren't the Vanir citizens?"

"Not after they took us prisoner. The Nakija may use their abilities against enemies, foreign and domestic. The Vanir betrayal marked them as a domestic enemy, thus I was freed from my restrictions."

"And when you consider us enemies?"

"If," Sif corrected her. "Then we will be enemies. I do not expect that. The Republic has wronged you. The actions of the Vanir reflect on the Aesir and Nakija. Their crimes are the crimes of all the Republic. I can only apologize and work to regain your trust. You have not lost *my* trust, although I understand I have lost yours. I accept that."

Winters stared at Sif. How could she know if she was being influenced or controlled? The thought made her skin crawl. Another person seeing and influencing her innermost thoughts? Could there be a crime worse than that?

"We should go to Zhukov," Sif said.

"Why?" Winters asked.

"The Republic is planning an attack against the SOG sector fleet," Sif said.

"Maybe you missed the part where I don't trust the Republic?" Winters said.

"Skadi will be there," Sif said. "She will help you find your gunnery sergeant and private."

"How do you know?" Winters asked.

The girl took a deep breath and looked troubled, like she didn't want to say.

"A psychic messenger told me," Sif said finally.

Winters digested that. A psychic messenger? Did that mean the Republic had faster than light communication? How well did it work? Could she send a message to Skadi or get a response?

"Why didn't you use your messenger service to tell them about Nasaraf originally?"

"I am passive," Sif said. "I listen, but if nobody is looking for me, there is nothing I can do or say. Even if I am listening, there is no guarantee I'll hear the messenger, and it's not reliable."

"What makes you think Skadi would help?" Winters asked.

"She helped you escape at Midgard," Sif said. "She has shown you loyalty and opposed the Vanir on your behalf. I trust her."

Winters stared at Sif. Was the girl trying to influence her? And if she was, why? Winters was sure Sif didn't always rely on her psychic abilities. Besides, there were other ways to lie and influence others without mental abilities. Lies within truths were the most dangerous, but the cold, hard reality was that Winters had absolutely no idea where they should go. *Tupolev* hadn't exactly announced their final destination.

"You should go rest," Winters said.

"Yes, ma'am," Sif said, giving a curt bow before leaving.

Winters looked around the CIC and her eyes fell on the bodies.

"I will have some robots remove them," Blitzen said. *"And fix up the CIC when other more critical items are fixed."*

"Thank you," Winters said.

"You can go rest if you like," Blitzen said. *"Lilith and I can keep watch while we work."*

It was tempting, but she didn't want to go through the dead captain's things right now. And sleeping in the bed of a dead man held no appeal for her.

"This chair is comfortable enough. I'll just doze."

"Aye," Blitzen said.

She closed her eyes, but it didn't mean she slept. Despite the exhaustion, her mind kept spinning and bouncing around. How long had the *Pankhurst* been there? Why did it attack when it did? What would it do now; where would it go? How was she going to get the gunny and Stathis back? She knew he would never abandon her and Levin. She would not leave the Marines behind. One reason she was a Marine Raider shuttle pilot was because she was crazy enough to risk her life for other Marines and skilled enough to survive and fly nearly anything. While she might not be a Raider she was a Marine, and now she was in command. She couldn't let others take all the risks, not anymore. Levin was a warrior, but he wasn't a pilot. This was her realm. She had to step forward and take responsibility.

Damn it. Why had the gunny been stupid and left her in charge? She hoped she wouldn't let him down, because she knew he wouldn't let his Marines down.

* * * * *

Chapter Forty-Five: Zhukov

Chief Warrant Officer Diamond Winters, USMC

The bridge door slid open and woke her up. She'd fallen asleep. She spun and drew her side arm. Levin froze.

"Sorry," Winters said, holstering the weapon.

"No worries, ma'am," Levin said. "Please don't tell me you have been here for the last six hours on watch."

"I have," Winters said.

She still wasn't used to the CIC. The walls appeared transparent, showing the space around the ship. With some experimentation Blitzen had drawn a simple wireframe of *Valkyrie 27*, showing Winters the dimensions and layout of the ship. It was a heady experience as she looked at it. What would it be like to have her own ship? To not answer to anyone? To go where she wanted when she wanted? To explore, or vacation at will?

"Ma'am," Levin said. "As senior Marine you really should be rested. Lack of sleep affects judgment."

"They are very picky about that for pilots," Winters said looking around her. There was a blue nebula; she could almost make out the shape of a sleeping dragon. Almost. "Sleepy pilots make fatal mistakes."

Sitting there, looking at the galaxy around her was as soothing as lying in the grass on a comfortable day watching clouds drift slowly overhead.

"Then you should go get some sleep, ma'am," Levin said. "I can hold down the fort."

"I'm fine," Winters said. She smiled as Levin scowled.

"Seriously, Sergeant," Winters said, "I cat napped while my SCBI monitored things."

"That's not as good as actual sleep, ma'am," Levin said.

Winters spun her chair around so she could look at Levin. "I've been thinking."

"Chiefs are known to do that well," Levin said cautiously. "But they tend to be well rested when they do."

"We aren't going to give this ship back to the Republic," she said.

Levin nodded.

"Can we handle it, ma'am?" Levin asked, looking around.

"I think we can, between us and the SCBIs."

"What about *Tikari*, ma'am? Is it still attached?"

"No. The Republic screwed us, put us between two warring factions."

"Three, if you count the SOG," Levin said.

"Sif wants us to go to Zhukov," she said. "She says Skadi is there and might help us find the gunny."

"You don't think Skadi will want *27* back, ma'am?"

Winters scowled. "She can't have it. Unless the gunny insists, but he'd better have a damned good reason if he does. I've always wanted my own ship."

Levin smiled as he looked around. "I could get used to something like this, ma'am, but then what? It isn't like we can run cargo, can we? The SOG strangles the free market. How would we do maintenance? What if we need a new engine or something?"

"Sergeant Levin?"

"Yes, ma'am?"

"You're a party pooper."

"Yes, ma'am."

"Good questions, though. We'll have to figure something out. You're right, we probably can't survive without support."

"But we can't be slaves either, ma'am. We need to find out more about the ghost colonies."

Winters nodded.

"So, Zhukov then?" Levin asked.

"We need to find the gunny, alive or dead. Marines don't leave Marines behind."

"Semper Fi," Levin said. "What about the prisoners? And Sif? Are we going to lock her down?"

"I don't know," Winters said.

They sat lost in their own thoughts for several minutes.

"Do you have a plan, ma'am?"

Winters sighed. "Yes, Sergeant. For now, we trust Sif but keep the others locked up. We'll go to Zhukov but stay out in deep space; we'll watch and wait. While we're watching, we can work on a better plan."

"If Sif is right, there's going to be a really nasty fight near Zhukov. Do you really want to go into something like that?"

"We know the Republic is going to be there. I don't want unwilling passengers on my ship any longer than necessary, and I'm damned sure not going to turn them over to the SOG."

"And Sif?" Levin asked.

Winters looked at the stars around her and shivered. It had nothing to do with the cold. She was alone in a strange world she did not yet understand. She had no home, no people, nothing. All she had was three fellow Marines, two of whom might be dead or dying.

"We'll see," Winters said. Could Sif be a friend? She obviously couldn't keep them safe, but then who could? Is that what she wanted? Someone to keep her safe?

Winters laughed. "First, we find our brothers, then we'll figure out what the future holds. We're going to Zhukov."

"Semper Fi."

* * * * *

Chapter Forty-Six: Patriot

Gunnery Sergeant Wolf Mathison, USMC

Seeing Stathis lying under a control panel working on delicate electronics gave Gunnery Sergeant Mathison the heebie-jeebies. It took a lot of willpower to not go and make sure he wasn't sleeping, drawing inappropriate pictures, playing some game, or screwing with something he shouldn't be. After decades of dealing with privates and second lieutenants, it was against Mathison's nature to rely on Shrek or Freya to tell him if Stathis was screwing off. Would Shrek even report something like that? The SCBI was supposed to be loyal to Stathis. Would it help him slack off? He was so worried about Stathis it was hard to concentrate on what Freya was showing him.

The heavy presence of SOG Guardsmen ringing the base didn't help his confidence. The Guard units had brought along air defense artillery and there were a hundred thousand troops being shuttled down from orbit and deployed around the base and city.

"How's it going, PFC?" Mathison said.

"The SOG is composed of masochistic bastards, Gunny. They don't make this shit easy to work on. I used to tinker with circuit boards and stuff in high school, and that is nothing like this solid-state stuff. The SOG makes everything modular and tamper resistant."

"So, what's the problem?"

"I'm tampering, Gunny."

"And?"

Mathison barely heard Stathis sigh.

"It's designed to be replaced with a different part, Gunny, not modified."

"I have faith in you." It was a lie, mostly, but he felt it was an appropriate time to do so.

"Thanks, Gunny."

"He's doing a good job," Freya said.

"He had better. Screwing it up will just get us killed."

"As I was saying, the buildup in space is subtle, but it's there."

"So what? The SOG is probably always building up their forces. Hard to put boot heels on everyone's neck if you don't have enough boots with heels."

"So, if they were just going to hit a pirate base or something, they probably wouldn't need so much hardware. And they wouldn't be so sneaky about it."

"What's the story on the Golden Horde? How can they challenge the SOG?" Mathison asked.

"It's hard to read between the lines with the SOG propaganda. It looks like the Golden Horde was once closely allied with the Republic, but they parted ways about fifty or sixty years ago. The Golden Horde comes from a planet named Tengerin. After China conquered Mongolia, they deported dissidents to Tengerin, a harsh and barely habitable planet. The forced immigrants survived and thrived. When the Asian Union was absorbed by the SOG and the SOG began merging all the far-flung colonies, the people of Tengerin rebelled. About ninety years ago, the Vapaus Republic helped and ended up evacuating most of the population to a homestar."

"Was this parting amicable?"

"Mostly. The SOG still believes the two groups maintain relations, but they have seen no joint operations in over fifty years since an incident on a planet. I see a reference to an Operation Razor? The SOG believes there was a falling out but has confirmed no open hostilities between the two groups."

"So maybe they're going to ambush this Golden Horde?"

"I don't know," Freya said. *"I'll send you more information on the Golden Horde. There isn't much, though. The SOG thinks they're more morally bankrupt than the Republic, and that they go crazy with cybernetics."*

Mathison's internal display indicated a received file. He opened it and began reading.

The Golden Horde was certainly more militaristic and aggressive than the Vapaus Republic, based on the reports. The Horde conducted a large number of raids and whenever they struck, they tended to eradicate any resistance with extreme prejudice. What really caught Mathison's eye was that the Golden Horde seemed obsessed with cybernetics and robots. Unlike the Republic or the SOG itself, the Golden Horde relied on robotics to an extent that made the SOG think they were working on artificial intelligence. The Horde used a tribal system led by a single ruler. Mathison wasn't sure about the rest, though. Cannibalistic, incestuous, subhuman intelligence, psychotic? It sounded like they were categorized using the same template that described the Republic.

"And we have a problem," Freya said as Mathison was reviewing the reports and trying to figure out if there was any truth in them.

"What kind of problem?"

"Captain Enlai Shan is on his way back from vacation. He just got a recall notice."

"Damn. Can you cancel or delay his flight? Is he taking civilian transportation?"

"Yes. I still have access to the civilian systems, and I have his ident codes since he left them on the system here. I'll just reroute his flight to another city."

"And his crew?"

Freya was silent for several minutes. *"They are still at their ideological re-assessment facility."*

"What is that?"

"It's a facility where they can send personnel to undergo indoctrination and evaluation. They aren't popular and are frequently used as a punishment. Some are no better than Nazi concentration camps."

"So, this Captain Shan doesn't trust his crew?"

"The SOG procedures state that when an entire crew is sent to an ideological re-assessment facility, the corresponding ship is grounded until assessment is complete. The commanding officer is temporarily re-assigned to standby duty. If there are no billets open, the captain may take a vacation. Rarely are there available billets for corvette captains."

"So, the prick sends his crew to an indoctrination facility while he goes on vacation?"

"So it seems," Freya said.

"Send him to the ass end of the planet if you can."

"His crew has been reported as minimally reliable. They are likely to be released early."

"I hate to do it, but can you delay them?"

"Maybe."

"Just in case, we need to be prepared," Mathison said.

How do you prepare for the captain of the ship you're trying to hijack coming back early? Tie him up and throw him in a closet? Were there closets on this boat?

* * * * *

Chapter Forty-Seven: Perimeter

Lojtnant Skadi – VRAEC

SOG troops were passing every couple of minutes. Skadi was sure Control Otto was counting, but Skadi didn't want to become depressed. She was sick and tired of this drab, boring apartment, with blue walls and red trim. The paint wasn't peeling, but only because it was covered in a lacquer to help protect it. Disgusting. Skadi was sick and tired of the dark blue drapes. Whoever had decorated this apartment had no fashion sense, or they hated people. It was pre-furnished, with cheap plastic furniture that was slightly less comfortable than the floor. The standard video screen covered a wall so the SOG could overwhelm people with propaganda. Watching the constant stream of public programming was mind numbing.

The local news reported that the valiant Guardsmen of the SOG were conducting a training exercise, using beautiful Zhukov City. They had taken over, even though the alert for Hermod had been taken down. This was no training exercise; the troops had live ammunition. There were no adapters on their weapons, and the troops behaved like they were worried about something.

Another armored personnel carrier drove by and made her think of the ones on Koros Nine. The hatches were closed so she couldn't tell if it was loaded or not. More than a few wheeled transports passed, and Skadi saw they were full of troops.

But Control Otto told her and her team to stay in place and keep a low profile. They were surrendering their initiative to the SOG. Didn't they see that? Time was not on the Republic's side.

How much longer before the Guards started going door to door? The Aesir had a few drones hidden around the area, and the Guardsmen were being watched every minute. When they cordoned off buildings and started searching, Skadi would know, but without a plan, that information would just be the final nail in their coffin.

All their gear was hidden, but if the shooting started, they would be able to get to it quick enough. Hopefully.

Vince, their MT protectee was even more nervous.

The wall video was full of pictures showing "valiant" Guardsmen in battle, helping needy people, or rescuing victims of pirate raids. Propaganda, pure and simple, with constant calls to remain calm and cooperate with the training exercise, which might seem real. Everything was fine, of course, and there was absolutely nothing to be worried about.

Only the absence of Peacekeepers kept Skadi calm. She had only seen standard Guard units. There weren't even any Orbital Drop Troopers, and if INSEC were present they were well hidden. The Peacekeepers and ODTs wouldn't be deployed until they had a firm target.

Bern was busy with his cracker unit, trying to tap into the local SOG channels. He had piped it through the Aesir link into some custom software that usually allowed him to crack the local channels, but so far they were useless.

For whatever reason, the SOG troops were intent on searching the sewers and basements for bodies. Skadi wished them well. So far, none had ventured into the apartments or any of the housing complexes.

"Maybe it *is* a training exercise," Vili said. "With live ammo. If I had to guess, I would say some general is pissed at them and is making them slog through the sewers."

"It shouldn't take them long to search the sewers, though," Niels said. "They have plenty of drones."

"The officers don't seem to be using them," Vili said.

"No drones? What are they looking for?" Bern asked.

"Nothing up here," Niels said. "It's all in the sewers."

"Unless they're setting a trap," Vili said. "Saturate the sewers with drones and sensors so we can't escape that way."

"What's with sunset?" Vili asked. "Why do most of the troops only come out at night. You think that's when they'll start going door to door?"

"Not unless they're coming up out of the sewers," Bern said. "I have several drones out. I see them scanning buildings, but they haven't entered any of them."

"Well," Skadi said. "We need to get food. We might have enough for a few more days before we have to start eating our bedding."

"I'm tiring of noodles," Vili said.

"That is the staple of Zhukov," Bern said.

"No wonder they're such little people," Vili said.

Vince started pacing again.

"What kind of trap are they setting?" Vince asked.

"No idea," Niels said. "It makes little sense."

"Contact," Bern said, catching Skadi's attention. Her eyes locked on the big Aesir.

"What?" Skadi picked up a headset to listen. All she heard was yelling and firing.

"They're fighting someone," Bern said. "Not sure who."

"Where are they?" Skadi asked.

"Sewers I think," Bern said. "7977th Guards regiment. I can't get video."

The screams and yells and gunfire continued. It didn't sound good, but whoever the Guards were fighting appeared to retreat.

"Is there a rebellion or something?" Bern asked. "Something we missed?"

"Remember Nugget?" Skadi asked. "How the creatures used the subways?"

"You think they're here?" Niels asked.

"I'm starting to," Skadi said.

"Didn't they end up nuking Nugget?" Niels asked.

"The whole planet from the sounds of it," Bern said. "Might happen here because these boys took heavy casualties fighting, whatever it was."

Outside, sirens pierced the night accompanied by the wail of an ambulance.

"So, who's winning?" Skadi asked.

"We really need to get the hell out of here," Niels said. "I don't think the SOG is going to win, and I would hate to be at ground zero when they discover that."

"Anything from Control Otto?" Skadi asked.

"Nothing," Niels said. "They're telling us to shelter in place; they're still working on an extraction plan."

Skadi scowled as she glanced at Vince pacing around the apartment. Were they being hung out to dry? Sacrificed? The MT was usually very good about taking care of their people, but was Vince and Skadi's team expendable?

"What was your mission?" Skadi asked Vince.

Vince paused his pacing. "I can't tell you."

"You'll tell the SOG interrogators when they capture and break you," Skadi said.

Vince opened his mouth, closed it, then resuming his pacing.

"Are you expendable to the MT?" Skadi asked him. The rest of her team watched the exchange.

"Of course not," Vince said.

"Do you think my team is expendable?" Skadi asked.

Vince's pause was all the answer Skadi needed but he said quickly, "Of course not. Nobody's expendable."

Skadi burst out laughing. Vince was too naïve or a terrible liar; he must be new to MT.

"If the Guard is fighting those creatures in the sewers and underground tunnels," Niels said, "we need to get out of here. We still don't know how that plague, or whatever it is, spreads."

"Could we be spreading it?" Skadi asked.

The Aesir looked at each other.

"Paska," Vili said. "Like plague carriers?"

Vince looked at them, worried.

"We went through extensive biowarfare analysis aboard *15* after Koros Nine," Niels said. "Extensive. I'm pretty sure if it was something like a virus or bacteria, we would have discovered it."

Skadi stared at the video screen, not seeing it.

Hermod had gone missing on Green Hope, which was where the Marines had gone. Now both Hermod and Gunnery Sergeant Mathison were on Zhukov and it looked like there was a plague or something similar taking over the planet. It was similar to what had happened aboard the secret base where the Marines had been found, and what had happened on TCG and Curitiba.

Sif was afraid of something destroying intelligent life, a great filter that eradicated all intelligent life on a planet. Could this be it? Some plague? Was Nasaraf spreading it somehow? How did the Marines play into this?

Paska. And she was stuck here, a nursemaid for an MT agent in a city that was being torn apart with no option except to hope her controller could come up with a plan to get them out.

Gunfire erupted outside their window.

* * * * *

Chapter Forty-Eight: Visitor

Gunnery Sergeant Wolf Mathison, USMC

When Freya woke him it wasn't exactly unpleasant, but it was always disconcerting. One minute he was deep asleep and dreaming, but then reality would intrude, dragging him up from the depth as the familiar voice whispered in his mind.

"Bad news. We have a problem," Freya said.

Mathison looked at the time on the wall next to his bed. He had been asleep for three hours. His fingers and back hurt from leaning over a keyboard and monitor getting Freya connected to the hard wire link of the ship.

The SOG was absolutely paranoid about mutinies and had fail safes within fail safes. The captain of a ship had a lot of control, so much control that when they replaced the captain, they had to replace most of the central data nodes. The captain was the god of their vessel. Even the executive officer was restricted, and they had to circumvent all those controls. Without the duly authorized captain, a ship was almost crippled. Mathison and Freya and Stathis and Shrek had been working every minute for the last couple of days trying to get control of the ship. It was a very slow process, but some things could not be rushed.

"Are Guardsmen on the way?" Mathison asked, sitting up and holstering his sidearm, which he had kept under the pillow. He even slept in his armor these days. If they were discovered, they would be overwhelmed, and Mathison wanted to make damned sure they killed him instead of capturing him.

"No, but Captain Shan is on his way. He just got off a transport."

"I thought you rerouted him?" Mathison said. *Damn.*

"He pulled rank and orders to get aboard a military transport. Every available ship is being prepped. The SOG is trying to be covert about it, but they are gearing up."

"So, the shit is about to hit the fan in space?"

"And the city. We have a much better link into the SOG systems now, and it appears they are still hunting Hermod. They believe he has been infected like the creatures on TCG. The commander of the Tupolev *Task Force is throwing his weight around. He's reporting a courier from Green Hope was hijacked and carried the virus from there. There is also a concern that the Republic is behind it."*

Mathison swore as he made his way to the bridge. All day, robots had been delivering and loading the ship with everything Freya and Shrek could get their digital hands on. There were a few robots on the corvette to handle basic tasks, and twice Stathis had gone out in a crewman's uniform to take custody of things. So far, he hadn't screwed up, and Mathison almost trusted him.

"What are we going to do, Gunny?"

"When he boards, we take him prisoner."

"The 2048th corvette squadron is having an all-captain's briefing tomorrow morning. Classified stuff."

"How do you know?" Mathison asked.

Stathis looked a little sheepish. "I checked his schedule. We have access to his personal account. Not much information, but a little. That stuff is wireless."

"Where?" Mathison asked sitting in the captain's chair.

"The meeting is online. What about having our SCBIs fabricate evidence of treason against him? Get him arrested?" Stathis asked.

"Then investigators will show up to search his ship and quarters," Mathison said.

"Just lock the door and keep him from coming in?" Stathis asked.

"Just as bad," Mathison said. "He'll get Guardsmen involved and set off a bunch of alarms." *"How long until we have full control?"* Mathison asked Freya.

"If we cut corners, maybe tomorrow afternoon."

Crap.

"He's boarding a transport for this ship now," Freya reported.

"What kind of transport?"

"Small, four-person transport. Automated."

"Can you control it?"

"Yes, but I can only delay so long before he decides to just walk."

"What about causing a fatal accident?"

"No. It's against my programming. I'm not a killer."

"Can you pass control to me?"

"Yes," Freya said, and Mathison imagined she sounded reluctant. *"I will put an overlay on your cybernetics so you can see what the transport sees. Your hand motions will control it like you are controlling a drone. Until you do something, it will follow its programming."*

A transparent viewscreen wrapped around Mathison's view. The colors were odd, but Mathison knew he was seeing something a human wasn't expected to see. A throttle indicated maximum speed. A light flashed, showing safety protocols had been disabled. Nearby, a corvette was on approach to land. Mathison might have smiled if this wasn't murder. There were two other SOG space officers in the transport with Captain Shan, but Mathison had no sympathy for them. All were captains.

He was forcefully disconnected when the corvette landed.

* * * * *

Chapter Forty-Nine: Tristan's Visitor

SOG Scientist Tristan Malloy

The vessel was VRS *Ovela Kostaja* and Tristan didn't know what to make of anything. Some Republic soldiers kidnapped him, along with Skadi and the Aesir, then another group rescued him. As near as he could tell he was just baggage. Now Skadi was gone, off to do whatever, and he was stuck on a Republic cruiser twiddling his thumbs and hoping someone would at least tell him before he was killed.

The only positive was that he hadn't seen the alien in weeks. It was as if when the Republic had whisked him away from Nugget, they had left the alien behind. There was so much he didn't want to think about, but they wouldn't give him enough alcohol so he could drink his way into oblivion. Instead, he was stuck with an endless number of videos and games. The Republic had asked him about the alien but then quickly seemed to forget about him and it.

Now, the *Ovela Kostaja* was lurking in deep space near some SOG system. Tristan didn't know which system, and he didn't want to know. They had promised him refuge and citizenship if he helped them, but so far he had only helped the Republic reduce their food stores and life support. He felt useless, powerless, and it was almost a relief when he felt the alien presence in the passenger lounge. He looked up from his drink and saw the alien.

Nobody else was present, not that that ever stopped the alien from appearing. Only he could see it, and Tristan was becoming more and more confident that he was going crazy.

"What?" Tristan asked, as if he would understand it any better than before.

"Crisis continues within you," it thought to him.

"As if I don't know? You're a figment of my imagination; I see that now. I just don't know why."

"This entity inscription within you. Initial influx of sanctorium bastille. Stableness contingent on reacquire of dimensional incarnate refuge."

"You make no sense."

"Enlightenment troublesome. Abundant evolution. You visualize expressions troublesome to recognize. Duration implies more cognizance."

"Whatever." Tristan looked at his drink.

"Negative ruination is purposed at you. Prevent unhindering of devourers. You are obliged to divulge. Additional unhindering imminent."

"I don't get it."

"Failure is excessive resurgence and oblivion."

"One would think that with time you'd get better at this."

"Negation of tangible cogitation feature hinders extensive cogitation."

"Which means what?"

"No brain." Tristan laughed, but the creature did not look amused. It looked frustrated. Its lips twisted, showing the creature's teeth as its eyelids lowered.

"Yeah, you sound stupid."

"Negation inadequate cogitation. Affirm adequate tangible faculty for interface with dimension."

"You're coming from another dimension?"

"Semi-permanent affirmation, inadequate continuation."

"Why are you bothering me? Why not bother someone else? Why not somebody who understands you?"

"This entity inscription within you. Interface melded through initialization and inscription.'

"Are you dead?"

"Permanent affirmation. Transition halted. End of line. Continuation prohibited due to influx and transfer to oblivion initiated by devourers."

'What are the devourers?"

"Initial origin correspondent dimension. Transition is conquest. Oblivion is aspiration. Adjudication dictated by sphere of causality."

'From another dimension?"

"Permanent affirmation."

"What do they want here?"

"Initiation of oblivion through conquest. Quest for ultimate transition."

'So, these devourers are from another dimension, and they want to conquer this one?"

"Initial section query, permanent affirmation. Secondary section query inadequate continuation. Progression is cyclic. Devourers association with dimensional migrants cyclic and inconsistent based on adequacy of tangible faculty of host and thrall."

'So, they come and go?"

"Semi-permanent affirmation, inadequate continuation."

"What is your name?"

"End of line reached. Identification irrelevant. Transition halted and oblivion imminent. Devourer victory pending."

"Were those devourers on Nugget?"

"Minimal affirmation. Thrall host in transition by directive of devourer primeval archetype. Devourer primeval archetype end of line. Transition confirmed as continuation undesirable. Unbindering of primeval archetype desired for undesirable transitory phase."

"They were servants of the devourers?"

"High permanence. Primeval archetype dictates host thrall conformation and end of line."

"How many of these devourers are there?"

"Defined sum is inadequate. Infinite across continuum. Multiple origin inconsistent with definition."

"So, how do we fight them?"

"Halt transition into dimension, limit tangible cogitation faculty. Host thrall cumulation yields ballast. Host thralls gain resolute intensity with cumulation."

"How do we kill them?"

"Complete end of line and transition cessation impossible. Eviction from sphere of causality is volatile. Dimensional cycles unpredictable, dictated by archetype casualty not accessible to current causality adjudication and entity tangible faculty. Imminent cycle merge unpredictable in duration utilizing durability. Previous merges of causality random and enfeebled by merge distance. Species experienced inadequate merge of causality. Species consciousness limited by longevity and understanding of dimensional adjudication. Merges noted in species knowledge, inadequate confirmation. End of line, end of merge. Enfeebled merge limited by limited host thrall cumulation required for full devourer primeval archetype tangibility. Defeat of devourer archetype implied omitting permanent confirmation."

"Can we kill them?"

"Negative affirmation. Complete ruination inconsistent with adjudication of archetype causality."

"Where have you been?"

"Dimensional interaction cycles unpredictable. Current entity interaction with inscription vulnerable to causality random enfeeblement. Time is localized causality construct of causality adjudication. Adjudication implied but inconsistent with current inscription interaction."

Tristan scowled. Maybe a different question? "So, they can kill us, but we can't kill them?"

"Ruination dependent on individual origin of entity, not dictated by localized causality. Query implies inadequate understanding of causality creation source. Current causality dictated by interaction of merging spheres of adjudication."

"Can you say how many devourers have been released?"

"Merge durability unmeasured by distance. Multiple devourers in conflict caused by thrall accumulation. Devourer primeval archetype intangibility in question. Full comprehension of infinite inadequate. Seven devourers tangible as causality violator assessed. More devourer primeval archetypes endangering causality consistency and integrity. Threats initiated in coincidence with transition to inanimate causality construct. Transition associated with causality weakness. Exploitation of causality integration enables vulnerability and entry to localized adjudication by devourer primeval archetype."

"There are seven like Nasaraf?"

"Nasaraf is a unique devourer primeval archetype. Seven unique primeval archetypes violate causality and adjudication. Additional primeval archetypes await violation and usurpation of causality adjudication."

The lounge door opened, and a Republic agent walked in. His name was Kari Ramo, but that was all Tristan knew about him.

Kari froze in the doorway as his eyes locked on the alien, and his hand dropped to the sidearm on his hip. The alien turned toward Kari but Tristan didn't know if they spoke.

"Who is that?" Kari said cautiously. He looked ready to shoot the alien.

"You can see him?" Tristan asked. Someone else could see the alien? Did this mean he wasn't crazy?

"Yes," Kari said cautiously. "How did he get here?"

"How can he see you?" Tristan asked the creature.

"Entity does not originate in current causality and translates adjudication."

"You can talk with it?" Kari asked.

"You can't hear it?" Tristan asked.

Kari looked at Tristan and shook his head, then looked back at the creature. Tristan couldn't read Kari's face or body language.

"He's an alien?" Tristan asked the creature, referring to Kari. Kari looked human to him.

"New entity did not originate in current causality within dimensional adjudication. Multiple transitions have been detected, implying corruption and adjustment of source cognizance. Destination transition not identifiable. New entity accepts multiple sources of adjudication and causality."

Tristan wasn't sure what to think. Were there other members of the Republic who were aliens?

The other door to the lounge opened and a pair of burly soldiers rushed in. They weren't armored, but both carried rifles.

Tristan froze and waited for them to tell him what to do. He knew any sudden movement would be met with violence. The two Aesir were big, like they had been genetically modified or something on a scale like some Guards and Peacekeepers were.

Both soldiers swept the room with their rifles and looked at Kari.

Confused, Kari pointed at the alien, but it was obvious to Tristan they couldn't see it. He wondered how had Kari summoned them?

"Really?" Kari said. The two soldiers scrutinized where he was pointing. "You don't see anything, Aesir Theisen?"

"Sorry, sir, I see nothing."

Kari looked thoughtfully at Tristan as the two Aesir checked the room again. The one named Theisen was a large, intelligent-looking brute with sharp eyes; he seemed eager to find a threat, like he was letting Kari down by not finding one.

"Okay," Kari said. "Carry on, gentlemen."

The two soldiers looked confused for a few moments before filing back out.

"So, you can hear him?" Kari asked.

"In my mind," Tristan said.

"What's he saying?" Kari asked.

"I'm never sure," Tristan said.

Kari walked up to the alien and passed his hand through him. Tristan didn't miss Kari's shiver as if a frigid chill had passed down his spine.

"Maybe we should start again," Kari said, sitting where he could look at Tristan and the alien.

*****

Chapter Fifty: Zhukov System

Chief Warrant Officer Diamond Winters, USMC

Valkyrie 27, now rechristened the USS *Eagle*, slid into the Zhukov System. Winters and Levin sat at their consoles watching everything, trusting their SCBIs to tell them if they needed to do anything.

This was the first time Winters had entered an occupied system, so she wasn't sure what to expect. The goal was to transition into the outskirts of the system, past the local Kuiper belt, below the system's ecliptic, where she could look around and hopefully avoid any SOG or Republic ships. The chances of encountering another ship there should be astronomically low. Unlike previous transitions, she had to match the local system's movement, not something she'd ever encountered before. Like Sol, and every other body in the universe, the Zhukov system was hurtling through interstellar space at over eight hundred kilometers per hour. Just jumping into the vicinity wasn't enough because the solar system would zip right past you if gravity didn't rip you apart. Shorr, or wormhole space, was also moving, and they understood even less about that phenomenon, but it was noted and documented.

There was so much Winters had never expected with FTL travel. The first problems was that everything was moving; nothing was stationary. Everything was moving at high speeds. It was only the vast distances that made things appear stationary.

When someone looked at a star in space, they were looking at where that star was, thousands or even millions, of years ago. The distance and speed of the target had to be calculated in order to know where it was now. If that wasn't complicated enough, other objects could alter the trajectory of a solar system. Just because you could see a star didn't mean you could slip through a wormhole and arrive next to it. You really had to figure out exactly where it was based on speed and distance. The mathematic calculations were mind-boggling once you realized the distance between Earth and the Sun was an astronomical unit and the Solar System traveled that distance almost every week. If any calculations were off—the distance to be traveled, the movement of the target system, direction and distance—then the ship would arrive far outside the system. An additional jump was usually required to correct any mistakes, but that took time. Getting to the system was just half the problem if your velocity was off. It was far more difficult than managing a shuttle or gunship.

Information flooded into the bridge, and Winters looked skeptically at the readout. She assigned it to luck. *Eagle* had successfully arrived in the system and at the proper velocity. The astrogation files of *Eagle* were spot on, and Winters realized just how impossible it would be to find the rest of the Republic fleet.

Velocity was as important entering the wormhole as it was coming out. Which was why it sometimes took days between wormhole transitions. The ship had to match the velocity and direction of the destination star system so they wouldn't shoot out of it the second they arrived. There was also a very minuscule chance of trying to arrive in a physical body.

Eagle was right where Winters wanted it to be.

Numerous passive sensors reached out to learn about the system while the two Marines struggled to learn the basics. It would have been impossible without the SCBIs which could memorize manuals and procedures in microseconds.

"I'm not seeing any battles," Levin reported as he looked around. Sif was also looking, but the SCBIs were confident they had locked down what she could do.

Winters scanned the displays with Blitzen, putting an overlay on her vision of anything in the distance that was important. The Zhukov star was quite a distance away, and either the battle was occurring right now, or had occurred and the light from the explosions had passed them already. If the battle had not yet begun, then somewhere in this vast, lonely space was at least one Republic fleet.

Winters had spent most of the journey poring over space combat and tactics manuals, so she was relatively confident that she knew what to expect. Any attackers would approach from out-system behind waves of missiles and clouds of pellets. The attackers would push for a long duration acceleration then coast in. By the time the defenders saw the attackers decelerating, the first waves of pellets and missiles would be reaching their targets.

Current doctrine said there was no way to defend against an attacking fleet. Planets and their orbits were very predictable. Gravity gradients were also well known and predictable. It could take weeks for an attacking force to be detected.

Another option for attackers was to transition into the outer edge of a system, assemble, then transition into place on top of their target. The problem with this was that it gave the defenders a chance to shoot back and inflict casualties.

The SOG had almost perfected the deep space attack, and they kept themselves in form by hitting Torag systems, frequently eradicating all life on a planet to inspire fear and hopelessness in the Torag.

Finding a fleet in the outer system was nearly impossible; there were still plenty of undiscovered planetoids in the outer reaches of most systems.

"Now what, Captain?" Levin asked.

"We wait," Winters said. She liked that. Captain. Could she keep the ship and the title?

"I'll plot several jumps to take us in closer," Blitzen said.

"Thank you. I want to get closer, but we don't dare risk alerting anyone we're here."

"The chances of that are astronomically low."

"Didn't you say that about us being found after the Jefferson *was destroyed?"* Winters asked. Blitzen remained silent.

"Something very bad is happening," Sif said, staring toward the inhabited planet. "Something very bad."

"Is the attack starting?" Winters asked.

"No. Worse."

"Open the channels," Winters told Blitzen. *"Let's see if we can find out what's going on."*

* * * * *

Chapter Fifty-One: Fall of Zhukov

Lojtnant Skadi – VRAEC

Skadi opened the door for Vili, who had his hands full of groceries. The firefight the night before had been brief, and not even the drones had seen who had attacked the Guards.

"They didn't have as much as I expected," Vili said, handing the bags to Bern. "The clerk said shipments were being delayed. He didn't know if it was because of the military or something else."

"Nothing on the regular military channels," Bern said.

Skadi looked at the bags and wanted to scowl. Noodles. Lots of noodles.

"They didn't have anything other than noodles?" Skadi asked.

"Of course, they did," Vili said with a shrug. "I just didn't want to spend the extra scrip. Didn't want to draw attention to myself."

"You don't think buying a crate of noodles is unusual?" Skadi asked.

Vili shrugged. "That's what everyone else was getting. Two bags was small. I think people are getting noodles because they're cheapest and they store easily. If I had to guess, I would say people are preparing for the long haul."

"That isn't good," Skadi said. "Are they expecting a protracted siege?"

"Well, the sun is setting, and people are getting paranoid. There was lots of talk about people disappearing. I don't know how many people, though."

"Disappearing?" Skadi asked.

"Yeah. One clerk mentioned how she hadn't seen as many people as she would expect."

"If they're changing they probably would not go shopping," Niels said.

"That is what I was thinking," Vili said. "Any word about us getting out of here?"

A loud buzzer sounded, and everyone covered their ears. The video changed to an alert.

"Attention, full curfew is now in effect. Anyone except Guards on the street will be shot on sight. Hate-filled capitalist fascist elements of the Vapaus Republic have released a virus causing the wonderful citizens of Zhukov City to rebel. Under no circumstances is anyone allowed to leave their home. Guardsmen will sweep the neighborhoods looking for these vile, repugnant, evil dissidents, and they will provide food and critical supplies to our brave citizens. Anyone with special needs should contact their block warden immediately by phone. Anyone with pale skin and red eyes should be reported immediately to emergency services. Failure to comply will result in death."

"SOG is losing," Bern said.

"Paska," Vili said. "Nothing from control?"

Bern shook his head.

Gunfire erupted in the distance. Then the tempo increased.

Skadi looked out the window and watched an armored personnel carrier stop in front of the building but the ramp didn't drop. Another APC pulled up next to it, both turrets facing the street where Skadi heard the gunfire.

"That's close," Vili said.

"Armor up," Skadi said. "Full kit. Be ready to bug out."

"What about me?" Vince asked.

Skadi winced. They didn't have an armored suit for him. All he had were the clothes he was wearing, and they weren't exactly fresh after the last couple days. "Bern, you need to get Control Otto and tell them we may have to depart quickly; the fighting is starting up just outside our window. We need exfiltration *right now*."

"Zen," Bern said, stripping and pulling on his kit.

Skadi did the same. She kept looking out the window. The two APCs hadn't started firing, but the fighting down the street was getting more intense.

She was watching the APCs when a figure leapt off the roof of a nearby building onto the nearest one. Skadi zoomed in her view.

It was Hermod, but his skin was pale, and even from her position she could see his red flashing eyes as he leaned over and literally ripped the hatch off the APC turret. In the blink of an eye, he reached in and pulled out a Guardsman.

Skadi stared in shock as he pulled off the Guardsman's helmet and sank his teeth into the screaming man's throat.

She expected a spray of blood and she watched as Hermod held tight to his victim. Instead, the Aesir team leader sat back as if temporarily content. Another figure landed next to him and scrambled headfirst into the open hatch, moving with a speed that was unnatural.

Shuddering, Skadi stepped back.

"Hermod is outside," she said.

"Why does that sound like a bad thing?" Niels said.

"He isn't human anymore," Skadi said. She couldn't get his flashing red eyes and the commander tattoo on his pale skin out of her mind's eye.

"Paska-lounas," Vili said, testing the sling retention of his armor.

"I just watched him rip the hatch off an APC," Skadi said.

"Is he wearing armor?" Vili asked.

Skadi shook her head.

"Paska-lounas," Vili said. "What do we do?"

"We go to the spaceport," she said. "We need to get off planet. What does Otto say?"

"Control Otto is not responding," Bern said.

"Not responding?" Skadi asked, and Bern shook his head. "Do we have a link?"

"Yes, but Otto isn't listening or transmitting," Bern said. "We have a connection with five nodes."

"This is so much worse than Haberdash," Vili said. "At least there we had a ship to escape to. Do you think we can steal a SOG ship?"

Skadi swore. There would be no way to hijack a ship. She wasn't about to ditch their armor and weapons.

"Cancel that," she said. "We head out to the wilderness. We need transport."

"Do we have the coordinates for any nodes outside the city?" Bern asked.

"Get in touch with Otto and get some," Skadi said. "We can't stay here. Everyone and their grandmother will be trying to get to the spaceport to evacuate the planet."

"Why do you think that?" Vince asked.

"Because *that* is behind those APCs," Skadi said. She glanced outside and saw the second APC't turret hatch had been ripped off, but Hermod was nowhere in sight. "He is gone."

There was a body lying beside the APC, but Skadi could only see it was wearing a brown Guard's uniform. The gunfire in the distance was dying off. The shots were coming faster, but there was less of it. It sickened Skadi to realize the SOG was not winning, and for once, she wanted them to.

The Aesir put on their helmets and readied their weapons, scanning the doors and windows. Vince crouched behind Bern.

"The quickest way out of the city is to the north," Niels said.

"Toward the fighting," Vili said. "The space port is in the other direction. The creatures are trying to take the spaceport."

The ground shook and plaster fell as cracks appeared in the ceiling and walls. The video screen flickered and died. It was almost a relief, but the silence was ominous.

"What was that?" Vince asked trying to make himself smaller.

"Kinetic strike," Skadi said. "A few miles away. That's very bad."

"Never thought I'd root for the SOG," Vili said.

The ground shook again.

"We need to go! *Now!*" Skadi checked outside. There was no more gunfire but she saw movement in the shadows. SOG Guardsmen did not move that stealthily.

Then she saw someone, or something, break a window on the other side of the street.

Someone kicked the apartment door open, and Vili put a burst from his silenced wire gun into the creature's head. The creature fell backward, but another quickly took its place. Skadi fired a short burst and it collapsed.

The Aesir watched the door, waiting for another one to come in.

The one Skadi had shot was missing most of its head, but then it twitched and pulled its hands underneath it. Skadi stitched its spine with several rounds, shooting below the base of the skull. Outside, the other one sat up, and Vili shot it in the chest, center mass.

"When you kill them they're supposed to stay down," Vili said. "Were those bodies trying to get up?"

The one Skadi had shot was still trying to move.

"Out, now," Skadi said and led the way out the door. They were on the second floor so they could go out the window in case of an emergency, but Skadi was pretty sure that would be a bad idea right now. Wherever Hermod was, she wanted to go the opposite direction.

Who in their right mind kills by biting a man's throat? The Hermod she knew was well-versed in weapons. That thing he had become was a bloodthirsty monster that didn't need weapons.

* * * * *

Chapter Fifty-Two: Spaceport

Gunnery Sergeant Wolf Mathison, USMC

The sun set, and Mathison hoped things would quiet. Transports were still bringing down troops, but as soon as they landed, they headed into the city. From where *Patriot* was, Mathison could see troops moving around at the edge of the tarmac. The entire starport was now surrounded by a bunker system that was crammed full of Guardsmen. The spaceport perimeter looked like they were preparing for an attack.

Over the bridge speaker, Mathison was listening to Guards units being deployed. Based on what the Guards were saying, a team of Aesir had released a biowarfare agent among the civilians which made them attack the Guardsmen. Anybody with pale skin or red eyes was to be shot immediately and repeatedly. Headshots were recommended because body shots did not always drop the target fast enough.

Instead of things quieting down with the setting sun, Guardsmen were becoming more active. Most of the corvettes had already lifted for orbit except for three that had lost their captains. Mathison was looking at a nearly empty starport. Freya had blocked or delayed several attempts to order new captain's computers for the ships, and had finally sent the installation teams to a base far from the parts that needed to be installed. The corvette squadron commander was frustrated because he wanted to get his last three corvettes into space.

It was looking more and more likely that the commodore would just write them off because he did not dare come down in person.

Mathison watched the screens as several gunships slid into the sky and headed toward the city.

He felt the first artillery rounds being fired.

"Artillery, Gunny?" Stathis asked.

"I'm guessing things aren't going well," Mathison said, cycling through the different screens. Freya had tapped into the spaceport security systems, so he now had access to several thousand cameras.

There was a flash of light and the ground trembled.

"Kinetic strike," Mathison said. He pulled up a display and saw the impact zone was in the city. The SOG was launching kinetic strikes against neighborhoods now.

"They're going to lose, aren't they, Gunny?" Stathis said.

"Yes."

"Will we get out of here in time, Gunny?"

"Yes," Mathison said. "We're much better off than those Guardsmen. We've handled those creatures before."

"Aye, Gunny."

Mathison didn't like lying to Stathis. Two Marines, no matter how well armed and equipped, couldn't stand against hundreds, or thousands, of those creatures. There was interference with SOG communications as well, so the Marines were only getting part of the picture.

"How is the ship's integrity?" Mathison asked Freya.

"This corvette is an armored brick. We are locked up tight. They'll need heavy weapons to get in."

"If they're pushing back the Guards, they might have heavy weapons."

"We have received no incoming fire, so I can't say for sure," Freya said. *"But nothing on the Guard's channels indicates the enemy is heavily armed. They are numerous and hard to kill, but not well armed."*

"Show me the city," Mathison said, looking at the holographic plot in the center of the bridge.

The area lit up, showing the city wrapped around a bay. The spaceport was along the shore, where the heavier and more awkward ships could land in the water and dock at piers. About thirty kilometers to the north, the suburbs gave way to forested land, and in between were numerous warehouses, factories, schools, commissaries, hospitals, and recreation centers. Everything looked clean, pristine, and organized. Each block had its own commissary, recreation center, and other community facilities. Several blocks often shared schools and there was an occasional warehouse or factory that separated the blocks. To the west was more ocean, so the city sprawled to the east and then down and around the bay.

Freya began lighting up the different areas.

"Red is what the SOG Guard claims is under rebellion," Freya said. *"SOG-controlled regions are amber. I marked contested areas in flashing red and amber. This data is based on what I can hear. SOG communications are unreliable right now. It may be the attackers jamming communications."*

Mathison looked it over and noticed there was a lot of red. He watched as new areas started flashing.

"It looks like the creatures are waking up and engaging the SOG," Freya reported. More and more areas flashed. *"Communications are getting worse."*

"SOG is getting their ass kicked," Stathis observed and pointed at an area with a river running through it. "Do they know they're going to get cut off there?"

Mathison looked at it. There were three bridges, though two looked to be destroyed. There were several amber areas on the far side of the river and the red was moving to capture the last bridge. Freya popped up identifiers showing the SOG 882nd Guards Regiment was in that area. Another unit was holding the bridge. If the enemy made it there, they would cut off the 882nd.

"Maybe," Mathison said. "Not our problem, though. Maybe they'll get gunship support."

Mathison felt a rumble and black spots appeared to show more kinetic strikes.

"Gunny? What if they decide to blow up the corvettes so the creatures don't capture them?"

"Shut up, Stathis. I'm pretty sure our SCBIs thought about this." Freya remained silent and Mathison hoped she was busy.

Freya and Shrek had reprogrammed some of the smaller robots so Freya could manage some of the engineering herself instead of relying on Mathison or Stathis. Mathison wasn't really keen on giving them that much autonomy, but the only other real alternative was death. What had been really awkward was when Freya asked him to bleed a little on the robot so she could infect it with some of the nanites from his bloodstream.

Now Mathison watched the graph and saw the SOG slowly getting pushed back. He listened to the 882nd Guards Regiment get slaughtered after they were surrounded, and he listened to other units screaming for help or mercy as they were overrun by the enemy horde.

"No creatures with telekinesis," Mathison said around midnight.

"What, Gunny?"

"I have heard no reports of creatures using telekinesis. All the SOG Guardsmen reported that the enemy is fast moving, which makes them near impossible to kill. They look human except for the red eyes and pale skin."

"And mouths full of razor-sharp teeth, Gunny."

"Right. The creatures we fought on Nugget and at the secret SOG base were a lot less human."

"What does that mean?" Stathis asked.

"I don't know. Maybe the creatures are morphing to be more like humans?"

"But what's making them change and why?" Stathis asked.

"No idea," Mathison said as he watched Guardsmen retreat to the spaceport.

Around the space port, Guards engineers began flattening nearby buildings, allowing for better fields of fire. They were getting ready for a showdown. The nearby space elevator was in almost constant motion, going up and down. There were countless civilians huddling around the space elevator, waiting their turn.

"I kind of expected the SOG to abandon the civilians," Stathis said.

"This is Xray-niner," a voice said. "We can see at least twenty of them coming at us. We need more ammunition. Where's our support?"

"Xray-niner, this is Bravo-three," said another voice. "No support is available at this time. Pull back another block."

"Negative, Bravo-three," the first said. "Civilians are still evacuating. We'll hold a little longer."

"Negative, Xray-niner," the second voice said. "You are ordered to pull back, now."

"No copy, Bravo-three," the first voice said. "We will hold. Just a few more minutes. Shit. Here they come. There are more than twenty this time."

"Xray-niner, retreat, I say again retreat!" Bravo-three said. "Xray-niner? Respond, Xray-niner?"

"This is Xray-niner-three." This voice was hard to hear because of the constant fire of someone nearby. "Xray-niner is dead. We can't retreat. They cut us off. They are massacring the civilians. We will hold as long as we can. Maybe we can take more of these bastards with us. Long live the Social Organizational Governance!"

"Xray-niner-three," Bravo-three said, "I order you to retreat. I say again. Retreat! Xray-niner-three, how copy? Xray-niner-three, respond."

Mathison grunted in sympathy. This was a side of SOG he hadn't expected. The Guard was fighting hard and had to be inflicting heavy casualties, but they were still dying. Listening to them on the radio, there were plenty of them fighting and dying like heroes. Some were dying a coward's death, but there was plenty of heroism. Xray-niner was one example of many. Poor bastards.

There were fewer kinetic strikes, but the artillery continued nonstop and the gunships constantly strafed targets in the city.

"Gunny, you need to hear this," Stathis said, monitoring another channel. "Looks like other cities are experiencing similar outbreaks."

Mathison scowled as he listened to some general order a retreat from a city with about a million people a couple hours away. All the SOG troops were being pulled back to guard the space elevator and capital city.

A section of the starport perimeter began firing. Checking the cameras, Mathison saw fewer and fewer troops were coming through the fences. The starport would be heavily engaged by morning.

"If they think it is an infection," Stathis asked, "why aren't they checking people coming through the gates?"

"Dunno," Mathison said. "I haven't heard of any cases of a person just changing."

"That makes little sense."

"Maybe you should go ask one of the creatures."

"Only if you provide cover fire, Gunny."

Mathison grunted and went back to listening to the radio intercepts.

The situation got worse.

*****

Chapter Fifty-Three: River Route

Lojtnant Skadi – VRAEC

Hiding in a basement until the fighting passed them by didn't seem very brave, but then everyone, including Vince, was still alive. Screams from above told Skadi there had been civilians in the building who hadn't fled. The screaming didn't last long, though, and the creatures didn't seem intent on searching basements or attics.

She heard the constant hum of gunships and the *pop!* of their weapons as they strafed the streets. Artillery slammed into the area, but it quickly moved on, staying close to the active fighting. A small window let them see into the street.

"How could they assemble so many troops so fast?" Vili asked.

"SOG was calling it an infection," Niels said.

"What vector?" Vili asked.

Niels shook his head.

"The creatures will probably start a more methodical sweep to find and capture any survivors," Skadi said,

"So, you think the creatures plan on infecting everyone?" Niels asked.

"Why wouldn't they?" Skadi asked. "This is an invasion and a genocide. I haven't seen or heard anything from the creatures except a bloodthirsty desire to kill the uninfected."

"They don't seem that smart to me," Vince said.

"Hermod got here from Green Hope," Skadi said. "That takes intelligence."

Silence reigned as everyone thought about that.

"Nothing from Control?" Skadi asked and Bern shook his head.

"We've been abandoned," Vince said.

Skadi scowled, which Vince couldn't see because of her helmet. Was he right? What had happened to Control Otto?

It had been a long hard night as they hid in the apartment building's basement, and Skadi's nerves were frayed. They could still hear distant artillery fire, but the streets and buildings nearby were dark and silent. With no word from Control Otto, she knew they couldn't stay in the city. There was more movement outside as sunrise approached. A few civilians ran past, heading toward the spaceport. Skadi doubted most of them would survive. They seemed to be heading toward the fighting, not away from it. They were probably seeking the safety and security of the SOG forces.

When the sun rose, the streets looked deserted. Silence blanketed the city. Even the artillery had fallen silent. Had the spaceport been overrun or had the enemy finally been defeated?

Skadi didn't care. She just wanted out of the city. Maybe out in the forest or hills she could contact other Aesir or Republic forces. Zhukov City was too dangerous now.

Vili led the way. The Aesir moved out, with Vince in the center of the formation. They hugged the buildings and avoided open areas. Skadi felt the eyes that followed them, but nobody called out. Zhukov City had become a ghost town overnight. Even the bodies were gone. She looked inside the two APCs outside the apartment building and saw they were burned out and inoperative. Charred bones showed some people had died, but there were not nearly enough bones and no complete bodies.

"Where are the bodies?" Vili asked, but everyone remained silent.

"Maybe the creatures took them away to eat them?" Vince said.

"We'll figure it out later," Skadi said and pointed Vili toward a street. "Let's see if we can find transportation or something. I'll feel much better once we're out of this city."

"There's the river," Vili said. "Maybe we could find a boat?"

"We would be very exposed," Niels said.

"I haven't seen them shoot weapons," Niels said. "Or swim."

"Do it," Skadi said.

Everyone took cover as a pair of gunships flew overhead.

"Well," Vili said, "the SOG still controls the skies, if nothing else."

"I wonder how trigger-happy they are," Bern said.

"Let's not find out," Skadi said.

"You think they won't fire on a boat?" Niels asked, and Skadi swore.

"Keep your eyes open," Skadi said. "If we have to walk then we walk. We just need to get out of the city."

"This is a painajainen," Vili said. "Just a paska-painajainen."

"We aren't dead yet," Niels said.

"Yet," Vili said.

* * * * *

Chapter Fifty-Four: Sunrise

Gunnery Sergeant Wolf Mathison, USMC

By the time the sun's rays touched the skies, the gunfire around the perimeter had fallen silent. Mathison knew some creatures had made it into the bunkers despite the robotic guns, and the SOG was still removing the bodies and laying them out. The creatures were absolutely lethal in close quarters, or else the SOG troops were next to harmless. Three of the creatures' bodies were dragged out and burned. The four rows of SOG troopers in body bags made the math obvious. They placed the bodies in the area next to the *Patriot* where a corvette had sat a few days earlier.

After a few hours, there were well over a hundred bodies laid out, side by side.

All around them, people worked, but nobody approached the corvettes. One corvette had a crew, but Mathison watched them lock up their ship and head to the space elevator. Without a captain, the ship couldn't fly. The squadron commander had finally given up. The last Mathison heard, they had redirected the upgrade team to a base that had been overrun the night before. They wouldn't be coming.

"Good news, bad news," Freya reported at noon.

Mathison had only been expecting her to report they had full control of the *Patriot.*

"Good news first," Mathison said.

"Shrek and I have full control of the ship, lock, stock, and barrel. Additionally, we have several back doors planted in various systems so we can get remote control. Mutiny protocols will be worthless."

"The bad news?"

"The planet is now under interdiction. All ships that take off will be subject to boarding. Any ships not boarded and searched will be destroyed. We cannot be boarded and searched. People are being screened at the space elevator for infection, but from the sounds of it they aren't sure what they're looking for."

"So, we're stuck here?"

"For the moment."

"What if they decide to bomb us from orbit to make sure the creatures don't capture the ship?" Mathison asked.

"According to their systems, all the grounded corvettes are non-operational. I've added additional details about non-functional drives, burned out electrical systems, malfunctioning mutiny protocols that have locked the ship down, and I'm watching channels and notifications for any orders to destroy the spaceport. I think we are safe. All ships have also received a lockdown command to prevent anyone from boarding or otherwise using the ships. This command does not affect us."

"What's the planetary population of Zhukov?"

"Slightly over nine hundred million."

A lot of people were going to die. *"Any idea on how people are infected? Airborne? Touch? Injection?"*

"Nothing. The SOG is baffled by this. They have not detected any contagion. They have not captured a living subject, although they have body parts."

"Why don't they attack in the sunlight, Gunny?" Stathis asked.

Mathison shrugged. "Probably because they have better night vision. Smaller forces have the advantage at night. Darkness generates a lot of confusion for regular forces."

"The SOG has excellent night vision equipment, though, Gunny."

"Doesn't mean they are used to operating at night."

"Where did the enemy go, Gunny? SOG patrols are only finding bodies. No pasty skinned, red-eyed monsters."

"They probably pulled back to lick their wounds. They must have taken heavy casualties, and they aren't completely stupid. Maybe they're sweeping through the overrun areas, cleaning up civilian holdouts."

They cycled through the cameras and radio intercepts. The SOG was intent on strengthening the perimeter, and it sounded like it would take a few days for them to evacuate the remaining surviving civilians. Every elevator that went up was full of civilians. Everything that came down had supplies and food for those clustered on the tarmac waiting their turn.

Something was happening. The attack last night had been too fierce. What was the enemy up to?

Mathison and Stathis both dozed off while Freya and Shrek monitored the ongoing situation and continued exploiting the SOG hard links.

Mathison thought the SOG had beaten off the enemy attack, but then the sun set.

*****

Chapter Fifty-Five: Ghost Town

Lojtnant Skadi – VRAEC

Moving through the city was a disturbing experience. It was a ghost town. There were bloodstains, but no bodies. Some buildings had caught fire, but most fire suppressions systems still seemed to be working. Everything was quiet, and Skadi felt people watching them from the shadows. None of the buildings had power. Occasionally, gunships could be heard in the distance, but the Aesir didn't see or hear anybody else as they headed north through the streets.

None of the vehicles they found were operational. They were either burned out wrecks or intentionally sabotaged.

Control Otto had not come back online, and Skadi feared the worst.

The Aesir could be alone on the planet for all she knew. Only the distant gunships provided any evidence they weren't.

"Was everyone killed?" Vili asked during one break. "Or did they flee to the spaceport?"

Skadi shook her head as she stared around them. If the civilians had fled to the spaceport, then it was probably overcrowded, and the SOG would be struggling to feed and take care of everyone. Bern had found a commissary shop where they could take a break, but it had been ransacked. Again, there was blood but no bodies. Most of the food had been removed and what was left had been opened and ruined. Flies buzzed around, and Skadi had a hard time believing things had been normal the day before. Or had they?

Niels had a couple drones circling the area, watching for SOG gunships or patrols. He caught sight of a pair of teenagers furtively slipping from shadow to shadow, heading toward the spaceport, but there was nobody else.

"Where are they? Where are the bodies and the creatures?" Vili asked.

"Probably surrounding the spaceport," Skadi said.

"I don't hear any firing," Vili said. "Do you think the spaceport is still holding?"

"The gunships are coming from somewhere," Niels said. "The spaceport is well fortified because it also protects the space elevator. That will be a very tough nut for anyone to crack. The infected are probably licking their wounds, waiting for nightfall. Maybe that was their goal, to trap the SOG at the elevator."

"What about Control Otto?" Vili asked. "What do you think the deal is there?"

Niels looked at Skadi, and she shook her head. "They might have been planetside. They might have been overrun by the infected."

Vili shook his head. "Paska-lounas, this stinks. Makes me miss Haberdash or Lisbon. You would think they would have a backup system."

"We are Erikoisjoukot," Skadi said. "We do the impossible."

"Because someone has to," Bern said.

Aesir nodded.

Vince had found a coat and backpack, and was looking for food supplies, but he wasn't having much luck.

"We need to move out," Skadi said. "I want to be out of this city before nightfall. Those creatures are going to be scouring the city looking for survivors, and I don't want to be found."

"Zen," everyone echoed.

They weren't far from the edge of town, but sunset wasn't far either. A chill ran down Skadi's spine, and she knew if that they were still in the city when the sun set, they wouldn't live to see the sun come back up again.

*****

Chapter Fifty-Six: The Dead

Gunnery Sergeant Wolf Mathison, USMC

The sun was setting, and Mathison was confident nobody was going to bother them. The corvette was a veritable fortress.

Stathis was sitting in the XO's chair while Mathison sat in the captain's chair.

"What are you eating?" Mathison asked.

"Some noodle stew stuff, Gunny. We seem to have plenty of it. Want me to make you some?"

"No, I'll get my own in a few minutes. It smells good. The sun is setting."

The starport perimeter remained silent as the sun slid down behind the distant hills.

"Maybe they aren't going to attack, Gunny."

Mathison grunted as he cycled through the spaceport cameras.

"Gunny?" Stathis said, and the worry in his voice caught Mathison's attention.

"What?" Mathison looked at Stathis' view. It was focused on the rows of body bags next to the *Patriot.* The bags were moving.

Mathison watched as the dead Guardsmen, one by one, opened their bags. "Oh shit."

"Weren't they dead?" Stathis asked. "I thought they were dead!"

"That makes no sense," Mathison said. But maybe it did, and Mathison felt nauseous. It should have been obvious, but it made no sense. Not in this day and age.

The video from Hermod's team showed them finding bodies in a closed up school gym. The sun was starting to set when they discovered them. Then the bodies started moving. Seconds later communication had been lost.

"Gunny?" Stathis said as they watched the now-flickering cameras. The dead were pale with red eyes. They wasted no time spreading out and attacking nearby Guardsmen and civilians. They fell upon the surprised Guards; it was a slaughter. Mathison watched one Guardsman empty a magazine into one of them. The creature collapsed but got to its feet seconds later and lunged at the Guard.

All over the starport, wherever the dead bodies had been staged, it was a slaughter.

Mathison felt sick. He now knew how people were infected, even if he didn't understand it. And the enemy was now inside the perimeter.

"Gunny?" Stathis said again. "Those are freaking vampires!"

Mathison shook his head and wanted to argue, but Stathis didn't see him.

"Blood-sucking, unkillable vampires. How is that possible, Gunny?"

"Shut up, Stathis."

"If they're not vampires then what are they, Gunny?"

Mathison watched one of the newly risen creatures leap and land on a man and sink its fangs into the man's neck. Some blood spurted, but not enough. The creature began feeding. Mathison shuddered. What kind of hell was this?

"We need crosses and holy water," Stathis said, babbling. "I don't remember seeing any churches. There's no wood on this ship. We can't make stakes. Gunny, what are we going to do?"

"Shut up, Stathis."

"Freya?" Mathison asked.

"What we're seeing should be impossible. Maybe nanomachines? An infected attacker bites a victim and transfers the nanos to the target. The attacker gains sustenance, but the nanomachines in the victim replicate and animate the corpse."

"Probably nanomachines," Mathison told Stathis. "The vampire bites a victim and infects him. The machines work to reanimate the corpse."

"Is this ship airtight, Gunny? Can they turn into gaseous form and come get us?"

"This is a spaceship, Stathis. Think about it. We're safe."

"Nanomachines makes sense." Stathis started calming down. "How do we fight them? Why didn't they come out in the sunlight?"

"Freya?"

"Insufficient data. Might be a tactical decision. There are probably power limitations, and they need to recharge."

"Who knows," Mathison told Stathis. "Might be the same reason Marines prefer to attack at night and sleep during the day."

Stathis nodded. "Do you think I should make some crosses, Gunny?"

"Are you that stupid?" Mathison asked. "Do you think a cross will work against a tiny machine?"

"What if they're actual vampires, Gunny?"

"Listen to yourself, Stathis. How do you think vampires made it here? Do you think Count Dracula suddenly learned to make spaceships?"

"But—"

"But nothing. Some jackass mad scientist made the machines and got ideas from horror stories."

"Do you think the Republic did this?"

"Right now?" Mathison thought about Skadi and Sif. "I don't know, but I don't think that's the type of people Skadi, Sif, Bern, Niels, and all the others are. Not necessarily that Vanir general or the others. Not saying there aren't mad scientists in the Republic, but this doesn't seem like them."

"You sure, Gunny?" Stathis asked.

"No," Mathison said.

Once the slaughter ended, would the vampires try to break into *Patriot*? How would the SOG respond? Would they hit the spaceport with kinetic strikes?

Cameras started going offline as the reception deteriorated. Everywhere the Marines looked, people were being slaughtered. Finally, Mathison turned off the videos.

He didn't feel safe anymore knowing what was going on out there, but he knew they wouldn't be able to rip the door off the corvette. The infection gave the vampires strength, but no more strength than he had in his armor.

The SOG Guardsmen didn't have powered armor, so the vampires could rip the helmets off their prey. Only blazer weapons seemed to do much against the vampires, and the SOG didn't have many of them, preferring to arm most of their Guardsmen with traditional slug throwers or wire guns. If a Guardsman fired with a blazer the nearby vampires stopped what they were doing and killed the gunner. Regular weapons only dropped the vampires for a short amount of time.

Mathison felt like he was watching a bad horror film where the producer was trying to see how much gore and death he could get onto the screen.

He turned off the last monitor and sat there in silence.

Stathis stared at Mathison. "What are we going to do, Gunny?"

"We are going to survive, Stathis. We are Marines."

"Those are vampires though, Gunny."

"The USMC has never lost a war against vampires," Mathison said.

"When did we fight vampires?"

"Were there vampires in the United States? No. Vampires knew better than to mess with the United States."

Stathis looked at Mathison like he was going crazy.

Mathison smiled. "We will survive. The SOG couldn't kill us, the Republic couldn't capture us. I'll figure something out."

"Aye, Gunny," Stathis said, but he didn't sound convinced.

"We're also going to find Chief Winters and Sergeant Levin." *Somehow.*

"Aye, Gunny."

"Have I failed yet?"

"No, Gunny."

Mathison grunted.

Maybe he would have a better idea of what his options were in the morning. For now, he and Stathis were safe in the middle of a vampire-infested space port.

Vampires. Shit.

* * * * *

Chapter Fifty-Seven: The Forest

Lojtnant Skadi – VRAEC

The hills were rugged and thick with trees. It was harder going than Skadi had expected. Vince was hanging in there, but he wasn't in the same shape as the Aesir, and he didn't have powered armor to help him. Skadi was surprised he had lasted this long. The smell of pine was strong and relaxing, and when Skadi took off her helmet there was a slight chill that helped her focus. The stars twinkled above, and she wondered how many of them were SOG warships planning to drop nukes.

The sun had set almost an hour ago, but Skadi wanted to keep pushing on. She wanted to put as much distance between her team and Zhukov City as they could manage. The hills looked like ideal places to hide. The trees provided some cover from overhead observation and ground transport would have a difficult time following them, but walking was slow and difficult.

Vince found a stick and Bern was carrying the agent's backpack, but they had to rest soon, or Vince would collapse. Skadi felt her legs cramping, and she knew everyone was tiring. Powered armor was great, but it didn't do all the work for you. Going up and down hills still took its toll.

"Break time," Skadi said, pointing to a place at the side of the road that was uphill.

It was hard getting up the gradient, but once they were there the Aesir had a good view of the road going in both directions.

It was past midnight, and they had seen and heard no one. Not even the distant drone of gunships or artillery. Were they alone on the planet? Bern's drone showed nothing nearby, just a two-lane road that went on and on into the hills. Her maps said it led to a logging facility and some farms, but she did not know if they had been attacked, too.

"Grab some sleep," Skadi said. "Niels and I will take first watch. Bern and Vili, you have second."

"What about me?" Vince asked.

"You don't have any night vision gear," Skadi said, which was mostly true, but he looked too tired to be of use and probably needed the sleep more than the Aesir.

Vince scowled and nodded.

"I have cybernetics, but nothing like your helmets. Nothing from Control Otto?" Vince asked.

"Nothing," Niels said. "We've lost several relays, but we still have a few. Do you know where Control Otto was located?"

"No," Vince said. "Need to know, and I didn't."

Skadi nodded. Yeah. MT was like that. Kusipas.

"We aren't leaving this planet, are we?" Vince asked.

"I'm not looking to retire on a SOG world," Skadi said.

"Do you have a plan?" Vince asked.

"Don't die," Skadi said. "We improvise things from there."

Vince shook his head and looked around him, squinting into the darkness.

Vili and Bern wasted no time finding a flat place to sleep while Skadi and Niels sat back-to-back. It gave them both half the perimeter to watch and ensured they wouldn't fall asleep. Also, with their suits in physical contact, they could talk without anyone hearing them.

"Vili's right, this is a paska-lounas," Niels said on their private link.

"Yes."

"Before, we at least had a plan."

"Yes," Skadi said.

"Do you have a plan?"

"No. Except maybe stay alive until the attack. When the Republic fleet attacks, maybe we can contact them and get extraction."

"Will they come far enough in system, or will they just hit and run?" Niels asked. "We don't have enough troops for a planetary invasion."

"I don't know. Need to know, and we didn't."

"Maybe Zhukov is a good place to retire."

"You retire. I'm pretty sure that when the SOG comes back, it will be with overwhelming force, like Lisbon."

"You have to retire first."

"You want the team?" Skadi asked.

"Hell no, that commander's tattoo would ruin my boyish good looks."

Skadi laughed. Niels was full of shit.

One thing was certain, the SOG response wouldn't be coming this week, and a week was a long time to avoid detection. Her team didn't have enough food for a week, maybe three or four days, and tree bark wasn't any good. The logging facility might be the answer, unless the creatures were occupying it, but there had been no evidence so far that the creatures had left the city.

Niels and Skadi took turns flying the drone around the area. Skadi spotted some deer, which could help with their food problem. There were plenty of smaller animals, as well. The SOG had tried to import most of the Terran ecology, and that gave Skadi hope.

* * * * *

Chapter Fifty-Eight: Apocalypse

Gunnery Sergeant Wolf Mathison, USMC

Nobody had tried to get into the corvette, and when the sun rose the bodies and vampires disappeared into the buildings. Freya reported they had retreated into the bowels of the space elevator where there was a warren of warehouses and tunnels burrowed into the ground. None of the elevators were moving.

Looking through the few cameras showed them piles of bodies everywhere in the lower levels. There was no movement anywhere. All the bodies were covered in blood, but there were no wounds visible on any of them. The chests were not moving, not even with light breathing, and their temperatures were consistent with lifeless bodies. That many warm bodies should cause air conditioning to kick on or something. But with the blood-red emergency lighting and a consistent, unchanging temperature, Mathison had no reason to believe they weren't dead.

Nearby, a gunship was still burning where it had crashed. Trash littered the tarmac, discarded clothes, body bags, ammunition wrappers, rifles, armored vests, and other sundry gear were everywhere, frequently stained with blood and pieces of rotting flesh. Except for the trash blowing in the wind, there was no movement, no sound.

"Anything from the SOG?" Mathison asked.

"The only survivors I can detect are in orbit," Freya reported. *"You and Stathis might be the only living people on the planet, although there might be hundreds of thousands of others outside the big cities. There are several large fishing vessels out at sea that are untouched."*

Mathison felt nauseous. An entire planet? What would the vampires do next? What would the SOG do?

They had packed the orbital section of the space elevator full of survivors. Efforts were still underway to evacuate them to ships. The troop carriers were the best choice, but Freya was picking up a lot of traffic about an ongoing crisis in orbit. Life support was being strained, and there wasn't nearly enough food or water. People were rioting, and that only made things worse.

"I'm picking up chatter about nuking the spaceport," Freya said. *"Right now it's just chatter, but they're worried the vampires will somehow get up the cables."*

"Time frame?"

"Probably tomorrow, or maybe tonight."

"I need a trench coat, Gunny."

"What?" *A trench coat?*

"All the cool vampire hunters have them," Stathis said.

"Shut up, Stathis. You aren't cool. You are a PFC in the United States Marine Corps. You have to be a lance corporal before you're cool."

"Can I open the hatch for the robots, Gunny?" Stathis asked.

"Robots?"

"I had Shrek put in a request through the local system for more small-arms blazer rounds. There are still plenty of automated systems throughout the spaceport, including inventory control. There are some robots about to deliver several crates of blazers and rifles. Since everyone is dead, nobody is asking questions, and I noticed the vampires really did not like Guardsmen with blazers. I figured since the dead Guardsmen don't need them, we could use them."

Mathison opened his mouth to yell, then closed it. The cargo hatch was underneath, so any SOG satellites would just see the robot go under the corvette, they wouldn't see people. There were still some automated robots moving around the spaceport.

"Fine," Mathison said. "But don't let the robots leave. I don't want any watchers in orbit realizing we're here."

"Aye, Gunny."

"We need to get out of here," Mathison said to Freya.

"If we boost for orbit, they'll shoot us down. They are on alert. If their attention is focused elsewhere, maybe, but right now there are too many eyes watching the planet. I can't fool those or divert questions from real people."

"Then let's go somewhere else. Not a city. What's nearby that might have a place big enough to land this thing?"

"The closest point is a lumberyard about sixty kilometers away. There's usually just a small crew there that services the robots. There's a field large enough for us."

"Sounds good."

"You don't think the SOG will notice a corvette moving to the lumberyard?" Freya asked.

"You tell me."

"Yes, they will. We'll need to camouflage the ship when we get there."

"Stathis said the automated supply system is still working. Would painting the top of the corvette be sufficient?"

"Not from detailed scans."

"Then order some paint. I'm assuming you know the right colors."

"Yes. We'll have to move at night."

"Fine. I don't want to hang around here after darkness falls. The bloodsuckers might get curious."

"What if the SOG nukes the starport before nightfall?"

"If you hear they're going to strike then you get us out of here."

"*Aye, Gunny,*" Freya said.

*****

Chapter Fifty-Nine: Corvette

Lojtnant Skadi – VRAEC

Skadi decided not to follow the road. It was harder going, and several times they had to retrace their steps to find a way past obstacles, like a cliff or canyon, but following the road was the best way to run into creatures, SOG patrols, or even survivors. The lumberyard was about twenty kilometers away, and Skadi doubted they'd be able to get there by sunrise.

Everyone was tired, and Skadi couldn't remember being this sore in a long while. She had to keep the team moving, though. Day or night, she wanted to get to the lumberyard so she could assess it. Hopefully, it would be a good place for them to hunker down and wait for the Republic attack. She was undecided whether she wanted to reach it at night or during the day.

"Down, down, down," Bern said. "Something is coming our way."

"High or low?" Skadi asked. Was it airborne or on the ground?

"High," Bern said. "Too big to be a gunship."

Skadi tapped into Bern's drone and saw what it had spotted. A large black mass was gliding low over the treetops. Far too big to be a gunship, almost the size of a corvette.

"Paska," Vili said. "The SOG is going to secure the lumberyard."

Skadi nodded. That made the most sense.

Bern put the drone in a tree and had it hide so it could get a better look at the ship.

"Corvette," Niels said. "What's it doing out here?"

"Some covert operation, probably," Niels said. "If they're scanning they're going to pick up Vince like a bright light at night."

That was bad, but a corvette could get them off the planet if they could hijack it. Special operations craft might not have as many mutiny or hijack controls because by nature they were crewed and controlled only by the most loyal. Right?

"Nothing from Control Otto?" Skadi asked.

"Silence," Bern said.

Skadi powered up her radio and changed it to the Aesir emergency frequency. She set the power low so it had little strength, but if the corvette was listening it would hear them.

"Aesir, Aesir, Aesir," Skadi said on the frequency. "Bertta-paavo-sakari-kuu."

B-P-S-K was an Aesir distress code. If the corvette was Republic, they would know.

"Who is this?" a voice said.

"Authenticate jussi-kalle-risto," Skadi said. The voice sounded familiar.

"We don't have those codes," the voice said. "Who is this?"

"The corvette has stopped and is hovering," Bern said. "I think they detected Vince."

"Paska," Vili said, aiming his blazer carbine like it could threaten the corvette. Skadi held up her hand.

"Vili," Skadi said on the frequency.

"Vili is a guy," the voice said. "Skadi?"

"Gunnery Sergeant Mathison?" Skadi asked, recognizing the voice.

There was a pause.

"What happened to you?" Mathison asked.

"We escaped the city," Skadi said. "Who's with you?"

"Escaped?" Mathison said. "Right."

"What are you doing here, and why did you shoot at me?" Skadi asked. The corvette had to have enough weapons to destroy a grid square, and she was pretty sure it could pinpoint her location. Had she doomed her team to death? Skadi motioned for Niels to listen in on her radio. Niels nodded as he adjusted the radio on his wrist panel.

"Skadi," Mathison said. "I liked you. Really. Why did I shoot at you? Well, I figured you were working with Hermod. After toasting Hanz and exposing Hermod, I kinda figured we'd be persona non grata."

"You killed Hanz?" Skadi asked. This didn't make any sense.

"I watched Hermod and Hanz kill some cops; they ripped their throats out. Hanz went all vampire on me, so I think I've figured out a few things. Nothing personal. I'm sorry they got you, too."

"Wait." Was he getting ready to fire?

"Why?" Mathison said.

"We are still human."

"Right. Sorry, but I've never seen you so pale. Seems to be a characteristic of the undead."

"Undead?" Was Mathison mentally unbalanced? What was he talking about? Undead? Pale? Paska. "I was wearing makeup. I was undercover, working security. Pale was some stupid SOG fashion at that club."

"What were you doing there?" Mathison asked.

"They sent us to provide security for a Musta Toiminnot operation. Sometimes Erikoisjoukot get missions like that."

"Why weren't you at Green Hope?" Mathison asked. "Or did you get there after Stathis and I left? Did you join up with Hermod and come here?"

"What?" Skadi asked. "Is Sif with you? Bluebeard?"

The channel fell silent.

"Why are you here?" Mathison asked. "We expected you at Green Hope."

Niels shrugged.

"This is not a secure channel," Skadi said. "I can't discuss it on an open channel."

"Convenient," Mathison said.

"Wait!" Skadi said, trying to think of what she could say or do.

The channel fell silent again, but the ship didn't start moving.

"That's a SOG corvette," Niels said. "How did he get onto a SOG corvette?"

Skadi shook her head.

"Is Winters and Levin with you?" Mathison asked.

"No," Skadi said.

"How did they die?" Mathison asked.

"They aren't dead," Skadi said.

"Damn it, don't fuck with me. I've got half a mind to erase that valley from the map, and I don't give a damn if the SOG fleet sees me. Tell me the goddamned truth, you bloodthirsty bitch."

"I don't know what you are talking about," Skadi said. This wasn't like Mathison, was it? "We left home fleet and came here. Our ship would not take us to Green Hope. It got complicated after you escaped."

"Why?" Mathison asked.

"I can't tell you," Skadi said.

"SOG has an ambush prepared," Mathison said. Skadi heard the pain in his voice. "They know the Republic is going to attack this system, and they are ready, in space at any rate. Are the vampires part of your attack? The main attack or a diversion?"

"Vampires? Gunny, what are you talking about? You aren't making any sense," Skadi said. She felt like she was negotiating with a psychopath who was getting ready to kill her, and there wasn't a damn thing she could do. Broadcasting the mayday might have been one of her last mistakes. "Those creatures came from the *Pankhurst.* The Republic would never do something like that."

Skadi hoped that was true. The Vanir had captured her and tortured her. Would they sink low enough to release a biological agent on a civilian population?

How did the SOG know about the Republic attack? Did the Republic forces know? How did the gunnery sergeant know?

"It's moving again," Niels reported. Mathison must have decided. She checked, but it wasn't coming toward her. Maybe he would not cleanse the valley with fire.

"Are you going to kill the survivors at the lumberyard?" Mathison asked.

"There are survivors?" Skadi asked.

"I don't know," Mathison said. "We are going there. I will kill anything that approaches my ship at night. We have plenty of blazers. Hanz found out the hard way how effective blazers are."

"What the hell is he talking about?" Niels asked.

"I don't know," Skadi said. "But I don't think he is working for the SOG, and he has a ship. If we can keep him from killing us, we might be able to get off this death world."

"Big if," Niels said. "He tried to kill you once. I'm thinking he isn't sane anymore. Vampires?"

Skadi shrugged.

"Maybe you missed how he killed Hanz and revealed Hermod's presence to the SOG," Skadi said. "I need more information before I classify him as hullu. If he *is* right, the *Pankhurst* has been very busy."

*****

Chapter Sixty: Lumberyard

Gunnery Sergeant Wolf Mathison, USMC

Stay or go? Damn it. There wasn't enough nighttime for him to find another spot, unless he landed in a lake or something. And there was no guarantee it would be deep enough or that he could lift off again using the gravity drives. Working with Skadi, he had heard one story where *Tikari* got bogged down in the silt at the bottom of a river and she had been forced to use explosives to break free. He didn't want to use explosives on *Patriot.* He was confident the SOG ship wasn't half as robust as a Republic ship.

Getting far away from Skadi would solve a lot of the problems he was having.

Freya slid the corvette into an empty space at the lumberyard. The yard itself had a large open area covered in a sprayed foam concrete. Freya had warned him the corvette would probably ruin the concrete, but it was better than nothing.

When it settled to the ground, Mathison felt the concrete crack but the corvette didn't sink too far, and Freya assured him they could still take off. No vampires came running at them from the silent buildings which made Mathison feel better.

The second the ship stopped moving, Mathison and Stathis leapt out of the top hatch and moved to different corners. Small, knee-high maintenance robots on wheels followed them out. While Stathis and Mathison kept watch, the robots wasted no time pouring paint over the top of the ship. In the distance, Mathison spotted the lumberyard offices. There were no lights and no hint that anybody was present. Mathison expected to see streaks of white, fast moving vampires, coming at him at any second.

"You think they can get through our armor, Gunny?"

"Let's not give them a chance to try."

"I ate a lot of garlic before we landed, Gunny. Now I wish the filters in this helmet did a better job with bad breath, and it's giving me gas. Do you think it would help if I smeared some of that garlic butter on my suit?"

"Stathis?"

"Yes, Gunny?"

"Shut up and watch your sector."

"Aye, Gunny."

When the first rays of the sun touched the clouds above the lumberyard, the robots had finished. As paint jobs went, it looked horrible up close, but at a distance, hopefully, it would be much less obvious.

Back inside, Mathison felt a lot better. If Skadi had been making good time, she probably wouldn't arrive until a couple of hours after sunrise. If she was still human. Mathison wasn't convinced. Why hadn't she made up a story about Winters and Levin?

"You still think she is telling the truth?" Mathison asked Freya.

"Yes. There was stress in her voice, but everything was consistent with what we know about her. If she has turned, then she's in full control of herself."

"Hermod was in control, too. I guess we will see. Do you think the vampires can be active during the day?"

"Do you think they're really vampires? We have so little information."

"They seemed pretty inert and dead during the day. The video from Hermod's team and Valkyrie 19 *seems consistent. Maybe they look and act normal during the day."*

"Do you know how stupid that sounds?" Freya asked. *"Vampires? In this day and age? They would have eradicated life on Earth if they had existed there. I'm sure there is a more scientific explanation."*

"The creatures on the SOG space station didn't morph into vampires. On Nugget, they were also very non-human, and they came out during the day. Those creatures also had telekinesis. On Curitiba they were also very different."

"It makes little sense unless there's some kind of intelligence seeking to eradicate humanity using our own fears and myths," Freya said.

"What myths did the creatures in Nugget come from?"

"Maybe it is learning?"

"What if more than one of those creatures escaped from that prison?"

"More creatures from the prison? Why would they be different?"

Mathison shrugged. *"Just thinking."*

"Are you there?" Skadi asked on the Aesir emergency frequency. Triangulation equipment on *Patriot* pinpointed her location as six hundred meters away, near the lumberyard offices. The corvette didn't have any ground-to-ground weapons except for some point defense turrets. Mathison realized the ship was a lot more vulnerable on the ground, but unless Skadi had heavy weapons, she wasn't getting in. Hanz had died. If Skadi had changed, she would die, too.

"Yes," Mathison said.

He checked the board in front of his chair which showed a map of the area. It marked her location in amber and Freya was working to get a firing solution on her position with the point defense turrets.

The sun rose as Mathison watched. Using *Patriot's* sensors, Mathison picked up a single figure. Was she alone?

"Are you alone?" Mathison asked.

"Why did you shoot at me?" Skadi asked, avoiding Mathison's question.

"If you had seen Hanz move as he came to bite me, you would understand."

"He really tried to kill you?"

"Yes. It was very hard to miss the pale skin and red eyes. He was a big guy. When the spaceport was overrun, we got to see more vampires in action. They're hard to kill without blazers. I was lucky that I had my blazer with me when Hans tried to get intimate. Why were you there?"

"I was working with an MT operative to contact the black market," Skadi said.

"Why didn't you come to Green Hope?" Mathison asked.

"Not on an open channel," Skadi said.

"Keep her talking," Freya told Mathison. *"I'm analyzing her speech pattern. I might be able to detect any lies."*

"Then tell me what happened after I shot at you," Mathison said.

Several minutes later, Freya seemed convinced Skadi was telling the truth. What she said matched what the Marines had learned of the SOG defenses. Mathison's biggest problem, aside from Hermod talking to the cops, was that he hadn't seen any of the vampires who swarmed the starport speak or otherwise communicate. Now Freya had eyes on her, and it didn't surprise Mathison that *Patriot's* systems couldn't detect Skadi because she and her team were armored, but visually Freya was able to pick up the smudges of moving people with active camouflage. It looked like her entire team was present, along with a single person who didn't have armor.

Skadi walked into the open, her helmet off, and let Mathison see she was no longer pale, and her eyes definitely were not red. She had bags under her eyes and looked tired, but makeup could do a lot.

"She isn't catching fire in the sunlight," Stathis said, but Mathison ignored him.

"Freya?" Mathison asked.

"Everything seems consistent with what we can verify," Freya said. *"Shrek and I agree, there is a ninety-six percent chance she is not a vampire."*

"Four percent she is?" Mathison asked.

"Based on current data," Freya said, *"we can't give you a hundred percent. If you want a hundred percent, shoot her dead and see if she gets back up?"*

"I'll pass," Mathison said.

"I'll need to see the rest of your team," Mathison said.

Skadi nodded.

* * * * *

Chapter Sixty-One: At the Lumberyard

Lojtnant Skadi – VRAEC

Skadi could see Mathison was nervous as she led her team aboard the corvette. Both Marines were armored with trauma plates and blazer carbines. Skadi also knew that most SOG vessels had internal anti-boarding systems that could be activated on the captain's command, and she was confident that Mathison and his SCBI would know those systems and have them under their control.

In all her years fighting the SOG, she had never been aboard a fully operational ship. She had fought through ships before, but they had usually been grounded and disabled. The HKT teams would be more versed on SOG anti-boarding systems and attack methods, but for Skadi, it was a surreal experience. She could sense the ship's network, but it was not offering her a network handshake or link offer.

The recreation room was small and cramped under normal conditions, but filled with oversized Aesir warriors, it was claustrophobic. Her team still had their helmets off so Mathison could confirm none of them were vampires, but he had not yet removed his. Skadi let it slide. He was holding all the cards right now, and he had trusted her and Sif. Now it was her turn to return the favor.

Hours later, she had explained most of what had happened, from their escape to the departure aboard the Nakija/Vanir cruiser. Then her team listened intently as Mathison and Stathis described their own experiences.

The videos of the vampires swarming the spaceport were frightening.

"What are your plans now?" Skadi asked.

"Find Chief Winters and Sergeant Levin," Mathison said. "Then I'm of half a mind to strike out and see what's on the other side of the galaxy."

"Really?" Vili asked, earning a frown from Mathison.

"No," Mathison said. "That's sarcasm. One of the many services I provide."

Vili laughed, but Skadi didn't find it amusing.

"The SOG Space Fleet is going on alert," Stathis reported. "They appear to be under attack."

"It has begun," Mathison told Skadi and headed for the bridge.

She followed him and saw it was cramped and unpleasant. There wasn't enough room for everyone, so she motioned for the others to go find places to sit while she and Niels took seats. The others returned to crash seats in the lounge.

Zooming out, the holographic display in front of Mathison's seat showed amber flashes, and Skadi tried to make sense of the SOG icons and display.

"We have an escape vector. Take us to orbit," Mathison said.

"Acknowledged," a strange voice said over the speaker system, surprising Skadi and Niels.

The holographic display showed the ship's escape vector. Light amber bubbles showed the location of the SOG fleets and their estimated sensor range.

"We still have access to the SOG battle net," Mathison said. "Information from their networks is streaming in. We can't inject anything without transmitting, but they are broadcasting encrypted data."

"And you have the encryption keys?" Skadi asked.

"Yep," Mathison said as the corvette lifted off. She could see the projected course, and it looked like Mathison was going to keep the planet between the ship and the SOG fleet.

Three new ships appeared in high orbit, already inside the SOG corvette screen. The SOG had them identified, but they were not obeying commands or responding. They were massive merchant ships, slow, ponderous, and laden with cargo pods, almost the size of a dreadnought. One had gone missing a few weeks ago according to the data Freya was pulling from the SOG battle net and displaying on a screen nearby.

"What's the Republic planning?" Mathison asked.

Skadi had no idea. Putting those three tugs so close to the planet was impressive, though. She hadn't known the Republic could do that.

"Freya," Mathison said, "start deploying the radio drones."

"What drones?" Skadi asked trying to remember the drone complement of a corvette.

"Sif gave us some frequencies to use," Mathison said. "I would like to warn the Republic about the trap."

Skadi said, "On the Aesir frequencies, transmit: This is Team Skadi. Authentication vihtori-kuu-zeta-aarne. Keep repeating that if you can. It's a code only my team knows that indicates a trap. If the Vanir hear it, they will understand."

Mathison looked at her for several seconds, then nodded.

"What are they doing?" Stathis asked, pointing to the display. "Boarding pods? The Republic is trying to board SOG ships?"

Alerts were going out across the SOG net that the cargo containers had shattered, and numerous pods were breaking off. Any humans aboard the pods would be jellified by the acceleration, though.

"Golden Horde, maybe?" Skadi said. "They have some method of boarding with robots. I didn't know they were this advanced, though."

One of the cargo ships flashed out of existence as missiles from the dreadnoughts slammed into it.

Seconds later, the other two cargo ships flashed into oblivion.

Numerous alerts went out over the net, warning ships to take evasive action and prepare for boarders.

"Alert," Freya said as the space high above *Patriot* lit with red lights.

"Shit," Mathison said.

A fleet was transitioning in on the back side of the planet in the SOG fleet's blind spot.

Beacons identified the ship, and Skadi saw one that froze her blood.

The *Pankhurst.*

There were several other ships as well, SOG warships that may have been from the Tau Ceti Gold defense force.

"Warn the SOG," Mathison said before Skadi could stop him. "Broadcast our sensor data on the SOG networks. They have to know."

"The SOG is now picking up missile volleys coming in from deep space," Freya announced.

Mathison turned to Skadi, his hand on his sidearm.

"Is the Republic now in league with Nasaraf?" Mathison asked.

"No," Skadi said. But were they? How could they be?

"Can we make an emergency jump?" Mathison asked.

"Negative," Freya said over the speakers. "We are still too deep in the gravity well. The vanhat fleet is launching missiles. Trajectory shows they will use the planet's gravity well to accelerate them at the SOG fleet."

"No routes out?" Mathison asked.

"Negative," Freya said. "I would recommend diving back into the atmosphere. Maybe they will ignore us."

An alarm went off, indicating the corvette was being targeted.

"Maybe not," Freya amended. "A corvette is breaking off from the fleet and coming our way."

"Just one? I've got this," Stathis said. "Give me weapons free, Gunny."

"Weapons free. Let's see what the *Patriot* can do."

Patriot was heading away from the vanhat ships, but the one corvette was on intercept.

"That is no longer a SOG vessel," Freya reported. "It is accelerating hard enough to kill any humans aboard."

"Do unto others before they do unto us, Stathis," Mathison said.

Skadi tried to remain calm. There wasn't a damn thing she could do except watch. Maybe linking up with Mathison hadn't been such a good idea.

*****

Chapter Sixty-Two: Space

Kapten Sif – VRAEC, Nakija Musta Toiminnot

Sif watched Chief Winters as the Marine maneuvered the ship closer to the planet Zhukov. The SOG fleet around the planet wasn't the smallest or the largest but they had a substantial layered corvette screen. It looked to be a standard deployment, with corvettes patrolling the lanes most likely to be used by incoming ships or missiles. Most ships preferred to conserve energy and use standard gravitational wakes and waves to maneuver. Long-range missile attacks relied on the same waves. Not using the gravity of the stars and planets required more fuel and energy. Missiles relied on a propellant since they were too small for mounted power plants, which meant they had a limited range and ability to maneuver.

Winters acted like a seasoned *Valkyrie* captain. Sif didn't know how much of that was Winters and how much was her AI, but it was a sobering experience to see someone from a pre-FTL society transition into the modern era using current technologies like a long-time veteran. Sergeant Levin was a rock for the chief, and Sif sensed his loyalty to the Marines like a physical force.

The prisoners were well-treated, and Levin was strictly professional when dealing with the Jaegers, never giving them an inch or an opportunity to escape. Sif had spoken with Sloss several times, and she sensed a grudging respect in the veteran Aesir team leader. She could also tell the Jaegers would seek to escape at the first opportunity and take control of *Eagle*. It was a tightrope between preventing the Aesir from escaping, which would lead to bloodshed, and not betraying them to support the Marines, though she knew she could find ways to justify it.

It was difficult doing what was best for the Republic, but like the Vanir who had betrayed them, it was all a matter of perspective and belief. The Vanir's betrayal had taught her that. They and their righteousness caused her to doubt her own righteousness. It was too easy to tell others you were doing it for their own good, but wasn't that robbing them of the choice? A certainty that you knew better than them?

Her indecision kept her following the Marines. They moved and acted with a sense of purpose she had lost, but that could be a trap too. It was easy to trust the actions of people you trusted. So many people got into the habit of trusting others. Sif knew this. Knew it to her core. But the Vanir's betrayal had cut her deeply.

The SOG fleet went on alert before the reason was obvious to *Eagle*. Ships appeared in the upper atmosphere, within the screen of corvettes. At first, they appeared to be dreadnoughts, but then the power profiles showed they were simply large transport ships. Although the transition had been closer to the planet than expected, Sif was about to dismiss it until missiles started launching from the SOG fleet and the merchant ships appeared to explode into a mass of pods aimed at the surrounding ships.

Chief Winters moved *Eagle* closer.

"We are decrypting SOG communications," Winters said.

"You aren't worried we might get caught between the Republic and the SOG?" Sif asked.

Winters glanced at her with a small smile. "Step outside, look around and tell me what you think the chances are of that?"

Winters was right. Space was vast and *Eagle* was keeping her distance from Zhukov, a quarter AU away, so the chance of being detected was minuscule. Everything *Eagle* was seeing had occurred over two minutes ago.

"I'm getting something on Aesir channels," Levin said.

"—eam Skadi. Authentication vihtori-kuu-zeta-aarne."

Skadi was alive? And here?

Winters looked at Sif. "What does that authentication mean?"

Sif shook her head. "Each team has a unique set of codes. The Vanir have them, but they keep them secure. I don't know those codes."

"Which we don't have," the chief said, her eyes locked on the holographic display.

"Zoom display on the far side," Winters said.

Ships were transitioning into orbit on the opposite side of the planet from the SOG fleet. Blitzen tagged them as Force Two. They would be in an excellent position to ambush the fleet currently fighting off the boarding pods.

"Republic?" the chief asked.

"I didn't know we could transition in so close to a planet," Sif said.

The space around the SOG fleet was chaos, and it was hard to see what was happening with all the explosions.

Moments after Force Two transitioned into space, another fleet transitioned in, higher than the first. It was much larger and dwarfed the first SOG fleet. Blitzen tagged it as Force Three.

"If Force Two was Republic ships," Winters said, "they just got boxed in by another SOG fleet."

Sif winced. How far did the Vanir betrayal go? The fleet in the lower orbit would be mauled by the one with the higher orbit. The first SOG fleet coming around the planet would be a hammer to shatter the trapped fleet. Was she watching the death of the Vanir?

Identification started coming in on the trapped fleet. Most of the trapped ships in Force Two were SOG.

"A civil war?" Levin asked.

Then one ship was flagged as the *Pankhurst*.

More alerts appeared as *Eagle* detected hard burns from incoming missiles.

Too much was happening to make sense of everything, but the trapped fleet wasn't being destroyed. Meanwhile, SOG ships were starting to maintain course and ceased firing. Some of those SOG ships fired on their fellow SOG vessels in support of the trapped fleet.

Even at this distance, Sif could feel the evil, the hatred, the desire to dominate.

"That trapped fleet, Force Two, contains the *Pankhurst*," Levin said. "SOG vessels in Force One and Three are firing at each other."

Sif felt an undercurrent of fear and panic seep through the hatred.

The *Pankhurst* and other ships launched drop pods toward the planet. The *Tiananmen* launched drop pods as it skirted the battle before changing course toward deep space.

Shortly after the *Tiananmen* retreated into wormhole space more SOG ships fled, leaving about half their number behind.

"Two more fleets inbound," Levin said, and the screen zoomed out. "I'm getting ID on one. Force Four is the Republic. The other fleet, designated Force Five, is the Golden Horde?"

"Sometime allies of the Republic," Sif said.

Missiles from both fleets slammed into the SOG survivors who had not fled, and the crew of *Eagle* watched as the fleet, led by the *Pankhurst*, accelerated toward the Golden Horde ships in Force Five.

Without warning, both the Republic and Golden Horde fleets transitioned into wormhole space and Sif let out a sigh of relief. She didn't want to think about what would have happened if the fleet containing the *Pankhurst* had reached the Republic. Someone was paying attention.

"Smarter than I expected," Winters said.

"They probably saw what happened to the SOG fleets too, ma'am," Levin said. "They should know what happened in Tau Ceti. Nasaraf can take over ships from a distance."

"They're also probably shitting their collective pants," Winters said. "Maintain stealth. Let's see what happens, but if they notice us or start in our direction, we are leaving. The gunny might still be on that planet."

"The *Tupolev* and the *Tiananmen* both escaped," Levin said.

"But the *Tiananmen* sent down a bunch of drop pods," Winters said. "Maybe a battalion, which means if the gunny is still with them, he could be on the planet or on the *Tiananmen*."

"Yes, ma'am," Levin said.

"Since we don't know where the *Tiananmen* went, we will stay and watch," Winters said.

"But if he's on the planet," Sif said, "we don't have a stealth craft to rescue him."

"Let's watch and see," Winters said. "I'll bet the gunny could make a shuttle out of duct tape, shoe polish, and cardboard if he had to."

Sif raised an eyebrow.

"Some Marine staff NCOs are like that," Winters said smiling. "I'll bet Gunny is one of them."

"He is, ma'am," Levin said. "He certainly is."

* * * * *

Chapter Sixty-Three: Battle of Four Fleets

Gunnery Sergeant Wolf Mathison, USMC

Of all the bad things that could happen, Mathison had to watch Stathis try to shoot the incoming corvette as he listened to the SOG battle fleet deal with boarders. Apparently, the boarders were not humans or robots, but a description of "monsters" did not give Mathison much information. People were also complaining about malfunctions, bleeding consoles, and demonic ghosts. It sounded like when the *Pankhurst* was first attacked.

The corvette coming at them, identified as "68402," seemed to effortlessly dodge Stathis' fire.

"Can't you let Shrek help?" Mathison asked.

"He is," Stathis said. "That is one slippery bastard, Gunny."

68402 was not firing and that worried Mathison. Was it going to ram them?

A chill ran down Mathison's spine and he felt a sense of wrongness about everything. What was happening? He checked the board. Were they getting ready to transition into a wormhole?

The missiles coming in from deep space heading for the SOG fleet were being intercepted by the corvette screen and fighter drones, but based on the panic he was hearing, there were problems getting the drone fighters away, there was interference and electronics weren't working right.

"The drones are now broadcasting," Freya said. "We are getting polled by the SOG, but I think they're a little too busy to ask us too many questions. They are thanking us for the warning, though."

The corvette screen was dying as missiles targeted them instead of the larger ships. All the SOG vessels were sending out a wall of half millimeter pellets to hit incoming missiles. There were too many incoming missiles and not nearly enough counter-missile fire.

"Those poor bastards," Skadi said, looking at the SOG fleet. They were going to get hit from two angles, from the vanhat and the Republic.

"They're too low in the gravity well to escape," Niels said. "The corvette screen is also way out of position. The Vanir aren't working with the vanhat, are they?"

"Those bastards better not be," Skadi said.

Turbulence rocked *Patriot* and Mathison heard whispers too faint to make out the words.

"I've got a bad feeling about this, Gunny," Stathis said.

Orbit was absolute chaos. Too much happening, too many groups, too quickly.

"Kill the bastard, then," Mathison said.

"I'm trying, Gunny." Stathis sounded worried. "I can't hit the bastard, though. He's too slippery."

The SOG long-range sensors showed two fleets coming in from different angles. Both had pirate icons, but one fleet was the Vapaus Republic and the other was the Golden Horde. They had a screen of lighter ships in front and Mathison saw several ships larger than the dreadnoughts: three Vanir battlestars.

Nasaraf's ships were coming around and the vanhat missiles slammed into the SOG fleet like a shotgun blast. Countless missiles exploded when they slammed into the screen of pellets, but many made it through. The SOG anti-missile missiles tried to stop the remaining ordnance, but they were near worthless. Numerous ships exploded, but not as many as Mathison would have expected.

Out of the corner of his eye, Mathison saw something float through the wall, but when he turned to look at it disappeared.

"I'm going hullu," Niels said.

"Wormhole effect," Skadi said. "Nothing is real."

"We aren't in a wormhole," Niels said.

The whisper became louder. Mathison still couldn't make out what it was saying, but he heard the anger and hate.

"I'm losing control of the ship," Freya said. "Something is interfering with the systems."

"You really need to kill that ship, Stathis," Mathison said.

"I'm a Marine, not a freaking squidbert, Gunny. I think I need to stick with rifles."

"Spacebert," Mathison said, correcting Stathis. "And you are a Marine. Marines kill things with whatever tools they have. And that thing needs to die."

"We're starting to drop like a rock. I don't have control. Power failure, control plane failure."

A beam leapt from the attacking corvette and slashed the side of *Patriot.* The ship shuddered and Mathison wondered if he was going to die because *Patriot* crashed or because the enemy corvette shot them to pieces.

The console started to bleed. Mathison stared at it. That couldn't be blood. No. He had pulled that console apart. There was nothing red in there, and there was no reason for it to bleed.

"Do something," Skadi said. "Can't your SCBIs do something?"

"More emergences," Freya reported. "Almost right above us in high orbit."

Or they'd be shot down by the additional forces, and there wasn't a damn thing he could do. Another beam from the corvette reached out and cut into *Patriot.*

"New emergences identified as SOG," Freya reported.

Crap.

"They're engaging Nasaraf forces," Freya reported. "We are in range. I'm counting a force of six dreadnoughts and numerous battleships, battle cruisers, and destroyers."

"Oh Gods," Skadi said, watching what was arriving.

The vanhat ships turned and headed toward the new SOG fleet.

Then, something that should have been impossible, a battleship noticed the corvette attacking *Patriot* and fired at it. Mathison expected it to fire at them at any moment.

Corvette 68402 spun and dodged but the combined fire from Stathis and the battleship were too much and it erupted in a fireball.

"Control is returning but we are no longer space worthy," Freya reported. "I think I can crash without killing us."

"If they don't shoot us down first," Mathison said.

"Incoming transmission from the battleship," Freya said. "This isn't good."

"This is the SOG *Tupolev* to corvette 7082. You are hereby ordered to stand to and prepare to be boarded or you will be destroyed."

"Seriously?" Stathis said.

"Open a link," Mathison said, hating the SOG with every fiber of his being. To be saved and betrayed so suddenly.

"*Tupolev*, this is *Patriot.* We cannot comply. You can either shoot us out of the sky or pick up our pieces after we crash. Your choice."

"Identify yourself," another voice said.

The ground was coming up fast. At least the console had stopped bleeding. There were no good options.

"This is Gunnery Sergeant Wolf Mathison of the United States Marine Corps. Go ahead and shoot. Even if we could heave-to we wouldn't. You bastards won't capture us alive, not again."

"Ooorah," Stathis said, but his heart wasn't in it.

"Is Skadi with you?" the *Tupolev* asked.

Surprised, Mathison looked at Skadi.

"You know him?" Mathison asked her.

Skadi shook her head.

"None of your business," Mathison said, letting his anger out. "Are you going to shoot? I've seen the SOG shoot; I'm not impressed. I'll bet we slam into the ground first. You guys suck."

The *Tupolev* remained silent as *Patriot* plummeted planetward.

"Do you have any control?" Mathison asked Freya.

"Some. Are you trying *to get the* Tupolev *to shoot us?"*

"I would rather get shot than fall to my death." Mathison felt the straps through his armor as gravity took hold of the ship. He never liked those amusement rides where it felt like you were falling. Like now.

"It isn't the fall that kills you, Gunny."

"Yeah. It's the sudden stop at the end. Har-har, Private. Now shut up so I can die in peace."

"PFC, Gunny. You promoted me."

"Private First Class is still a private."

"Can't you two be a little more relevant?" Skadi asked. "Your conversation is pointless and doesn't help."

"Why? Do you think there's something we can do about our situation? Maybe get out and flap our arms? It's a little too late to try the bean burrito blast off technique."

Stathis held onto his seat with his eyes closed. "Gunny, you and the lojtnant might have a few seconds if you want to share a moment."

"Hold on," Freya said.

Mathison didn't know what she was talking about. He was holding on.

Patriot lurched hard and slammed everyone into their seats. A roar drowned out everything and Mathison was thankful his helmet was on, or he would have been deafened. His stomach spun, and he wanted to vomit. He closed his eyes, which didn't help, but neither did opening them. For a second, the ship was in free fall, then it slammed into something again, then again before sinking slightly.

There was a sudden jerk, and *Patriot* stopped moving.

"Oh shit," Stathis said, groaning.

Mathison waited for the ship to move again. The red emergency lights were on, and he expected the gravity to shift any second, that the ship would reach its limit and fall again.

"*This ship won't fly again*," Freya said.

"*I may never walk again. You kind of alluded to that when you said it was no longer spaceworthy*," Mathison said. "*And then we fell*."

"Oh shit," Stathis said again.

"What?" Mathison said.

"I was just joking, Gunny, about you and the lojtnant. Please don't kill me."

"You've just been busted back to private," Mathison said, trying not to show his relief.

"I guess you win your bet with the *Tupolev*," Niels said.

"Damn," Mathison said.

"There's a small city about six kilometers away," Freya reported. *"I don't know if that's good or bad. We're several hundred kilometers from Zhukov City, but I didn't see any lights on in the city during our fall."*

"*Is it day or night here?*" Mathison asked, though he thought he should know.

"Night."

"What are the chances the Tupolev *lost track of us?"* Mathison asked, unbuckling.

"Not good."

"We need to get out of here ASAP," Mathison said. "There could be a kinetic strike on its way right now."

"Or Peacekeeper assault shuttles and gunships," Skadi said.

"Gunny?"

"What, Private?"

"I think you should stick to being a gunnery sergeant. I hate to tell you this, but as a ship's captain, you suck."

"Thank you, Admiral Stathis, for that wonderful gem of knowledge," Mathison said patiently. "If it's any consolation, you're just as competent a spacer as a Marine private fresh out of boot camp."

"Really?" Stathis said, sitting up and sounding hopeful.

"No, you're worse," Mathison said. "Now, shut up. We need to get out of here."

"Oh," Skadi said.

Mathison heard a tone in her voice that couldn't be good. "What?"

"Vince," Skadi said. "He didn't make it."

"I'm sorry," Mathison said.

"He had no armor," Skadi said. "Bern is seriously injured. Vili is trying to help him now. His arm and shoulder are crushed."

"How bad?" Mathison asked.

"It is bad, but he should live. Shattered arm and ribs. His legs are fine," Skadi said. "He's being filled with pain killers. Not sure if we can save the arm, but we probably won't have to carry him; his nanites are working."

"Let's get out of here, then," Mathison said. "Stathis, I want you to grab as much ammo as you can carry. Also, get some of those SOG blazer carbines and at least one of the long rifles."

"Aye, Gunny." Stathis pulled himself to his feet. He wasn't as steady or fast as Mathison expected, but he understood when he tried to stand. *Patriot* was tilted at a slight angle and his bones and muscles felt like jelly. The adrenaline was draining from his system, and he was exhausted.

*****

Chapter Sixty-Four: Gunny

Kapten Sif – VRAEC, Nakija Musta Toiminnot

The bridge was quiet as everyone watched the ships circle Zhukov. The SOG and the Republic had left, and Sif wasn't sure either would come back.

Half the SOG ships had not fled and were now flying with the fleet that included the *Pankhurst.* There was no formation and no apparent organization to the fleet. It was merely a mob of ships that somehow avoided colliding with each other. The passive sensors couldn't pick up any radio communications between the ships so they were using tight beam or something else, and that bothered Sif on several levels. They were not human, or they would be using a recognizable technology, but if they were using a different technology, why were they stealing human ships?

"The gunny is alive," Levin said smiling.

"How do you know?" Sif asked.

"My SCBI is getting a transmission on an Aesir emergency frequency," Levin said.

"In the clear?" Sif asked.

Levin smiled. "Encrypted. It'll probably take the SOG a few decades to decrypt it."

"What do you mean?" Sif asked.

"It's a language only the SCBIs understand," Levin said. "Then it's encrypted with encryption keys they share."

"Why is the language important?" Sif asked.

Winters smiled. "SCBIs are not human. They can talk at a more basic, more intuitive level. It's not the first time machines have communicated with each other in a language people can't understand. I think there was a company in the early twenty-first century that was experimenting. They shut down the experiment when two of their AIs started talking to each other in a language the developers couldn't understand. It scared the crap out of them."

Sif nodded, but thinking about it was disconcerting. It had been easier to think of the SCBIs as smarter versions of people, but if they could develop and use their own language? They frequently talked with each other but preferred to communicate only with their host.

"It doesn't scare you?" Sif asked, trying to sense the mood and attitude of the SCBI.

She thought Winter's SCBI felt amused, as did Winters herself, but Levin and his AI seemed distracted. It was something to consider. How tightly were the SCBIs integrated and dependent on their host?

"Maybe if I thought about it too deeply," Winters said. "But honestly, it's more like having a close friend who has other close friends who you don't talk to."

"So, you trust your SCBI?" Sif asked.

"Completely," Winters answered. "I haven't seen a reason not to."

"What did the gunnery sergeant say?" Sif asked.

"Well, Freya reported that he and Stathis were alive. He has linked up with Skadi, but the planet Zhukov is overrun."

"Where is he now?" Sif asked.

"The last transmission indicated that they were going to crash land on Zhukov," Winters said. "Freya reported she thinks they are likely to survive the crash. There's been nothing since then except a notification that Gunny, Stathis, and Skadi's team are still alive. Too much static after that."

"Do we know where?" Sif asked.

"Vaguely," Winters brought up a display of the planet and zoomed in on the northern hemisphere. "Near a place named Glastown. Looks like the same place the SOG sent an ODT battalion."

Sif looked between Winters and Levin. She didn't like the implications of that.

"Do you have a plan?" Sif asked.

"No," Winters said. Then, "Well, yes… The problem is that we don't have ground to space capability."

"Well, Chief, maybe the Gunny can arrange something. We just need to get word to him that we're here and what capabilities we have."

Winters nodded. "Can we put a comm package on a drone?"

"Lilith says we can. I'll get to work on it."

"And those vanhat-controlled cruisers in orbit?" Sif asked.

"Those might be a problem," Winters said. "But we need to review our options."

*****

Chapter Sixty-Five: The Forest 2

Lojtnant Skadi – VRAEC

This part of Zhukov was hilly and covered with plenty of trees, but there was far too much rock and rugged terrain for it to be useful for anything other than growing the short, stunted pine trees, sycamores, and lichen. This far north probably got more snow than usual. Skadi hated the snow more than the desert. Not that she hated the cold, she was usually wearing powered armor. You couldn't walk through the snow without leaving tracks. Rugged terrain like this just slowed everyone down.

It wasn't summer, though there was a lot of green. It was chilly and everything was damp, like it had rained recently. She was tempted to remove her helmet to breathe the fresh air, but without sampling for biological warfare threats, she didn't dare.

Looking up wasn't helpful. Gray clouds covered the sky, hiding the stars and the ongoing battle. It looked like a meteor shower, but those weren't meteors.

"Drop pods," Niels said.

"This mission, without a doubt, is worse than Haberdash and Lisbon," Vili said. "Paska-lounas for everyone. This is so not good."

Skadi stumbled and almost fell because she was looking at the sky instead of where she was going. "SOG or Nasaraf?"

"I would like to discourage that line of questioning, Skadi, ma'am," Stathis said.

"Really?" Skadi said.

"Yes, ma'am. Because if I know the gunny, I'll be the one who has to go ask. I don't think either of them would be friendly."

"Stop calling me ma'am. I'm not your mother."

"You are old enough to be my great-great-great-great-grandmother though," Stathis said. "I'll bet if my grammy knew I wasn't respecting my elders, she'd beat me."

Skadi heard Vili chuckle.

The drop pods were coming down toward the city, which was behind them.

"That's a lot of drop pods," Niels said. "The entire battalion, maybe? ODTs most likely."

"If they're going to Zhukov City they're going to need more troops," Stathis said.

"Zhukov City's too far away. No gunboats?" Vili asked. "Or assault shuttles?"

"Maybe the next wave," Skadi said, looking around. Only the ODTs used drop pods. Each drop pod held at least four troopers and a lightweight buggy they could assemble quickly.

"I think if we head toward anything resembling civilization, they'll be looking for us," Mathison said.

"Anything near the city of Glastown at any rate," Skadi said, checking her computer.

Glastown was a small town of about a thousand, located at the foot of some mountains. Everyone was classified as employed or immediate family, with most people working on servicing the robots and equipment used to mine the nearby mountains. The mined metals were then sent to the electronics factories near Zhukov City. Her records didn't show any nearby military facilities or anything of strategic importance. Unless there was something Republic Intelligence didn't know about.

"I wish we knew what was going on up there," Vili said, echoing her thoughts. "The Republic should know we're here if that Marine sent your message."

"And the Vanir might chew on a paska-lounas in orbit," Skadi said. "There's no guarantee they'll win or be able to send help."

"So, the plan is business as usual? Don't die and do our best to kick the SOG in the teeth?" Vili asked.

"As usual," Skadi said.

"Zen," Vili said.

"At least they didn't hit us with a kinetic strike," Mathison put in.

"Little pleasures," Bern said, and Skadi didn't miss his sarcasm. The pain medication was making him loopy, and his nanites were working overtime.

Mathison changed direction and started heading away from the mountains, at an angle away from Glastown.

The first vampire came up over the ridge and slammed into Mathison, knocking him over. The second ran straight into a burst from Stathis' blazer carbine and practically exploded from the heat. The Aesir brought up their weapons, but Stathis beat them to it.

Mathison roared in anger or pain as Skadi tried to aim her weapon so she wouldn't shoot him. The big Marine punched the vampire while holding it by the throat. His fist had crushed its skull, but the hands were still slapping at Mathison—wicked-looking things trying to cut into his armor. Stathis stepped forward, placed his muzzle against the creature's torso and fired. The creature twisted, throwing Mathison aside but giving Stathis a better shot, which he took. The vampire screeched and died.

"Why is it you can crush their skull, but they don't die?" Mathison asked, getting to his feet, his carbine covering the direction they had come from.

"Well, they don't like blazers for a reason, Gunny."

"Why's that?" Mathison asked.

"I don't know, Gunny," Stathis said. "Maybe it is the heat and plasma?" Stathis paused for a minute. "Or maybe the change that makes them vampires renders them more vulnerable to heat and plasma." Then to Skadi. "Shrek thought you might want to know. That's the current working theory, ma'am."

Skadi nodded, half tempted to lecture Stathis again about calling her ma'am. Maybe later.

"Are there more?" Skadi asked.

Stathis shrugged.

"We need to keep moving," Mathison said. "Someone might've heard the weapons fire."

"Zen," Skadi said. Who had put him in charge, damn it?

Hours later, the sun was rising, and they hadn't been attacked again. If Skadi was honest, she'd rather fight the SOG than vampires.

Mathison signaled, and they formed up into a circle, facing away from the center. As they were finding their positions, weapons fire erupted in the distance. A vicious roar echoed through the hills, and the weapons fire intensified.

"Skadi, ma'am," Stathis asked. "We don't have any information on a creature that makes that sound. Can you please tell me it's some bird or something?"

Skadi checked her data systems. They had a lot of information from the SOG about Zhukov. There were no major predators. Where necessary, the SOG used traps and hunter bots to keep the population of herbivores in line. That had definitely sounded like a predator.

"I would be lying to you, Stathis," Skadi said.

"Could the vampires be morphing or something?" Stathis asked Mathison.

"Are you volunteering to go ask?" Mathison asked.

"No, Gunny. I believe there are some answers to life's mysteries that we don't want answered."

"For sure," Vili said. "At least we aren't the only prey out here."

"Those creatures have ODTs to hunt," Niels said. "I say let them enjoy each others' company."

"Better them than us," Stathis said. "When we kill monsters that were once human, are we still killing people?"

"Doesn't matter," Mathison said. "Anything trying to kill us dies first."

A private link opened from Vili. He sounded unsure. "I have a confession to make. I'm sorry."

Skadi looked at him. This didn't sound like Vili. Something was bothering him, and he expected her to be angry.

"What?" Skadi asked. And then he said the last thing she expected.

"I killed Vince."

"You what?" Skadi asked.

"I'm going hullu. I thought you should know. It isn't Bern's fault."

"What? What the hell happened?"

"It was when we were getting shot at by that other ship," Vili said. "Everything was getting crazy, like we were in a wormhole without an inkeri generator. I heard whispers, and it was getting louder. It was that feeling, Skadi. You know, the Kiska Syndrome? I lost it. I'm sorry."

"What the hell happened?"

"I thought he was changing."

She couldn't see his eyes, but his helmet was angled like his eyes were looking at the ground between them. "It sounded like he was growling and his eyes were red. I thought he was turning into one of those creatures."

"Paska," Skadi said. What was she going to do?

"I'm sorry. I thought he was changing, so I shot him in the head. Afterward I placed the cracked beam in his head.

"Did Bern see?"

"Yes… I think so. He was injured by that time. Yes. No. He probably didn't see."

Skadi stared at Vili. He had done it. He had snapped.

"Bern." Skadi added him to the private link.

"Skadi."

"Did you see what happened to Vince?" Skadi asked.

Bern was silent for a few moments. "Yes. I swear on Odin's axe that Vince was changing. His eyes were glowing red, and I think I heard him growling. He was turning into something else and he was trying to get his safety harness off. I could feel it. Vili did the right thing. It had to be done. I couldn't reach my sidearm. It had to be done."

"Paska." She couldn't lie. There would have to be an inquiry. Her team could be tied up for years for killing an MT agent. She doubted the Musta Toiminnot would understand or forgive. They would want blood. At a minimum, Vili would be taken off the Erikoisjoukot teams. He would be lucky to remain an Aesir. His career was over. Right or wrong, the MT wouldn't tolerate it.

"He *was* changing Skadi," Bern said again.

Which didn't make it acceptable. Could she lie for Vili? Convince a reviewing authority that Vince had died in the crash because he wasn't in armor?

Skadi nodded. "I need to think about this."

"Zen," Vili said. He paused "Skadi, if it looks like I'm going hullu again, please don't let me hurt anyone else. Do anything you have to. Please?"

"*Don't* go hullu, Vili," Skadi said. Could she pull the trigger on Vili? Or Bern? Or Niels? What if one of them started changing? No.

"Zen, Skadi," Vili said. "But please don't take any chances. Put me down."

"You let me worry about it," Skadi said. "You don't go hullu ever again. Zen?"

"Zen, Skadi," Vili said and dropped off the link.

"He wasn't hullu," Bern said. "If he was hullu, I was too."

"Zen," Skadi said. "You heal. Let me worry about it."

"Zen, Skadi," Bern said and dropped off the link.

Paska, she was going to have to tell Niels. As her second in command, he had to know.

Paska.

*****

Chapter Sixty-Six: Vampires

Gunnery Sergeant Wolf Mathison, USMC

Their first warnings were a chill along the spine and the feeling that something was very wrong.

The sun was still high in the sky but hidden by threatening rain clouds. It had rained earlier, and everything was damp. Greens and browns dominated the landscape, and it was getting warmer, but that feeling worried Mathison.

They found a house, probably some politician's country home, built on a hill overlooking a valley. There were no vehicles. The windows were covered with retractable slats and all the doors were closed. A vacation home and the owners were away?

While the others provided cover, Mathison moved up to the building and tested the door. There was no apparent glass to look inside, and the dust and grass covering the area showed that nobody had been there for weeks.

"Probably some commissioner's private residence," Skadi said. "They do that. A place they can 'get away from it all,' so they can concentrate on how to better 'help' their people."

"Or a place they can hide their vices," Niels said. "Be careful. Sometimes they can be very aggressive about hiding their secrets."

"Thanks for the warning," Mathison said. This wasn't a house; it was a fortress. Who the hell built a fortress? How did they get away with this?

"It looks defensible, Gunny," Stathis said on a private channel. Mathison couldn't argue. It looked tough. But what kind of nastiness would they find inside?

"It looks like it'll draw attention," Mathison said. "Attention draws fire. Didn't I tell you how drawing fire makes you unpopular?"

"I wonder if the shower works though, Gunny."

"Did you shit your pants again?"

"You ever going to forget that, Gunny?"

"Mama," Mathison sang, approaching another heavy door. "I just killed a man. Put my butt against his head, cut a fart, and now he's dead."

"Gotta admit that was funny, Gunny."

"Yeah," Mathison said, deadpan. "I laughed so hard, I shit my pants."

Mathison returned to the back door and looked it over. It was a heavy-duty door designed to keep intruders out. Probably led a storage room or the basement.

"Get up here, Stathis." Mathison waited until Stathis stood behind him and tapped his shoulder to let him know he was ready. "When life closes a door on you…"

"Breach and clear, Gunny. I've got your back."

Mathison watched Skadi pair up with Vili while Niels and Bern waited at the corner of the building to provide security. Mathison hoped that when he kicked in the door it didn't explode.

Once Skadi was in place, Mathison stepped out and slammed his boot into the door near the handle. The door was built strong, but not strong enough to handle powered armor worn by a Marine, and the lock shattered. As the door was still swinging open, Mathison followed it into the room, immediately moving to the side, his carbine sweeping the room. The door slammed into the wall and bounced into Stathis, who was on the threshold, but the door was like a bird flying into a wall. The door hit the wall again as Stathis entered opposite Mathison.

"Clear," Mathison said.

"Clear," Stathis echoed. The Marines found themselves in a living area with a couple couches, tables, a large video screen, and a large pool table. The video screen was off, so Mathison knew someone very rich and powerful owned the place.

There were two more doors. Approaching the one closest to Stathis, Mathison found himself behind the little private. He stacked up next to the thin interior door and tapped Stathis on the shoulder to indicate he was ready. Stathis reached over and found the door unlocked.

Stathis pushed the door open and moved inside with Mathison right behind him, but Stathis stopped suddenly and Mathison plowed into the private, almost knocking him over.

Pissed, Mathison looked around Stathis to see it was a small, windowless laundry room with three bodies on the ground, two men and a woman. There wasn't enough space in the room for Stathis or Mathison unless they stepped on the bodies.

"What killed them?" Stathis asked.

Their clothes had blood on them but no visible wounds.

"Me," Mathison said and stitched each one with a burst from his blazer.

The bodies blazed, caught fire, and seemed to move as if writhing in pain, before falling still.

Stathis grabbed a fire extinguisher from a nearby wall and sprayed them, but they were now charred beyond recognition.

"You okay?" Skadi asked on the squad link. She must have heard the blazer fire and was worried.

"Yes," Mathison said. "Three bodies. Just making sure they're really dead."

"Zen," Skadi said.

"I've never seen a body so flammable," Mathison said to Stathis.

"Vampires, Gunny. Or they were."

Mathison shrugged.

"Dead now, anyway. Though, how does that work, Gunny? Are they dead or deader? Can they die if they're already dead?"

"Shut up, Stathis. Let's clear the rest of the house."

"Aye, Gunny."

The Marines backed out of the room.

"Skadi coming in," Skadi said.

Didn't these Aesir understand they needed to secure the outside so nobody snuck in or out?

"The building isn't clear yet," Mathison said.

"Something big is coming," Skadi said.

"What do you mean big?" Mathison asked as Skadi came in helping Bern.

"I mean we can discuss it inside."

Niels and Vili appeared behind her.

* * * * *

Chapter Sixty-Seven: Zhukov Orbit

Chief Warrant Officer Diamond Winters, USMC

Eagle was getting closer to the planet. The *Pankhurst* and most of the ships had left, but there were still a few cruisers in orbit, and Winters knew *Eagle* couldn't take them in a fair fight, and maybe not even in an unfair fight.

"What are they doing, Chief?" Levin asked. "Guarding the planet?"

"Or preventing escape," Winters said.

"I'm detecting an emergence," Levin said. Winters looked at the holographic plot. A single ship had appeared and was on approach.

"SOG or vanhat?" Winters asked.

"Looks like a cargo vessel," Levin said. "It seems to be squawking SOG ident codes and requesting authorization. It is not getting any responses, though. Cruiser is jamming wormhole transitions."

One cruiser accelerated toward the merchant ship and Winters watched as two pods shot away from the cruiser. Winters winced. Probably boarding pods. The cruisers were here to trap incoming cargo ships.

"Cargo vessel is trying to run," Levin said.

The cargo ship was doomed.

"The cargo ship is broadcasting a mayday," Levin said.

"Turn it off," Winters said. There wasn't a damned thing *Eagle* could do except commit suicide.

"Can I monitor?" Blitzen asked. *"It would be helpful to know the range of boarding pods. I noted that targeted craft were infected before the pods contacted the target. The SOG fleet suffered, but the Republic and Golden Horde fleets appeared unscathed."*

"Whatever you need," Winters said.

She didn't want to think about the poor bastards on the cargo ship that had just stumbled into a trap. Would it be possible to warn other ships without risking *Eagle*?

Four hours later, the mayday stopped. The radio waves were silent, and the cargo ship began leaving the gravity well before disappearing into wormhole space.

The infection was spreading.

* * * * *

Chapter Sixty-Eight: Wandering Monster

Gunnery Sergeant Wolf Mathison, USMC

Peering out the door toward the forest, Mathison saw something moving through the trees. He couldn't get a good look at it, but he saw it was almost four meters tall and it moved fast. It circled the building a couple times, and under his armor Mathison felt his skin crawl and the hair on the back of his neck stand up, but the creature didn't come out of the trees and let Mathison get a good look at it. He was confident that if it did come out he could place a couple rounds in it. No matter how big it was, blazer rounds would hurt it, a lot.

"Sounds like it is leaving," Stathis said. "Why don't we go after it?"

"And if it has telekinesis?" Mathison asked. "Remember Niels? It sees you, and it slams you against the tree a couple of times? No. We stay here. I'm the only one who gets to slam privates into trees."

"Is that tree-to-tree counseling, Gunny? Or is it still considered wall to wall? Did you get a good look at it?"

"No." Mathison ignored his other comment.

"So, it could come back?" Skadi asked.

"Yes," Mathison said.

"The rest of the building is clear," Skadi said. "Looks like somebody's summer home or something. Nothing unusual. Those bodies in the laundry room were it."

"Any vehicles in the garage?" Mathison asked.

"Nothing," Skadi said.

The three dead vampires and how they had gotten there were probably going to remain mysteries.

"You have a plan?" Mathison asked.

"Don't die and do our best to kick the SOG in the teeth," Skadi said.

"I think the SOG is the least of our worries," Mathison said. "I expect that if they had won, or the Republic had won, we would have heard something."

They both stared out the door and up at the sky.

"Do you have a plan?" Skadi asked.

"There were two other corvettes at the spaceport. They were locked down during the fall of the city because they didn't have captains. They're still there for all I know."

"That's about four hundred kilometers away," Skadi said. "That city is also probably very full of hungry vampires. Walking there is not a good option."

"If the space elevator is operational, there might be ships in orbit," Mathison said. "We can move around during the day."

"Four hundred kilometers in a day? The creature that was wandering around a few minutes ago was moving around in the day," Skadi said. "I'm pretty sure it isn't native to the planet and I'd bet the SOG didn't bring it here."

"There are spaceports on the other continents," Mathison said. "I doubt they're any better off."

"And crossing the oceans won't be easy," Skadi said.

"We should hunker down," Skadi said. "I'm sure the Republic or the SOG will return with overwhelming force."

"Did you miss how the vampires overran Zhukov City?" Mathison asked. "Their numbers are growing, and I don't think the SOG forces really stood a chance. There's no reason for the Republic to land troops and attack the vampires."

"Why are you so hell bent on getting yourself killed?" Skadi asked.

"Because I have two Marines that may need my help," Mathison said. "They're the only family I have left. Your vaunted Republic has betrayed me and them. I may be all *they* have."

"Oorah," Stathis said from nearby.

"When I know they are safe, and not in some Republic prison or about to be overrun by monsters, I'll be more amendable to hiding. Until then, I'm going to find my Marines because no Marine is left behind." Mathison glanced at Stathis. "Well, I have one dumb as shit private that likes to kill things and cause trouble."

"Yut!" Stathis said.

"Don't you want to get back to your people? Continue the war against the SOG?" Mathison asked her.

Skadi turned away without answering.

"I wonder what her problem is, Gunny," Stathis asked. "Do you think she's pissed at the Republic?"

"No idea. But I'm sure she has problems we know nothing about."

"Aye, Gunny."

*****

Chapter Sixty-Nine: SOG

Lojtnant Skadi – VRAEC

She looked at Bern wondered what was going to happen. Vili could face execution when they returned. The recordings from his suit were corrupted. The investigators would call that convenient. Vili seemed resigned to his fate, but Skadi was not. Vili was a brother. He had saved her life countless times. But the MT agent was also a member of the Republic, a special agent whose job was just as dangerous and valuable as Vili's. Even if he was found innocent of murdering Vince, they would list him as susceptible to Kiska Syndrome and that would be the end of his military career.

"Company," Mathison called from the other room.

Skadi looked out the broken door and saw several buggies stopping in the yard.

The buggies were from drop pods, and they were covered with ODTs.

Skadi swore. The troopers surrounded the building. They looked ragged and exhausted, but the officers were directing them to set up security. One NCO looked at the building and noticed the door off its hinges. A command was yelled out and the troopers dropped to the ground, some aimed toward the forest, some at the building. There had to be over fifty troopers out there.

So much for a quick escape.

"They can turn this building into swiss cheese," Mathison said.

"Paska-lounas," she said.

The SOG soldiers were armed with blazers instead of slug throwers, and she saw there were wounded on the buggies. They had seen hard fighting and had probably come here hoping to find shelter or establish a base. Mercy or cooperation would be the last thing on their mind.

The building had excellent fields of fire, but the walls were no better than cardboard against blazers and only the Marines had heavy trauma plates that would provide any protection against blazers.

"Breach team," Stathis said, motioning at a team coming toward the door.

"Warning shots," Mathison said.

"Warning shots?" Stathis asked.

"Do it," Mathison said.

Stathis fired a burst from his carbine at the feet of the approaching troopers. A return burst from the troopers near the buggies cut up the wall close to Stathis and the Marine dropped so fast Skadi was worried they had hit him. As quickly as the shooting started it stopped, and everything fell silent.

As quickly as they had advanced, the troopers backed up. The grass smoldered where Stathis had shot it.

Everywhere Skadi could see, the drop troopers were taking cover and aiming at the forest or the building.

A single figure in black ODT powered armor approached the building.

"You have a plan?" Skadi asked. Maybe if the Aesir and Marines had struck first they could have inflicted enough casualties and forced them to retreat. Unfortunately, the SOG Orbital Drop Troopers weren't the kind to retreat because of casualties. Did the Marines know that?

"Don't die," Mathison said.

"Hello in there," the single trooper said in English. His rifle was slung on his back, and he was holding his hands so they could see them.

"Get off my lawn," Mathison yelled back.

"Is that who I think it is?" Stathis asked, and Skadi looked at him. How did Stathis know a SOG Orbital Drop Trooper?

The trooper reached up and pulled off his helmet. He was of Chinese descent. A small thin mustache covered his upper lip, and his short hair was cut nearly to the scalp.

"I hardly think this is your house or your lawn. This all belongs to the people of the Social Organizational Governance. May I ask who I'm talking to?" the man asked politely. Skadi pegged him as an officer. Arrogant bastard. He had enough troops that if she shot him she would have more holes in her than a strainer. Keeping him talking was the only thing delaying the violence.

"The new owner," Mathison said.

The officer smiled and nodded.

"Gunnery Sergeant Wolf Mathison, I presume?" the trooper said.

"I don't think we've met," Mathison said.

"I am Colonel Commissar Feng," he said. "It is a pleasure to finally make your acquaintance."

"The last commissar I spoke with promised to ship me off to Earth for execution," Mathison said. "Sorry if I'm not thrilled that you know my name."

"We mean you no harm," Feng said.

"Don't believe him, Gunny," Stathis whispered. "That is him, the guy I ran into on the *Tiananmen*."

"The last commissar said something like that, too," Mathison said. "Nothing personal, just following orders. It is a shame you have to die. You seem like such a nice guy."

Feng nodded, but didn't look angry or worried.

"I understand your concerns," Feng said. "My battalion was dropped to find you."

"Just a battalion?" Mathison asked. "The last time I was in SOG custody I vowed to never be captured alive."

"I understand your concern," Feng repeated. "Really. Under other circumstances, I would be quite willing to put you up against a wall and have you shot. However, as my commander, General Duque, so eloquently pointed out, these are not ordinary circumstances, and we must serve the greater good. We must preserve the human race, even if that requires us to act in ways we would otherwise find repugnant."

Skadi tried to remember if she had ever heard of Duque. If Feng was from the *Tiananmen,* then he was talking about the person in charge of the task force that had been hounding her for so long.

"Which means what?" Mathison asked.

"Which means we must work together," Feng said. "Is Skadi with you?"

Mathison looked at Skadi.

Skadi shrugged. What did it matter? Both sides would either start firing or not.

"What if she is?" Mathison shouted.

"I would like to finally meet her," Feng said. "She is very elusive and very dangerous. Under other circumstances, I would nuke this building, even with me standing right here. Alas. the general was very clear about her, too. Telling me that was probably harder on him than it was on me."

"What do you want?" Mathison asked.

"To talk," Feng said. "What else? The general believes you may have more information on what happened at 402. This threat is bigger than the Republican anti-socialists or a few ancient capitalist slaves."

"So, he sent a battalion down to talk?" Mathison asked.

"He would have sent the entire regiment, but things were a little rushed, as you might imagine. Would Tristan or Ganya be with you by any chance?"

"No," Mathison said.

Feng looked disappointed and nodded.

"Perhaps that is better," Feng said. "Can my men fortify the area? I give you my word of honor, we mean you no harm."

"I'm not sure I can trust you," Mathison said. "The last commissars kind of ruined that for me."

"I'm sure," Feng said. "There really are things we need to discuss. I can share information with you if you can share with me. We returned to Base 402 and recovered the data cores. We have a good idea of what happened there, but there are some gaps."

"Nothing a little torture won't help answer?" Mathison asked.

Recovered the data cores? They must have been in an armored, nuke proof vault. Damn.

Feng sighed and looked around. "402 is not the only base that was affected. Base Romeo-903 also had a, shall we say, accident? There was another incident at Base Yuma 441, and several artifacts are missing. Nasaraf is not the only one who has escaped. There is even a base on a planet named Snowball that we have lost contact with, though I'm not sure where that is."

"Paska-lounas," Vili said. "This is getting worse and worse. Can we fight our way free?"

"Not with Bern like he is," Skadi said.

"He carried me," Vili said. "My turn?"

Skadi shook her head.

"What assurances do we have that you won't betray us?" Mathison asked.

"Honestly?" Feng said. "Not any really. I'm sorry. I can give you my word of honor, but you said you wouldn't trust that. I have no other assurances that I think you will accept."

"What happens after we have exchanged information?" Mathison asked.

"I'm hoping we will find a way to fight this problem," Feng said. "You have proven very resourceful. We must stand together against this threat. The SOG, Marines, and the Republic united, because this threat is a danger to all of us."

"And after we defeat this incursion?" Mathison asked.

"I like this Marine," Vili said to Skadi.

"I don't know," Feng said. "I would like to say we part and return to our previous enmity, or perhaps you will join the SOG as we bring peace and enlightenment to the galaxy. This is probably not something that is going to happen in the next month or two, though."

"Do you have a way off the planet?" Mathison asked.

"Sadly, not readily available," Feng said.

"So, how do you expect to get this information to your general?" Mathison asked.

Feng nodded, as if expecting the question.

"At a pre-arranged time, we will deploy drones with data that will send a burst transmission," Feng said. "I feel confident the *Tupolev* will receive these transmissions. They may then initiate a rescue."

A not-so-distant roar caught their attention.

"Another troll," Feng said, looking in the direction of the sound. "Hopefully just one and not a full pack."

"A troll?" Mathison asked, and Feng shrugged.

"A young trooper called it that before he became one," Feng said, sounding sad. "How many creatures have you identified? Time is running out. We are either fighting for the human race or you are fighting against it. Please let me know so I can act accordingly. We need to establish a perimeter before the vampires awake as well."

"Where's the rest of your battalion?" Mathison asked.

Feng looked around him. "This is all that is left."

Mathison leaned out the door and looked around at the shattered remains of an entire battalion. The battalion aboard the *Tiananmen* had been around a thousand.

He turned to her, and Skadi wished she could read his face.

"I don't trust them, but Feng is right. Sif knew this before we met, didn't she? The human race could be facing extinction," Mathison said.

Skadi looked at Feng, who was looking toward the roar and speaking softly. Probably an implant. Drop troops moved around, establishing a line facing where the roar had come from. Two of the buggies spun around so the riders could bring the heavier automatic blazers to opposite ends of the line.

She saw Feng was now looking toward the sun and knew what he was thinking.

"Temporary allies," Skadi said. "Don't make me regret it."

"No shit," Mathison said and then raised his voice. "You hold your fire, we hold our fire, and we can work together. Don't make us regret it."

"Understood," Feng said, and put his helmet back on. "May we bring in our wounded?"

Mathison stepped out. "I'll help."

Stathis stepped out with him, not sure where to point his rifle. He kept it pointed down as he scanned the SOG ODTs.

Feng saw Stathis and paused. "Spacer Bobylev I presume?"

Stathis looked at Gunny.

"My apologies, Private Zale Stathis," Feng said, and Skadi heard a smile in his voice. "It is good to see you again."

"You wanna play games or get your wounded inside?" Mathison asked.

Feng pointed toward the buggies and then strode toward the lines. Something was coming through them.

Skadi took a knee away from the door and aimed at where the creature would appear as the colonel yelled out to his men about the rear and flanks. He seemed more concerned with those than with what was coming through the forest.

Her skin itched and a chill ran down her spine.

The creature appeared. It looked almost exactly like one of the creatures from Nugget, except much bigger. Skadi began placing rounds in its head, along with nearly every trooper on the line. The creature stumbled and fell before the buggy gunners had time to fire. Two troopers ran up to it, primed grenades, and threw them on top of the body. A small *pop* and *fizz* sprayed phosphorus in a small radius and burned the troll.

Skadi stared at it. The creature may have been human once, but it had grown into some oversized creature with brown-scaled skin, claws, sharp teeth, and large, hate-filled eyes.

When the grenades went off, Skadi's skin stopped itching.

"They can heal fast, you know," Feng said, looking again toward the sun. "Not as fast as the vampires, mind you, but I do not want to have to waste ammunition on it later."

Feng turned toward Skadi. "None of the recordings do you justice."

Skadi didn't know what to say. Standing this close to a commissar and not trying to kill him felt unnatural.

"It is an honor to meet you, Lojtnant," Feng said and motioned for some troopers to help Stathis and Mathison.

"Colonel. I must admit ignorance of you."

"I am actually pleased by that," Feng said smiling. "It means you are not as all-knowing and all-powerful as some claim you are. The house is clear of vampires, then?"

"It is now," Skadi said, staring at the colonel. He didn't seem like a bad man, and his troops moved quickly to obey his orders, not in a terrified way, but in a competent, trusting way. Which made him even more dangerous.

Feng turned to a nearby trooper. "Captain, take some men and sweep the area. Get some sensors out."

"Yes, Colonel." The captain jogged over to a cluster of troops.

"Your troops don't seem to fear you," Skadi said.

Feng turned to her. "I would hope not. Fear is not my style. We need to get busy, though. When night falls, the vampires will hunt far and wide."

"How many troops did you land with?" Skadi asked.

"Nine hundred and eighty-seven," Feng said, and she heard the emotion in his voice. "Now I am down to eighty-six. I hope to get as many home as I can, Lojtnant. Please excuse me. I would like to talk, but we must move fast. There may be more trolls about, and while that will be okay tonight, now is not a good time. We have discovered trolls hunting in packs. While the decoy does not move silently, the others do."

She watched as he got the buggies arrayed around the area and ordered the other troopers to dig. It would be nearly impossible to get everyone in the building, but Colonel Feng seemed to know that as he moved his people around.

An hour later, nothing had emerged from the woods, and the area looked more like a military camp. There were several wounded ODTs and a couple medics helping them. The buggies with mounted guns were strategically placed so they had good fields of fire and each was protected by at least a squad of troopers busy digging in. Other troops moved in and out of the woods, stringing up wire.

Once everyone was moving with a purpose, the colonel looked things over and nodded.

"Good men," Feng said as he came toward Skadi. "If the vampires come, they will suffer. Now might be a good time to talk, before night falls."

* * * * *

Chapter Seventy: Feng

Gunnery Sergeant Wolf Mathison, USMC

The only other SOG trooper in the room was Captain Evanoff, a stern, quiet man who seemed to have a permanent scowl stamped on his face and bags under his eyes. Mathison suspected he probably hadn't slept since they had landed. It was Skadi's team, him, and Stathis. Outside, the sun was sinking lower.

"First," Feng said, looking at Mathison, "I must ask: are you in any way responsible for the release of the demon Nasaraf at Base 402?"

"No," Mathison said. "Your scientists managed that without us. Me and my Marines were in our cells scheduled for execution."

"We did not find any significant sign of network intrusion until after the release," Feng said nodding. "It would be irresponsible of me not to ask."

Feng turned toward Skadi. "I would ask Lojtnant Skadi if the Republic has been capturing or destroying more ships than usual?" Feng asked.

Skadi scowled, and Feng shrugged. "I understand you are Erikoisjoukot, not Vanir." Feng sighed. "Captain Evanoff, Can you please go check on the men?"

"Yes, Colonel," Evanoff said and left.

When he was gone, Feng looked at the Marines and Erikoisjoukot.

"I realize you have many reservations about sharing information with me. This is understandable. Expected. However, I realize you are not the vile human beings that the SOG paints you as. You are, in your way, patriotic to your cause and cultures. I respect this. You are men and women of honor. We, the general and I, know this." A small smile came to Feng's face as he looked at Skadi. "Understanding you is our only advantage." He turned his gaze to Mathison. "That makes it easier to understand you."

Mathison remained silent. Hopefully, the colonel would get to the point.

Feng shrugged and looked at everyone. "You may or may not know that the Kiska Syndrome is becoming more prevalent, stronger in its effects. It is making space travel more and more difficult. Already, military ships must double their transits in order to minimize the problem. This has been bothering social scientists for a while. We are also losing more ships in Shorr space. Officially, this is the fault of the Republic, the Golden Horde, and other pirates. Unofficially, we fear something may be happening in Shorr space, something related to the Kiska Syndrome. These entities, such as Nasaraf, are something we do not understand—where they come from or what they are. There are several theories. One theory is that they are demons from Earth's past. Another is that they're alien intelligences, criminals that started a war in the Tomb Worlds and were banished to Shorr space, where they are working to return to the real world."

Feng turned to Mathison. "Some think they are artificial intelligences."

"He knows about us," Freya said.

"No shit," Mathison said.

"Regardless of what they are," Feng continued. "They can manipulate our world in ways we did not think possible and cannot yet understand. Some say that sufficiently advanced technology appears as magic to less advanced creatures. From what we have seen, these creatures defy the laws of physics. This shows possible familiarity with other dimensions and the laws of physics in those dimensions. We lack data." Feng frowned. "If you have any additional information, please share."

"Tristan said an alien from the original prison was appearing to him," Mathison said. "It was warning him about devourers."

"Where is Mister Malloy now?" Feng asked.

"Not with us," Mathison said, and Feng nodded. "But he's alive."

"Good," Feng said. "His supervisor, Mister Ogienko, thought he was insane and had him dumped at Nugget in case he needed to use him later. Mister Ogienko made Mister Malloy sound mentally unbalanced and did his best to hide Mister Malloy's warnings. This is something he will have to answer for, but that is a different issue that does not concern us here, now. The Republic has acquired several artifacts. Are the artifacts safe? You are not experimenting with them, are you?"

"They are safe," Skadi said. "After what happened at 402, we wouldn't dare experiment with them. We captured Tristan and Ganya because we needed more information."

"Thank you," Feng said. "Right now, we are not sure if we can return them to their tomb or not. Obviously, some prisoners have escaped, and we do not know how to put them back. If Tristan really is seeing some alien ghost, then we need to ask it how to put these creatures back in their prison."

"Yeah, we would love to help with that, but we are a little trapped on this planet," Mathison said.

"Why did you come here?" Feng asked.

Mathison and Skadi remained silent.

"I understand," Feng said. "Again, allow me to share. We have one or more agents in the Golden Horde and the Republic and have known about the plan to attack this system for a while now. We expected ground-based activity to support the space borne assault. Higher authority believed it would be better to strike a blow against the Republic and the Golden Horde so we could more fully concentrate on this new threat. It was thought that Lojtnant Hermod and his team were operational. We did not want to reveal our preparations, so we attempted to suppress that report. In retrospect, I do not think that report came from the proper authorities. Did it?"

Mathison shrugged as Feng looked at him.

"Interesting. Is the Republic having a problem with Kiska Syndrome as well?" Feng asked.

"We've noticed it getting worse," Skadi said grudgingly. Mathison noticed she did not mention the inkeri generator.

"Thank you," Feng said. "So, it is not specific to drive tuning or travel paths. Do you know of any instances where creatures have found their way onto ships in Shorr space?"

"What do you mean?" Skadi asked.

"People who change? As if infected or subverted by something in Shorr space?" Feng clarified.

Skadi glanced at Mathison. Curitiba?

Feng continued, "We have encountered this. People have changed, sometimes visibly, sometimes mentally, when the ship leaves Shorr space. The longer the exposure, the higher the chances of someone becoming infected."

"This is new information," Skadi said.

"I suspect as much," Feng said. "The Governance is over two hundred planets with tens of thousands of colonies, outposts, and other facilities throughout known space. We can collect more information. My contacts keep me well informed. This was a major problem, and it is getting worse."

"Why share with us?" Mathison asked.

Feng looked surprised and then thoughtful. "I serve humanity and the greater good. As misguided as your selfish ideologies may be, you are still humans, still trying to find your way toward enlightenment. This threat we are facing is as much a threat to you as it is to us. Surely you can see this?"

"Yes," Mathison said. Condescending prick.

"No offense," Feng said. "Under other circumstances, I would exterminate you. Not with pleasure, mind you, but as an unpleasant and necessary step toward the enlightenment and growth of humanity."

"For sure," Vili said and Mathison could almost hear the big Aesir rolling his eyes.

Weapons fire outside interrupted the conversation.

"A troll," Feng said. "Probably a pack."

Mathison put on his helmet and followed the colonel out. The distant mountains almost hid the sun as Mathison looked around. In just an hour, the ODTs had dug fighting positions. His skin itching, Mathison looked around. He almost missed the two gigantic eyes staring at him from the woods. There was nothing about those eyes, or that face, that appeared human.

He raised his rifle to fire. The creature shifted, and he lost sight of it.

"There was one over there," Mathison said, pointing. A machine gunner in a pit moved his gun to face that direction.

"Are these things telekinetic?" Stathis asked out loud.

"Telekinetic?" Feng asked. "What do you mean?"

"You haven't met them yet, Colonel?" Stathis asked. "I think that is a good thing. There were some on Nugget that could move things with their minds. One flipped a bus from a distance, but they didn't look like that."

Stathis pointed at the scorched remains of the first troll.

"That is interesting to note," Feng said. "None of the survivors from Nugget reported anything like that."

"Maybe we were just special, Colonel," Stathis said.

Sudden weapons fire cut the conversation short as ODTs opened up on a troll that was rushing from the woods. Most shots were to the face, and the head disintegrated almost instantly. Not all the troopers fired though, most started looking in other directions. Another section started firing and a pair of the buggies opened up on a cluster of trolls rushing them. Five trolls sprinted at the line, but the alert troopers were ready.

Green troops would all look in the direction of the firing. Veteran troops trusted their buddies to handle the threat or call for help.

"Disciplined," Mathison commented.

"Thank you," Feng replied. "These are the surviving veterans. There might be one or two newer troopers. Most of them changed shortly after landing."

"Changed?" Mathison asked.

Feng pointed at the trolls. "They could be our brothers, changed. I suspect it may have to do with experience in Shorr space. The more time you have spent in space, the less susceptible you are to being transformed by whatever force changes people. What you see around you are the more senior members of the battalion. They frequently have over a hundred hours in Shorr space."

"Which might make sense," Freya said. *"Why it seemed random aboard the space station when so many people changed into creatures? However, I would think that you and the other Marines would be more susceptible since you had never been in Shorr space. There may be flaws in his logic and data."*

"Are you infiltrating their network?"

"Yes. Shrek and I almost have their encryption algorithm."

"Good, I don't trust them."

"If he suspects we exist, then I would proceed with caution. Feng is very dangerous. He knows they compromised the systems aboard the station. He also might be more than a mere commissar."

"Agreed," Mathison said.

"Do you have a long-term plan, Colonel?" Mathison asked.

"Yes, Gunnery Sergeant. Don't die as we defeat these demons."

"Simple, Colonel," Mathison said.

"Simple plans are most likely to succeed, even if they are very difficult in execution. It will be a difficult night. We will discuss it later."

The sun was now almost completely gone from the sky.

The ODTs were in their fighting holes, with two troopers to a hole. At present, only one was visible in each, and Mathison realized the second troopers were trying to sleep. None of the troopers challenged him as he walked around, but he saw that most of them were corporals, sergeants, staff sergeants, and captains, and at least one major. The rank and file were corporals and sergeants, which explained the intense discipline.

"Am I the lowest ranking person in the area?" Stathis asked Mathison on a private link. "The lowest rank I've seen among these ODTs is corporal."

"Yes," Mathison said.

"There was a pair of corporals digging a latrine," Stathis said. "They don't have privates?"

"Sounds like they all died," Mathison said. "Or transformed into trolls or something."

"Don't let that happen to me, Gunny. Please?"

"Hasn't happened yet. But I promise to put you out of my misery if you promise to put me out of my misery."

"Deal, Gunny. Are we going to get out of here?"

"We haven't found Chief Winters or Sergeant Levin, yet. We aren't allowed to die until we make sure they're safe."

"You have a plan, Gunny?"

"Yes." It was a lie, but Stathis didn't need to know that.

The sky was overcast, and it was raining a little. It was going to be a very dark night and Mathison was thankful for his night vision.

Stathis was quiet, and Mathison knew he wanted to ask. He looked at Stathis.

"I'm not sure I want to know anymore, Gunny."

"Now you're sounding like a lance corporal."

Several thermite grenades went off, burning the trolls.

"Do you think the demons, trolls, and vampires are learning our history, or were they part of it, Gunny? What if they've just been absent for a while and now they're returning?"

"I don't know," Mathison said.

Weapons fire from the other side of the building shattered the night.

"I wonder if dragons will be blazer proof," Stathis said as the two Marines ran around to see what was going on.

"Shut up, Stathis."

Dragons? Hell no. Mathison did not want to deal with dragons.

* * * * *

Chapter Seventy-One: Vampire Battle

Lojtnant Skadi – VRAEC

That bad feeling returned as Skadi looked at the forest.

The ODTs had clear fields of fire for about fifty meters. Skadi thought they should push it out, but then they would have to cut down trees, and if she was honest, she wasn't sure how long they would stay here. Not with this many people. She didn't want to think about how many trolls were out there, and she knew they would eventually come here. Something would draw them.

She walked the perimeter. It was surreal to be among the ODTs and ignored. There were no privates or lower-ranking troopers, which made it even more surreal. She knew she had probably exchanged fire with some of these people, done her best to kill them. Now they were working to keep each other safe and prepare for what would likely be an onslaught.

With their helmets on, she could only imagine the looks of hatred directed at her, but none made comments or spoke to her as she walked around inspecting their work.

They knew what they were doing. She watched the officers walking the lines, checking people's fields of fire while one trooper in each position slept and the other watched over the barrel of their blazer, their eyes sweeping their portion of the perimeter. Automatic blazers were well placed so they could sweep the front, covering likely avenues of approach like the road and the fire break in the trees. There were troopers inside the building as well, ready and peering through windows.

The light drizzle was unpleasant, and the temperature was dropping. In her armor, her only concern was whether it would freeze and cause problems with footing or sensors. Most sensors didn't work well covered with a coat of snow or ice. If they had batteries, they died more quickly, and other things could easily go wrong.

She saw troopers waking up their sleepers. They were going on alert.

"Ma'am," one of the ODTs said, coming up to her, "we have sensors dropping off. They'll probably hit us shortly. It could be a few or a thousand. You might want to get inside."

Skadi saw his rank emblem. "Thank you, Captain."

She looked around one last time before she returned to the command center. The second she turned away weapons fire shattered the silence.

Skadi spun and saw shadows flickering out of the woods toward the line. Without thinking, she brought up her rifle and fired.

The people sprinting at the ODT perimeter could have been civilians, men, women, and even children, barely a flash of pale skin and shadow as they crossed the distance with blinding speed. One vampire, a woman with long blonde hair, was coming straight at Skadi. She fired and missed as the vampire dodged her first shot. Skadi fired again and the woman slipped to one side, a cruel smile on her face that revealed razor-sharp, bloodstained teeth. Solid black eyes were locked onto Skadi as the vampire came closer. A shot from one of the ODTs caught the vampire in the chest. Superheated plasma caused the vampire's chest to explode in a way Skadi had never seen. The vampire crumpled, and Skadi turned her attention to another vampire that wasn't watching her. This time, her round caught the creature below the neck and the vampire stumbled and collapsed as it caught fire and died.

The ODTs were far too calm as they shot down the approaching creatures. The last vampire made it within ten meters of the fighting positions. The buggy-mounted machine guns hadn't bothered to open fire.

"That's the first wave," the captain yelled so everyone could hear. "Just a probe. Our fire will draw more trolls, too. The night has just begun. We are ODT. We will prevail, for the greater good. Never quit!"

"Never quit! Hurrah, hurrah, hurrah!" the troopers yelled back.

"Would you like an escort inside, ma'am?" the captain asked Skadi.

"Are you ordering me back?" Skadi asked.

In the distance, there was loud music, along with what sounded like a car horn going off.

"No, ma'am," the captain said. "The colonel ordered that if anyone survives, it's to be you and those cappie Marines. We'll follow his orders, but I would feel more comfortable if you were inside. We have encountered vampires using weapons before and I would prefer you not be exposed when those creatures make their appearance."

Skadi scanned the woods and looked back at the captain.

"Thank you," Skadi said and walked back to the command center.

She arrived as another side of the building opened fire. It didn't last long. Another probe?

The colonel looked up as she entered.

"These are just probes," Feng said. "If they behave like they did last night, they'll keep probing with small numbers until maybe midnight, by which time they'll have built up their numbers. When that happens they'll swarm us. That's when it will get difficult. This position is slightly more defensible than we had last night and our perimeter is much smaller. It was the trolls that caused the most damage."

"How were the trolls more problematic?" Skadi asked. They seemed large and easy to handle. They didn't move half as fast as the vampires.

"In their presence, troopers changed," Feng said. "When a trooper began to change, they would turn on their fellows. This opened gaps in our line that the vampires exploited, after they tore apart the trolls."

"They aren't working together?" Skadi asked.

"No," Feng said. "If they had been, we would have been wiped out that first night. We hope to draw the vampires and trolls together, at which point we hope they'll fight each other and ignore us."

"Are you responsible for that music?" Skadi asked.

"Music?" Feng asked. "Oh yes. I suspect the Marines already have access, but you are watching our screamer in action. We have placed some loud-speakers with batteries and timers in some pipes under the road. So far, it's working. The trolls are drawn to the noise and the vampires are drawn to the trolls. We're watching them fight via a drone we have up. Those two groups that hit us appear to be fringe groups."

Clever.

"We use timers so that when one stops, the next starts. Hopefully, that'll keep them away from us. If we survive the night, then we can continue our journey to Nuvo Gagarin," Feng said.

Skadi checked her database. Nuvo Gagarin was a smaller SOG space port about two hundred kilometers away.

"What's there?" Skadi asked.

"It's not a large city," Feng said. "It is a military base, so it should be defensible. It might still be held. We had communications with them during our drop. They warned us what we were dropping into, but they were hard pressed. Apparently, some drop pods from Nasaraf's fleet had targeted them and the smaller city of Novi Ufa. We have not heard from them since, but radio communication has been unreliable."

"Then?" Skadi asked.

"Then we hold and wait for the *Tupolev* to return," Feng said. "I don't think we have a lot of options. Do you think your Republic fleet will return?"

"I don't know," Skadi said truthfully.

Feng nodded. His eyes weren't focused on her, probably watching the drone's view on his cybernetics.

"How are you doing, Bern?" Skadi asked.

"In pain," Bern said. "It's hard to think. The nanites are struggling."

"Hang in there," Skadi said. "We've been in worse situations."

"I don't know," Bern said. "Valhalla awaits. We will have our Ragnarok."

"Not fighting shoulder to shoulder with our enemies," Skadi said.

"I'm tired Skadi," Bern said.

"Then take a nap. We're getting you out of here. I promise."

"Zen," Bern said. "But Valhalla won't be kept waiting. Don't make promises you can't keep. I won't hold you to that."

It struck Skadi that this was probably going to be their last mission together. If the MT were going to take Vili away for killing one of them, it would break her team.

"We are Aesir, bound together through blood and tears," Skadi said.

"We are the blades of our people. Zen."

Paska. She wanted to make Valhalla wait, but she didn't have that much control.

* * * * *

Chapter Seventy-Two: Assault

Gunnery Sergeant Wolf Mathison, USMC

The drone relayed the battle from the road. It was quite high and Mathison watched as hundreds of vampires attacked a group of thirty trolls, large lumbering behemoths. These trolls were larger and fiercer than what had attacked earlier. He wondered how big they could grow, but it was hard to tell their actual size because they were covered with vampires that had leapt on them and sunk their sharp teeth and claws into the trolls' tough, leathery skin. The vampires and trolls were both covered in blood, and despite the gaping wounds, the trolls continued to fight, grabbing vampires with both hands and smashing them into the ground or a tree or anything solid. Neither side fought with any tactics, just sheer, brutal savagery and blind hate.

Half frozen droplets began to fall from the sky.

One troll fell to its knees as more vampires piled on top of it like land-bound piranhas. They leapt at the troll and tried to take a bite or to tear with their claws. The troll stopped fighting, but the vampires continued to leap on it until they buried it under a pile of squirming, pale-skinned creatures that had once been human.

The battle was only five kilometers away, and it made Mathison nauseous to watch it. When the vampires were done with the trolls, they would likely turn toward the house.

"Frightening, is it not?" Feng asked, catching Mathison by surprise.

"What?"

"Please don't insult my intelligence," Feng said. "Surely you have gained access by now. The drone's view of the road. The savagery and violence. If they turn their attention toward us, I dislike our chances."

"Do they know about us, Colonel?" Mathison asked. How had the colonel known? Or was he guessing?

"Probably," Feng said. "It is said a shark from old Earth could smell a single drop of blood in the ocean from many kilometers away. While this is a myth, there is some truth in the fact that sharks have an acute sense of smell. These creatures are not entirely physical, and they do not seem to adhere to our laws of physics. I suspect there is something in their nature that draws them to people, like blood draws sharks, or wolves. It may be their senses extend far beyond this planet and system. If not the individual creatures, then perhaps Nasaraf and others."

Mathison stared at the colonel. His eyes were locked on Mathison and it was hard to read what was going on behind them.

"He is probably correct," Freya said. *"If they are projecting, or otherwise tied to another dimension, then the physical laws from that other dimension could bleed over into ours, which can cause inconsistencies and other problems. This merging or confrontation of physics will further confuse what we know."*

"So, this really could be the end of the human race?"

"Look how quickly the SOG fleet was defeated, and they reduced this planet to ruin in a matter of days. What if these vanhat can follow humanity to other systems, can find the ghost colonies?"

"What do they want?"

"With different laws of physics, can we even understand what they might want?"

"What's the story with Tristan?" Mathison asked Feng.

"He was a scientist that served under Mister Ganya Ogienko. Based on reports we have recovered, it appears this Tristan was having visions of an alien who was trying to tell him something. Mister Ogienko thought this was a symptom of exposure to alien technology and feared that he could be contaminated further, so Mister Ogienko had Mister Mallory transferred to Tau Ceti Gold. Mister Malloy never admitted to this, but we have recordings of him in a room, alone, having a discussion with nothing."

"Now you think he really was seeing an alien?"

"Yes. He could be the key to solving these problems, to understanding how these beings were defeated in the past."

"How do we know they were defeated?"

"Please understand this information is confidential and the SOG will deny it should you share this with others. I will tell you because we need your help. Do you understand?" Feng asked.

"Yes. I'm familiar with classified material."

Feng nodded. "Other expeditions have recovered genetic material from these ancient aliens. They were human, or they had many similarities. They are also related to the Torag. We do not know if genetic experiments caused this diversification or planetary conditions, but mankind and the Torag have a common ancestor. We believe it was the aliens from the Tomb Worlds. They survived, although they appear to have suffered devolution and a dark period where history was lost. We need to recover that lost history."

Mathison stared at Feng. Outside, the light drizzle turned to drifting snowflakes.

"This is a profound revelation," Freya said.

"And if we don't cooperate with SOG we might doom humanity to extinction."

"More sensors are going offline," Freya said, and Mathison's skin itched. *"Too many."*

"Incoming," Mathison said as Feng started to get the reports.

Blazer fire began to roar, and Mathison heard it increase all around the perimeter.

Feng ran for the stairs, and Mathison followed him to the top floor where there was a single room with windows that looked out in every direction. Someone had raised the slats so the ODTs could keep watch and fire, but not wide enough for someone to fit through.

Troopers in the windows fired as Mathison peered out. Everywhere, the forest was moving. They were swarming but not attacking, and Mathison wasn't sure what was stopping them, but they hadn't left the cover of the trees. With deliberation, the ODTs picked them off, conserving ammunition. They had moved all the spare ammo off the buggies into the trenches.

The ODTs were cool professionals, but Mathison saw one ODT get up and try to run inside and another ODT grabbed him and pushed him to the berm. The trooper who had tried to run stood firm after that.

"I'm tapped into the ODT's helmet cams," Freya said. *"This is not looking good. I estimate at least five hundred vampires assembling out there. Mostly to the north."*

Mathison moved to the north. It was hard to tell how many there were.

"They're trying harder to mask their numbers to the north," Freya said.

"Colonel," Mathison said. "Looks like they are massing to the north. They're trying to hide their numbers, though."

"Thank you, Gunnery Sergeant," Feng said and Mathison watched as a few troopers slid into the holes on the north, with about three per hole now.

Mathison didn't hear the signal, but as one, the vampires began their sprint. A wave of the creatures poured from the woods toward the defenders. The ODTs began firing. Mathison didn't waste any time. Freya helped guide him, fed him targets, and still Mathison nearly wasn't fast enough. He didn't count how many were felled before the machine guns began firing. Almost all of them began firing at the same time, right across the front of the dug in troopers. Two machine gun teams were positioned at each corner of the building, shoulder to shoulder, laying down a wall of blazer fire across the front of the trenches. It almost looked like the machine gunners were shooting at each other, but they had an offset of a couple of meters, so the rounds safely zipped past their buddy's shoulder. A wall of blazer fire protected all sides of the building, and when the vampires slammed into it they exploded, spraying gore and body parts all over the troopers trying to shoot them down.

"Definitely the north," Freya reported as Mathison fired, shifted, fired, shifted, fired. Beside him, Stathis and Skadi were also firing methodically. Niels had taken the east, Vili the west. Bern was watch-

ing the south, but because of his injuries, he was not as fast or accurate. An ODT staff sergeant was beside him, though.

Colonel Feng went from window to window, checking things and calling out commands.

One of the machine guns stopped firing, and Mathison glanced over to see the two troopers throw it aside and hurriedly try to attach another machine gun. A pair of vampires made it through the gap. One landed in a trench, but the other leapt toward the window. Mathison wasn't sure if it was jumping at him or just the window, but he sent two shots into its face and someone else put a couple rounds in its chest. The body hit the building below them and Mathison looked for another target. A gunner who had been firing nonstop fell silent. Mathison looked and saw a vampire leap onto the gunner. The ODT swung his fist, but the vampire slipped under it with blinding speed, reached for the gunner's throat and grabbed his head. Another vampire came at them from another angle and Mathison shot it down.

More attackers made it past the fire and now both north side machine guns were down.

"Stathis black!" Stathis dropped out of sight to change magazines.

"Paska," Skadi said, doing the same.

Mathison was low on ammo. Very low. The vampire who had the gunner twisted the trooper's head. Mathison heard the snap and the scream of triumph from the vampire. A trooper shot the victorious vampire as another trooper scrambled out of his hole. The dead gunner's assistant grabbed the gun and began firing at the same time the other gun started firing. It all happened in the blink of an eye, any longer and the lines would have collapsed.

"Stathis green."

Mathison's counter reached zero.

"Mathison black." Mathison dropped down. He heard Skadi cursing and firing above the sound of screaming vampires.

In seconds, Mathison stood. More vampires had made it into the trenches and while they could not sink their fangs into the trooper's bodies, they could snap necks, break arms, and throw hapless troopers into machine gunner fire.

The machine gunners didn't hesitate when a trooper was thrown into their wall of blazer fire. They killed their comrades without mercy because anything less would mean more vampires getting into the lines.

With Stathis and Skadi, Mathison leaned over and began shooting at vampires that had made it past the wall of fire.

Something slammed into the west window, shattering the slats. A vampire screamed as Vili roared.

Mathison spun in time to see Vili stick his fist through the vampire's head, then place his weapon against the creature's chest and fire. The explosion from the superheated plasma knocked the vampire back out the broken window. Vili leaned over and began firing in short bursts. Feng rushed over to look and also began firing.

"Paska-lounas. I thought Soggies were bad." Vili noticed the colonel was next to him. "No offense."

"I accept that as a compliment," Feng said in between shots.

"For sure," Vili said without pausing in his firing.

Hands grasped the edge of the window and a white face, splattered with dried blood and hatred, appeared in front of Mathison.

Mathison fired a single shot into the creature's face. Without another sound, the creature fell back out of sight.

Looking out, Mathison saw that nearly a quarter of the troopers in the trenches were dead and vampires were still streaming out of the woods.

A roar of anger and hatred from the forest caused several vampires to pause and look back. Nobody wasted any time; they continued shooting anything still moving.

More roars followed the first one.

"Trolls," Feng said, sounding tired.

Several vampires turned to flee and were shot in the back by surviving ODTs. The snow was sticking to the ground and patches of white were appearing.

The night fell silent except for the occasional shot from an ODT as they walked the lines, making sure all the vampires stayed dead. The sounds of battle echoed through the forest from the northwest.

Feng had a drone up and Mathison tapped in.

The adrenaline drained from his system and exhaustion set in. Mathison popped a stim to take the edge off and noticed Stathis do the same.

"It isn't even midnight," Feng said, and Mathison heard sadness in his voice as he looked out at his troopers.

"Maybe the trolls and vampires will keep each other busy for a while, Colonel," Stathis said.

"I appreciate the optimism of privates," Feng said. "I have learned that optimists rarely have many facts."

"Stathis, brown out," Stathis said on a team link, and swapped magazines.

"Mathison, brown out," Mathison said once Stathis was done.

"What do you think, Gunny?" Stathis asked as he pulled out used magazines and began transferring rounds from the partially spent magazines into a single one.

Mathison stared at the bodies strewn across the yard. It looked like a bunch of civilians had been massacred in a horrific orgy of death. None of them held weapons, and they were all wearing gray, mostly featureless clothes. The dried blood stains and fresh burn marks were at odds. Rarely were all body parts attached, and there were plenty of places where clothing had caught fire. Some bodies were burning, and Mathison was glad for the filters in his helmet that would block the smell.

That smell was unforgettable. He still remembered the stench from his time in the Philippines.

Feng headed downstairs. The Marines and Erikoisjoukot surveyed the woods, which were eerily silent.

"Sounds like they hate the trolls more than us, Gunny."

Mathison nodded. With what they had taken from *Patriot*, the ammunition reserves were at seventy percent. Not bad, but that could go far too quickly. The ODTs had plenty of ammunition crates still strapped to their buggies.

Winters and Levin seemed so far away.

"You think the sergeant and chief are okay?" Stathis asked, mirroring Mathison's thoughts.

"They're Marines. They are either okay, or dead, half buried in empty magazines and enemy bodies."

"The colonel appears to be preparing a radio drone," Freya reported. *"He's recording a message and will probably send the drone up as high as he can to broadcast into space. I could piggyback a message if you like."*

"Great," Mathison said, wondering if he was wasting his time. *"Attach a message saying where we're headed and with who, and why."*

"For who?"

"For the Republic. And for the chief and sergeant."

"Do you think they're listening?"

"Do we have anything to lose? They could be with the Republic fleet and watching for us."

"Aye-aye, Gunny."

Mathison looked into the forest. He heard someone screaming, most likely an injured trooper.

The scream fell silent, and Mathison wondered if it would be beneficial to watch the drone's view as it monitored the vampires and trolls fighting it out. The trolls were most likely to lose, but the more vampires they killed, the better.

Mathison tapped into the view and watched as more trolls joined the fight, then more vampires.

Where were the vampires coming from?

* * * * *

Chapter Seventy-Three: Colonel Feng

Lojtnant Skadi – VRAEC

Skadi followed Colonel Feng downstairs to see what he was up to and if she could help. The ODTs had fought well. None of them had panicked or tried to flee. She could respect that.

Outside the house, the colonel stopped to talk with various troopers while Skadi watched the tree line. In the trenches, she saw there were more casualties than she had thought. Despite a wall of fire, the vampires had made it through and killed men in powered armor. That was a sobering thought. She looked at the bodies of the fallen ODTs. Most had their necks snapped, one had his helmet caved in from a powerful blow. It couldn't have been from a fist, but there was no mistaking the cause of death. The vampires had even thrown a few troopers into the machine-gun fire.

The machine gunners themselves stood stoically, watching the forest and ready to lay down another wall of flaming death. Skadi saw they had put up stakes to prevent the mounted guns from going too far to one side, where they would fire at their own troops. Assistant gunners were busy going through the extra guns and pulling out ammunition, laying it out for rapid access.

Other troops were trying to put something large and heavy over the machine-gun nests, but there wasn't a lot to work with. Some troopers were building up the berm so the vampires wouldn't be able to see the machine gunners from the forest at all. With the light snow freezing the ground it had to be hard digging, but Skadi didn't hear any complaints. If the ODTs were talking, they were doing so privately.

Because she was watching the tree line, she saw the flash as a shot was fired. Beside her, an ODT collapsed.

Without thought, she leaped into the nearest fighting position, which was occupied by a single trooper.

Firing from the tree line?

Colonel Feng was in the next hole over.

Another shot rang out and the machine gun to her left fired a burst that ended up in the sky. Her suit and cybernetics triangulated where the shot had come from, and Skadi fired a burst into the area. They fired no more rounds.

There was a scream and the woods filled with vampires again. They wasted no time sprinting toward the ODT lines and Skadi faced them.

"That was a Republic weapon that killed Sergeant Mai," Colonel Feng said. "Do you have compatriots among the creatures?"

"Not that I know of," Skadi said and switched links.

"Aesir, Aesir, Aesir," Skadi said on an emergency Aesir frequency that they all monitored. "Any Aesir on link?"

Skadi shot two vampires running toward her. Another one made it into the machine gun's wall of fire and disintegrated in a spray of flaming blood and body parts.

The nearest machine gun stopped firing. The trooper next to her fell back, half his head missing from a blazer round.

"Somebody find and kill that damned sniper," Skadi said on the team link.

"Zen," Vili, Niels, and Bern said.

Bern's status went from yellow to red.

A pair of vampires ran at Skadi, a fat man and a small child. Skadi shot the child first since she was smaller and faster.

"Niels," Skadi said. "Check on Bern."

Skadi shot the fat man several times in the chest and he collapsed.

"Bern will meet us in Valhalla," Niels said. "Head shot."

Ice flowed through Skadi's veins. Not Bern.

Who was firing at them with Republic weapons? Who had killed their brother?

She spotted a flash out of the corner of her eye. She didn't know who had just died, but the shooter was a smudge, wearing adaptive camouflage armor. Skadi fired a sustained burst at the target and then to either side since she couldn't see it anymore. If the target was Aesir, he would shoot and move quickly. Skadi fired into the place he was likely to move to, but she couldn't be sure she hit anything as three more vampires broke from the tree line and raced toward her.

She shot the first one, but the other two made it through the machine gun's wall of death unscathed. She shot the second one as it leapt at her, but the third one slammed into her, pushing her against the body of the headless trooper.

The vampire was a man and Skadi grabbed his neck as he pushed her over and down. The creature batted her rifle out of the way and reached for her head as it kicked at her with its knees.

Pushed to the bottom of the hole, Skadi struggled to keep it from grabbing her helmet. Like ODT helmets, they did not design the Republic helmets to be twisted off with a head still in them. It wasn't something she would not have considered a weakness, until now.

The vampire slammed a powerful fist into her arm and Skadi grunted in pain. From her position, there was no hope of getting the muzzle of her blazer between her and the vampire. Anyone upstairs in the building might see the vampire on top of her, but any blazer rounds that went through the vampire would probably go through her as well.

Skadi kicked and dropped her rifle to punch the creature and grab its neck. Like a rabid animal, it struggled, hatred filling its solid black eyes. The teeth that were no longer human snapped open and closed, anticipating her flesh.

She squirmed and kicked and held her grip. It was like holding a cat that didn't want to be held. A normal human's eyes would bulge as their face turned purple from lack of breath, but apparently this thing didn't need to breathe as it struck her arm with fists like sledgehammers and pushed against her.

She tried to reach her sidearm but gave up as her arm almost gave way and the flailing claws came close to getting a grip on her helmet. This vampire had been a SOG civilian and was smaller than her, but his strength was unlike anything she had seen without powered armor. It took both hands to hold the creature at bay as she brought a knee up to keep its kicks from hurting too much.

The creature screamed at her, pushed and pulled.

A heavy weight slammed onto the back of the vampire, and at first Skadi thought it was another vampire. Her arms almost gave way under the weight. A hand grabbed the vampire's hair and pulled the head away from her. A powered knife slammed into the creature's neck, half severing it as the ODT pulled the creature up and pushed it out of the hole, a twist of the trooper's wrist severed the head completely. The soldier threw the body into the wall of machine-gun fire.

The ODT who had just saved her life brought up his rifle and resumed firing. She suddenly realized how close to meeting Bern in Valhalla she had come.

In a daze, Skadi grabbed her own rifle and stood to continue firing. Two more vampires raced toward them and she dropped them both.

Both machine guns were firing and then, without warning, the vampires stopped pouring from the forest.

"Cease fire," the colonel yelled out from beside her.

She stared at the colonel. She didn't know what to think. He had risked sniper fire to leave his hole and save her life. A SOG commissar had risked his life for her.

That made no sense. Commissars were cowardly, self-centered, political officers. Not warriors.

"Watch for the sniper," Feng said as he climbed out.

Staying low to avoid making himself an easy target, Feng went back to his hole and pulled out the bodies of the two troopers, lying them on the dirt behind the hole. Around her, other ODTs did the same, but she noticed the machine gunners remained hunched behind their weapons, eyes scanning the tree line.

It hit her again. Bern was gone. Killed in action.

There was a hole in her heart. One of her team was dead, killed by a Republic weapon. It had been a long time since she'd felt this. She had buried the feeling, ignored it for too long. How many more would she lose? Einar, Kerk, Dierk, Henrick, Eryka. The list was too long.

A Republic weapon. Hermod's team or MT agents that had defected?

How? Why had he joined the enemy?

"Cover me," Skadi said. She pulled herself out of her hole and walked toward the forest where she had seen the shooter.

"Skadi," Niels said. "Stay here, damn it. They could be preparing to attack again."

"I have to know," Skadi said.

Colonel Feng barked an order, and two ODTs leapt from their positions to join her.

She stalked into the trees, stepped over mangled bodies that were still smoking. Then she saw a body. It was almost invisible, the active camouflage was still partially working, but she had hit and nearly shattered the rifle, and the sniper's chest cavity had been ripped open. The corpse was still smoldering. She knelt and pulled off the helmet. She recognized Jord Lykken, one of Hermod's men. He was pale and his teeth were not human. Hard black eyes stared up at the drifting snow, and Skadi shuddered. Even with his helmet on, his face had been covered with dried blood.

Skadi shuddered. It was Jord, but it wasn't. Beside her, both the ODTs scanned the forest. Jord's suit should be melting, destroying itself to prevent capture. How had Jord done it? Kept his suit working despite his changes? How had he kept his intelligence when other vampires seemed to be nothing more than mindless animals? Were there other members of Hermod's team out here? Hunting with their animalistic companions?

Jord blinked.

In a flash, Skadi stood, drew her sidearm, and placed several rounds into his head.

Those eyes would never blink again.

She holstered her sidearm and transitioned back to her rifle. She began backing up, both ODTs mirroring her. It was almost easy to forget they were the enemy and not Aesir brothers, like the creature in front of her.

"Did you find the sniper?" Feng asked when she got back to the lines.

"Yes."

"And?"

"He belonged to an Erikoisjoukot team that went missing."

"This threat kills us both," Feng said. "We are no longer Governance and Republic; we are humans fighting to avoid extinction. The common good binds us and makes us brother and sister."

"Yes." Skadi was suddenly tired. The exhaustion wasn't just physical. The Vanir had turned on her, and now other Erikoisjoukot had turned on her, killing her brother. Her only friends were some Marines from ancient history and those she had once called the enemy. Looking at Colonel Feng, she sensed he was as thrilled with the situation as she was, but he was doing his duty.

"Watch out for other snipers," Feng said to his men. "Lojtnant, could you please return to the building? If there are other snipers, I would prefer you not make their job easy."

Skadi was tempted to argue but nodded and went inside as an officer launched another drone.

* * * * *

Chapter Seventy-Four: The Gunny Lives

Chief Warrant Officer Diamond Winters, USMC

The chair was comfortable enough, but Winters hated it. She was spending too much time on the bridge, waiting and watching, trying to remember what she was forgetting. The *Eagle* slipped closer and closer to the planet, and she had snuggled it close to the smaller moon that circled the ugly little planet. There were only two vanhat ships left, circling the world in high orbit, where they were probably invisible to anyone on the planet below. They were both SOG cruisers, and Winters didn't know what they were capable of. They both out-massed *Eagle* by a factor of two to one, and the database said they were dedicated warships.

Looking at them through the telescope, it was impossible to see anything that gave away their origin or the death they carried.

She watched one of the battle stations finally start its fall into the atmosphere and wondered if anyone was still alive. A quick calculation showed it would most likely land in an ocean, but plenty of other debris had bombarded the planet recently. She felt confident that nothing had landed on the gunny but the hardest part was waiting and watching. The SOG had resorted to saturation bombing TCG, wiping out all life on the planet, and it was likely they'd do it again.

If Gunny was still alive down there, she had to find him and get him off before the SOG returned.

If he was still alive. That was the hard part. Was she wasting her time, and how could she find two men on a large planet overrun by monsters? It wasn't like she could pick up the phone and call.

"Transmission detected," Blitzen said, and adrenaline coursed through Winter's veins. *"Interesting."*

"What?" Winters asked.

"A drone pushing through the atmosphere is transmitting an omnidirectional signal on some SOG frequencies. It's also broadcasting on Aesir frequencies, and there are SCBI data packets. The gunny and Freya are still alive."

Which calmed Winters a little.

"I can decrypt the SOG communication," Blitzen said. *"Apparently the gunnery sergeant has teamed up with Skadi and a SOG commissar for survival. They are making their way to the Nuvo Gagarin spaceport."*

"We can land there, can't we?"

"I believe we can. But I suppose the real question becomes who is there to oppose our landing? The SOG might still be in control, or the vanhat may have overrun it. If the SOG is still in control, will they shoot us down, and how do we get past the two hostile cruisers? We might be able to send a directional transmission to them, although we risk revealing ourselves."

"What did the SOG transmission say?"

"It was relatively low encryption, but it's nothing but a series of code words," Blitzen said. *"There's no way to crack that without a code book or a lot more context. The message was too short."*

"Okay. Let's send the gunny a message. Time it so there's minimal chance of one of those cruisers picking it up. We may have to blanket that part of the continent, though."

"Can do."

* * * * *

Chapter Seventy-Five: Winters

Gunnery Sergeant Wolf Mathison, USMC

Mathison didn't remember much of the rest of the night. After Bern was shot, there were two more attacks but no more snipers, and the attacks were little more than random mobs that rushed them without thought or planning.

After she came back from the woods, Skadi was silent. Grieving.

Now the survivors were tearing down the road in the dune buggies. With all the casualties, there was plenty of room to spare. Mathison rode shotgun with Stathis and an ODT gunner in the back.

The buggies themselves appeared to be lightweight frames, with suit-charging stations and plenty of cargo slots. There was no armor, but they were all-terrain and versatile. Unloaded, they were light enough for a single trooper in powered armor to pick up and throw a short distance. Fully loaded, a pair of troopers could still easily pick one up. There were four positions on the little buggies: driver, shotgun, a standing gunner, and a seat facing backward behind the gunner. They mounted the machine guns in skeletal turret frames that could swivel in any direction. The gunner couldn't be comfortable, though, since it looked like his seat was nothing more than a chair leaning forward. It kept the gunner low and the center of gravity of the buggy low, but Mathison couldn't imagine sitting there for hours.

Gray skies concealed the sun and moons while snow drifted lazily from above. The roads were covered with ice and a fine layer of snow, which meant the buggies had to move more slowly than normal or risk sliding off the edge.

Mathison popped another stim tab and swore. You could only take so many before they stopped working, and the only thing they managed to do was make sleep impossible once you had a chance. Ahead of him were the colonel and Skadi. Behind him were Niels and Vili. Too few ODTs had survived the night, and Mathison wondered if they could survive another night like that. When the sun brightened the gray clouds, thirty ODTs were still alive. Only one was injured because a vampire had made it into the building and killed the injured troopers before the medic had shot it.

Earlier in the day, a troll attacked from the woods. It was cut to pieces by the turret gunners. But now the forest was pushing in on the road and they would have less warning.

With heavy eyelids, Mathison watched the world around him, scanned the pine trees and tried to see if there were any trolls beneath them. The buggies were silent as they glided down the four-lane road, and they were moving too fast for Mathison to see properly. There were no other cars or vehicles, and Mathison wouldn't have been surprised if they were the last humans alive on Zhukov. Something was interfering with longer range radio transmissions, though, either the vampires or the trolls. Mathison wasn't sure and right now he just didn't care.

"Gunny?"

"What, Private?"

"What cutting score do I need for PFC in the New Marine Corps?"

"What?" Mathison tried to clear his head. It was like a fog had settled in. He watched the driver ahead of them swerve a little, but the colonel reached out and tapped the driver on the shoulder. Colonel Feng had gotten no sleep, but Mathison could have sworn the commissar wasn't tired.

"I want to work on getting PFC again. Then maybe lance corporal."

"You have a girl? Looking to get a bigger paycheck?"

"You mean we are getting paid now?" Stathis asked.

"Yeah. We're just paying higher taxes, so it just feels like they pay us nothing. We get a car and a chauffeur. What more could you want?"

"I hate socialism already, Gunny," Stathis said, and Mathison had to chuckle.

"Why does it matter, Stathis?"

"Well, if we get a posthumous promotion, I don't want to die a PFC. People might think I'm a boot or something, some noob who should have zagged instead of zigged. Privates and PFCs just aren't respected like lance corporals."

"You don't have my permission to die, so don't worry about it."

"Can I call you commandant instead of gunny?"

"If you do, I'll give you a dishonorable discharge," Mathison said.

"But you're the senior Marine. Isn't the senior Marine the commandant? Maybe I can call you general?"

"Do you want to start walking, Stathis? Because I'm about to kick you out of this buggy."

"But—"

"But nothing. Titles and rank don't mean shit right now. Technically Chief Winters is the senior Marine. See how she likes being called commandant, or general."

"What's above colonel?"

"You didn't learn that in boot camp?" Mathison asked, turning to look at the private.

"Sure, Gunny. Brigadier general. Can't you promote yourself to brigadier so you outrank Colonel Feng?"

"That's not how it works, Private." Mathison turned back to the front. Stathis was watching the rear and far too professional to turn around.

"How about this, if you die in the line of duty, I'll put sergeant on your tombstone."

"I'd like that, Gunny. Thank you."

"Unless you die without permission."

"That's cold, Gunny. I just can't see you giving me permission for that."

"Exactly," Mathison said. "Now shut up and watch your sector."

"Aye, Gunny."

"We're getting a transmission," Freya said. *"It's Blitzen."*

"Blitzen? The chief is alive?"

"Apparently. Long transmission. I'm getting a lot of data. But Chief Warrant Officer Winters is now in command of a Valkyrie *and she is currently hiding by the nearest moon. She says Sif is cooperating, but there are some Aesir commandos currently in detention."*

"Wait. What?"

"She says the Vanir have turned on us. They attempted to capture her and Levin. They killed the crew of Valkyrie 15 *during the assault.* 15 *has been destroyed. She is currently in command of the 27, now called the USS* Eagle.*"*

"Does she have a stealth ship?"

"Negative. She received your message and says she can land Eagle *if you can get to a starport. The chief realizes that might be difficult for us, and there are two former SOG cruisers in orbit that make it difficult for her. She says Sif is helping, but she doesn't trust the Aesir anymore. Besides the cruisers, all other forces appear to have left the system, or she can't see them on sensors."*

A weight lifted from Mathison's shoulders. Here he was wondering how he was going to rescue the chief and Levin, but it looked like she would end up rescuing him.

"Let Stathis know," Mathison said as he tried to think through the options. The lack of sleep was making it difficult.

A minute later, Stathis opened a private link.

"That is awesome, Gunny," Stathis said. "I hope she's a better captain than you were. Can you ask her not to do what you did? I don't want to get shot down again."

"I'm going to throat punch you, Stathis," Mathison said.

"Aye, Gunny," Stathis said, sounding far too happy for Mathison's mood.

*****

Chapter Seventy-Six: Transmission

Lojtnant Skadi – VRAEC

Skadi watched the forest pass by around her, waiting for the next troll to come stumbling out of the forest and attack. She was half tempted to nod off but didn't trust the driver not to fall asleep and wreck the buggy. She was sitting in the tail position, her feet almost dangling off the back as she watched the rear. Besides the forest, her only view was the buggy carrying the gunnery sergeant and Stathis and the line of buggies behind them. Far too many had died last night and this morning. It bothered her to leave behind functional buggies, but then it made little sense to have so many. At some point, the colonel would have to call a break and let people get some sleep. Driving on icy roads and watching for ambushers while trying to stay awake was nerve-wracking. The snow was gradually sticking to the roads, covering the ice and making their tracks more visible. One side of the road was covered with thick trees and the other side had a steep drop off. There was no rail but Skadi kept her eyes to the rear or on the trees. This was not the place for a driver to fall asleep. She was pretty sure nobody had slept in days.

The vampires stopped attacking a few hours before dawn, probably because they had to find a place to hide and sleep.

Her incoming transmission light blinked and her system stored the message in her buffers. It had come in on an Aesir auxiliary channel and it hadn't been Mathison or Stathis.

When she tried to view or listen to it, the message was nothing but garbage, but there was a lot.

"Good news?" Colonel Feng asked her on a link. He would be monitoring the various frequencies as well. How did he know what the Aesir preferred frequencies were?

"A garbage transmission," Skadi said. "Makes no sense to me. How did you know?"

"I am monitoring several frequencies," Feng said. "That one is known to me, for obvious reasons. Since I cannot decrypt the message, I suspect you can. Do you have help coming?"

"It was not using any encryption I'm familiar with," Skadi said.

"Your Marine friends perhaps?" Feng asked. "I believe they piggy-backed a message on my drone when I sent it up late last night. I don't mind because I think we are on the same team. At least I hope we are—the human team."

"I'll ask," Skadi said and opened a private link with Mathison.

"Was that message for you?" Skadi asked.

"Yes," Mathison said, and Skadi couldn't quite place his tone.

"Is there anything I can help with?" Skadi asked, fishing for information.

"Are you aware the Vanir have turned on us? And by us, I mean my Marines."

"I know they want to arrest you. They arrested me and my team. Tried to make us tell them where you were, although I think it was obvious."

"Some Vanir SEALs boarded *Valkyrie 15*, killed everyone, and took some of your Aesir and my Marines as prisoners."

"Bluebeard?"

"Dead. Along with the rest of the crew. You didn't mention the Vanir were killing each other over us."

"I didn't know," Skadi said. "How did they escape?"

"Sif helped. She is alive and with them. They are in a *Valkyrie* not far from the planet. The chief will attempt a rescue mission but there is no stealth vessel. She also has a squad of Aesir locked up, since they cannot be trusted."

Valkyries needed a space port. This was good news. Or was it? Mathison's tone was decidedly chilly, and he sounded angry. Was he angry at her?

"This is good news," Skadi said, trying to sound positive, but his tone was setting off alarm bells. "We can get off this painajainen planet."

"We still have some challenges," Mathison said, which did not sound good.

"Nothing we can't work through."

"That depends on whether my Marines remain a commodity to be fought over."

"What do you mean?" Skadi asked, getting a sinking feeling in her gut.

"If the Vanir are going to kill each other over us, then I'm not sure who I can trust. I know I can't trust Colonel Feng, but until now, I thought I could trust you."

"You *can* trust me," Skadi said, her world starting to fall apart. First the Vanir arrested and tortured her, then she found out she couldn't trust everyone she thought she could trust. Bern's death, and now Mathison was telling her he didn't trust her? Vanir were killing Vanir? Aesir were killing MT. The Republic was coming apart.

"I would like to, but right now there are only three people I trust. One is behind me and the other two are in a ship on the run from the people who wanted to execute us, the people who claimed to be our allies but are treating us like tools, and vanhat who just want to kill everyone."

"Let's just—"

The driver of the buggy slammed on the brakes, but the buggy kept sliding forward. Skadi tried to turn and see what was going on ahead of them.

A troll stepped onto the road and swung a massive fist at the second buggy, which was in front of the colonel's.

The colonel's turret gunner fired as the troll's target swerved. The small cart lost control and slid off the road and down an embankment. The buggy in front of the troll slowed as the turret gunner spun around, just in time for another troll to step out and swipe at them. The colonel's buggy tried to turn and almost hit the troll, but the colonel's driver lost control and the jeep spun.

The first troll erupted in a spray of superheated flesh and plasma, almost ripping it apart as the colonel's gunner opened fire.

Standing almost four meters tall, the second troll's attack caught the gunner of the first cart in its massive grip. The gunner was wearing a seat belt, so the troll lifted the entire buggy, while crushing the gunner's machine gun into his armored torso. The troll squeezed and the gunner's scream was cut off as the troll's other fist came down on the trooper riding shotgun, slamming the buggy into the ground and crushing the ODT. The trooper in the tail end position leapt out and rolled, as did the driver.

The troll roared in anger or victory, and Skadi placed several shots into its body. The troll reeled as the colonel's gunner used his machine gun like a saw and cut it in half.

Skadi glanced back in time to see other buggies slowing and pivoting to cover opposite sides of the road. The gunners staggered their attention, each watching the opposite side of the road from the one in front of it. The last buggy gunner watched behind.

Only two trolls?

The colonel got out of his buggy and Skadi followed him as he looked over the ledge. The bottom was ninety feet down.

None of the four troopers were moving. The colonel shook his head.

Even though they were SOG, it bothered Skadi they had died such an ignominious death. The colonel could see their vital signs, and Skadi saw that the driver's body was bent unnaturally. The others didn't look too good either.

Feng waved his hands. Skadi couldn't hear what he was saying, but two buggies sped up and took point as the colonel got back into his seat. The two ODTs from the smashed jeep climbed onto other buggies.

Skadi checked her map. The spaceport was about a hundred kilometers away. The convoy started back up. It was almost noon.

* * *

Several hours later, the lead buggy turned down a dirt path covered with hard dirt, gravel, and patches of snow. The trail narrowed, and the buggies bunched up so they could see and support the one in front of or behind them. The going got more difficult as the trail wound up a hillside before stopping in front of a concrete bunker. Trees hid the entire installation.

"What's this?" Skadi asked Feng.

"Surface-to-space missile silo and a tertiary command post," the colonel said motioning a couple jeeps forward. "The location is a secret. It's unmanned and automated, though I do not know if any survivors from the port came here. We'll hide out here until tomorrow, if it is safe. It will give us a chance to rest and we should be able to easily defend it from vampires and trolls."

The colonel waved his hand in front of the security panel and typed in a code. He glanced at Mathison, who was watching him as the door slid open. The ODTs held their weapons ready. An underground vehicle laager greeted them but there were no vehicles. Skadi had hoped for a tank or anything with a big gun and thick armor. Lights came on as the door opened further.

"Do all commissars know about the secret facilities?" Skadi asked, looking around.

"I'm afraid not. Being a commissar in the *Tupolev* battle group gives me more access than most," Feng said. The ODTs spread out and swept the area, looking for vampires or trolls. "This should make an excellent base of operations while we reconnoiter the space port. If you do not have friends coming to help, we can remain down here until the *Tupolev* returns."

Skadi didn't like that idea.

"Did you know the *Tupolev* has been hunting you and other Erikoisjoukot for nearly a decade?" Feng said, perhaps noticing her reaction.

"It does seem to show up at the most inconvenient times," Skadi said.

"Yes, the Republic had become quite a threat."

"Had?"

Feng shrugged. "I think we both have a bigger threat to deal with."

"And after?" Skadi said.

"After? I suppose we return to our cat and mouse ways. I will not be merciful."

A chill ran down her spine. She knew he meant all of it.

*****

Chapter Seventy-Seven: SOG Command Post

Gunnery Sergeant Wolf Mathison, USMC

The buggies drove into the bunker, and Mathison looked around. Concrete walls and LED lighting revealed little; it looked like any number of underground facilities he had seen. Large meaningless numbers on the wall, a section, maybe a level, and numerous doors. It felt like a tomb, unoccupied and dusty, a place where people rarely came. Why the SOG would need a tertiary command center for a starport was a mystery Mathison didn't feel like investigating at that moment. Bureaucracy or paranoia, it didn't matter. What did matter was that it seemed like a safe place and a possible base.

"There have been no intruders," Feng announced over the general frequencies that even the SOG troopers had access to. "This does not mean you should drop your guard, people, but I think we should be safe. We'll set up around the entrance. Another team will sweep the base."

"This base has a lot of shielding, so I'm not picking up much," Freya reported. *"Should I work on the network?"*

"Nothing hostile or destructive, but I want at least trooper-level access."

"Can do."

Standing to one side, Mathison watched the commissar organize the ODT survivors, sending some to sweep the base and others to establish firing zones around the garage entrance. Once everyone was inside the massive doors slammed shut and the commissar had squad leaders organize a rotation so most people could get some sleep. The doors to the base could withstand nearby kinetic strikes, so the chances of a troll getting in were slim to none.

"It looks like the trolls and vampires can't get in, Gunny," Stathis said on a private link, "but how are we going to get out if nobody can find us?"

"I would hope this base has a back door or two," Mathison said.

"But we'd be back to walking, Gunny. I only see the one entrance for the buggies."

"We can create a diversion or something," Mathison said. "Regardless, I want you to find a safe spot and go to sleep."

"Where will you be, Gunny?"

"Not far. Don't argue, go get some sleep." Stathis was probably sleep walking anyway.

"Aye, Gunny."

Stathis headed for a corner near a main door while he looked around for Skadi or Feng.

"They're not responding," Feng was telling Skadi. "Links to the base are also down, so it's anybody's guess what the status is there. It could be a big battle ground between vampires and trolls."

"What's the plan?" Mathison asked, joining them.

"Maybe you should leave that to the officer, Gunnery Sergeant," said an ODT major.

Mathison locked eyes on the officer and was trying to think of something cutting to say when Feng spoke up.

"Major Marashov," Feng said, "do not assume the US Marines were like other organizations. In the Marines, the NCOs and staff NCOs behaved more like officers than any other military I've read about. They called them the backbone because it was the NCOs who did the lion's share of hard work and stiffened the spine of their military. I will explain to you later in greater detail, but for now you should understand that this gunnery sergeant was more than capable of commanding an elite platoon and if I am not mistaken has done so with skill and honor. Perhaps I will share his combat record with you sometime. You may consider a Marine gunnery sergeant to be the equivalent of an enlightened captain or senior lieutenant. I dare say he has more leadership and combat experience than any of our own. He is no glorified private."

"Understood, Commissar Colonel," the major said without emotion. "My apologies."

Mathison nodded. The colonel had access to his combat record? SOG gunnery sergeants were glorified privates?

"My apologies as well, Gunnery Sergeant Mathison," Feng said. "As I was explaining, we will rest here until tomorrow, at which point we will attempt to reconnoiter the starport. We'll maintain surveillance of the port until rescue comes. This is a defensible position. We should be ready to move at a moment's notice. If it's the *Tupolev*, then they should be able to provide covering fire and gunship support."

"What assurances do we have that you won't throw us in a cell the moment we board the *Tupolev*?" Mathison asked before Skadi could.

Feng frowned. "Well, I could give you my word of honor. I would dare to give the general's word of honor as well, assuming you cooperate with us against these creatures. We are both servants of the greater good. Sometimes that requires we do things we may not like or commit lesser crimes to avoid the larger ones. We both feel that the extermination of humanity is the biggest. We will not force you, of course—I don't have the troops for that—but if your only other option is to stay here on the planet, will you?"

Mathison didn't like those options either, and he was pretty sure the colonel wouldn't let them stay in this fortress. Of course, the colonel didn't know about *Eagle* watching from deep space, and he wasn't about to bring it up.

"And if we aren't as much help as your general or you think?" Skadi asked.

"Lojtnant, I'm very sure you will be a great deal of help, but this is not about you. You see, it isn't just your Erikoisjoukot team, it is the entire Republic that we seek to ally with. The Golden Horde as well. As I said, the bigger picture. Who knows what can come of it? Socialism is about inclusion, everybody working for the benefit of all. Perhaps this enemy will help unify us as we should be unified, as one people."

Mathison was beginning to trust Feng even less. Being stranded on the planet was becoming more appealing by the minute.

"Who are you to promise alliances with the Republic?" Skadi narrowed her eyes.

Feng's smile was patient. "My rank of colonel commissar is merely a convenience for now. I do not have ultimate authority, of course, but I have a significant amount."

"Are you a member of the Central Committee?" Skadi asked.

"The members of the Central Committee are a secret, and that is not my secret to divulge."

Which, Mathison noticed, did not answer the question in any meaningful way.

"Is he lying?" Mathison sent to Freya.

"He has no tells I have been able to identify. He might have the fewest tells I have ever seen in a person."

"Is he human?"

"As near as I can tell. If I had to guess, I would say he's a lot older than he looks."

"Like Skadi."

"Yes," Freya replied. *"I would also wager he has an array of non-standard cybernetics, as well. Occasionally I pick up odd signals."*

"You should get some sleep," Feng said to them. "I also need some sleep. We should be safe enough here and should have plenty of warning of any attack."

That was one thing Mathison could agree to.

* * * * *

Chapter Seventy-Eight: Space

Chief Warrant Officer Diamond Winters, USMC

Classical music was playing in her ears as she looked between the display screen and the holographic map. She could re-draw every detail about them in her mind as she searched for something she hadn't already seen. Some option, something they could exploit.

She had heard the gunny tell Stathis and Levin that when the situation became static, to do something to make the enemy react, because Marines thrive in chaos. What could she do to cause the enemy to react in such a way that she wouldn't get hunted down and destroyed? What could she do to get rid of those two cruisers?

She saw the intelligence in their actions. They randomly changed course and speed, which would be typical if they were worried about stealth missiles or a long-range attack. It showed a cunning intelligence and a good grasp of human combat tactics and capabilities. They knew what humans could do, but humans had no such understanding of what they could do. All *Eagle* had was several missiles with the stealth classification and a few multi-function drones.

"Sergeant Levin?" Winters asked.

"Yes, ma'am," Levin asked from his console. Winters wasn't sure what he'd been doing, probably reading technical manuals.

"Do you think we could set up a couple drones with those Aesir relay units and drop them on the planet in the gunny's region? Would we be able to use them? That would allow us to send him the coordinates and link information."

Levin was silent for a few moments. "That sounds like a good plan, ma'am. I can't think of a reason that wouldn't work. The range isn't too bad; the manuals say the range is almost a quarter AU. It would certainly get us more real-time information and a better understanding of the situation on the ground."

"Check with Sif," Winters said. "See what she thinks."

"Want me to prep a drone?" Blitzen asked.

"*Prep three*," Winters said.

"Aye-aye," Blitzen said.

"*Also*," Winters said. "*Let's prep some drones as radio relays. If another cargo ship comes in, I want to be able to warn them without giving our position away.*"

Winters watched everything going on around her. Blitzen displayed the status and estimated completion time for the drones.

The door to the bridge slid open.

"Chief Winters," Sif said. "I would like to report that the Republic fleet is still in the system."

Winter's blood went cold, and her hand unconsciously dropped to her sidearm. There was nobody with Sif.

"I have been in contact with Kari, another Nakija who is with the attack fleet. They saw what happened to the SOG and felt the violence. Fleet doesn't understand what is going on, but they are keeping their distance for now. They are also having problems, though he did not discuss those with me."

"How did you communicate with them?" Winters asked. Had Blitzen or Lilith missed something?

"On the astral plane," Sif said. "Communication is unreliable using that method, but it can be effective."

"Change position," Winters told Blitzen. *"Get us far from here. They could have HKTs vectoring in."*

"On it. I'll maintain the bridge displays to keep her from realizing we are moving."

"I have not told them where we are or what we are doing," Sif continued. "I expect you would like to return the Jaegers to their home?"

"Yes, but I would prefer to do it without a Vanir HKT coming for us," Winters said.

Sif nodded. "Do you know why your gunnery sergeant would shoot at Skadi?"

"Maybe he met some Republic HKTs?" Winters said.

"I'm not your enemy," Sif said.

Winters scowled at the girl. "You aren't in the brig with the Jaegers. If I thought you were, they would be enjoying your company."

"Do you think you could hold me?" Sif asked.

Damn, the girl had a point. Maybe. Could she influence Blitzen though?

"We are keeping the ship," Winters said.

"Since when did Marines become pirates?" Sif asked.

"Since the original Marines wore horns on their helmets," Winters said.

"Technically, the original Vikings did not have horns on their helmets," Sif said.

"*Technically*, the Vikings were the original warriors from the sea. Marines are just a more evolved version. Horns on helmets are irrelevant."

"There is no doubt you and your sergeant were wronged," Sif said. "The Republic will not make the same mistake again."

"The Republic won't get the chance."

Sif nodded, which Winters didn't like. Was Sif agreeing or disagreeing with her?

"More of the creatures have escaped their prison," Sif said. "You have seen what happened to the SOG fleet. I would not be surprised if half the SOG ships and crew are already dead. The vanhat are like a plague, and they are spreading quickly."

"Tell me something I don't know," Winters said.

"The SOG received a report that Hermod was here," Sif said. "Then when your gunnery sergeant saw Skadi planetside, he shot at her before retreating. They know your gunnery sergeant is here. We also believe Hermod is here."

"That makes no sense."

"We know."

"Why is the fleet still here?"

"They didn't say. I think there are problems with the fleet. But there is a more immediate problem for us."

"What?" Winters asked. What kind of problem were they having?

"I think we need to retrieve the gunny and Skadi from the planet."

"Why?"

"Kontra-amiraali Carpenter wants his daughter back. However, he has started on a path he cannot change."

"Do they know about the Vanir betrayal?"

"Yes."

"And?" Winters prompted.

"And it is complicated."

Winters stared at her. "Can we just put the Jaegers in a pod and drop them off?"

"No. Task force Ragnar doesn't know where we are and the vanhat are not all gone. Would you risk that?"

"No."

"If I could promise their good behavior, would you let them out?"

"No," Winters said, then thought about it. "I don't know."

"Something is happening," Blitzen reported. *"Missiles inbound on the vanhat."*

"Another thing," Sif said, sounding pained, "the Republic has been watching. It understands this infection cannot be allowed to spread. As I said, they have taken actions they cannot reverse."

"Which means what?" Winters asked, a lump in her throat because she was sure she already knew.

"The Republic will render Zhukov uninhabitable since the SOG is unable to do so. The SOG understood this on TCG. The Republic will do the same here."

"On screen!" Winters said, not caring if Sif saw it now. The gunny was down there, and if the Republic was about to destroy all life on that planet, she had to get him off.

Right now, she wasn't sure who she hated more, the SOG or the Republic.

* * * * *

Chapter Seventy-Nine: Race

Gunnery Sergeant Wolf Mathison, USMC

Something large slammed into the base door, waking everyone up. Mathison was up and had his weapon aimed before he remembered what was going on.

"A couple trolls," Major Marashov. "They can't get through that door. It's designed to withstand kinetic strikes."

"They're hitting it pretty good," Stathis said so only Mathison could hear.

"There's a camera viewing the approach," Freya reported. *"I can show you."*

"No," Mathison said.

If they weren't getting in and there weren't many of them, he didn't care. A queue light appeared on his display. A message on the Aesir channel.

"I'm receiving a transmission from Chief Winters," Freya reported. *"I have tapped into the base's receivers, otherwise we wouldn't get it. Decrypting."*

Leaning back against the wall, Mathison tried to relax.

"Good news, bad news, and we have a huge problem."

"We have lots of problems. Give me the good news first."

"The chief is on her way to pick us up," Freya said.

"I hope she's a distance out. We aren't going anywhere for a bit."

"Well, that's the bad news. Like the SOG, which has been driven away, the Republic realizes this incursion is an infection that must be sterilized. The SOG sterilized the infection on TCG. Can you figure out what the Republic plans to do? They're still in system, by the way, but have no plans on coming anywhere near the planet for what should, hopefully, be obvious reasons."

"How much time do we have?" Mathison asked.

"If you leave now, you might make it to where Eagle *can land, and escape before the missiles wipe out all life on the planet."*

"Those trolls are a problem."

"And here I was thinking I might have to explain the minor problems to you," Freya said.

Mathison got to his feet and looked around. Stathis nearly leapt to his feet when he saw Mathison.

"Shrek told me. Want me to take out the trolls? Do we need to ditch these ODTs? I would rather not ditch the Aesir, but let me know what your plan is, Gunny."

"Wake Skadi and explain it to her. I'll talk to the colonel."

"Aye, Gunny," Stathis said, looking around.

A sentry told Mathison the colonel was sleeping on a cot in the nominal command center, an office down the corridor from the main doors.

"The colonel is sleeping," an ODT corporal said as Mathison approached.

"So was I," Mathison said pushing the corporal out of the way.

The corporal went for his sidearm, but Mathison grabbed the corporal's arm.

"If you draw that I will kill you. Then we'll all die. You'll just die first. If you want to play stupid games when we are about to get nuked, then go ahead."

Mathison stepped past the corporal, almost hip to hip, still holding the corporal's hand. With his other hand, he grasped the corporal's neck, used his leg to sweep the corporal's leg, and slammed the big ODT to the ground in front of him. He stepped over the ODT, now grasping for breath, and opened the door.

Colonel Feng was sitting up reaching for his helmet.

"What did I miss?" the colonel said looking up at Mathison. His eyes flickered to Mathison's empty hands then the corporal struggling to his feet.

"We need to get to the spaceport now, Colonel. The SOG fleet has been defeated in orbit and fled. The Republic fleet did not flee but is lurking in deep space. They have determined that this planet must be purged, and they are going to do it. Soon."

"You have a ship coming to pick you up?" Feng asked.

"Yes," Mathison said, and the colonel nodded.

The corporal entered the room, his weapon pointed at Mathison.

Stathis stepped up behind the corporal and tapped the back of his helmet with the muzzle of his rifle before stepping back.

"Holster it," Stathis said. "Or I blow your little brain out."

"Stand down, Corporal," Feng said.

The corporal hesitated before lowering and then holstering his weapon.

"Go outside and play pocket pool," Stathis said, not taking his muzzle or eyes off the corporal.

The corporal looked at Feng.

"I'm okay. Wait outside please, Corporal."

When the corporal stepped out, Stathis lowered his weapon.

"Good," Feng said, looking at Mathison. "I was thinking the *Tupolev* was being detained."

"You were expecting them?" Mathison asked.

"When we left, the battle was going badly. When I spoke with the general on my way down, he said his ship had been infected."

"We need to get moving."

"A Republic ship?"

"An *American* ship."

Feng looked confused as he followed Mathison.

* * * * *

Chapter Eighty: Coming In

Chief Warrant Officer Diamond Winters, USMC

The two cruisers didn't pay any attention to the smaller *Valkyrie* with the massive wave of missiles coming at them. The two hostile cruisers were concentrating on knocking Republic missiles out of space, but Winters figured there would be more missiles coming in, and different types of missiles.

Sif was talking with the Jaegers and Winters didn't know what to think. Levin had spent some time hardening the bridge, stocking it with food and other supplies in case they tried to retake the ship. The bridge would be their last holdout.

Blitzen and Lilith had removed several system back doors and believed they had full control of the ship's boarding defenses, which didn't make Winters feel as comfortable as she would have liked since the HKTs had demonstrated how worthless they were.

Now the biggest dangers were the two vanhat cruisers and what was waiting for them below.

Since the invasion, it was like the entire world had been covered in rain clouds, masking the surface from orbital surveillance. *Eagle* had maps and plenty of information, but no real-time information. The landing field of the starport could be full of rusting wrecks or it could have been destroyed in a kinetic strike. It could also be full of monsters standing shoulder to shoulder, screaming at the sky.

If that wasn't bad enough, it was nighttime and the vampires would be active.

Mathison had to make his way about fifty kilometers through a troll- and vampire-infested forest to the starport, most likely now a vampire lair, where he would have to find a clear spot where *Eagle* could land. Then he would have to get through the hordes to board the ship while she and Levin kept the vampires away.

But if anyone could do it, the gunny could.

Eagle's point defense weapons could sweep an area and would work well as anti-personnel weapons, but not if those creatures got too close to the gunny.

Winters turned as the door to the bridge opened and drew her weapon.

Sif paused and held up her hands.

"Jaeger Sloss and his Aesir will provide support on the ground," Sif said. Winters scowled. "Nothing else. Sloss will defer to Skadi when she is aboard. She will be the ranking Aesir and he knows her."

If she survives, Winters thought. "I thought you were the ranking Aesir."

Sif shrugged.

Did Sloss consider Sif a traitor?

"Does he know there might be SOG ODTs?" Winters asked.

"He understands," Sif said. "He does not yet believe there are monsters. I have shown him video and shared information, but he remains skeptical. He is a man of honor."

"You don't think his loyalty is to the Vanir who captured us and killed Bluebeard?" Winters asked.

"I do not think so," Sif said.

"Think?" Winters asked. Wasn't the girl a mind reader or something?

"Yes," Sif said. "My powers are not as reliable as I wish they were."

Eagle began to shake as it entered the atmosphere. They were one hour out.

"Do we have a link with the gunny yet?" Winters asked Blitzen.

"He is very busy. We have linked with Freya and Shrek."

"Status?"

"We might be wasting our time. They could be the only survivors on the planet and every creature is coming for them."

*****

Chapter Eighty-One: Death Road

Gunnery Sergeant Wolf Mathison, USMC

Mathison slapped another magazine into his weapon and kicked at a vampire leaping at them from the side of the road. His armored boot smashed the creature's skull and threw it backward. He regained his grip on the rollbar and fired his rifle one handed as the buggy sped down the road, trying to stay close to the one in front.

There would be no stopping, no waiting. The convoy wouldn't go back for anybody. When they left the bunker, they all knew there would be no stopping or slowing down. To fall behind was to be left to die because there was only a small window and anyone who didn't make it never would.

The driver swerved to avoid a troll's body in the road but didn't slow down much. The only thing that kept Mathison from flying out of the buggy was his iron grip on the rollbar.

In front of them, the ODT turret gunner was firing almost non-stop as Stathis alternated between firing his rifle and feeding the gunner more ammunition.

They only had ten kilometers to go, and Mathison didn't think anybody had stopped firing the whole time, except to reload. Ammunition was dwindling, and Mathison was glad the ODTs had dumped the food, water, and medical supplies in favor of ammunition and spare weapons. With all the trolls and vampires coming at them, there were only eight buggies left.

Skadi, Niels, Vili, and wounded ODT Captain Kristoff were now in the lead buggy. They had started in third place. Vili was driving like a madman, while Niels manned the turret, and Kristoff sat in the tail gunner spot, being slammed from left to right as the buggy dodged the bodies and monsters.

Sergeant Hammer was Mathison's driver, and he seemed focused on climbing onto Skadi's bumper. The sergeant seemed to know what he was doing and probably could have been a race car driver in another life. The turret gunner was a Corporal Pronin—a short man who seemed to think the machine gun was a sniper rifle as he fired precise, accurate shots instead of short bursts like Niels ahead of them.

Mathison wasn't sure who was in the buggy with him, but the colonel was directly behind them, followed closely by the remaining buggies.

"We are not doing well with ammunition," Feng said over the standard channel.

A troll stepped out and swung a ladder at Mathison's jeep. Sergeant Hammer swerved expertly as he avoided debris in the road. The troll missed and was left behind. The colonel's gunner fired a burst and chopped off the troll's arm. His jeep dodged the staggering troll and zipped past. When the troll fell, it landed on the jeep directly behind them and flipped it. The gunner and a passenger flew out. The next buggy tried to avoid them but must have hit an ice patch because they slid off the road and smashed into a tree. Mathison glimpsed pale white faces rushing toward the buggy. The remaining buggies had to slow to navigate the hazards and Mathison saw more white faces rush them from the trees. The passengers and gunners fired desperately.

Ahead, the road curved.

"Save a round for me, Gunny," Stathis said on a private link as Pronin yelled for another ammunition block.

"What makes you think I'll outlive you, Private?" Mathison asked as he fired at a pair of vampires waiting in the road ahead. They were watching Skadi's buggy too closely. Mathison got them both.

Mathison's buggy swerved to avoid a body he hadn't seen and he felt the buggy slide on the slick road.

A short burst from Corporal Pronin mangled the road enough for the jeep to regain traction and keep them from sliding into the woods.

A vampire leapt out of the forest, taking advantage of Pronin's inattention, but Stathis stitched it with a burst from his rifle.

Steaming blood and gore splattered the corporal and Stathis, but most of the body landed behind them. Feng's buggy slammed into it, launching it back off the road.

Pronin resumed firing at potential threats to either side of Skadi's buggy and Mathison tried to cover where Pronin wasn't.

Ahead of them, a pair of trolls battled a swarm of vampires. Niels sprayed the entire group with a long burst from his machine gun.

Skadi's jeep slowed down to push the bodies aside, and more vampires came out of the woods. These vampires were wearing blue SOG fleet uniforms. The convoy was getting close to their destination.

Niels and Pronin made quick work of them.

"Are they having a party on this road, Gunny?" Stathis asked.

"They forgot the beer," Mathison said, firing a burst at a flash of white.

"Gunny," Stathis said seriously, "I think we're the kegs."

"Worst. Party. Ever."

"We're running out of party favors. Stathis black."

Mathison glanced behind and saw at least one buggy behind the colonel had survived and caught up, but none of the others.

The ODTs were brave bastards.

The snow fell more heavily.

Winters came over the Marine link. "Gunny, I hope you're moving fast. Those cruisers have launched drones or something at us. Our window is getting smaller."

"Any eyes on the port?" Mathison asked as he fired into the woods ahead.

"We're a little busy," Winters said. "Our drones are fighting their drones. I would like to say it's a one-sided fight, but it's not. They have more drones, and I don't have any to spare."

"Copy that. You take care of yourself. That's an order. It's better that some of us escape than none of us."

"Marines never leave their own behind," Winters said. "If you don't want me coming to collect your body, you and Stathis will be at that port. If your LZ is the gates of hell, we will be there."

"Aye, ma'am," Mathison said.

Pronin fired a burst into an oversized troll that stepped onto the road. It took the combined fire of Niels and Pronin to knock it back and finally kill it.

"Are the trolls getting bigger, Gunny?" Stathis asked. "I think the trolls are getting bigger. That was almost six freaking meters tall.

Please tell me I was seeing things. It didn't have any pants on. What does it need a pecker that big for?"

"Shut up, Stathis!"

"Ammunition!" Pronin yelled.

"You need to use less, Corporal," Stathis said, "we're starting to run low; only two boxes left."

"Then we'll use our knives," Pronin said.

Hammer accelerated to close on Skadi. Behind them, Feng's buggy sped up as well.

A vampire sprinted out of the woods, but someone behind Mathison shot it with a rifle before it got too close. The colonel's gunner got busy shooting a troll coming from the other side.

Skadi's buggy skidded around a wrecked truck as Mathison shot at vampires swarming onto the vehicle, preparing to jump down on the convoy. There wasn't a lot of road left for the buggies to maneuver.

Pronin began sweeping the top of the truck clear, but as they got closer he would lose the angle on anything staying low. Feng's gunner picked up the slack but the bodies couldn't be confirmed as completely dead.

Pronin and Mathison were too slow to catch the vampires that leapt at Skadi's buggy. The first vampire slammed into Niels and the machine gun, the second vampire missed completely, but managed to grab the vehicle as it sped by. It whipped around from the momentum and almost landed in Kristoff's lap.

Mathison saw the turret was cracked and broken from the impact and the gun came off the mounting bar. Hammer swerved to miss the bouncing gun. Mathison fired at another vampire as it jumped toward Pronin.

Vili swerved and fought to regain control as the now-top-heavy buggy slid on the ice.

Mathison tried to get a shot as Kristoff struggled feebly against the vampire on top of him when another vampire leapt from the wrecked truck. Niels swung his fist into the vampire's skull, spraying blood everywhere as the vampire tried to grab him by the head.

Niels barely beat the monster, finally throwing it off the buggy into the woods.

He reached down, grabbed the vampire attacking Kristoff, and threw it off, but Kristoff wasn't moving. Mathison didn't see any more because the buggy swept past the truck and almost collided with another troll.

Pronin stitched it from chest to head and it fell backward just as the colonel's jeep cleared the wrecked truck. The vampires swarmed the trailer and Mathison knew the following jeeps didn't stand a chance as an avalanche of vampires fell upon them.

"And then there were three. Three little buggies."

"Shut up, Stathis."

An entire battalion chewed up and spit out.

"Take point," Skadi said to Mathison. "We need a machine gun up front. We have a spare, but Niels won't be able to hit paska with it."

Mathison tapped Hammer on the shoulder and motioned for him to move them ahead. "We have point."

"I am the Hammer of righteousness," Sergeant Hammer said. "Let's see if those Republican scum can keep up with me."

"Your colonel is back there, too."

"The colonel will keep up." Hammer slammed the buggy into a body, knocking it aside.

"You'd better hurry," Winters said on the Marine channel. Mathison ignored her.

"You want to let the Hammer know we're supposed to go around things, not hammer through them?" Stathis asked on a private link.

"You wanna drive?" Mathison asked as he shot a vampire standing in the road. "Then shut up."

"But I *do* wanna drive, Gunny."

"You won't be able to shoot."

"Oh. Never mind. But if we don't get there soon, we won't have anything to shoot with and then I can drive."

Pronin concentrated on their route while Mathison tried to watch everything else from his perch.

"Just few more kilometers," Mathison said, checking how much ammunition he had left. It was not good.

Minutes later, the buggy emerged from the woods.

The area around the spaceport fence was clear and there was a trench or moat in front of the fence. Mathison saw several armored personnel carriers blocking the road.

Blazer rounds started coming at them and Sergeant Hammer swerved to dodge them as Pronin clamped down on the trigger and leaned into the gun. Vampires ran at the buggies as Skadi's jeep cleared the forest.

Hammer took a turn too fast and two wheels came up. As if in slow motion, the buggy began to roll toward the roadblock. Blazer rounds flashed around Mathison as he felt himself rising higher and higher into the air.

"Those are vampires firing at us," Freya reported.

"Crap!" Pronin abandoned his gun, trying to avoid getting pinned as the buggy rolled over.

Blazer rounds sliced through the buggy. The buggy rolled twice and came to a stop, upside down. Mathison shook his head. The vampires would be on them any minute.

A cannon fired and the forest behind them erupted.

"They aren't very skilled," Freya said as Mathison crawled out.

"You okay, Gunny?" Stathis crouched beside Mathison. How did he get out so fast?

"Yeah," Mathison said, not sure if he was lying. Stathis had other things to worry about. There was an explosion between the APCs and the overturned buggy, and several vampires were vaporized.

"We need to move," Stathis said.

"Come," Pronin said, pulling Mathison up. Sergeant Hammer was kneeling and firing. A ditch along the road looked like it might provide some cover.

A shot from one of the APCs caught Pronin and the corporal exploded, spraying the ground behind them with gore. Mathison and Stathis hit the ground.

Behind them, Niels had dismounted and was firing. Feng's buggy was also firing.

More rounds slammed into Mathison's buggy, ripping it apart. The two Marines tried to become one with the ground. Blazer rounds flashed overhead. Either Niels or Feng's gunner hit something on the APCs. The explosion lit the night. The armored personnel carriers had plenty of armor to stop bullets, but blazers chewed them up. More APC blazer rounds hit near Sergeant Hammer, who was hugging the ground.

"We aren't getting past them," Stathis said, bringing up his rifle picking off the vampires running at them.

Vampires would soon start coming out of the woods if the APCs didn't finish them. Regular projectiles hit and chewed up the ground. Apparently, the vampires didn't have many blazers.

"Someone needs to watch the rear," Mathison said.

"At least they had decent cover at the Alamo," Stathis said. "They had walls and shit."

"This isn't the Alamo," Mathison said, firing and taking off a vampire's head. The body flopped to the ground.

"If we die here, nobody will know."

"We'll know. But we aren't going to die."

"What do you know that I don't, Gunny?" Stathis asked between shots.

"I ordered you not to die," Mathison said, picking off another vampire. "I thought you wanted to be a lance corporal, or something anyway. Not a PFC when you died."

"Never thought I'd die fighting beside capitalists," Hammer said. "My mother will be so disappointed."

"I always wanted to die fighting monsters," Stathis said.

Hammer, Stathis, and Mathison put their heads down as a blazer chewed up the top of the ditch. Stathis started crawling along the ditch.

"Don't run now, cappie," Hammer said.

"I don't run, I flank. Let them shoot at where I was."

"We almost made it," Skadi said on the main link. "So damned close. I can see the port. Just over the fence."

"Must be about a hundred vampires," Feng said.

The incoming firing on his position slowed, and Mathison popped up to fire.

A shadow passed overhead, and the unmistakable crack of supersonic missiles drowned out the blazers.

The roadblock erupted in flames and coil guns took out the advancing vampires as *Eagle* slowly passed overhead, an avenging angel armed with heavy weapons. The tree line behind Skadi and Feng erupted as the coil gun cut down the forest. Trees shattered as high-velocity two-millimeter pellets shredded everything.

"You'd better start moving, Gunny," Winters said over the link.

"Aye, ma'am," Mathison said, smiling.

Skadi's buggy came up the road. Mathison grabbed a roll bar and found a spot for one of his feet. His other foot hooked into an empty ammunition slot. Stathis jumped on the other side, opposite Mathison. The colonel pulled up and Sergeant Hammer jumped on the colonel's buggy. Niels and Skadi fired at moving targets, but it seemed the vampires were reluctant to approach them now.

The buggies didn't move as fast with the extra weight, but they were much better than walking as they sped toward the spaceport. *Eagle* hovered over them, a massive shadow blocking the snow, providing a ring of death around them.

Minutes later, *Eagle* moved toward an empty spot.

Behind them, something roared and was answered by several more. Trolls.

Eagle dropped to the concrete and a ramp opened. Aesir poured out, weapons ready.

Blazer rounds from surrounding buildings lanced out to strike at the buggies, hitting one trooper and throwing him from his spot. The

Marines, Aesir, and ODT's couldn't fire in all directions as they sped across the tarmac.

There was too much open ground to cover, and they were too exposed. Coil guns on the Eagle opened fire, shattering buildings and vehicles, but Mathison knew it wouldn't be enough.

The Aesir coming down the ramp went prone or kneeled to provide accurate and lethal fire. Their pinpoint fire sought out snipers and other targets the coil guns couldn't see. Their blazer rounds smashed through the attackers' cover.

The two buggies reached the ramp, and the Aesir began to fall back, covering each other as blazer rounds slammed into the *Eagle*. They left Kristoff's body as they abandoned the buggies and ran up the ramp. Once aboard, the Jaegers followed, and the ramp slid closed, but Mathison realized it wasn't over.

Inside the cargo bay, the Jaegers and ODTs stared at each other. Weapons were pointed down, but they were pointed at the space between the two groups.

"Stand down," Skadi said.

The five SOG troopers were outnumbered, but they didn't look the least bit intimidated by the Aesir.

"Unload, lock, and clear," Feng said to his men, removing the magazine from his own rifle. "We are guests aboard this vessel. We have exchanged fire in the past, but today we are allies. Look at the big picture: we serve the greater good and will demonstrate our resolve and strength of character by setting an example and being first to trust our hosts."

Slowly, the ODTs unloaded their weapons. They put the magazines back in their pouches and slung their rifles on their backs.

The Jaegers remained motionless. Mathison couldn't see their faces. Would they open fire on the SOG troopers?

Mathison motioned to Stathis, who removed the magazine from his blazer and cleared the round from the chamber.

"Stand down," Sloss finally said, and the Aesir put their weapons away.

Mathison felt the ship shake as it rose through the atmosphere.

"Can you get up here, Gunny?" Winters said on a private link. "Before those psychos start shooting at each other."

"Is Sif here?" Mathison asked.

"She is here on the bridge," Winters said. "She's talking with Sloss, trying to keep him from killing the ODTs. We all think it would be best that the ODTs not know who she is or anything about her."

"Excuse us," Mathison said. He felt self-conscious walking between the two groups, which seemed ready to start shooting or brawling.

Feng was taking his helmet off as the door closed behind Mathison and Stathis.

"I thought they were going to kill each other," Stathis said.

"They still might," Mathison said.

"I'm linking into Eagle's *systems,"* Freya said. *"Blitzen and Lilith appear to have complete control."*

"Great," Mathison said, wondering if he could finally get a good night's sleep.

* * * * *

Chapter Eighty-Two: Briefing Room

Lojtnant Skadi – VRAEC

Skadi expected to see her breath as she looked around the room at Sloss, Mathison, Winters, Feng, and Niels. The icy stares should have dropped the temperature in the room enough for the heaters to kick in. Sif was conspicuously absent, but she knew the girl was listening.

Eagle had left Zhukov's upper atmosphere hours ago. Skadi had watched the display as bombs exploded all across the planet, shoving the world into a new ice age. Zhukov was going to have a nuclear winter that would probably kill every organism on the planet, and if that wasn't enough, Winters mentioned the Republic had also changed the orbit of several asteroids, and within the month those would slam into the planet.

It was highly unlikely any humans were still alive on the planet. It was a sobering thought. Several hundred million people had lived there. Two massive SOG fleets had been guarding it. How could you fight an enemy that turned your own people into an assailing force?

"We have several problems," Winters said, looking at everyone. "I could fix most of them by shoving most of you out the airlock."

Winters' eyes moved to Sloss, Feng, and Skadi.

"Unfortunately," Winters continued, "that wouldn't solve the larger problem, which is the survival of the human race."

"I'm not sure most of it is worth saving," Sloss said, glancing at Feng.

"You are welcome to leave," Winters said, pinning Sloss with her glare. "The airlock is that way. I'm looking for answers, ideas, and suggestions, not hatred and stupidity."

"Zen," Sloss said.

"Trust me," Winters said, still looking at Sloss. "I want you off my ship more than you want to be here. I'm not ready to throw you out the airlock. Yet. But I won't stop you from taking a walk off my ship."

"This is a Republic ship," Sloss said.

"It's mine now," Winters said. "When you try to imprison or kill me, I take your ship. Spoils of war, asshole. Get over it."

Feng looked surprised. Sloss scowled. Skadi wasn't sure how she felt about it. Valkyries were some of the most advanced vessels in the Republic's arsenal. Having foreigners in possession of one didn't sit well with her. Sif had explained what had happened in the Green Hope system, and Skadi understood Winters' hostility, even if she didn't agree with it. She had spent a lot of time aboard this vessel, and it still felt like hers.

"So, that is how this is an *American* ship," Feng said.

Winters glanced at Mathison.

"Is this a problem?" Mathison asked.

"No," Feng said. "We are no longer facing death on Zhukov, so I cannot complain about specifics. I am hoping to make contact with the Republic in order to coordinate a defense against this threat."

"We're working on that," Winters said.

"How?" Feng asked.

"That is our concern," Winters said. "When that happens, we will return Skadi's team and the Jaegers to the Republic. They are not our prisoners."

"Nor do they appear to be allies," Mathison said.

"That's not true," Skadi said.

There were only four, but she preferred not to have the Marines as her enemy, not when there was the Governance and the vanhat threat to contend with.

"Maybe not for a lojtnant," Mathison said, "but last I checked, lieutenants don't dictate national policy."

Skadi frowned. He was right, but Sif had been adamant that she would stay with the Marines, even if given the opportunity to return home. She said, at this time, her loyalty was to the Marines, not the Republic. Which didn't make any sense. *What did Sif know she wasn't sharing?* Damned Nakija and their secrets.

Winters looked at the colonel.

"Considering that," Winters said, "what is your intent? We can drop you off at a SOG colony."

"I appreciate that, thank you. However, I think it is more important that I contact the Republic and the Golden Horde. If I am not mistaken, your team leader Hermod has gone over to the enemy and may have been instrumental in the fall of Zhukov. Or was he working under Republic directives?"

"No directives that I know of," Skadi said. She trusted Mathison. Hermod was no longer human, but he had been more than a mindless, bloodthirsty vampire.

"Until we can confirm the destruction of his ship, *Stalkkeri,*" Skadi continued, "we still have to consider him to be operational and a threat."

Feng nodded. "So, you see, only the Republic understands Hermod and his ship's capabilities. As with Zhukov, he can slip past Governance defenses to infect a population. He is a spearhead."

"And the *Pankhurst*?" Winters asked.

"Yes," Feng said. "I suspect that is a different enemy. It is this Nasaraf and the *Pankhurst* which appear to be the force behind the trolls. I expect there may be another force behind Hermod and the vampires."

"There are probably other vanhat as well," Sif sent to Skadi on a private link. Dutifully, Skadi repeated what Sif said.

"Exactly," Mathison said. "Who knows what additional horrors we'll face?"

"Mister Tristan Malloy might," Feng said.

"And he is with the Republic," Skadi said.

"That settles it, then," Mathison said. "We have to find the Republic and talk."

"That won't be nearly as easy as you might think," Skadi said.

"Why?" Mathison asked.

"We have incoming ships," Winters reported. "One is the *Pankhurst* and the Republic fleet just entered Shorr space. We can't stay here. Standby for transition."

Staying in the Zhukov system had just become a terrible idea.

"Get us somewhere safe, and we'll come up with a plan," Mathison said.

"Aye, Gunny," Winters said.

USS *Eagle* slid into Shorr space.

#####

About William S. Frisbee, Jr.

Marine veteran, reader, writer, martial artist, computer consultant, dungeon master, computer gamer, dreamer, webmaster, proud American, and best of all, dad.

Growing up in Europe during the height of the Cold War and serving as a Marine infantryman through the fall of communism shaped Bill's perspective on life and the world. When most Marines were out trying to get lucky he was studying tactical manuals. Years later, he shared much of his knowledge to a website for writers of military science fiction.

These days, he's brushed off the pocket protector and is a top gun computer consultant.

Learn more at http://www.WilliamSFrisbee.com.

*****

The following is an

Excerpt from Book One of Abner Fortis, ISMC:

Cherry Drop

P.A. Piatt

Available from Theogony Books

eBook, Audio, and Paperback

Excerpt from "Cherry Drop:"

"Here they come!"

A low, throbbing buzz rose from the trees and the undergrowth shook. Thousands of bugs exploded out of the jungle, and Fortis' breath caught in his throat. The insects tumbled over each other in a rolling, skittering mass that engulfed everything in its path.

The Space Marines didn't need an order to open fire. Rifles cracked and the grenade launcher thumped over and over as they tried to stem the tide of bugs. Grenades tore holes in the ranks of the bugs and well-aimed rifle fire dropped many more. Still, the bugs advanced.

Hawkins' voice boomed in Fortis' ear. "LT, fall back behind the fighting position, clear the way for the heavy weapons."

Fortis looked over his shoulder and saw the fighting holes bristling with Marines who couldn't fire for fear of hitting their own comrades. He thumped Thorsen on the shoulder.

"Fall back!" he ordered. "Take up positions behind the fighting holes."

Thorsen stopped firing and moved among the other Marines, relaying Fortis' order. One by one, the Marines stopped firing and made for the rear. As the gunfire slacked off, the bugs closed ranks and continued forward.

After the last Marine had fallen back, Fortis motioned to Thorsen.

"Let's go!"

Thorsen turned and let out a blood-chilling scream. A bug had approached unnoticed and buried its stinger deep in Thorsen's calf. The stricken Marine fell to the ground and began to convulse as the neurotoxin entered his bloodstream.

"Holy shit!" Fortis drew his kukri, ran over, and chopped at the insect stinger. The injured bug made a high-pitched shrieking noise, which Fortis cut short with another stroke of his knife.

Viscous, black goo oozed from the hole in Thorsen's armor and his convulsions ceased.

"Get the hell out of there!"

Hawkins was shouting in his ear, and Abner looked up. The line of bugs was ten meters away. For a split second he almost turned and ran, but the urge vanished as quickly as it appeared. He grabbed Thorsen under the arms and dragged the injured Marine along with him, pursued by the inexorable tide of gaping pincers and dripping stingers.

Fortis pulled Thorsen as fast as he could, straining with all his might against the substantial Pada-Pada gravity. Thorsen convulsed and slipped from Abner's grip and the young officer fell backward. When he sat up, he saw the bugs were almost on them.

*****

Get "Cherry Drop" now at:
https://www.amazon.com/dp/B09B14VBK2

Find out more about P.A. Piatt at:
https://chriskennedypublishing.com

*****

The following is an

Excerpt from Book One of the Echoes of Pangaea:

Bestiarii

James Tarr

Available from Theogony Books

eBook and Paperback

Excerpt from "Bestiarii:"

"Mayday Mayday Mayday, this is Sierra Bravo Six, we've lost power and are going down," Delian calmly said as Tina screamed from the back. He and Hanson began frantically hitting buttons and flipping switches. "Radio's dead, I've got nothing." He had to yell it so Hansen could hear him over the wind.

Mike's eyes went wide. He felt his stomach come up into his throat as the helicopter dropped and began rotating. "Shite," Seamus cursed and smacked the button to drop the visor on his helmet.

"Keep transmitting," Hansen told his co-pilot. "Damn, I've got no electronics, can we do a manual re-start?" He stayed on the stick and the collective, trying to control the autorotation.

Delian had been hitting every button and toggle switch possible. "No, I don't think this is a short, it looks like everything's fried. Mayday Mayday Mayday, this is Sierra Bravo Six, we are going down." He told the younger pilot, "You know what to do. Keep it level, autorotate down, try to control the rate of descent. Time your glide. You see a place to land?"

The helicopter was spinning to the right as it fell, which traditionally was the reason the pilot was the right stick. Hansen looked out the window as he fought the controls. "We're in the mountains, nothing's flat. I've got trees everywhere. Hold on back there!" he yelled over his shoulder.

The helicopter began spinning faster and faster and Mike found himself being pulled sideways in his seat. The soldier on the door gun lost his footing and floated up in the air, then was halfway out the open door, one hand still on the mini-gun, restrained only by his tether as the G-forces made Mike's face feel hot. He vomited, and the bitter fluid was whipped away from his face. The world outside the open doorway past Todd was a spinning blue/green/brown blur. Tina was screaming wildly. The wind was whistling around the cabin.

"We've got smoke coming from the engine," Delian said, peering upward. "What the hell happened?"

"Brace for impact!" Seamus yelled at the cabin, and wedged his boots against the seat opposite.

"Coming up on the mark, keep it level," Delian said calmly. "Get ready for the burn!" he yelled over his shoulder at the passengers. He switched back to the radio, even though he thought it was a waste of time. "Mayday Mayday Mayday, this is Sierra Bravo Six—"

"If they work," Mike heard the pilot respond, then suddenly there was a roar, and he was pressed down in his seat, getting heavier and heavier. The helicopter was still spinning, and out the open doorway and windshield there was nothing but a blur of greens and browns. Mike got heavier and heavier, and Tina stopped screaming. Then the roar stopped, and they began falling again, pulling up against their seatbelts. Tina opened her mouth to scream once more, but before she could draw a breath the helicopter hit with a huge crunch and the sound of tearing metal.

*****

Get "Bestiarii" now at:
https://www.amazon.com/dp/B0B44YM335/.

Find out more about James Tarr at:
https://chriskennedypublishing.com.

*****

The following is an

Excerpt from Book One of Chimera Company:

The Fall of Rho-Torkis

Tim C. Taylor

Now Available from Theogony Books

eBook, Paperback, and Audio

Excerpt from "The Fall of Rho-Torkis:"

"Relax, Sybutu."

Osu didn't fall for the man steepling his fingers behind his desk. When a lieutenant colonel told you to relax, you knew your life had just taken a seriously wrong turn.

"So what if we're ruffling a few feathers?" said Malix. "We have a job to do, and you're going to make it happen. You will take five men with you and travel unobserved to a location in the capital where you will deliver a coded phrase to this contact."

He pushed across a photograph showing a human male dressed in smuggler chic. Even from the static image, the man oozed charm, but he revealed something else too: purple eyes. The man was a mutant.

"His name is Captain Tavistock Fitzwilliam, and he's a free trader of flexible legitimacy. Let's call him a smuggler for simplicity's sake. You deliver the message and then return here without incident, after which no one will speak of this again."

Osu kept his demeanor blank, but the questions were raging inside him. His officers in the 27th gave the appearance of having waved through the colonel's bizarre orders, but the squadron sergeant major would not let this drop easily. He'd be lodged in an ambush point close to the colonel's office where he'd be waiting to pounce on Osu and interrogate him. Vyborg would suspect him of conspiracy in this affront to proper conduct. His sappers as undercover spies? Osu would rather face a crusading army of newts than the sergeant major on the warpath.

"Make sure one of the men you pick is Hines Zy Pel."

Osu's mask must have slipped because Malix added, "If there is a problem, I expect you to speak."

"Is Zy Pel a Special Missions operative, sir?" There. He'd said it.

"You'll have to ask Colonel Lantosh. Even after they bumped up my rank, I still don't have clearance to see Zy Pel's full personnel record. Make of that what you will."

"But you must have put feelers out..."

Malix gave him a cold stare.

You're trying to decide whether to hang me from a whipping post or answer my question. Well, it was your decision to have me lead an undercover team, Colonel. Let's see whether you trust your own judgment.

The colonel seemed to decide on the latter option and softened half a degree. "There was a Hines Zy Pel who died in the Defense of Station 11. Or so the official records tell us. I have reason to think that our Hines Zy Pel is the same man."

"But... Station 11 was twelve years ago. According to the personnel record I've seen, my Zy Pel is in his mid-20s."

Malix put his hands up in surrender. "I know, I know. The other Hines Zy Pel was 42 when he was KIA."

"He's 54? Can't be the same man. Impossible."

"For you and I, Sybutu, that is true. But away from the core worlds, I've encountered mysteries that defy explanation. Don't discount the possibility. Keep an eye on him. For the moment, he is a vital asset, especially given the nature of what I have tasked you with. However, if you ever suspect him of an agenda that undermines his duty to the Legion, then I am ordering you to kill him before he realizes you suspect him."

Kill Zy Pel in cold blood? That wouldn't come easily.

"Acknowledge," the colonel demanded.

"Yes, sir. If Zy Pel appears to be turning, I will kill him."

"Do you remember Colonel Lantosh's words when she was arrested on Irisur?"

Talk about a sucker punch to the gut! Osu remembered everything about the incident when the Militia arrested the CO for standing up to the corruption endemic on that world.

It was Legion philosophy to respond to defeat or reversal with immediate counterattack. Lantosh and Malix's response had been the most un-Legion like possible.

"Yes, sir. She told us not to act. To let the skraggs take her without resistance. Without the Legion retaliating."

"No," snapped Malix. "She did *not.* She ordered us to let her go without retaliating *until the right moment.* This *is* the right moment, Sybutu. This message you will carry. You're doing this for the colonel."

Malix's words set loose a turmoil of emotions in Osu's breast that he didn't fully understand. He wept tears of rage, something he hadn't known was possible.

The colonel stood. "This is the moment when the Legion holds the line. Can I rely upon you, Sergeant?"

Osu saluted. "To the ends of the galaxy, sir. No matter what."

*****

Get "The Fall of Rho-Torkis" now at:
https://www.amazon.com/dp/B08VRL8H27.

Find out more about Tim C. Taylor and "The Fall of Rho-Torkis" at:
https://chriskennedypublishing.com.

*****

Made in the USA
Columbia, SC
29 December 2024